The Dream Traveller: Dark Rising

The Dream Traveller Series
Book One

John Nassari

John Nassari

The Dream Traveller: Dark Rising

November 2024

This is a work of fiction. Names, characters, places and incidents either are the product of the author's imagination or are used fictitiously. Any resemblance to actual persons, living or dead, events or locations is entirely coincidental.

All rights reserved

Copyright © 2024 by John Nassari

Third Edition. First Edition May 2024

ISBN 978-1-0686068-0-9

No part of this book may be reproduced in any form or by any electronic or mechanical means, including information storage and retrieval systems, without written permission from the author, except for the use of brief quotations in a book review.

Digital art and maps by Chris Knapman

Typography and cover design by Andy Snow-Ellis

Pitstone Publishing

www.thedreamtraveller.pub

For Mum

A Note To The Reader

For your reference, a *Figures of Note* list can be found at the back of this book. It includes descriptions of the Dream Travellers, the people of Rathnell, and other prominent individuals from the realms and factions of this world.

THE UNCHARTED TERRITORIES

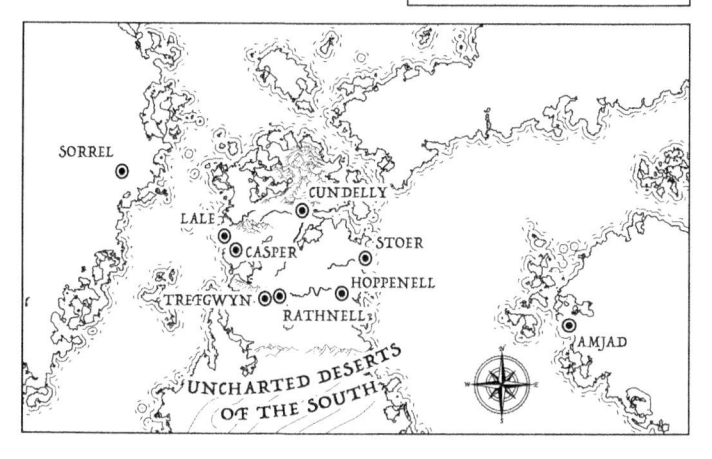

THE CHARTED TERRITORIES
THROLLS REACH
VOIMREN
DREBERG
FATES KEEP
SPIRE'S PASS
GOWER STRAITS
TORE
ALADRE
CLOG MARSH
LOFTEN MOUNTAINS
PRYN
HIGHLANDS
BRINDAL
LETCHDEAD
HOON
DANNEN
ALDEN
STONEPIT
RIDDON SLOPE
TAINS CROSSING
CAPELS RIVER
CUNDELLY
GLOOM MARSH
RAGON'S CURRENT
CLEREN RIVER
KLEVIS
PINE KEEP
YARNIK
DUNNET
LALE
LUBIN FOREST
BREWER LAKE
WITHINS MARSH
CLAY LAKES
CASPER
ORRAN RIVER
HALLWICH
STONE
FERN RIVER
STOER
GAMBOL WARD
ORRAN FOREST
FERN WOOD
CALPAN BAY
MERKIP
PLAINS OF DEEN
SALT LAKE RIVER
GATHSCAR
RATHDANGON SLOPE
HOPPENELL
TREFGWYN
RATHNELL
DEDISLE RISE
ASPEN PLAINS
WIGGINTON ESTATE
ANDERGINE
LEVERSTOCK
BLAREN WOOD
ALERGON
TETONS RIDGE
BERUJA
UNCHARTED DESERTS OF THE SOUTH
FOR COLOUR, SCAN Q R
0
100
200
300 Miles

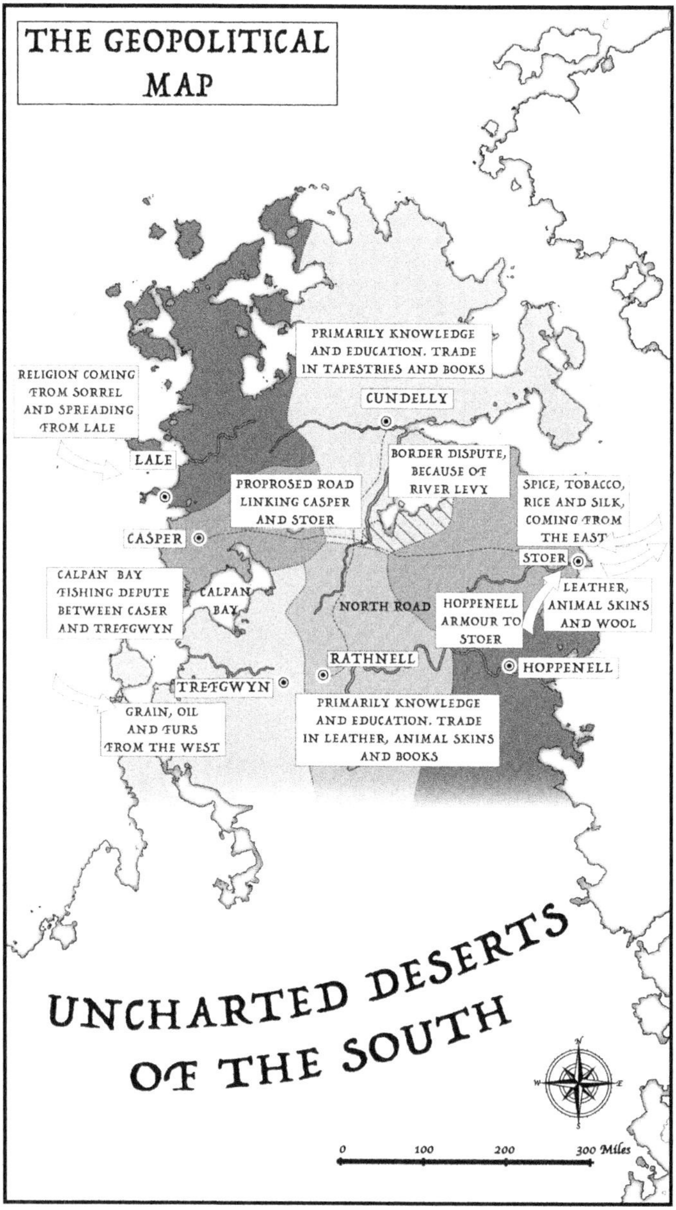
THE GEOPOLITICAL MAP
PRIMARILY KNOWLEDGE AND EDUCATION. TRADE IN TAPESTRIES AND BOOKS
RELIGION COMING FROM SORREL AND SPREADING FROM LALE
CUNDELLY
LALE
BORDER DISPUTE, BECAUSE OF RIVER LEVY
PROPROSED ROAD LINKING CASPER AND STOER
SPICE, TOBACCO, RICE AND SILK, COMING FROM THE EAST
CASPER
STOER
CALPAN BAY FISHING DEPUTE BETWEEN CASER AND TREFGWYN
CALPAN BAY
NORTH ROAD
HOPPENELL ARMOUR TO STOER
LEATHER, ANIMAL SKINS AND WOOL
RATHNELL
HOPPENELL
TREFGWYN
PRIMARILY KNOWLEDGE AND EDUCATION. TRADE IN LEATHER, ANIMAL SKINS AND BOOKS
GRAIN, OIL AND FURS FROM THE WEST
UNCHARTED DESERTS OF THE SOUTH
N
W
E
S
0
100
200
300 Miles

Dark Rising

One

Hazel froze on the moonlit tree branch, bracing herself for a quick death. Below her, on the shadowed forest floor, she watched the unworldly shape sniff and snort, wisps of smoke rising from its fur. It had appeared out of nowhere, emitting a putrid stench. She held her breath, careful not to make a sound, praying its burning stare wouldn't find her among the leaves.

Then, it vanished. She remained suspended in disbelief, her heart pounding in the silence, questioning what she had seen. Yet the unsettling feeling that something was terribly wrong lingered as if the ancient forest itself paused in fear with her. She scanned the tree huts, barely visible in the high branches. Receiving no reply to her urgent bird calls, she clutched a vine, swung her legs forward, and descended cautiously to the ground.

She knew she had to warn the others but was torn between choosing the night watchers or the Mothers' hut. She ran towards the campfire, towards her father, the chieftain. As she approached, relief washed over her at the sight of Faygon and his band of young warriors.

'Father! I had to leave my post. I needed to warn you, to warn everyone. There's something out there. This is no Highlander assault. It's worse.'

'Isn't that a relief!' came the mocking voice of Killian. 'Will you use the delusions of a headstrong girl as an excuse to increase the watch and divert more men from the hunt, Faygon?'

'You forget your place, Killian,' Faygon growled, his voice laced with fury. 'And you forget our history.'

'On the contrary, Chieftain, I refuse to let paranoia cloud my judgment. It's about time someone reminded you that…'

A bloody talon came through Killian's chest. An instant later, he was yanked into the darkness.

'Move, Daughter!' Faygon bellowed, pushing her. 'Awake the clan. Save the children.'

Gripping twin swords, Faygon sprinted in the direction Killian had vanished. Hazel dashed toward the great sycamore, towards the sanctuary for Mothers and infants, determined to ensure their safety.

Out of nowhere, a fireball illuminated the night sky, devouring treetops. A sentry horn blared. Agile figures bounded on all fours. Foresters scattered in all directions, struck down by the darting attackers.

Something barrelled into her, and she went crashing to the ground. Her bow snapped beneath her and she rolled to her feet, her knife drawn.

'Run! They will kill us all!' She recognised one of the tribe's strongest fighters, his face a gibbering mask of terror.

Hazel stood transfixed as a shape swooped down and carried him away. A creature resembling an ape, but with a horned nose, burst into the open area. From elevated positions, a group of archers unleashed arrows at it. The ape was undeterred, roaring defiantly, leaping into the branches to attack them.

Only when her back bumped into a tree did Hazel realise she'd been retreating from it all. Foul forms were uniting from all directions. Smoke blanketed everything, stinging her eyes. Could she hide? She wondered if she could shroud herself in the ruins of her tribe's home, below the aura of orange flames.

A deafening explosion reverberated above her, and the Mothers' hut burst outwards; from the gloom overhead, she felt a weight on the branch above her, shuddering the ancient wooden bough. Then a figure in blood-red armour, towering half the height again of the tallest man, landed on the ground before her. At first, she thought some great knight had come to save them, but as it turned its enormous frame, its slick helmet revealed the contours beneath. A Forester ran at it and was sliced in two by a single sweep of its blade. It savoured the scent of death, and only now did Hazel notice the bulging sack it carried. The hessian writhed, and from it rose the sound of terrified mewling – the babies! The young of the clan!

Hazel fought the urge to charge at the thing and sweep the bag away from it, but her survival instinct won, some guilt-competing impulse for self-preservation. From the dark scuttled spiders, except massive ones. They paused at the dead Foresters, spinning webs around them and lifting them onto their hairy backs to carry.

She knew she had just moments left to live, to fight or to be slain where she stood.

Then, Hazel noticed the handle jutting against her pelvis. She grasped it, twisted, and pushed, revealing the hidden storage space within the tree's base. She slipped in, greeted by the mingling aromas of ripe fruit and musty air.

Tears streaming down her face, she grappled with her fear and guilt, hearing her clan's dying cries outside. She, a chieftain's daughter, hiding in a storage nook while her people fell. Steeling herself, she wiped her tears and peered through a slit. In the flickering orange light, new creatures circled the red-armoured giant, casting her kin's bodies onto a mounting heap.

What she saw next made her gasp.

Two apes roughly handled her father, pushing him before the giant. Despite his right arm being a mere stump, with tendons like roots, and his body marred by wounds, her father stood defiantly, embodying resilience in the face of agony.

One of the apes raised a curved blade and pointed. 'We did not kill this one, sire, because it fits the profile you wanted for your experiments.' It spat on the ground, its free hand nursing a welt across its cheek.

The armoured giant let out a harsh, grating laugh, but the voice of another spoke. A voice emanating from the thin frame of a man concealed beneath a hooded purple robe. There was a jaded intelligence in that voice that instilled terror, eroding any remaining glimmers of hope.

'Bring him closer. Hmmm,' the voice whispered, 'a druid adds body and taste to my special formula.'

Faygon scowled at him.

The man's cowl nodded fractionally, voice amused. 'Chieftain knows himself by another term, perhaps a tree-diviner?'

All around, the creatures chuckled.

'He's a proper bark licker!' one sniggered.

Faygon somehow pulled free of the red giant. He drew his knife, but instead of attacking them, he held it to his own throat. 'Scum. You will not take me.'

'Careless!' The robed figure's tone filled with annoyance. 'You didn't check him for a weapon?' He hissed at the horned creatures. 'Extinction Day looms upon mankind, so I had hoped to keep this souvenir.' He redirected his attention to a gangly figure cleaning its talons, a creature similar to the one responsible for Killian's demise. 'Are there any others left besides the babies?' he asked.

'Nar,' it spat. 'I think not.'

'You think?'

'The cursed trees obscure my sight, Master. It is unclear. There is one faint heartbeat that eludes us close by; it could be an animal or perhaps something more. I do not like it. We should leave, sire.'

'A witness? How amusing, a hunt! I want my souvenir. When this one finishes himself off, conduct a detailed search in case there is another survivor.'

Faygon had been standing tensed and ready, but now his widening eyes jumped to Hazel's hiding place, the blade loosening in his grip.

Hazel watched. 'Do it, Father. Please,' she whispered.

But instead, he unleashed a resounding howl and charged at the robed figure, brandishing the dagger. The red giant intercepted him before he could reach his target, but even as he was restrained, weapon stripped away, Faygon continued to fight and yell.

'Ah! What skills you have to last this long, and such bravery. My souvenir may not know what he is but is a druid all the same. How fortunate! As your soul burns in the transformation, consider that those talents will make you a leader in my army. You should have taken the chance when it presented itself and ended your life,' said the robed figure. 'An eternity of torment awaits you. Come,' he snapped at his demonic battalion. 'He will make a fine servant!'

A fiery doorway materialised beside the hooded figure, emitting a blue glow. The gangly demon paused at the entrance, seeming uncertain about stepping through.

'But sire, what if there is a witness? We never leave one alive.'

'True, but the time arrives to take credit for our work.'

One by one, the creatures passed through the door, hauling the sack containing the babies of Hazel's clan and the bodies of her kin. Then her struggling father, whom she knew had just made the ultimate sacrifice for her, disappeared into the unknown. An eternity of torment, that thin figure had said, and she believed him utterly.

Finally, the robed figure stepped through, and the doorway vanished, and she was left alone in the forest. Overwhelmed with grief, she collapsed to her knees and began to sob.

Two

Forty leagues away, in the walled city of Rathnell, Girvyn tried to get some sleep. He could hear his uncle pottering in the lounge. The bitter smell of wood smoke wafted into his bedroom. It wasn't a huge house like some of the noble mansions on the far side of the coppice: a two-bedroom, single-floor cottage. But it was big enough, and it was all theirs.

Suddenly, he lurched, feet kicking sheets away from his body. His face distorted into an expression of agony.

'No-no-no! Please, not again!'

He shut his stinging eyes, willing sleep to take away the pain, but then he saw something in the vista of his eyelids. What was that? Stars beckoned like a night sky. Was he losing his vision? Finally, after all these years of headaches, he would be blind…at fourteen.

If he could somehow find sleep, it would relieve the…

In a snap of a finger, he was gone.

'Hello?' he called out. 'Is anyone there?'

Where am I? What just happened? He found himself in an endless expanse of milky space. The floor was white, too, but not the uneven floors he was used to in the castle. This was smooth and perfect.

Why bare feet? He wiggled his toes, felt the surface under his feet, felt the rustle of his clothes. The sensation of cloth on the skin felt so real.

What was this? A hallucination? Had he died? Was this a lucid dream? It didn't feel like a dream. Dream memories are recalled upon waking, and he was sure he was awake. Yet, the headache had gone in a blink. Normally, the pain took time to subside.

He reasoned, he must be dreaming.

A calm logic took hold. If this was a dream, he was the author. This meant he was in control, and unlike so many of his dreams, it wasn't a jumbled composite of his day. It wasn't particularly frightening. It was just weird.

He was on the verge of setting out, to walk into the vastness, when he heard a noise.

Swoosh. Swoosh. Swoosh.

He looked up and saw an object hovering in the space above him. He watched it curiously; it was a rectangular picture, like a piece of art that had fallen from the grand assembly hall and was rotating in mid-air. But not an abstract painting, not paint at all, this looked real.

He listened to the throbbing rhythm of the swoosh, felt the wind generated from the object's constant turning.

More pictures popped into view, but he was captivated by the first one. Both sides showed a chamber; leaking walls, strips of glass hanging from the ceiling. It was a cave. He had seen pictures of them in a book in the Rathnell library, titled: "The Hidden Realm: A Celebration of Hoppenell's Cave Structures." Girvyn laughed to himself. So that was what he was doing: making dreams out of remembered illustrations. It made sense.

Before he knew it, he was transported into the picture.

It wasn't glass he was looking at but shards of stalactites hanging from the ceiling. He wondered at the colours and textures of the cave and the echoing "plop plop" of water drops from a hollow below him.

Perhaps this was what he needed to do to return home, to wake, see his uncle, explore the cave until the dream ended. Pebbles crunched as he stepped forward; he followed the cave trail, barely noticing the walls leaking, trickling like tears of pain.

Slowly, he began to get the feeling he was not alone. In the white space he'd felt protected, as if it was secure, or even, he dared think it, safe like home. Whereas here, this place through the window, felt wrong. He couldn't shake this feeling, and it got worse.

A survival warning kept him from screaming. If he was being observed, he didn't want whoever was watching to perceive any weakness. Equally, that analytical part of himself, supposed that he was doing this to himself.

He attempted the deep breathing technique his uncle had taught him to combat stress. This situation was unfamiliar, but stress was not; it was an old, unwelcome companion. He tried to think rationally to regain his composure. Soon he would be awake, or the dream would change; this would all be forgotten.

But when?

He noticed that the illumination within the cave was residual light from a lower cavity, hinting at the possibility of an exit. He crouched down and crawled through the short tunnel until he came outside the cave. It was dark, save for what seemed like moonlight, but he couldn't see a moon. He caught a stench on the wind. It almost made him retch. What recess of his mind had given rise to this?

A track led in front of him. He edged along it, longing for return. Even the headaches were better than this. He held his breath, straining to listen. Something sounded. There it was again: moaning emanating from obscurity. On either side of the track, whispers danced at the edges of words.

Hands reached out of the earth, clenching and unclenching.

Wake! Wake! he ordered.

Nothing happened.

Nor did the hands try to grab his feet.

Was his mind adding extra props to scare him?

He sped along the path, feeling the rush of adrenaline coursing through his body. He tried to divert his thoughts, focusing on pleasant memories like playing chess with his uncle or a forest trail at sunrise. He kept moving, grateful for the moonlight that guided his route. Gradually, a building emerged; a towering edifice blending with the night sky.

He dug his thumbnail into his palm, and experienced pain. *Wake up! Wake up*! he urged, desperate to change the course of this bewildering narrative. He frantically patted his pockets, searching for a weapon, a dagger, or even a pencil, attempting to will one into existence, but to no avail. Nothing changed, no matter how hard he thought or what he attempted. If this wasn't a product of his own actions, as he increasingly suspected, then whoever or whatever had created this reality must possess intelligence. Were they inside that structure? With a growing sense of resolve, he convinced himself that stepping towards it was a better course of action than aimlessly wandering further.

The door slid open, both left and right panels retracting, revealing a passage lit by flaming torches. A new sense of unease replaced the previous disquiet. He heard the door close behind him. He swung round, but it didn't reopen.

Who opens their door to a stranger? And why is it now shut? The sense grew again that someone, or something, was watching him.

He waited a minute, listening, and then continued. The corridor grew colder as he walked further. Soon, his breath formed in the dim light ahead of his face. At the end, he found a dome as vast as the sky. Rising from the ground to the apex, glinting lights dotted the blackness. Observing the entirety of it would strain his neck to the limit. The closest lights were to his left, seemingly the easiest to reach. Could they offer an escape back to his bedroom? He had to find out, to see, or risk being trapped indefinitely.

The light emanated from glass containers, and now he was close enough to see what was inside.

Each housed a monster.

All remained still, yet their eyes tracked him. He realised he wasn't just an observer; they could see him! The overwhelming danger struck him like a blow. Fear crept through his mind to where all his worries festered. He felt himself sway and grasp for breath. 'No, please, not here. No-no-no-no-no.'

Concentrate on breath. He heard his uncle's voice, trying to ease him out of his panic attack. He saw his uncle's warm, concerned face in his mind's eye. *Concentrate on breath.* He did. Saw his feet, then saw his hands. He was on all fours. He needed to move, hide.

Get up! he urged.

He raised his head, looking at the monsters in the glass boxes; they weren't watching him any longer. They were staring somewhere else. He followed their gaze to another part of the chamber and frowned; it was as if a fragment of cloud had detached from the sky and been trapped here.

There was a snap. A spark cracked through the cloud. The air thickened, emitting a pungent scent.

Get up! Run! he heard himself urge again.

Something was unfolding; a growing heat, vibrations, crackles cut the air. Girvyn sprang to his feet and dashed toward the glass boxes. One stood empty, and he thrust his palm against the door, forcing it open.

He'd barely managed to climb inside and shut the door when a brilliant light erupted from the disturbance. In that blinding moment, he saw hundreds of glass containers illuminated in the chamber, and then the radiance subsided, revealing a blazing blue doorway, sizzling sparks snapping along its frame.

Through this strange door, he saw a fiery forest. A beast with a wolf's head entered the chamber, followed by spiders carrying corpses on their backs. The dead wore the attire of the forest folk. Girvyn had never met a Forester, but he'd seen illustrations in the city library.

Then he noticed one person alive, a man being led by a giant in red armour. The Forester was missing a left arm. Despite this, he appeared oddly peaceful.

Finally, a figure in purple robes entered the chamber through the blue-hot door. 'Transport the deceased to the processing plant for sustenance. Retain the Forester for modification. Escort him to the pod,' he commanded.

'Do what you want to me, I don't care,' the man said, his accent heavy.

'You seem unafraid, Forester? Such limited imagination! We will show you, though, and then you will scream for the mercy of death.'

The Forester cast his gaze across the watching monsters and raised no sign of concern, which seemed to annoy the purple-robed man.

'Do you bathe in peace for the witness I left behind? A loved one, was it? We will see how bold you are when you join us.'

The armoured creature pushed the man towards the pods. The occupants descended into a frenzy.

There was one exception, isolated in its stillness.

The hooded figure pointed a scarred, bony finger. 'Let it out.'

The door opened. The creature jerked, suckers on its skin twitching.

Girvyn stared in disbelief.

The monster unfurled, revealing its true shape. The size of a human, with a single tentacle serving as a mouth.

'Get on with it!' the cloaked figure ordered.

As the tentacle attached to the man's face, he pleaded for death.

'So, now you want mercy?' the figure mocked.

'Please!' the Forester cried out. 'No!'

His painful cries filled the dome until the sounds ceased altogether. Girvyn slid back into the pod, back pressed against the inside wall, watching in horror. A liquid pumped through the tentacle into the man's mouth. The creature seemed to relish his pain, savouring his transformation and drawing out each dripping drop as if the process itself provided pleasure. The Forester went to fall but was held aloft, dangling.

His body began changing. At first it was hard to see, something inside, which made his agonising scream all the more harrowing. Then, across his torso and neck, swellings spread. With bone-crunching sounds, his head enlarged, and a new limb began to emerge from his torn shoulder, completing the grotesque transformation.

The Forester now loomed twice his original size, a ghastly appearance with jet-black eyes. His body was covered in glistening worms. Stick-like demons busied themselves around him, attaching pieces of red armour onto his skin, shaping it to match his terrifying new form.

Girvyn whimpered helplessly. Life wasn't supposed to be like this. He cleaned the house while his uncle worked or slept, worked at the market, and studied in the library, always bringing the books back on time. He didn't like talking much to strangers, but when he did, he tried to be nice. He wasn't a bad person.

Just then, he panicked and hit the door, causing him to lose his balance and fall onto the chamber floor. The hovering doorway seemed to come alive, emitting a roaring sound and casting its blue light onto Girvyn. Creatures surged forward and formed a circle around him. Yet, they refrained from closing in.

The hooded one approached leisurely, his voice a smug drawl. 'So, now we finally meet, Rosein's son, in the shadows of my Realm. You are thoroughly disappointing.'

'Wait! This is all a mistake. I wandered in here,' Girvyn pleaded desperately. 'I won't tell anyone what I saw.'

'Convert him.'

The tentacled creature slid towards him but then froze.

'What is wrong with you? Do it!' The crackling doorway emitted a roar as if it were in harmony with the robed man, amplifying his anger.

The tentacle creature tried to move, but its skin pulled backwards, ensnared by invisible threads, causing it to stretch and contort as it struggled to inch forward. Evil visages filled his vision, but all were immobile, just shifting, blinking eyes.

'What is this?' It was the first time Girvyn had noticed alarm in the robed man's voice. 'You!'

Then Girvyn noticed another presence there: a man

awash in a golden light. He snapped his fingers and the creatures were propelled across the chamber and disappeared.

Ignoring the robed one, the stranger extended a glowing hand towards Girvyn. 'Take it, Girvyn. We don't have much time. I cannot hold them off for long. Come.'

Girvyn couldn't discern if they made contact, for the hand appeared ethereal.

In an instant, they found themselves back in the safety of the white space.

'At last, a rescuer! I saved myself from my own dream!' Girvyn exclaimed, words streaming out of his mouth. 'What was that? What happens now? How do I wake?'

'Do you know, I've always admired your ability to recover so quickly.'

Was his face relaxing? The man's features were no more than a golden blur, like the surface of the sun.

'Hold on, who are you?' Girvyn started to panic again.

Perhaps the man could sense it. 'You are safe now. But you must be cautious when entering another structure.' Something familiar in his voice compelled Girvyn to listen and trust. 'Always be wary of the beckoning of windows. No matter how enticing they may be, you are always vulnerable within another author's construct.'

'I don't understand,' Girvyn replied, voice trembling. 'Why does this feel so real?'

'Because it is.'

Girvyn shook his head. 'I don't understand all this.'

'You will in time,' the stranger assured. 'That man you saw in the purple robe tonight, his name is Crane. Stay away from him in both dimensions.'

'Who are you?'

'A friend.'

'What was that place?'

But the man vanished.

Girvyn blinked and sat up in his bedroom, surveying the familiar surroundings. His headache had disappeared. The scent of wood smoke lingered in the air. Despite the chill and dampness, it felt comforting and secure. He could hear his uncle snoring in the adjacent room.

Girvyn drew the sheepskin cover closer to his cheek and nestled his head back on the straw pillow, and the horror of the dream faded away.

Three

Two months had elapsed since that harrowing night, and Girvyn had been plagued by headaches every day, serving as an unrelenting reminder of his ordeal. He tried to dismiss the memories as mere nightmares, shoving them aside like uncomfortable conversations or unwanted thoughts. Yet questions continued to swirl in his mind.

He assumed the dream was his own but was disturbed by what his imagination had conjured: a purple-robed figure standing before a fiery doorway, which served as the entry point for both monsters and victims. He couldn't shake the image of the injured Forester, growing a new arm and then donning armour. And then there was the appearance of his saviour, a mysterious golden figure. Girvyn grappled with the challenge of deciphering the significance behind these vivid yet cryptic images.

He loved to carve, striving to capture nature's beauty. However, since that dream, a dark torment had entered his work, and now everything he'd done before looked naïve and innocent. He held one of his carvings in his hand, a fusion of a wolf and a bear, his thumb tracing the contours of its twisted countenance.

'C'mon nah, ten apples for a quarter bronze!' the voice boomed across the market.

Girvyn put the figurine on the table and looked across the promenade, which teemed with late afternoon crowds vying for end-of-day bargains.

The voice boomed again. He glared at the neighbouring merchant, annoyed by the repetitive announcement. Surely any patrons desiring apples would come and purchase them and didn't need shouting at. Sometimes the chant echoed in his mind on the way home.

A new, softer voice poked his awareness. 'Tell me about this piece?'

Girvyn refocused, meeting the gaze of an older man resembling his uncle, a face marked by creases and patches of grey stubble. 'Well,' he replied bashfully. 'It's from a dream.'

'Don't be ashamed of that. I paint,' the older man said. 'And dreams are a great source of inspiration to me. Can I have a look?' He picked it up and turned it over in his hands. 'That's one strange dream, boy!'

'Yes, it was!

'Hmmm. Keep parchment by your bed so you can pen them down before you forget them.'

Girvyn almost laughed in his face. 'Forgetting it is harder than remembering it.' He regretted his bluntness immediately.

The man fell silent for a moment. 'How much for it?'

'One piece,' Girvyn replied happily.

'No, it's three,' interrupted Fedrick.

Fedrick, the stand owner, appeared beside Girvyn and folded his arms.

'Which is it?' the man grumbled, glancing between them.

'Three,' Fedrick snapped.

The older man shook his head and left.

Fedrick rounded on Girvyn. 'One piece?! The raw wood costs almost that much. Were you dropped on your head as a baby or something?'

'I don't know,' Girvyn muttered. 'I never knew my parents, remember?'

'Alright, alright. But why one piece to the old man when you asked that woman for three earlier?'

'Because he understood it.'

Fedrick shook his head. 'Like I'll never understand you. Don't talk to the customers. You're no good at it. Leave that side to me.'

'But that's why I am here, to gain experience with talking to strangers.'

'Yes, exactly: talk, not sales. That's what I agreed with your uncle. Talk about your carvings and let me do the transactions. I am here to take my 50% cut from you, for taking up my time and my display space. You're supposed to be a child genius, aren't you? A record holder in Rathnell City.'

Girvyn held his breath, unsure of what to say, feeling a bit awkward about self-praise. 'I was the first child in Rathnell to read and write by the age of four,' he confessed.

'Exactly. A child genius. But sometimes you're dense.'

'I'd rather have someone enjoy my work than not,' he replied defensively.

'Your uncle has let you hang out in that library for far too long. You have no street smarts.' He waved a dismissive hand. 'Have your little chat about the work and gain some social skills. That's it!'

'It's not my fault people don't understand me.'

Fedrick snorted. 'Why don't you do more of them nice animals like you used to, eh? Bunnies. Shepherds and their lambs. Wood nymphs. Not too many clothes on them. There's money in that.'

Girvyn blushed furiously. 'That stuff doesn't mean anything. These do. People have to know about what's coming.'

Fedrick raised an eyebrow. 'What's coming?'

Girvyn stammered, unsure what he meant or why he even said that. 'Life's not all rainbows.'

'Our customers don't need to know about strife. Think about the bunnies and the wood nymphs. I know Laglen earns enough to keep you both fed,' he rolled his eyes, 'somehow. But a few extra coins wouldn't hurt, would it? Give the good people what they want; that's all I'm saying.'

Girvyn picked up a piece. A fox-bear hybrid. 'I call it Foxer.'

Fedrick buried his head in his hands. 'Let's start packing up. We haven't sold much today and have a lot to load.'

∼

Girvyn left the market as twilight approached, painting the western horizon in a vibrant palette of red and orange hues that faded into a sombre grey on the eastern side. As sunlight brushed through the keep, casting faint shadows on the castle turrets and parapets, he wondered why he had to go to the market with its unbearable noise. Was it just this chimera of "being able to deal with ordinary people"? Because it wasn't like he was getting any better at that, and as soon as he turned sixteen and could become a scribe, he wouldn't even have to try anymore. He loved the library, sought solace in the world of books. Why change what works? None of it made sense. Girvyn suspected sometimes that his uncle simply wanted him out of the house, but to do what? Sleep more? The sleeping sickness always came the same way: Laglen would turn distant, then a strange mix of evasiveness and sheepishness. Soon after, he would make excuses to go to his bedroom, and if Girvyn ventured there minutes later, his uncle would be impossible to wake.

His attention was diverted by a clamour and loud shouting coming from a junction ahead. A crowd had gathered at the gate to the bailey to witness the final moments of guard practice. The ferocity and strength of the soldiers overwhelmed him. He was hoping to see Elaya Faith, the Queen's Protector – his uncle's friend – leading the class. However, she was not there, most likely occupied with her duty of protecting the queen. Elaya approached her job with unwavering dedication as if it were her life's calling.

He kept going, the copse offering respite and a welcomed solitude. His home sat below towering pines which hid the other huts among the trees. Although Girvyn liked the solitude found below the tall trees, he was aware they could also provide cover for bandits. He'd once mentioned as much to his uncle, suggesting they might move to one of the narrow streets nearer the library. Laglen had laughed dismissively. 'What, live jammed in with no light, the smell of sewers, and bad cooking? No, we're protected better than you know here, and one day people will call this kind of house a cabin retreat, and all the richest merchants in the city will want one.'

As Girvyn reached the front step, the wood creaked and yellow candlelight wavered in the window. He wiped his shoes on the doormat and went inside. 'Uncle?'

Silence greeted him. It always did at this hour. He closed the door and surveyed the mess. It could be worse; tidying the scattered scrolls and half-eaten snacks wouldn't take long. The hearth smouldered. He added logs to it, blew on the flames, cleaned up the kitchen, then settled into a chair and opened a book. Girvyn knew his Uncle Laglen worked tirelessly, providing shelter, food, and income through his scholarly pursuits.

Yet, he was always rushing for the next nap.

Outside a dog barked, accompanied by voices, the night watchmen patrolling the city grounds. Girvyn's gaze drifted towards his uncle's bedroom. He saw Laglen's feet protruding from the bed, motionless as the oak beams in the Great Library.

Knock-knock. Girvyn paused, contemplating whether the queen's guards were collecting taxes. It was that time again, and he had spotted collectors milling about the castle grounds on his way home. He considered trying to wake his uncle, though it was wishful thinking; it had never succeeded in the past.

'Laglen,' a voice murmured in a soft foreign accent. 'Open up.'

Girvyn hesitated, recognising Elaya Faith. It was one thing to engage with her on his own terms, like during guard practice, where a chance greeting sufficed, and he could leave. But here and now he was unprepared to have a conversation with her. Yet his uncle was still asleep, leaving him with no exit strategy unless he claimed to have another headache.

As he gripped the doorknob, he summoned a smile, felt the crack of the fake lines reach down his cheeks. Elaya had a knack for uncovering the truth from the most tangled situations.

'Hello, Elaya,' Girvyn said through the door. 'He's asleep.'

'Open up, Girvyn.'

He did, and she brushed past him, hands on hips, scanning the room. Her face contorted into a pinched expression, forming creases on her dark-black skin; her cheekbones curving like the dunes of her homeland. 'How long?'

Embarrassment overcame Girvyn more than anything else. He knew he appeared indecisive when lost in thought, but he was merely considering his options. Raising a tanned, slender finger, he said, 'I don't know. But it's soup night, he'll wake for that.'

They entered Laglen's bedroom. Elaya glowered at Laglen.

'I can try to wake him?'

'What's the point. No, I'll wait.'

'Will you join me for dinner?'

'I don't like the way he leaves you to do all the work. I never have.'

'Is that a yes?'

She smiled and gave a slight nod.

Girvyn went to the kitchen and called over his shoulder, 'It'll take about an hour to simmer.'

Elaya removed her double back-scabbard with its two short swords. She placed it on the floor, then unbuckled the knife belts from her ankles and upper thighs and sank into a chair beside Laglen's bed.

About an hour later, they ate at the kitchen table, savouring slow, silent mouthfuls, careful not to disrupt the tranquillity with slurping sounds. Elaya was a perfect dinner guest, short on words but steadfast in her presence. Girvyn never quite understood the discomfort people felt in silence; to him, those moments were the most cherished in conversation. He cleared the bowls and his throat.

'Tea?'

'No, thank you,' she replied, resting her palms on the tabletop.

Girvyn feigned a yawn. This whole waiting thing was

starting to feel awkward. 'Do you mind if I go to bed? I'm tired from today.'

'Of course not.' Elaya rose from her seat and headed towards Laglen's bedroom.

He shut his bedroom door and lay on his bed, head on the straw pillow, sheepskin drawn up to his chin. He felt his stomach churn, like he was jolting on a galloping horse. Shapes began to form on the inside of his eyelids. He watched them for a while, tracing their contours, like seeing faces in clouds. Then, in a single moment, stars began to twinkle through the darkness. He had seen these stars in his mind's eye before, and usually, he could blink them away. However, tonight was different. They grew brighter until a blinding blanket of white consumed his entire field of vision. He remembered experiencing this phenomenon; accompanied by the headache before that awful dream. He thought the headache caused the visual disturbance, yet, now, as he gazed at the white light without any pain, he realised it felt like a welcoming presence, as if it were calling out to him in some way.

He had tried to archive the dream, dissolve it into mystic history, half flashbacks, half folklore in his mind, but now it rushed back in one overwhelming instant: a hellish landscape, reaching rotten hands, monsters in glass pods, a Forester tortured, altered into one of them.

Then the memories were gone, and so was he.

He stood in the white expanse, breath hitching in rapid, rising anxiety. He braced himself for that hellish picture scene to materialise again.

'Please. No-no-no-no-no.'

As he fretted, a rotating frame blinked into existence, confirming his fear. How could it be happening again? How could he be making this up? Where would his ravaged, detached mind take him this time?

The picture hovered closer, wafting his hair in the breeze. This time, the scene was different. He didn't see a hellish landscape; he saw something else.

He pointed at it and said to himself, 'What is that?'

In what felt like the time it took to wink, he was swept into it.

His next few moments were spent in incomprehension. He was standing in a massive gathering of jostling bodies, crammed into some floating platform in the sky. It was a two-tiered structure with downward pillars between the top tier and the lower section where Girvyn was. High above, the roof was an undulating shape of frosted glass, curving right over them like the base of a boat.

Girvyn pressed his palms against his ears, attempting to block out the deafening noise, but the roar vibrated in his stomach. It was a sense mugging, but with no smell. Nor, come to think of it, any change in temperature either. Being so close to people, he would have thought it would get a little stuffy.

He tried to move, only to find himself face to face with some strange, indistinct man who stared through him; his gleeful expression and wild jumping motion adding to his oddness. And he wasn't the only one who looked odd. From what Girvyn could see the other people around him had that same, vacant sense about them. Like they were intoxicated, but without the slurring or the falling over bit. And their movements were all identical; whether they were close or high up in the second tier; like they were in a choreographed dance, but with unclear gazes and that same set of waving, springing displays.

Around the platform floated more gigantic structures

crammed with people. A cluster of hovering boxes the size of fruit crates, with a glass eye that protruded from the front panel, came in close to the stand and panned across the people. Beyond that, several colossal windows hung higher in the sky, each showcasing a stream of perplexing, shifting images. Girvyn wondered what it all meant.

Yet everyone around him seemed unbothered about being suspended in the sky. Neither did they look at what was on those windows. They seemed to be enjoying something else.

Girvyn looked down at his feet to try and anchor on something familiar. Yes, himself. The one thing ordinary in this bonkers place. He heard his uncle's gentle voice guiding him in moments of stress: *close your eyes, regulate your breath into long inflated intakes and exhalations.* Tried to let his own voice rise above the crushing din. 'Stay calm, Girvyn,' he said to himself.

How was this happening? Unlike that terrible dream of two months ago there was no darkness or demons, but the same questions remained. Where was he? Where was this coming from? Himself? It must be. And what was this floating stand he was crowded into? It was beyond any reference, actual or imagined, he had ever had. And yet here he was. In a dream. A dream so bizarre and so foreign it was like dropping into another world at another time. You have your thoughts, he said to himself. No one can take that away from you. Concentrate on yourself.

He kept his stare on his feet and couldn't help noticing the ground he was standing on. Smooth and grey. Not a blemish anywhere. Quite unlike the broken, cobbled streets back home. Yet, the shoes of the people packed in beside him and their clothing were rather uniform. He tried to scan the crowd, see into their eyes, but no one looked at him. There was something unnatural beyond that inane glee on their faces. He had been to jousting festivals – if this was what this was: some show for a crowd. But families would talk amongst themselves, watch over their young. Yet these people appeared captivated by what was happening in the basin beneath.

Far below in that distant bowl, a shape flew past, then another and another. The boom boom boom echoed like thunder. People hollered in excitement, and the sound reached a scalding point, burning his ears. The air felt heavy, thickened into something tangible, which he could wade through if he tried. He wanted to move his hands from the sides of his head but was too worried his eardrums might burst.

Then, a soaring, god-like voice reverberated, and then another joined the first, but he couldn't see where they came from.

'Rick Wells leads the pack with a new track record.'

'That's three personal bests in the last three laps.'

'He's recording speeds never seen on this track before.'

A shooting object, like a flying metal box, hurled into the air and exploded into a ball of fire. 'Oh my days, Edderson Jetson is out of the race. He's going to need a cold bath after that one!'

'Oh, he is, and it won't be his last.'

Five more shapes flashed past, followed by multiple booms.

'The chasing pack is on the move. Laglen is in fourth.'

Girvyn uncovered his ears and fixated on the floating windows. The noise faded, or perhaps his rising thoughts drowned it out.

Laglen. The voice mentioned Laglen.

This must be a mistake. Another Laglen? Or maybe he'd misheard.

Then there, on the display, was a picture of his uncle, like a painting, but ultra-realistic, giant, and moving, caught within that frame of the vast window. It was Laglen, but more muscled, and sporting a flowing mane of golden hair.

Words began to scroll across the bottom of the screen. They didn't mean anything to Girvyn. Lap 32. Position 4. Fuel Cells: 42%. Pressure Valves: Green. Dampening Fields: Green.

Girvyn's thoughts had lingered on his uncle before sleep took him, and now, within this dream, his uncle was a central figure. Girvyn rationalised this dream was an amalgamation of his subconscious thoughts, a blend of signs and metaphors. Girvyn supposed, the dream's landscape represented an allegory of Laglen's life. Symbolising their reality. Girvyn was waiting for his uncle to finish the game, like he waited for him to wake up. He quite enjoyed this systematic analysis, and it helped him stay calm.

Laglen! Laglen! Laglen!' The crowds sang.

Whatever Laglen was doing, and whatever that metal thing was, it energised the crowd.

'Go on, Laglen, you can do it!' Girvyn shouted, laughing.

He'd always liked games as long as no-one threw anything to or at him, and now he had adjusted to the sensory assault, he started to pick this one up: like a horserace back home.

'Do you hear that, Bran?'

'Yes, I did, Ray; the Laglen fan club has finally arrived.'

Laglen nearly lost it there and then. The metal shape he was sitting in went into a spin. The metal box behind him tried to overtake but couldn't. They came together. The other swerved sideways, flying out of control and into the wall, where it came to a dead stop.

'Mic Kenkra is stuck on the magnetic race barriers!'

'We are down to the last eight!'

Two more loud booms were followed by objects flipping into the air, arcing out of the basin in balls of lightning.

'Now six.'

'What we are seeing from Laglen is unbelievable!'

New voices, this time crackling and tinny, sounded out:

'Laglen, do you copy? Hang back from the front two; let them fight it out.'

'Affirmative. I copy, Ernest. But there is no time for that,' Laglen said; the screen showed a close-up of his determined expression. Sweat beaded down Laglen's nose. 'There are three laps left. It's now or never.'

With a few inches between them, Laglen followed the second-place metal thing as if their movements were synchronised. When they entered the straight, Laglen flew past.

'Second place! Only Jit Kay to pass,' Ray said.

'With one lap to go!' Bran replied.

Girvyn began jumping and cheering his uncle on, lost in the mass frenzy of the uniform crowd. The din reached deafening heights, and the hysteria washed out even the god-like voices. They came into the final straight, Laglen nose to nose with the leader. Just then, Jit Kay tried to swerve into Laglen and throw him off his racing line. Laglen veered leftwards and punched at a control on the panel below the wheel he was gripping.

Great jets of fire burst from the rear of the metal box, and it blasted forward, almost taking him into the race barriers, but with hard steering and hair flying, he took the corner, came into the straight, and crossed the finish line.

'Super burn! Did you see that?' Ray exclaimed. 'Laglen won with a dangerous thrust manoeuvre!'

Coloured red mist and bits of falling pieces of gold paper dropped from the skies.

Much slower now, Laglen came to a marked platform flush in the floor and waited while the second and third-place metal shapes came onto the blocks next to him. Once they had, the floor rose, lifting them into the air, with Laglen held the highest.

Girvyn noticed his stand was descending, and the crowd grew increasingly enthusiastic. When the platform reached the ground, the front of the crowd spilt onto the track, but they remained disoriented, littering the area with repetitive movements. Girvyn broke away and hurried towards where he'd last spotted his uncle, pushing through the aimless throng.

His uncle was being congratulated by a group of men in red outfits. Beautiful women were giggling flirtatiously, brandishing pieces of paper they were keen to impart.

Girvyn gawped at Laglen, wondering what screwed-up motivation he could have for altering his uncle in his dream this way, and why he would surround him with all these dallying followers. Girvyn pushed forward, flustered by the noise and hubbub, trying not to look at the ladies, which was hard to do.

Then, Laglen saw him, his expression changing into pure, unadulterated terror. 'Girvyn! How?' he spluttered.

Girvyn beamed. 'This is my dream, Uncle.' He spread his arms out to present it as a gift.

A newcomer popped into existence. He was identical to Laglen, though much younger, dressed in a long white coat. 'Oops. Embarrassing.'

'Stop it!' Laglen rounded on the younger version of himself. He clenched his teeth and came back to Girvyn, a forced calm in his voice 'No. It's my dream, not yours.'

'I think this is about you sleeping all the time. Elaya is waiting for you at home. I fell asleep. You should wake and see her.' He laughed to himself. 'But you can't. This is my dream! I can't wait to tell you about this when I wake up.'

'Girvyn, sit down.' Laglen gestured to the pavement, and they sat next to each other.

Girvyn was still grinning. 'This is so lucid!'

Laglen let out a long sigh. 'How have you done this? You shouldn't be able to Travel until you are trained.'

'Is this one of those existential talks we have sometimes?'

'Girvyn, you are not dreaming. Normal dreams are surreal.'

Girvyn clapped. 'This is so crazy, cow-popping surreal!'

'He doesn't know,' the younger Laglen said.

Girvyn frowned at him. 'Who is this person?'

Laglen shook his head. 'Ignore him. First, you must understand *this* is my dream, and you have entered it.'

'Hmmm, why would I create two of you?' Girvyn mused. 'But I guess none of this makes sense, even though I interact with it.'

'Did you pass through a window to get here?'

Girvyn frowned. 'Do you mean a floating picture?'

'They are not pictures, exactly. They are windows to people's dreams. And were you in a white space when this happened?'

'Yeah. So? I am inventing this, so you know I did.'

'You are so annoyingly clever.'

'Well, you made me go to all those after-school clubs. Debate, philosophy, carving, cooking.'

Laglen seemed frustrated. 'Stay seated,' he motioned before Girvyn could get up, 'and watch this...' Laglen waved his hand, and everything stopped.

It was unsettling. Clothing in mid-movement. A sudden quiet. Expressions frozen.

'If this was your dream, how did you do that?' Laglen asked him.

'I did that, not you.'

'No, you didn't.'

Girvyn frowned at him. 'Yes, I did; I am creating this situation.' He faltered. 'I wonder what all this means?' he said to himself.

'Complicated one!' the other Laglen said. 'How do you prove it to him?'

'Be gone!'

The younger version of Laglen vanished, leaving them to talk.

Laglen waved dramatically, and the scene transformed. It wasn't a slow fade-in, fade-out; instead, it was sudden, as if they had jumped into another place. They found themselves sitting on a mountain ledge, overlooking a valley.

'I did that,' Girvyn said, explaining.

Laglen shook his head. 'Look, I know this is hard to take in. And if I had brought you here from our side, together, prepped, informed, it would have been easier to show. But here we are, Girvyn.'

Girvyn laughed. 'I have no idea how or why, but I'm doing all of this.'

The view changed. 'Girvyn, this is the view from the citadel in Cundelly, but you've never been there. Explain that.'

Girvyn looked across the sudden, breathtaking cityscape. 'Ah, but I only have your assurance this is the view, and you're a figment of my imagination.'

'Aha! Jurgun's conundrum. You remember we discussed it, and you couldn't solve it?' A pen and paper appeared, and equations started to sprawl across the page. 'Look! Here's the answer, you see? Something you didn't know but now recognise to be true and therefore proof this is my dream, not yours.'

Girvyn scowled at his uncle's smug expression. 'I could be solving it now within my dream.'

Laglen threw up his hands in exasperation. 'You can doubt everything if you're going to be like that. Will you for now accept what I'm saying, Girvyn? Just on the off chance it's actually true?' He sighed. 'I wasn't supposed to tell you all this for a few years. Somehow you have started early. Has this happened before?'

Girvyn felt his stomach stir. A slow unsettling uncertainty. He wasn't enjoying this dream at all now. Not one bit. The insistence of Laglen and these shifting spaces brought a chill to his bone. To his marrow.

Laglen persisted, a concern in his voice. 'Has this happened before, Girvyn? Have you crossed before?'

He went to answer, to tell him about that dark fortress in the night, but a wave of distrust and questions surged through him. 'How can I pass into your mind? What evil is this?'

'Now that is a good question. That is the right question. And it's not evil. You are not in my head. We have met in another dimension. We are special, Girvyn. We are called Dream Travellers. This is a dream, yes, but it's mine. It's something I have chosen to do. And when you went to sleep in the Waking, you entered it.'

'The Waking?'

'The world we live in. The world you know.'

'This is not my dream?' Girvyn's breath began to shorten. 'I don't understand. What is this place? But I am dreaming!'

Laglen spotted his rising angst at once. 'Control your breath. Be in your place of calm. Close your eyes and think of the library. It is okay; I am with you.'

They stood in the library beside the towering shelves and ancient heavy books; some were older than the shelves they stood on. Girvyn glanced around, mesmerised, and went to sit at a desk, reassured by the familiarity of his safe place. Something struck him. 'There is no wood grain. I saw this before in the festival race. The people, their uniforms, it was unfinished.'

'We can create anything we want from our imagination on this side. It can be disconcerting, but I chose them like that. I could have added more detail, like those officials on the racetrack. They were more life-like.'

'And the women? Were they your fan club?'

Laglen blushed. 'Yes, they were.' He seemed keen to continue explaining. 'We call the scenes constructs. Once we save them, they become dream structures in the white space inside windows you can enter. They are saved in a place called the Atrium.'

'And you said this side. Meaning what, exactly?'

'The Dream Realm.'

'Who was that man?'

'He is my assistant. He helps me file my constructs. When you save a lot, they are hard to go through. Imagine having hundreds of books.' He stopped and tried again. 'Think of it like each daydream you have is real and can be saved. He helps me file them.'

'I can hear you. And I protect you from yourself,' the assistant appeared. He shrugged at Girvyn. 'I get the younger face because he created me many years ago. It is an honour to make your acquaintance.'

'Where did you get those stupid names from? Ray, Bran, and Jit. This is mad!' Girvyn groaned. 'I want to wake up.'

Laglen nodded. 'That's a good idea. We should continue

this chat at home. Then you will know it's true. That's the one way I can prove this to you.'

'I am scared. How do I wake up?'

'Shut your eyes and think of black stars in the white.'

Girvyn sent him a stabbing stare and vanished.

~

Girvyn woke, sucking in air abruptly as if he had been underwater too long. The coldness of the hut sank in. Vacillating candlelight danced across the walls. He rose and left his room and entered Laglen's. He found Elaya there, her presence steadfast beside Laglen's bedside, awake and alert despite how late it was, looking at Girvyn, no doubt seeing his distress aura.

'What happened?' she probed.

Laglen stirred.

Elaya looked at Laglen, eyes narrowing.

The memory of his dream was as clear to Girvyn as any lived experience. Not like those wavering, declining dreams he usually had that faded away as he woke. Surely what Laglen had said could not be true? He felt as if he was looking at an unfamiliar person. It was as though a great weight of betrayal had transformed Laglen into someone else. Hoping it was all a bad dream, he folded his arms and waited for his uncle to sit up.

'Girvyn! What happened?' Elaya pressed.

Girvyn ignored her. He barely heard the question.

Say something, Uncle, that's not related to the dream! He cursed. *Anything!*

If the dream was mentioned, it would attest that Laglen was right. For all these years, he'd believed his uncle was afflicted by a sleeping sickness. Every decision his uncle had made he began to see in a new, deceptive light. Was it all to get him out of the house? The trips to the library, the various clubs, and now the market. All of it.

Come on, Uncle, speak!

He saw an expression marked by an equal measure of shame and guilt.

Laglen sat up in bed, then glanced away. 'I am sorry,' he groaned. 'Now, do you believe me?'

Girvyn loomed over him, his face twisted into a fervent snarl. He stared down at a man he didn't recognise. Spittle burst from his mouth. 'All this time, you have been sleeping and entertaining yourself. All these years. And you didn't tell me. What is wrong with bringing me up? A distraction, was I?'

'Look, I know you are angry.'

'Angry, confused, bewildered, to name a few.'

Elaya's eyes widened. 'He knows?'

Girvyn glared back and forth between them. 'You knew?'

Elaya smiled thinly. 'I'm sorry,' was all she said.

'Who else knows?'

'Elaya and Brennen,' Laglen told him, finally meeting his stare. 'And the other Dream Travellers.'

Girvyn stepped back and folded his arms. Questions were fighting to get out. 'Who do you visit? Do you have another family there you prefer to spend time with?'

Laglen snorted in surprise and stood up, moving in for a hug.

'Don't touch me.'

Laglen faltered. 'No, Girvyn, it's nothing like that. It's recreation, experiments, and investigations. Yes, I have some attachments to things, but not another family.'

Elaya shook her head. 'Investigations? You mean indulgences. You know I don't approve, Lag. I never have. You have responsibilities here. And you have shirked them.'

Laglen glanced away. 'I get my scribing work done in the library. We pay the taxes.'

'Barely!' Girvyn shouted. He held his hand up before Laglen could speak. 'All the cooking I do, all the tidying up, is it because you prefer to be somewhere else? I thought you had fatigue problems!'

'I am not saying I don't get tired,' he replied, wiping his brow. 'I thought you didn't mind cleaning: that it was a sort of solace for you? Something you could control, where outside is disorder you find difficult.'

'Oh please. I am not saying there's not peace in it, but I thought it was a necessity because you were ill. You lied to me.'

'I'm sorry, Girvyn.' He sighed, pausing. 'Let's continue in the lounge.'

In silence, they moved to the other room.

Girvyn slumped into a chair before the hearth and glared into its embers.

Laglen continued. 'Once you get over the lie and I get over the shame and guilt, there is relief.'

'Relief?' He shook his head. 'So I don't have to go to the market anymore? There *is* some relief in that!' He threw his hands in the air melodramatically.

'There is relief in you knowing the truth. Now we must start your training.'

'Train me? What, to waste my life away in self-indulgent fantasies like you?'

'Look, I know you are angry, but you are slipping into the Realm by yourself and need to learn. And, besides, the Dream Realm is more than escapism, it is what you want it to be. I must impart knowledge in a careful, sustained way.'

Girvyn fed logs into the flames and watched the fire grow; stinging trails of black smoke entered the room. Girvyn was inundated with conflicting emotions. Life was already challenging, struggling to communicate with people, always perceiving or uttering things in conversations that others couldn't comprehend. That frustrating knack for remembering obscure details – it had been both a gift and a burden, but mostly a burden. Yet, deep down, a part of him had always sensed his uniqueness. He'd attributed it to his idiosyncrasies, but he now understood he was different. What he had witnessed in his uncle's dream had blown his mind. The notion that he could conjure places from his imagination, sent a thrilling shiver down his spine.

Girvyn lifted his head. 'I am intrigued about all this, and I want to protect myself, so I agree, it makes sense to train me.'

'Listen, you and I have to talk every aspect of this through. I admit I've been absent too much, and it won't happen again.' A stern stare told Girvyn that absolute privacy was needed for whatever came next. Laglen regarded Elaya. 'I guess the truth is all out now.'

She returned a gentle smile. 'You can be honest with Girvyn, and that is a good thing.'

Laglen frowned. 'How long has the Queen's Protector been watching over me tonight? With the envoys arriving for the summit, I'm sure you don't have that time to waste readily. What's wrong, Elaya?'

She drew a breath, unusually hesitant. 'As you know, we've been trying to understand why the Foresters and the Highlanders have agreed to talk civilly in the same room. Both have suffered attacks where babies were stolen, but two months ago there was a survivor in The Orran Forest. This Forester girl speaks of a figure in purple robes, Laglen. Controlling an army of what she calls demons but that sounds to me like Realm creatures. I hoped for your thoughts, and there's also a question of whether you could use your talents to investigate this where others can't.'

'You mean in the Realm?! I know why you are saying this; you mean Crane. But firstly, purple robes: it's not that unusual. Monks wear hessian robes. Nobles wear cloaks, and those with royal blood wear outlandish or gilded outfits. Outside of that, anything is possible. The world is full of differences and copies. Anyone could instruct a clothmaker. But even if it was him, I can tell you that he can't bring whatever he creates in the Realm into the Waking. It's impossible. Equally impossible to what you ask, which is that I seek to enter his construct and see what's inside. It's far too dangerous, Elaya, not even if...'

'Well I did it.'

'What?' stammered Laglen.

'I went into purple robe's dream about two months ago. I saw him and his demons.'

They both looked at Girvyn in silent amazement as he recounted what he had seen in the dream: a giant clad in red armour, dead Foresters being dragged into hell, one transforming into a monster.

Laglen listened with a deepening scowl. 'It doesn't work like that,' he interrupted. 'Crane can't drag people through to the Realm. What you saw must have been within the confines of a construct. You must have entered Crane's window as you did mine. Crane has a preoccupation with hell. That's why we don't talk to him anymore. What you saw in my construct, they were made up people, props. These actors make it more thrilling and immersive. But you could create a community, let them evolve, free thinking sentients with feelings. So if you start torturing them, it's not right, even if you create them for that. I'm sure what you saw in

Crane's hell was very unfortunate and upsetting, but the mind transcends dimensions, not the body. But you must be careful, Girvyn. Going into another author's construct is forbidden. Well,' he corrected himself, 'it's just not the etiquette. Think of it as a stranger's house. It might be open, but you always knock, don't you? In fact, how often do you look through another person's window? Especially if they are in. And going into Crane's structure was dangerous. The author has the power, not the visitor. Crane would butcher you instantly if you entered his domain uninvited.' His brow wreathed into a yet-more-troubled frown. 'How did you get out?'

Girvyn turned his thoughts to the glowing man, but he didn't know what to say or how to describe him. It seemed so surreal and fleeting. 'I got lucky. I escaped.'

'To where?'

'The white space.'

'You were very lucky,' Laglen breathed heavily, impressed. 'You returned to your Atrium without training.'

'See? That's my point,' Elaya said disapprovingly. 'You should have been at his side; you might have noticed Girvyn's transitioning if you had caught it before he crossed. Then you could have trained him early to not make that mistake. You have asked me to watch over Girvyn all these years, and I have. But why, if not to respond to moments like this?'

Girvyn glared at them both. 'Watch over me?'

Elaya sent Laglen a refuting look. 'He needs to know.'

'You need to take this slowly,' Laglen sighed. 'What I am going to tell you will upset you.'

'I'm already upset, so tell me.'

'There is no easy way to say it, Girvyn. Crane killed your mother.'

Girvyn threw his arms up. 'You told me she died in a fire!'

'There was a fire, but that came after. I couldn't tell a child that his mother, my sister, was killed in a wolf attack!'

Girvyn gasped, eyes welling, anger raging in him. 'A wolf attack?'

Laglen went to say something, lowered his head, and then remained silent for a long moment. 'I planned to tell you when you were older.'

'How noble of you.'

Laglen looked away, his eyes wide with distant memories. 'He came for all of us that night, including you. We were all in her shack, then outside we heard their hollow howling. We tried to escape, but they charged at us, sending us back inside. The wolves threw themselves at the door. Your mother saved us all. She took an axe to the hut's back wall and carved a way out for us. She told me to keep you safe and not train you until you came of age. Then she went back to delay the wolves while we got clear. We expected the beasts to catch our scent and give pursuit, allowing her to escape, but they didn't. We waited for her in the forest, but she never came. You were a few months old. I am sorry I haven't told you this before.'

Girvyn held back a sob, felt the pain in his throat soar, biting at his words. 'Did she suffer?' he managed.

Laglen went to speak, but laughed unfeelingly; the sound seemed inappropriate. He let the noise fade until it seemed like it was never there. 'We did nothing. We listened to her screams and then fled into the dark.' He let out a long, caught breath. 'But Crane is just a man. This side he is weak, frail, and cowardly. Sending his sentinels to do his dirty work. I am sure these terrible kidnappings are not him.' He looked at Elaya. 'I think it's a gang, Elaya.'

'Then how do you explain this sighting of purple robes, demons, and missing babies? It's so sadistic,' Elaya said, unconvinced. 'Very Crane.'

'Hmmm, indeed. It's a very unsettling situation. We have babies missing near sightings of a person in a purple robe and a Forester girl who claims to have seen creatures in her camp. It all seems telling, does it not? But maybe these are the wrong conclusions some other party hopes we'll jump to. Crane is not the only schemer in this world. I posit that we should advance with caution and a measure of restraint until further evidence casts a light on this puzzle. What do we do? Run with fear when Girvyn needs stability and training? Try to hunt down a man I have not seen in fifteen years? Execute him? What's new is this Forester girl survivor. But she could have seen nothing more than rabid madmen in a killing rage. Or her life was deliberately spared to be the innocent messenger of a lie. Hmmm.'

Girvyn knew Laglen was settled in himself in an intellectual inquest, a wordsmith in his element with rapier-like thinking. Shame and guilt were unfamiliar modes to him. But Girvyn now detested that reflected, studied way of his.

After a measured moment, Laglen said, 'It's all come at once, and I need time to think.'

'You always said Crane might come. We need to get Girvyn out of the city. I can have one of my men escort him into hiding, somewhere only a few of us know about, until we know he is safe,' Elaya urged.

Laglen pressed his temples in thought. 'You are right of course, Elaya. Always juggling everyone's safety.'

'Laglen, I know you've wondered why Crane would murder Rosein and never found a satisfactory answer. What if she was collateral damage and the real target was the other person in the cottage with her?'

'You mean Girvyn? But he was a baby.'

'A baby who turns out to be a Traveller with a talent to do

things even you can't. Girvyn escapes Crane's domain without training. What if Crane foresaw that somehow?'

'Is that your professional druid opinion?'

Elaya blinked. 'What? No, not exactly, but a siege is not always what it seems.'

'If only Crane was here in front of you now so you could read his lifeforce and know for sure.'

'I can't read minds, Lag. I read auras and get impressions. I don't ever get actual thoughts. But that helps to anticipate the other, yes.'

'How we could have done with your skills that night.'

Elaya sent Girvyn a concerned stare. 'I am sorry so much has been thrown at you this evening. How are you feeling?'

'Numb,' Girvyn replied quietly.

Laglen reached over and squeezed Elaya's arm. 'Thank you for bringing this to my attention. Give me a few days to investigate it. I need to speak with the other Dream Travellers. Actually, I need to get into that summit and hear what this Forester girl has to say. Can you help?'

Elaya shook her head. 'I can't get you inside, Lag. You are not one of my guards or an envoy. It's invite-only. Royals, diplomats, emissaries, witnesses; it's heavily controlled. Even though I am running security, old friend, I cannot get you in.' As she finished speaking, a smile began widening, and it was her turn to squeeze his arm. 'But I know a man who can! Brennen has ways to listen and see in the castle that others do not. Ask him for help.'

'Of course! Brennen.'

Elaya gave a small nod. 'In the meantime, I am putting a guard on Girvyn. The summit is in three days. We listen to it, then we decide what to do.'

'Elaya, you are my dearest friend, a natural protector, and a druid. Whatever you say goes!'

'Good. Then you should heed my words more next time.'

Four

The next morning, Girvyn woke from a dream. A normal dream of haziness and fusions in uncertain settings. As he swung his feet out of bed, the dream's characters drifted away like ghosts vanishing into shadows. He sat blinking, thinking. Since the revelation of what he was, of what Crane had done to his mother, Girvyn was left with an unrelenting sense of focus: to seek retribution for his mother's death. He just needed the training to do it.

He found his uncle poking a rod at the hearth.

'Morning,' Laglen said without looking up.

Girvyn came over. 'Last night,' he shifted and squirmed, searching for the right words. 'Look, I didn't mean to come over unappreciative of what you've done for me. You have looked after me my whole life, but mistakes were made, Uncle.'

'Yes, I know, and I will correct that. So why don't you go to the library while I go to sleep!'

'Uncle!'

Laglen had that twinkle back in his eye. Those drawn

expressions from last night were replaced by a mischievous, keen brightness. 'At least our humour is still intact.'

'Too soon, Uncle. Poor taste.'

'Agreed.' Laglen stood up. 'Look, I am sorry. Sorry about everything. But most of all, I have let you and myself down.'

'I'm sorry too. I understand your reasons for not telling me. It's okay.'

Laglen spread his arms. 'Can we hug now and move on?'

Girvyn hesitated. Was he still hurt? Was he more excited than angry? He threw himself into Laglen's arms and lost himself in the hold, in his shielding love. That smell of wood smoke and sour body odour that smacked of onions. It all felt delicious.

'I promise to make it up to you,' Laglen told him. 'There will be no more secrets. Elaya is right. You are both right. I have shirked my responsibilities. But my failure was not because I don't love or appreciate you. It helped the pain. I don't think I've ever got over what happened. Or come to terms with my new reality when your mother died, when I became your guardian. From the moment we came here, I sunk into the Realm as a place of escape. It made it manageable. It's remarkable how easy that was to do when you can create anything.'

'I'm keen to learn more about all that. I want to know it all.'

'You will.'

Girvyn glanced across the neat worktops. 'Does that mean you are going to tidy up a bit more?'

'You've noticed!'

'Uncle, it's hard not to! Did you commission the queen's housekeepers? Pull in a few favours?'

Laglen beamed. 'Nope, I did it all myself.' He turned his attention back to the pan. 'Eggs?'

'I am loving this new you!'

'I want to be there for you. Not just in honesty, but for the training you'll need, and in protecting you.'

Girvyn paused. 'What is the threat to me? Is Elaya overly worried?'

'I don't know.' Laglen made a face. 'Crane could have come for you years ago, but why would he be interested in an untrained Dream Traveller? I trust Elaya's instincts to keep you safe though.'

They ate, chatting about nothing and everything, enjoying the ease of familial conversation.

A rap rap rap came at the front door. More than a fist. Something solid against the wood.

They glanced upwards, momentarily taken aback.

'It's okay,' Laglen reassured, before proceeding to open it.

A man stood on the doorstep, his very presence dominating the surrounding space. His broad shoulders tapered to a slim waist; while the tight vest he wore hinted at sculpted muscles beneath.

'Are you Laglen?' the man said. He sheathed the dagger that he had used to knock against the door. 'My name is Tarith. Elaya sent me. Can I come in?'

'Elaya said she was sending you. Thanks for coming.'

Tarith entered, making direct eye contact with Girvyn. He extended a hand, which they both shook. 'I would do anything for that woman,' he said, his face softening.

Laglen smiled, glancing at Girvyn. 'So,' he said, hands on hips. 'I have some errands to run in the castle. What's the plan today?'

Tarith pointed to a chair. 'I'll sit with your boy.'

Girvyn went to object to being called a boy, he could write better than any adult he had met, but his fast, direct way was halted by his inner voice telling him to be less blunt and more polite. 'Is it possible to go to the library, please? I'm happy to read all day. I like it there.'

'I don't see why not,' Tarith answered. 'I will station myself outside the door, though. That stale silence and shuffling book pushers are not for me.'

'That works,' Laglen said.

Girvyn found himself surprised by Tarith's articulation, realising why Elaya depended on him and assuming his proficiency with a sword was at least as good.

'Would you help me put my boots on?' Laglen asked Girvyn.

They went to Laglen's room and shut the door. His uncle kept his voice low. 'It's not that I don't trust Tarith, but I want to protect my friend Brennen from being discovered in the castle tunnels.'

Girvyn nodded in understanding. 'You mean your recluse friend in the loft?'

'Yes. I'm hoping he can hide me somewhere in the castle so I can hear the summit tomorrow.'

Girvyn helped him put his boots on. 'When can I get to meet Brennen?'

'When you are older, he doesn't like people.'

'But he likes you. I am sure he would like me.'

'That he might.'

'Why doesn't he like people, Uncle?'

'Something happened in his life long ago that made him want to stay away from everyone else,' Laglen said. 'And now he has got used to hiding in there, listening to meetings and only seeing me and Elaya.'

'Why does Elaya let him stay there?'

'Because he is our friend. He means no harm to anyone and sees and hears many things from those hidden corridors.'

'I won't say anything about Brennen to anyone.' Girvyn hesitated. 'How long will I have a bodyguard for?'

'Until we get to the bottom of all this.' Laglen sent him a sympathetic look. 'Elaya wants to make sure you are not in danger. You have immense resilience. You always have. Yes, you get anxious at new things, but once those things become familiar, you adapt. For now, immerse yourself in books; it will help you take your mind off things.'

Girvyn blinked rapidly. 'Is there anything in the library I can read to help me learn about the Dream Travellers?'

Laglen returned an amused expression. 'What? On the public shelves? No, we're a secret to Orts.'

Girvyn frowned at him. 'What are Orts?'

'It's the name we give to people who don't Travel.' Laglen raised a finger to stop his reply. 'But I have a few diaries, journals and such, that you can browse.'

Laglen approached a trunk and unlocked it using a key hanging from a cord around his neck. As he raised the lid, Girvyn couldn't help but gasp. It was a rare occurrence for that trunk to be opened, and he had always wondered about the contents of the pages within, despite asking countless times and always being dismissed.

Laglen pulled a book out and brought it over, holding it for Girvyn to take. Girvyn froze, unable to do anything but stare at it as if it were the Book of Death. That sick feeling rose from his stomach to his chest, turning into a shiver of fear.

'It's okay,' Laglen reassured, pulling it back and out of view as if the sight of it alone would cause a curse. He stuffed it into a satchel and lifted the strap onto Girvyn's shoulder.

Back in the lounge, they greeted Tarith again.

'Shall we?' Tarith nodded at the door.

Girvyn took a breath and nodded back. Why was he

feeling so tense? He was going to the library. Was it the revelation that *he was* different that fuelled his anxiety? He pushed his brooding away.

They left the house and felt the chill of the morning breeze. Girvyn drew his coat tighter. Tarith didn't even notice. He was scanning the path ahead.

'After you, Girvyn,' Tarith gestured, following behind.

Girvyn liked him. There was something reassuring and no-nonsense about his new protector.

They didn't speak on the way to the castle, and Girvyn took his usual route. Through the copse, into the residential district on the city's east side, past low-roofed wood dwellings. Smoke trailed from stubby chimneys, and cooking sounds and morning chatter drifted across their path. After a few minutes' walk, stone structures grew visible through the scattered trees. The Tower of Rathnell rose the highest, guarding its networks of dungeons and cells. Then came the looming walls and arches of the castle, ramparts and rising turrets, seeming as primordial and permanent as the ancient glinting mountains on the distant horizon from where the stone had come.

After navigating through the inner walls and courtyards, they finally arrived at a bailey. The entrance was unguarded, allowing them to pass by a training session where some soldiers were preparing for sword practice.

Tarith acknowledged a few of them, ignoring their raised eyebrows.

'Nice day off?' one said.

'On baby patrol?' another sniggered.

'Just ignore them,' Tarith told Girvyn.

'Oh, I will; I doubt they can read.'

Tarith let out a short laugh. 'Of that, you might be right.'

Inside the castle, chambermaids and officials busied in

ant-like frenzies, and those of the court swept along the corridors, their trailing cloaks discharging airs of self-importance. When they reached the library, Girvyn felt his excitement stir.

Tarith scoped inside, checking each occupant with a scrutinising glare. There was one entrance in and out, so, once satisfied, he waited outside the door in the lobby, stationing himself in a wooden chair with his unbelted scabbard lying over his knees.

As Girvyn entered the great library, the scent of candle wax and aged leather-bound books rose to greet him. Wooden shelves stretched into darkness where the unknown lingered. A dozen monks clad in stone-coloured hessian garments worked behind tabletops, duplicating the archives for offsite storage.

Girvyn considered browsing through the map sections or reading about castle architecture, but the weight of the book in his satchel prickled his shoulder and his consciousness.

He laid the book on the desk before him and checked to see if anyone could see what he was reading. A few scholars were scattered nearby but were deep in work.

He felt a tightness in his chest as he faced the book; the first time he had ever been nervous about reading. Titled "Concerning the Infinite" in Laglen's script, it might hold answers to his life. Despite his apprehension, he was compelled to read it.

The book's cover, made of soft, dyed cowhide typical of the era, opened to crisp, substantial pages. He brushed his fingers across the parchment, his attention caught by the flickering lantern casting wavering light over the text. This was not a technical manual or a philosophical treatise, but a collection of Laglen's dream logs, many illustrated in his uncle's proficient hand. They weren't in chronological order either; the first was from ten years ago. Fantastical possibilities filled his mind. As he delved into the changing worlds within, he found not just diaries and descriptions but pictures, population graphs, and designs for innovative inventions. Then he stopped, staring in disbelief at the page before him.

Dearest Girvyn,

I write these words with trembling fear knowing that one day you will read this and see my fantasies. Assuming you are now eighteen and are reading this, I have kept these secrets my whole life; some innocent, some shameful, but always indulgent pastimes. I have used these worlds to escape my guilt for the loss of so many. The greatest is that of my sister, your mother, taken from us by Crane. I know I am not the only one to share the cowardice of indecision – we all waited in the night for your mother to come, only to flee when we saw the flames. I hope now you understand why I chose to hide from my past.
Judge, if you must, pity if you will, but please, forgive me for my cowardice.

Uncle Laglen.

Girvyn turned the page and gasped. There was a drawing of a woman's face strikingly like his own. Below it, his uncle's familiar handwriting read: 'Rosein, my laughing little sister. Was it fair of me to bring the part of you I knew back in a construct? She says so, but she is incomplete, making me realise how little I understood you. I suppose I thought to seek counsel on how not to repeat this with Girvyn, but have

I done nothing more than give form to my continuing failure?'

The next page showed a man on a mountainside, peering down into a valley below. The man resembled Laglen, though it was hard to discern from the reverse perspective, and he was adorned in a flowing golden cloak. Girvyn gazed upon a city nestled in the valley, a sight beyond his wildest dreams. It was a city of glass and mirrors, its walls and jagged buildings soaring into the sky.

Girvyn squinted at some notes below the picture. 'Behold, Jacarn! The city of the future. Population 400 million. Pollution 0%, Technology: sustainable, democratic, smart.'

Girvyn felt his pulse quicken as he tried to make sense of it all.

The subsequent illustration showed Laglen hand in hand with a woman. They both looked young. The picture showed Laglen leading her along a path, a gated homestead behind them. A poem lay beside it.

Dearest Marlena,

In the heart of four walls, love finds its place,
Where laughter and warmth sweetly embrace.
A haven of solace, a refuge so true,
Home is where love blooms, just like morning dew.

Hold close to your heart this love so pure,
In the place you call home, forever secure.
In its walls, in its hearth, in its laughter and song,
Love finds its dwelling, where we all belong.

Girvyn found himself unable to breathe, forcing his eyes

shut in a tight squeeze. He leaned back in the chair and slowly opened them, regaining his composure. Why would Laglen leave behind gateways to such secrets for him to discover? Did Laglen create these places, worlds, and scenes over his lifetime and then forget their contents? Was this book intended not just for study, but as a record for his uncle to remember?

A cascade of ideas raced through Girvyn's mind. Scenes of nature where he could find solace. Imagined conversations with talking animals and hybrid beings. The prospect of constructing a city like his uncle had. And then, the idea of having a real, understanding companion overwhelmed him with excitement.

He was a training programme away from sharing such unchecked power with his uncle. His life now had a clear division, a before and after this pivotal moment. All his previous thoughts about what he might do and become when he grew older had faded into insignificance, replaced by a new reality teeming with boundless possibilities.

At the same time, the image of his uncle had changed forever.

∽

Laglen wandered through the castle, but his mind was elsewhere. So much had transpired since Girvyn had entered his dream that it was hard to keep pace. Once his nephew had moved past his anger, he'd adapted swiftly to his new reality, even expressing a desire for rapid training. There was no denying his intelligence, and he grasped the potential of the Dream Realm, but he was impulsive and lacked caution. Which, of course, was unsurprising since he was only fourteen. Laglen felt apprehensive about all of this. His primary focus had to be to restrain Girvyn while ensuring he acquired the necessary grounding and knowledge.

Further ahead, kitchen staff appeared carrying trays of wine and cheese, en route to the courts. Laglen acknowledged them, nodding. Loitering in this area was not unusual for him, as he was a close friend of Wrin, the queen's chef. When the corridor emptied and the voices faded, he halted and faced an unremarkable wall of bricks. He followed them horizontally and vertically until he found it, the secret trigger brick. It never ceased to amaze him how the original architects had integrated this feature into the plans, now lost in the sands of time but still known to a few. He pushed it, and a door in the wall was revealed, scraping slightly as it swung inward to reveal a narrow, curving stairway. He envisioned a waiter leaning on the wall and stumbling upon it, discovering a person dwelling at the top.

Inside, it was dimly lit. A corridor to the left connected to a network of concealed passages. Laglen, however, ascended the stairs ahead. Brennen had resided beyond the wooden hatch at the top of these steep stairs for close to fifteen years, and the climb was long enough for old memories and intermittent flashbacks to resurface.

Elaya had felt indebted to Brennen for the kindness he had shown her when she first arrived in the city as a refugee minor. It had been her suggestion that Brennen utilise the concealed lofts and passages to take respite and recover from a traumatic experience. As time passed, she had encouraged him to reintegrate into society, but he never quite managed it. The longer he remained secluded, the more accustomed he became to solitude. He posed no security threat, so as Elaya rose in responsibility she opted to overlook the situation. There had been a benefit too: Brennen's profound interest in current affairs and his unique position, which allowed him to overhear unseen Privy Council meetings, corridor gossip, and chamber secrets, had proven to be valuable assets to Elaya on multiple occasions. She also owed a debt to Laglen. Between the two of them, they had played a significant role in guiding her toward her ascent.

Laglen reached the top and opened the hatch. He peered in. Numerous piles of books littered the floor. In the far corner was a writing table; a candle burned merrily.

'Hello,' he called out. 'Brennen?'

A throat cleared nearby. It took a few attempts, as if it hadn't been used for a while. 'Laglen?' came the growly reply.

'Yes, it's me.'

A tall man appeared, holding a dagger. 'Lag! I wasn't expecting visitors. Apologies for the blade.'

'Why would you expect visitors? You are a recluse.'

'Lag, it's been three months!' he said furiously. Then, a broad smile widened his face. 'It is good to see you, old friend.'

'And you, too. Been out much since we last met?'

'You know me.' He winked. 'I do come out from the hidden passages from time to time. I can't survive on vegetables I grow on my windowsill, so I steal from the kitchen. And the Great Library is too tempting to avoid when an occasion so demands to borrow a book.'

Laglen rolled his eyes. 'No wonder there are so many missing items on the shelves. Most of the time they blame Girvyn!' He measured Brennen's face, eyes tracing smoky patches of hair. 'You look well.'

Brennen pointed to a wooden chest. 'Please, be seated. Nettle tea?'

'Yes, thank you.'

Brennen searched through his belongings, then retrieved two cups. He lifted a pot from a contained fire on the window shelf, and a wisp of steam spiralled up. 'It's been steeping, so it should have a rich flavour.'

'A little for me, thank you,' Laglen replied.

Brennen handed Laglen a petite cupful, and Laglen took a sip, his features lighting up with pleasure. 'Excellent!'

Brennen grinned and sipped his own drink. 'And you? Are you venturing out more, or still immersed in the Realm?'

'Truth be told, too much the latter, my friend. I've realised my mistake.'

Brennen chuckled. 'We're both recluses in a way! Finding ways to escape things we don't want to face.'

Laglen couldn't deny it. His Realm addiction had brought distractions, indulgences, and sacrifices. It was not only Girvyn who had suffered: his interest in geopolitics and visiting his life-long friend Brennen had suffered too. Running away the night his sister died, the Realm had helped replace grief and guilt with vacuous gratifications.

Brennen knew him inside out, just like Elaya. However, Brennen was unaware of what had transpired yesterday, what Girvyn had experienced in his dream, so Laglen shared the details.

Brennen listened, blinking the whole time in astonishment. 'That's quite a story. So Girvyn knows. Hmmm, how did he take it?'

'Disbelief, denial, then anger. I don't blame him. He is a beautiful boy, and his unique way of thinking might be an ideal servant for him. Now all he wants to do is train. It's like water off a duck's back with him sometimes. He is in the library now, protected by Tarith, one of Elaya's trusted guards.'

Brennen nodded. 'Girvyn is resilient.'

'Yes, and often rash and immature.' Laglen leaned

forward. 'But listen, I need to get into that summit to hear what this Forester girl says. Can you help me?'

'Ah, yes, the Forester girl. The messenger from Cundelly told the queen the girl had seen demons. Stasnier seemed to believe it too; he looked most put out.'

'Brennen, have you been spying on the queen again? You promised Elaya you wouldn't.'

'Ah but, Laglen, if information is like fine wine, then the queen has all the best vintages. If I don't just a little bit then my pictures aren't complete, you see?'

'You are more privy than the Privy Council!' Laglen sniggered.

'I love the queendom, politics, and protecting the queen; I just can't stand people. You and Elaya visit, and I get engagement by wandering the secret passageways, helping where I can.'

'Well, can you help me listen to the summit?'

'Of course I can. You can have my hiding place. Anything for a stimulating conversation with you! You keep coming, and I will keep spying. And besides,' Brennen gave him that mischievous look again. 'Someone has got to collate the news for you.' He slapped his legs. 'The irony that a supposedly worldly man requires a recluse for that never ceases to amaze me.'

'I want to change that,' Laglen admitted again, his expression distracted. 'Indeed, I have neglected many things in the Waking. Girvyn is one of them, and current affairs is another.'

'And self-hygiene.'

'Excuse me?'

'When was the last time you washed? You look scruffier than me, and I never need to make myself presentable!'

Laglen waved it away. 'Yes, yes, all noted. So, tell me; your spying extends far across the castle: how is Queen Amelia's mood?' He sat back. 'Or do I need a longer battering before you update me on what you know?'

'I think the character assassination is done. I will not add anymore on top of what Elaya and Girvyn have dished out.'

'That's so generous.'

Brennen hunched forward. 'Queen Amelia's health is waning, but her mind is still sharp as a rapier. Her authority has steadily weakened with many decisions passing through the Privy Council, though, and I fear Stasnier pulls the strings there. He is as slippery as a snake. There is more to him than the loyalty he pretends.'

'Pulling the strings? But isn't that the job of the head of the Privy Council anyway, to lead in minor matters?'

Brennen mocked his gullibility, shaking his head. 'What? To direct funds to the Rathnell Armouries for a consignment of weapons that never reaches the barracks? What about a recent shipment of grain that never made the kitchens: was this for his own consumption or for sale in the great markets of Cundelly and Stoer? Lale are wanting to build their basilicas in Rathnell, but their applications keep getting lost!'

'Can you prove this? One never knows the full intent of a slithering snake. Resisting the religious press from Lale has been wise for the queen so far. She keeps state and faith apart, unlike the rest.'

'Are you defending Stasnier!?' Brennen hiked an eyebrow, seeming surprised by his up-to-date knowledge. 'True. But more emissaries arrive at our ports from Sorrel each day. Trefgwyn now has multiple applications for faith sites. It has its benefits. Religion unites the lost, creates belonging for the disenchanted, provides for the poor, and it's a mouthpiece for the state to communicate with the masses.'

'So why does Amelia resist it then?'

'Land at first. Faith is becoming a giant landowner in our

continent, but more I think she's resisting power. A focused religious voice in court sways the direction of politics, and there is the small issue of holy intolerances for otherness and non-believers!'

'Hmmm, you mean the Druid Guild?'

'Yes indeed, they have a lot of sway in Rathnell, especially since the Queen's Protector is a druid. Lady Adara of the Druid Guild has sent numerous messages of warning about religious-based anti-druid sentiments reaching right across the continent.'

Laglen released a low whistle. 'Very complex indeed. And the summit! Everyone is coming here; it's incredible to get them all in one room like this.'

'Elaya would say a hearth ready to explode. It's not just the Foresters and Highlanders that are warring, though theirs is a traditional conflict scenario. Do you know about the fishing wrangle between Trefgwyn and Casper?'

Laglen shook his head.

Brennen slapped his legs. 'Not to be tackled lightly' His expression grew serious. 'What's more, Lale continues to lobby for this road from Casper to Stoer, facilitating their emissaries' journey to The East. Cundelly oppose this, fearing a shift in power if it's built. Our queendom trades in books from the Great Library, animal skins, and farm produce. We are old in our exports, while other kingdoms exchange much more sought-after items like weapons, grains, grapes, tapestries, ores, and a wealth of riches from Amjad via Stoer. I fear there will be many discreet corridor meetings in the days ahead. Emissaries have been arriving for the summit since yesterday, frequenting the courts with their own officials, some hoping to forge minor alliances not seen since the days of the Great Knights.' Brennen topped up his tea.

Laglen sat forward. 'What a mess. Everyone is competing for advantages over one another?'

'More or less. Rathnell still holds strong trade routes with Cundelly, Trefgwyn, and the southern region. Yet although we have been impartial for many years, before long we may have to take sides on some disputes.'

'I know we wish to remain impartial, Bren. I have not been asleep that long!'

Brennen snorted. 'Anyway, where do you hear about politics?'

'I hear some gossip in the library.'

'The monks don't know anything!' Brennen rolled his eyes. 'But you can't even find the time to click a brick and come and see me more often because you want to rush to your escape place!'

Laglen folded his arms. He understood why Brennen was frustrated with him. The difference here, Laglen thought, is that everyone has their way of escaping the past; he didn't attack Brennen for his decision to isolate himself all those years ago – escape takes different forms! 'I hear things in corridors too, you know.'

'Oh, do you?' Brennen countered, eyebrow raised. 'Hmmm, did you know that Counsellor Praleck hopes to hold a private meeting with Casper representatives to discuss this road agreement?'

'Everyone knows about this plan for a road!' Laglen said. 'But no, I didn't know about the private meeting. Why is this road so important to all of us?'

'Because it creates networks, and networks forge allegiances. It's not just the road. The shipping industry is growing, Lag. Sorrell brought faith to our shores over thirty years ago. Lale introduced it to Casper, which is like a sister capital to Lale now, and applications for basilicas have been granted in nearly every city since then. Rathnell are the only city to not build one.' Brennen sent Laglen a rueful smile. 'Times are changing, Lag. Trefgwyn's shipyards have seen them build several trawlers these last years, which has helped their exports grow. They fish the Calpan Bay and trade up the north coast. Casper trawls the same waters which is where the fighting has begun between fishermen. Ships! Ships are key to expansion, and we are not near water, Lag. Cundelly and Rathnell are seen as old powers, entrenched in our time-worn models, and are being left behind.'

'But Cundelly is on the coastline…' Laglen mused.

'Cundelly can't sail through the Ragon's Current because of how treacherous those waters are.'

'But Rathnell is surely still a powerhouse, as it's always been? We have the trade routes to the south, as you said?'

'To what, the deserts? No, Stoer and Lale – even the smaller kingdoms of Casper and Hoppenell – are expanding, trading, modernising, partly due to the waters and partly due to their unique resources, which we don't have. If Stoer builds this road to Casper then faith has a route from The West all the way to Amjad, which they want, and Stoer has a route to export their unique resources to Sorrell and beyond.'

'Is that why Cundelly want to stop the road?' Laglen asked.

'Not exactly, though like us, they fear Stoer's growing might and the armour they have from Hoppenell. No, it is because of the dispute over the water lanes of The Orran River, which passes through both Stoer's and Cundelly's kingdoms. It all started some years ago when Stoer put a water levy where the river crosses into their land. Cundelly didn't pay it. They clashed. Cundelly at first won some ground and pushed them back so the river fell into their control. They then populated the banks with river settlements, but now Stoer's might has grown, and we have a border dispute through The Orran Forest as they want their land back. And these new communities that are not so new anymore want to stay under Cundelly's citizenship. This proposed road goes across this disputed area, and if built would make Stoer a superpower in the region.'

Laglen raised his hands in admission. 'I guess my racing time has seen me lose touch with large-scale politics. Thanks for explaining that.'

'Anything to make my point that a recluse knows more about global politics than you!' he beamed.

Laglen rolled his eyes. 'But why are we hosting the summit? We are not central enough to be convenient for everyone and bringing all the kingdoms into one place is like bringing the broth to a boiling point.'

Brennen raised an eyebrow at him. 'Where did you hear that?'

Laglen slipped a cheeky grin. 'I may have overheard the odd comment in the kitchen. It's like a politics club in there sometimes. Hence the broth analogy!'

Brennen laughed and dropped his head in his hands. 'So you are only picking up news while you are trying to get food from Wrin. I knew it was too good to be true.'

Laglen ignored the jibe. 'I still don't understand why we must host this summit?'

'I can say that Elaya would agree with you. She fought hard for it not to be held here.'

'She would never win once Queen Amelia decided.'

'No. Stasnier.'

'What?' Laglen shook his head in confusion. 'It was his idea?'

'I know. He has gone above and beyond to ensure that

Rathnell hosts this. I do not know what he is up to, but he uses this to his advantage.'

'Elaya will have something to say about that.'

Brennen gesticulated and slurped some tea. 'She is but one person. And Elaya has to concentrate on the queen's safety.'

Laglen blinked. 'Do you think she is in danger? There is the Hoppenell Peace Accord between all kingdoms to not invade each other or attempt regicide.'

'But what if an assassination came from within?'

Laglen frowned. 'The barons pledge loyalty to Amelia for land and, in return, are bound to stipend military service to her. Their soldiers are here to support the queendom, not attack it. I know that much!' Laglen protested.

'Unless all eight Barons collude together. They would make one mighty force.'

'A collective rebellion? Never! They are all as ambitious as each other and would want command.'

'Well, I agree there, Laglen! Baron Kerrick Shadstone would not allow it. Not unless he was the one plotting it, in which case, once they were in command of the crown, he would probably assassinate all the other barons in court and take power.'

Laglen nodded, expression crunched up. 'And you think this is what Stasnier is doing? Working against Amelia?'

'I cannot say. I try and listen to him, but he is very erudite in the way he says things. It is almost like he knows I am there, on the other side of the wall. Sometimes he intentionally whispers.'

Laglen leaned back and sighed. 'If a contested succession might arise soon then a prince of another kingdom would present in some beneficial alliance. This isn't my area of expertise, but the House of Trefgwyn has many male suitors.'

'Even as a charade, can you see her accepting an alliance at this late stage in her life? But Amelia is wise. An alliance would make sense, and her love for the queendom outweighs her personal interest, so I think it is the Privy Council working against the idea. It is a troubling situation, but who would they have lead us when she is gone?'

'Stasnier? Surely not...?' Laglen gasped.

'It's the most logical choice. Stasnier is Privy chair. Without a ruler, the queendom would collapse unless Queen Amelia nominated another to take the title after her. Curse my words, but Stasnier runs everything anyway and holds sway over most of Her Majesty's advisors. If you ask me, he deceives the queen, asking her to sign this and that, contents of which she is not even aware. That I know for sure!'

Laglen crossed his arms. 'Have you told Elaya this?'

'Of course I have,' Brennen replied. 'She shares my concerns. She's witnessed enough to doubt Stasnier's intentions.'

'Thank the night for your vigilant eyes!' Laglen exclaimed.

Brennen chuckled. 'I do what I can for the greater good.'

Laglen's smile faded. 'Kerrick Shadstone can't be trusted. I remember that from the earlier years.'

'I agree. Numerous smaller estates and minor barons have pledged loyalty to him. His influence grows every year, and there are rumours that he's manipulating Stasnier, compelling him to undermine the queen.'

'You believe Kerrick is a problem then?'

'The real problem is too many kings and kingdoms.' Brennen shook his head, and his thin mop followed. 'I believe there should be a single high ruler to rule all the continent, and each state has a member in assembly.'

Laglen laughed. 'I don't know much about all this, but that seems rather radical. That's more like something from one of my constructs. I used to let societies run into the future and see what happens to rule, power, and technology.'

Brennen pursed his lips. 'It's such a shame you became addicted to racing. You could have been such a useful, independent consultant in court.'

'What, convey power-sharing models from my futuristic constructs to the very people they would displace? They won't listen to a democratic model that would put them out of power. Years ago, I tried to present a flushing toilet invention, and the Science Council laughed at me.'

Brennen slapped his legs. 'I remember that!'

'But back to the business at hand. How can you get me in the assembly hall?'

'A hidden passageway leads to the top of the dome where the summit occurs. I can get you there. On the day of the summit, you must arrive before sunrise. You can crawl right up to it and hear everything. But on one condition?'

'What is that?'

'That you visit more. Like once a week!'

Laglen reached forward, eyes gleaming. 'Agreed!'

'Oh, and another condition.'

'What now?'

'Have a wash.'

Five

'The fishing conflict between Trefgwyn and Casper continues. Whoever controls Calpan Bay will dominate food resources for years,' stated Stasnier Glencast, chair and advisor to the queen, his voice laden with that usual self-satisfaction. 'Have we decided where we will place their representatives in the room?'

A throat cleared; Elaya waited for the voice to resonate. It was Berenger, vice chair. That grovelling faker. He was never far away from Stasnier and, from what Elaya could see, rarely offered any ideas of his own, but passionately agreed with the majority. 'That's not our concern. Elaya Faith runs security; she can keep them apart. She is always over worrying; it will give her something to do.'

A few mutters and sniggers sounded through the chamber door. Elaya stood on the other side of it, using her druid powers to eavesdrop.

Stasnier continued, 'On another note, The Orran River remains strategically important for the shipment of oils and furs from south to north.'

'Then let it be us that claims it,' Ellis remarked. 'Cundelly are our friends, we can make a joint declaration to the channel.'

Ellis belonged to the old guard, having been a Council member even before Stasnier's tenure. Elaya, recalling him from her teenage years, trusted in him.

Stasnier persevered, 'Indeed, it should be us; it will be us, either singly or in partnership. I'm trying to negotiate that. The summit offers a unique opportunity to present side-line proposals.'

'Everything needs to run through the Privy,' Elaya heard the disapproving voice of the only female on the committee, Cargya. 'You have no authority to act unilaterally, Stasnier.'

Stasnier muttered something Elaya couldn't hear.

There was a pause. Elaya strained to pick up any auras, but through the door she sensed nothing. 'Cundelly and Stoer remain entangled in a border dispute; and this proposed road between Stoer and Casper proves to be the biggest indicator of future war. We will have to keep many Houses separate during the summit as well. Add that to Elaya's list!' Berenger laughed.

More sniggering.

Elaya Faith grew tired of hearing about the progression of their entrenched plans; she forcefully pushed open the door and entered the Royal Committee chamber. Stasnier Glencast stood, theatrically ending the meeting while displaying his annoyance. The four committee members averted their eyes as Elaya strode to the table, slamming down a stack of papers she had been holding.

'What is this?' she snapped, pointing to the papers.

Stasnier flicked through them and looked up at her, a pinched expression on his face. 'We are in discussion. You are not allowed in here.'

'I go anywhere I like.'

'You are interrupting a private session. Can't this wait?'

'Why wasn't I notified of the feast tomorrow?'

'It's a formal reception. Most appropriate under the circumstances,' Stasnier said. 'What is there to tell?'

'That it is happening!'

'The first multi-state summit in a generation. With communities never brought together before. Here, under disturbing circumstances. Of course there is going to be a welcome dinner. This gives us a chance to boost Rathnell as a geo-political player on the continent,' Stasnier said.

Berenger shrugged. 'Elaya, I am sure you can handle it.'

'I accept a feast is appropriate, but in the grand hall, which as you well know is impossible to secure? And with the queen on a raised dais, making her a clear target? And you've only decreed no blades Stasnier, but did it occur to you that a Forester's walking staff can be strung into a bow in a matter of seconds with a range of forty yards? You have no right to make decisions that affect safety.'

'Look at the bottom of the page, Elaya.' Stasnier picked up the lowermost sheet and held it for her to see. 'Signed by Queen Amelia.'

Elaya's face flushed. Her voice lowered, and with it came an even deeper breath of her accent. 'Of course she is going to sign it. She signs everything you slyly pass in front of her!'

Stasnier showed an expression of surprise, inviting support from his colleagues. 'That is why the committee is here, to support the queen in running the queendom. We take on the burden of minor decision-making to save her worry.'

'Whatever. I should have been told about this. You expect me to keep everyone safe in an open room where people can mingle freely?'

Cargya smiled sympathetically. Ellis averted his gaze.

'We have the queen's best interests at heart,' Stasnier said.

'People need to meet. They are here to tell the stories of settlements wiped off the map. It's a perfect opportunity to strengthen Rathnell's reputation as a modern, tolerant society, and to help heal old wounds across the continent.'

'Or cut new ones.' She sighed vexedly. 'I want all weapons left at the gate by everyone.'

Stasnier touched his heart in pretend hurt. 'Such minutiae have always been your responsibility, my dear. No-one is trying to take that away from you.'

'Good luck with that, Elaya,' Berenger said.

Elaya tugged her ponytail and felt the tight, sinewy strands pull across her scalp. She was deciding whether to reply with a fist or a terse retort. They knew that pause well. She felt their stares. 'Where is the queen?'

'Calm down, Elaya,' Stasnier said, for the first time, his weasel-like expression less self-satisfied. 'She doesn't need to be disturbed.'

'You don't decide what's best for her.'

She adjusted the sleeve of her tunic, pausing. Then she moved to the window, sensing their eyes following her. Before entering she had counted the people in the room and assessed their strengths, weapons, and possible threats. Apart from the two guards by the back wall, trained by her, they were all physically feeble. However, these adversaries boxed with pointed words and sly silences.

She lingered for a while longer, keeping her back to them so they could see her crisscrossed short swords strapped to her back, hilts rising over each shoulder. Then she took a deep breath, loud enough for them to hear, showing them she was wrestling with something. She retained an impassive façade but sensed a snake in this decision. Stasnier wanted a large audience and to put the queen in front of it, but why? For what revelation or performance? Or was it to foster some side plan, something advanced by advisors in corridors rather than in open meetings. It was infuriating that her sword could not cut to the truth of this as it did with flesh, but she would have to play along. A blade would not serve Amelia. For now she needed to focus on security and show contrition.

She turned to find Stasnier's measured stare following her every movement. 'Everything alright, Queen's Protector?'

'I can keep them apart. I have the men.'

'Indeed. Indeed,' Stasnier waved a hand at her. 'Even your kind are coming, Elaya.'

'What?' Elaya was unable to hide her surprise. She had not seen her kindred since she left the deserts as a young girl some twenty-five years ago. She came back to the table. A slight scent of jasmine followed her.

'Yes, a clan from the deserts of the south are coming to speak to us,' Berenger told her, looking across the table at his colleagues, then back at her. 'The Tologon tribe. Do you know them?'

'I remember little from back then. I was nine when I left, and I don't dwell on the past.'

'Will you greet them?' Stasnier asked her.

'Yes, I'll greet them,' she said, pausing again. 'But I don't speak their tongue. Have not done so for many years.' She stared, voice softening. 'Have they suffered too?'

'We have yet to hear.'

She looked away, then nodded. 'I will need interpreters from the library with me at the gate.'

'Of course,' Berenger said.

'Okay, continue with your meeting then,' Elaya turned on her heel and left.

Outside, she leaned against the wall, taking a moment to breathe deeply, attempting to clear her mind. Visions of her clan's perishing faces intruded her thoughts. 'No, stay focused,' she whispered to herself, struggling to dispel the haunting memories.

As she proceeded down the corridor, a staccato crack of steel-heeled shoes on the stone floor grew louder. Stern-faced guards passed by, nodding. She came to the queen's chamber. There, she found two more men from her team guarding the door. She knocked and waited for the chambermaid to answer, scanning those inside before it opened: as well as the chambermaid there was another guard, the head dresser, and the queen.

Queen Amelia sat beside a window, an afternoon breeze wafted in, scented by sage fragranced candles. The head-dresser stood behind her, tending to a knot in her hair as part of her afternoon routine. Amelia attempted to shift her gaze towards the door, but the constraints of her current position hindered her head's movement.

'Amelia, it is I,' Elaya told her.

'Come closer, so I can see you. This insufferable comb is keeping me facing forward.'

'I'm sorry, Ma'am,' the head-dresser said.

She flapped her hand. 'That is enough for today. You can carry on the untangling in the morning.' Finally, she considered Elaya and then frowned. 'You seem troubled, my dear?'

'Well, it's just,' she faltered. 'Just usual committee posturing.'

Amelia wheezed. 'Everyone out. I want to talk to Elaya privately.'

The head-dresser and the others in the room froze.

'The queen commanded you all to leave,' snapped Elaya, 'so that she and I may talk privately. Did you not hear her?'

With mumbled apologies, the room was vacated, leaving Elaya to walk over to the queen and continue untangling her knotted locks. The old woman cackled.

'Was that a test, Your Majesty?'

'If it was you would always pass them, my dear. My voice would not go so loud without failing, and my eyes can no longer read the small print of the documents Stasnier brings me. My end approaches and I like to see which way those left behind will fall.'

'It's Stasnier and his kind. I honestly don't know why you can't run the queendom yourself as you used to.'

'That was a long time ago. I am old now. I can barely remember to eat meals.'

'I do not see that in you, Your Majesty. I still see your mind as keen as my sword edge, at least if you do not allow harmful voices to dull it.'

'Indeed. But time weakens the body for all of us. I cannot keep up with all the signings, visits, openings, hearings, and weekly meetings with the lords and barons.'

'Talking about signings, did you agree to a feast tomorrow?'

She shrugged. 'I do not know.'

Elaya shrugged back. 'I guess it doesn't matter.' She exhaled exasperatedly. 'It's just that I am not convinced they always work in your interests.'

'Perhaps. But, Elaya, if I look weak or an invalid for one public second, opponents will rise and move against me. Only a strong queen at the head of this queendom keeps the barons in check. Each sees himself as king, and they would tear the peace apart to crown themselves. I cannot allow that, no matter what the cost to me afterwards. I must continue to perform, Elaya, and for that I must rely on and trust the Privy Council. But I am more grateful than you could know to have your support.'

'You have my arm to lean on, my eyes to guide your step, and my sword to protect you. Always.'

Amelia laughed. 'Yes, they do not make many like you, Elaya.'

'Don't let the Privy Council take too much away from you.'

The queen smiled gently as if talking to a child. 'They are my Royal Advisors. Of course, they are not working solely in my favour. They are hedging, dodging, circumventing, trying to gain goodwill with me and advantage over one another.' Amelia grabbed the arm of the chair and began coughing.

'Water?' Elaya offered, gesturing to the jug beside her.

'Water will not help.' She went quiet and glanced away. 'It is harder without my husband,' she continued. 'But it is my job to work out what is good advice and what is not.'

'I miss the king,' Elaya said quietly. 'Why can't they advise and be straightforward? Do their job? I don't sometimes defend you and sometimes not. I always defend you!'

'Maybe you could advise me?' Amelia winked.

'I am a woman of impulse. I say what I feel; I don't strategise as some do.'

'I was actually joking. No, I would much rather have your swords and loyal confidence. Much more safeguarding.'

She reached out her hand. Elaya offered hers and felt a frail squeeze.

'Yes, they really do not make many like you.' The queen kept staring at her. 'There is something else, though, is there not?'

Elaya sighed. 'Don't you feel it? All these babies going missing. It's everywhere now.'

'It disturbs me also, my dear, that the innocent should befall harm thus.'

'Yes.' Elaya blushed. 'But that's not my only preoccupation.'

The queen tilted her head around and looked up. 'Please explain. Without fear of causing offence.'

'Well of course the taking of babies is an outrage, but what happens to them? If they were being stolen to be trafficked as slaves we would be seeing scores of pale children in the trading pens of the south, but we are not. If they were being slaughtered for foul witchdoctory, our eastern spies would have reported the sale of such potions, but they have not. The numbers are so many, and with no sign of those taken thereafter. That is what disturbs me most. I sense a most evil threat but can discern nothing of it.'

'Ah, Elaya, it is good to talk with you. When I do, my old self comes back to me and I feel the fog around me start to lift.' She patted her hand. 'It disturbs me also. I cannot recall an incident as ominous as this in sixty years. That is why we have this conference tomorrow, to discuss it.'

'The nomads are coming.'

'Are they?' the queen said. 'Has this reached so far south? That is sad.'

'It must be serious for them to come to the green land. They never leave the sand.'

'You did.' Amelia paused for a moment. 'Will it pain you to meet your people again?'

'My own clan is dead. I will greet these visitors as I would any other delegate or House...'

Elaya brought a finger to her lips and stepped towards the door, sword drawn. There was a creak outside. Then, a shadow moved across the bottom of the door.

She frowned, shook her head, and then sheathed the blade. Gripping the door handle, she swung it open and stepped back as a man fell inwards. 'Counsellor Stasnier, you should try knocking next time. It's much easier.'

'Ah, thank you for opening the door, Queen's Protector. I had my hands full.' Stasnier was holding a tray of drinks. He puckered his lips. 'Twice in one afternoon; I didn't expect to see you here.'

'What is this?' Elaya asked, her voice gruff.

'I have brought the queen refreshments.'

Elaya knocked the tray away and the drinks flew across the chamber.

'You overreach yourself, Elaya!' Stasnier snapped, his button eyes glaring at her. 'This outrage will be...'

'Elaya deserves commendation for her attention to protocol,' replied Queen Amelia. 'I only consume liquid certified by my testers.'

Stasnier tilted instantly into a stiff bow. 'Of course, my queen. Queen's Protector, my mistake.'

Six

Later that night, after a near-silent dinner in which both had been absorbed in their thoughts, Laglen broached the subject of Girvyn's day to find out what questions he had. He hoped any remnants of anger would be replaced with eagerness.

'So,' he said. 'Did you do any reading today?'

'I did! It's amazing. I can't believe this is something that is a thing. That it's happened to me! You are blessed!'

'So are you! Let's sit by the fire and talk,' Laglen beamed, feeling relieved.

They slumped into chairs. Laglen adjusted a log. When the hearth crackled merrily, he sat back.

'Did you find my note to you?'

'I did. Did you always know you were going to give me this book?'

'Yes, of course.'

'I forgive you,' Girvyn continued, explaining himself. 'You asked for forgiveness in your note to me. So, I have.'

Laglen nodded slowly, grateful for his understanding. 'Thank you.'

Girvyn patted his hand, his smile widening. 'But now I want to learn more! I want to go there!'

'But you don't just jump in. I learned theory as a child and considered the ethics of construction, so when I came of age and Travelled I was a responsible adult and had self-control. We are talking about skipping years of tuition. You shouldn't have been able to follow the lights to the dream dimension without instruction.'

'They beckoned me, drew me into the white expanse.'

'And that worries me.'

Girvyn fell into a momentary silence. 'I thought it was my dream,' he murmured, 'but it belonged to Crane. His face was now set with determination. Just as quickly, the expression was gone, and Girvyn seemed to jump to another thought. 'And the extent of your imagination! So many constructs. Can I visit some of them if they are still active?'

Laglen felt his cheeks flush with colour. Girvyn seemed to embody creativity at its finest, his unique carvings and unconventional worldview standing as proof. In contrast, Laglen saw himself as a dishevelled academic, perpetually hurried, living amidst chaos. Yet, he was aware that his true creative spirit flourished within the Realm, where his attention was devoted.

'Yes, but we must proceed carefully,' Laglen told him. 'A fellow Traveller, Kalamayn, has a book that could be a good starting point for your training. I'm drawn to high-level concepts,' he confessed. 'I transcribe, interpret, and manage the archive with my colleagues, but I've authored no public essays or research in the Waking. Even logging my creations for you was tedious. In the Realm, however, my imagination constructs castles and mountains. You witnessed a glimpse of this last night during the race game.'

Girvyn's gaze shifted to the satchel as he spoke. 'Tell me

about that community you evolved. In six months, you wrote, it jumped eight hundred years. What was that like?'

Laglen pondered, recalling numerous worlds he had created, but not this one. 'I need more details. Did this place have a name?'

'It's not important!' Girvyn pressed on, his eyes flickering with the rapid onset of new inquiries. 'Can you freeze these worlds and return to them later?'

'Yes, and erase them, but it's all about controlling your thoughts.'

'Could I create a duplicate library to read books I'm not allowed to touch? And make a friend to read with me?'

'Hold on! No, you can't create a book you haven't read before.'

'But you create worlds that grow. That must be harder than creating a book?'

Laglen leaned forward, squeezing the bellows to stoke the fire, which responded with a fierce roar. 'That's a different matter, that's about setting a progress parameter,' he explained. 'However, you could indeed create a friend who lives in the library, or in a house identical to this one.'

'I wouldn't do the smell; it stinks of wood smoke!'

'But you get my point. You have a very good memory, Girvyn. Use that to help fashion realistic places.'

'And the structure where time sped up?' Girvyn continued. 'Why didn't they remember you when you moved among them?'

Laglen sat back in his chair, his eyes tracing the dancing flames. 'Your mother used to create worlds where the inhabitants knew she was the creator. It complicated things when she revisited,' Laglen said. 'I prefer observing how futures unfold in a possible timeline, moving around unnoticed. This way, their timeline's trajectory remains unaffected by my presence.'

Girvyn inclined his head. 'How do you manipulate time?'

'Time differentials.'

'Could I cross over for a minute and experience ten hours there?'

'Yes, but why? Your body needs to rest, so using parallel time is better. He folded his arms. 'You don't want to over do it. Some people have been known to have confused realities. At this stage, you dip in and learn.'

'I want to understand it all,' Girvyn insisted.

'You will. But you are asking all the wrong questions. The question is what you create not how long you are there for.' He swivelled his chair to face him. 'Look, time spent inside doesn't age you, as your body is asleep in the Waking world.' He observed his questioning face. 'Don't worry about time.'

'What if I don't want to come back though?'

'Now that's a good question. You have to fight it.'

'Like you have,' Girvyn said churlishly.

Laglen rolled his eyes, and continued to explain. 'Adept Travellers can extend their sleep sessions to a maximum of thirty-two hours. But why, when eight hours is right for the body.'

'That's cow-popping amazing,' Girvyn exclaimed.

'Girvyn, I'm not fond of that phrase. Could you use "in night's name" like everyone else?' Laglen suggested.

'That phrase favours darkness. I prefer the light,' Girvyn retorted playfully. 'But why does the body automatically wake up after thirty-two hours?'

'It's unknown; it might be a safeguard to prevent the sleeping body from deteriorating. Dehydration is a lethal risk.'

'The people in your world, are they like normal people?'

Laglen hesitated at this. 'Oh, we are moving on now, are

we?' Everything was out of sequence to how he had wanted to explain it. It felt like a hearing dominated by erratic inquisitors. 'People are a whole other thing,' he answered finally.

'But in the race, I don't think I could talk to the people in the stands; they didn't even notice me.'

'I created them thinking more about how a crowd animates as an entity.'

'I would have added detail, made them more real.'

Laglen shrugged. 'I'm racing around at super speeds. I couldn't be bothered with the effort of making them more real when I can't see the detail anyway. Like I said, I like quick, high-level fixes. Sometimes,' he corrected.

'Those floating displays during the race, what were they?' Girvyn inquired.

'They were screens, projecting real-time images of me and the other racers,' Laglen explained. 'The concept was inspired by an evolution I've observed in another world.'

'But, Uncle, flying metal boxes?! We have swords and horses here.'

'Yes, we do. But my references have changed. We are gods in the Realm, subject to possibility, and here we are subject to inequality and external forces. Do you see why it's so enticing?'

'I can't get my head around it. I can't decide if I just want to sit in a library where there are no snoring monks ruining my reading, or speed worlds up to see a possible future.'

'I think you will love both! Haven't you ever wondered what life would be like in 2000 years? You can try things out. Tasmin used to make water features and simply relax.'

'Who's Tasmin?'

'Another Traveller I know.'

Girvyn's eyes glimmered. 'It's mind-boggling. Do you not

want to influence society in the Waking with inventions you have learned from your structures?'

'I use it for entertainment. I am not an inventor. Also everything is interlinked; to create a prototype of a flying metal box you'd need every technology that goes into it like propulsion power and metal alloys. It's way too much. I can steer it; that's all that matters to me.'

'That seems like a missed opportunity if I am honest.'

'I have tried it; I mean, introducing advances to the Waking, but,' he faltered, feeling his cheeks heat up with embarrassment. 'But I got push back, and now I just enjoy the escapism.'

'Push back?'

'It was once when I was young, but it was too far beyond where our world was. Immediately I started encountering hostility and suspicion, and I noticed a real risk I might be denounced and locked up or executed. I thus pretended to be a bit nutty until the threats subsided, and I learnt my lesson. You can't push progress in a world much faster than it's prepared to go.'

'When was this?' Girvyn shook his head in awe.

'Years ago. Not long after I trained, in my twentieth year.'

'I get it that you can't introduce new metal ores, but you could introduce ideas.'

'Kalamayn did.'

Girvyn sat forward. 'Tell me! Wait! Can I guess?'

Laglen laughed and waved a hand for him to try.

'The queue?'

'I don't think that's practised much.'

Girvyn chuckled. 'Have you been to the market lately, everyone does it!' Girvyn looked down, thinking. 'Toffee apples?'

'Hmmm. Now you mentioned it, that does seem out of

place.' He paused. 'No, let me tell you... It's something you use every day,' he said with a wink.

After a long moment, Girvyn threw his hands in the air. 'I give up.'

'Kal brought modern referencing systems to the libraries in the Waking!'

Girvyn squealed in delight. 'That's amazing!'

'About ten years ago, he walked into Cundelly library and introduced cataloguing, inter-library exchanges between the cities scholarly networks, reading areas, loan logging systems.'

'Is that all new? All from Kalamayn?'

'Before then,' Laglen continued, 'it was a closed shop with no referencing or order systems. Kalamayn is a man for details. He learnt it from a future library he had seen in one of his structures. Within six months, he had changed every library across the continent.'

Girvyn clapped his hands. 'I can't wait to make a difference too. Is he famous for this?'

'I wouldn't call him famous.'

'Got any more examples?'

'It's hard to know what changes have been made to society by Dream Travellers, as there is no council, no community meeting point. I am unsure if it's even 0.05% of society who can cross. I only know five families, one of which is Crane's lineage and so not given to co-operation. We're a small and closed sect. How do you even bring up a conversation with a stranger or even a friend about it? There might be people I know who can do it! But it's a trade secret. You could get your head chopped off for being the devil!'

'Why don't you go into their windows and say hello?'

'Because you're weak in their house and they might not

be friendly! They could kill you with a thought. It's not worth the risk. I'm too old for risks.'

Girvyn shrugged. 'I guess you are nearly fifty!'

'Thanks for that.'

'So, Traveller-supplied inventions could be everywhere? Could cutlery be one of them?'

'I doubt it.'

'I saw a map in the library based on a new navigation instrument. Could that be one?'

'Sounds like it could, you could track down the inventor but how do you prove it?'

Girvyn cocked his head as another random thought struck him. 'It's a bit cheating though, Kalamayn stealing ideas from the future, I mean. Good for him though for doing it.'

'I don't think Kal did it for notoriety; he did it to make things better.'

'There must be more!'

'Your grandfather introduced sanitation. Though not all kingdoms have deployed it.'

'I know, you should see the mess in the east district. People poo out of their windows.'

'Take a shovel and bury it. That's what I say.'

Girvyn shook his head in disbelief. 'All these things I thought were part of society's contradictions, and some of them come from Travellers.'

'What contradictions?'

'People get stabbed in the street for no reason and with no justice, unless the Royal Court gets involved, which rarely they do. Yet people queue in the market for apples.'

'Yes, we are strange. I hadn't thought of it like that. But I think society is full of contradictions anyway.' He winked. 'Ah yes, and then there is the eyeglass.'

'Did Kalamayn introduce spectacles as well?'

'No, Tasmin's mother did. I do wonder about mechanical clocks, though. A trader in Cundelly sells these timepieces, and he won't disclose who the inventor is. He says it's a confidential arrangement, and I wonder if the inventor is enforcing this because he is a Traveller.' He made a face and shrugged, voice distracted. 'I admire Kalamayn, that he saw this opportunity to do something non-threatening which will benefit the dissemination of knowledge and the world's progress.'

Girvyn hesitated. 'There were some sad structures in your journal, Uncle.'

'Like what?' He couldn't remember every structure log he had made in the journal.

'Like the one you created of my mother so you could talk to her about me.'

Laglen exhaled a deep, relieving sigh, feeling a wave of liberation sweep over him. For years, the weight of his secret had driven him into the arms of his hidden indulgence. Now, with Girvyn privy to his truth, having witnessed him in the act, Laglen experienced an unburdening. He pondered why he hadn't found the bravery to disclose this truth earlier.

'I found the loss of your mother terrible, and I still think about her. Recreating her was a perfect way to deal with that grief. I know it's not her, but my construction of her was close.' He muttered. 'She is probably softer in my version. She could be firm at times and direct. When you create someone based on your view of them, it's your perception, my construction. The colour of their true self is not the same.' Laglen stopped and offered him a small smile. 'Did you want to meet your mother?'

Girvyn was silent for a moment. 'I don't think so. It's not really her, but maybe another time.'

Laglen regarded him quietly. 'I guess you don't need the

distraction. You might get addicted to visiting my Rosein-memory and not concentrate on your training.'

'Is this advice from an addict?'

'I like to consider myself as an ex-addict.'

Girvyn went to say something and stopped.

'What is it?' Laglen asked.

'Some of your constructs, they shocked me, that's all.'

Laglen pursed his lips. 'I'm sorry, I can imagine. I am not making excuses but think of it as every daydream can become something real. Daydreams are supposed to stay private. You have just had an inner view of my mind.' He knew he had taken a massive risk, giving Girvyn the truth – warts and all – about his catalogue of created worlds. 'I think we should start your first training session,' he said, changing the subject. He rubbed his hands and gestured to the bedrooms. 'What do you think? Shall we cross?'

Girvyn stared back. 'What, now?'

'Yes, theory with practice.' Laglen kept his grin in place and hoped Girvyn was too excited to see beyond it. In this new spirit of openness there was one thing he was determined to hide from his precocious nephew, and that was his shock at the description of Crane's construct from the dream and the icy suspicion that the warped Traveller might actually have found some way to bridge Realm and Waking after all. If his fears about what Crane had achieved whilst he'd been off idling his time away in hovercar races were in any way correct, then introductions that should take years might have to be done in a matter of weeks. It was therefore imperative that Laglen hide his concerns. That was the very least he owed for his negligence.

Girvyn started to tremble 'I'm not sure I am ready.'

'I will be with you. I will find you in your Atrium and lead you to mine. I will set up a construct where you can take ownership of The Pull and test things safely.'

'The Pull?'

'Let's hold that topic until we have crossed.'

'What if I can't get it right?'

'It's stress-free. The act of creating is the easy bit. Control is the issue.'

'Uncle, nothing is stress-free for me. After reading your journal, I feel I am not ready.'

'But you said you were!'

'I know, I am a bundle of contradictions. I'm feeling the stress in my chest again.'

Laglen was acutely aware of the need to avoid overwhelming Girvyn. Reflecting on his own introduction to the Realm at age ten, he recalled how his parents and community members discussed their experiences with him. This slow and steady approach, spanning years, involved sharing insights about the constant sleeping, the effects of the Realm, and candid conversations with both adults and peers. His contemporaries, like Kalamayn, Mora, Tasmin, and even Crane, provided a support network. They shared their fears, growing as a unit, so when Laglen first entered the Realm, he was prepared and educated about its dangers.

'It's up to you. We can cross, and you can watch me if you like?' Laglen could tell his anxiety eased at this.

Girvyn gave him a thin smile. 'What do we do?'

'Something you do every night. Sleep.'

They walked to Girvyn's room. Then he lay on his bed. 'Now what?'

Laglen pulled the sheepskin up to his chin. 'In case your body gets cold.'

'This is a bit weird.'

Laglen agreed. 'Feels like I am putting you to sleep.'

'Ah, such great childhood memories,' Girvyn said sarcastically.

Laglen ignored the quip and considered the next steps. 'You know in my construct the vehicles I was driving were flying above the ground?'

'Yes. I was going to ask how they did that?'

'In this case, magnetism…let's put that to one side for now. Where I took the vehicles from, they have other machines that fly high up above the clouds. If you go in one at night you see the lights of cities and towns stretching for miles and miles in every direction. That's the dream field you'll see when you let The Pull take you. It maps the real-world sleeping locations quite well because Traveller's dreams cluster like city lights. These are the stars you see when you close your eyes. Travellers are drawn into these fields, taking you to your Atrium. You've already done it, so all I am doing here is explaining it; do what you did before, and I will see you on the other side.'

∼

Girvyn waited in the quiet of his bedroom. He heard his uncle's voice calling out from the room across the hall. 'Count to ten and cross.'

The moment he shut his eyes, the star field swept him away. Was this The Pull reaching to him? Beckoning him closer? It felt warm and soothing, like sun rays.

There was no sense of movement, only a blink between dimensions, and he stood in his Atrium: a vast expanse of white accompanied by a pervasive tingling sensation that weaved through and around him. Gradually, floating windows materialised before his eyes, some presenting still image, while others displayed looping movement.

He waited for his uncle, unsure what to do, when he suddenly popped into existence.

'Uncle! That was fast!'

'I am used to this, and with the help of my assistant, I filtered through the windows quickly and found you.'

'But there are thousands of them,' Girvyn murmured.

'Most of these are Orts' dreams.'

'But I thought Orts couldn't Travel?'

'That needs clarifying. They can cross, but they don't know they do. For them it's just a dream. They are usually abstract, surreal stories, often based on some nagging issue they never know about. Usually, repeats of traumatic matters.'

'And we can enter them?'

'Oh yes. But don't.' Laglen looked away as if there was more to say, but Girvyn sensed he seemed uncomfortable saying it. 'It's their private thing. If you tamper with their dreams, people can have heart attacks. And you will never even know who they were.'

'Have you ever entered them?'

'I am not proud of it. When I was younger. We all did.'

'Uncle, shame on you. And these other ones? I feel the tingling from them?'

Laglen seemed happy to move the conversation on. 'That's The Pull, an energy that surrounds us and turns our thoughts into things. Travellers' dreams vibrate stronger Pull signatures. Do you feel The Pull?'

'The tingling?'

'Yes. I think of it as a pulsing energy, connecting your thoughts to the Realm.'

Girvyn felt something alive and vast.

'Beyond The Pull lies The Source, a powerful energy. If you imagine The Pull as a river binding your creations, then

The Source is an ocean of deeper magnitude, which The Pull flows to.'

'What is it?' Girvyn swallowed, sensing the enormity of it.

'Some believe it's alive,' Laglen replied.

Silently absorbing, Girvyn sensed a presence at the edge of his perception.

'Come.' Laglen smiled. 'Shall we cross into my Atrium? I can make sure you are safe there.'

'Which of these windows will lead to you?' he said worriedly. 'What if I get lost? What if I get sucked into someone's terrible trap? What if I fall into Crane's hell again? I am not sure this is a good idea,' he said.

'Look, you didn't know before. Now you are in control. Just look for me; that will be the invitation.'

Girvyn frowned, feeling overwhelmed. 'I don't get it.'

'As new windows appear flick through them and find me.'

It sounded simple. So why was his heart hammering? 'There have been about another hundred added since I got here.'

'We are near bedtime so more dream spaces are coming live. Send a thought to arrange them into a presentation, and filter just the tingling ones, which are Travellers' windows.'

The windows were reduced to around fifty stacked displays, rearranged in a circle around him. 'Did I just do that?'

'See how easy it is.'

Girvyn's eyes cast across the waiting windows: landscapes, abstracts, objects, houses, portraits. 'Are these invitations to enter?'

'Not really. These are houses on a street with the door open; open, I assume, for a meet. Only enter the one with me on the screen.'

'Got it.'

'I am going to leave you now. Look out for me.'

'I'm scared,' Girvyn blurted. 'Can we go back to the house?'

'It's going to be alright,' Laglen reassured, then vanished.

Additional windows, showing strangers' faces, joined the array. The seconds passed like repeated blows to his chest. He reasoned, was this any different to standing in the market and watching passersby? Surely, that was worse, and he managed that. These people couldn't look back at him.

Suddenly, a new window disrupted the carefully arranged spacing, making it easy to notice. At this, he couldn't help but laugh. The screen displayed his uncle, who was performing twirls much like a court jester, his movements exaggerated and filled with playfulness, culminating in a theatrical bow. Girvyn observed this looped action for a moment, entertained, before stepping into the scene.

'Okay,' he said, admitting it. 'That was easier than I thought.'

'See, it's easy!'

'You should be on stage.'

'Oh, I am.' He pointed at the mounds of window stacks.

Heaps and heaps, trailing into the distance.

'Are all those your saved dreams?'

'Yes. And somewhere in there is a theatre play, and I am the lead actor! Did you want to watch it?'

The assistant popped into view. 'Girvyn, the curtain is rising in five minutes; you will have enough time to grab a drink and take your seat.'

Girvyn gave a slow shake of his head. 'No thanks.'

Laglen glared at the assistant.

The assistant vanished.

'I can see why you spend a lot of time here,' Girvyn admitted. 'Did you tell your assistant we were coming? He came out of nowhere.'

'No, we are the same person. He is an embodied version of separated thoughts. So, I don't have to do two things simultaneously and get distracted. He can do the boring stuff.' He clapped his hands like a teacher calling for class attention. 'Would you like to try something? You can change your form. Think of something and do it.'

'No, I don't think I should...' Suddenly, Girvyn stood as a book. 'What is this?!' the book said.

Laglen laughed. 'You did it! That's why thought control is so important. I love it. Very fitting. But I was thinking something alive.'

Girvyn changed back, face flushing with excitement.

'Okay, now add some height, change your weight.'

Elaya appeared before Laglen.

'Girvyn!' Laglen exclaimed. 'Most people start with tightened stomachs or add some muscle. Not appear as someone else! It's so accurate. You look just like her.'

'I remember every detail I see, Uncle. You know that.' Girvyn spoke in a faultless Elaya accent.

'But the scar on her neck, the ponytail, even the tone of her black skin, all perfect.'

Un-Elaya like, she curtsied.

'Astonishing. I didn't see that one coming.'

'This is great.' Girvyn returned to his original likeness, grinning. 'Could I become dust, light, or even nothing?'

'Yes, but I have never tried that. You take the form and retain your consciousness. Observe how your mind adapts to the form.'

'I feel the same,' Girvyn's disembodied voice said. 'No, wait...' He did indeed feel something different. He could move wherever he wanted and project the form he had become, but he didn't feel what it was like to be wind. He just had thoughts.

'Girvyn, are you still there?' Laglen asked anxiously. 'What did you do?'

A breeze tousled Laglen's hair.

'Yes, I'm here,' Girvyn responded.

'I can't describe what you just did.'

'It was a breeze-hug!'

There was a sudden splash of water beside Laglen. 'Oops!' Girvyn returned to his original form. 'I transitioned from wind to rain, then myself,' he explained.

The assistant appeared, signalling with a raised finger. His form flickered, vanishing and reappearing as if being pulled elsewhere. 'I'm receiving a call from a Traveller,' he informed them.

Laglen raised an eyebrow. 'Really? Are you certain?'

'Absolutely,' the assistant affirmed.

Laglen cursed under his breath, looking at Girvyn 'I forgot to set our presence to private.' He slapped his head. 'There is me warning you about this, and I forgot to do it myself!' He motioned to his assistant. 'Block their access and conceal my structures.'

With a nod, the assistant replied, 'Done,' and disappeared.

Girvyn felt his pulse quicken. 'Who is it?'

'I don't know.'

'Does this happen often?'

'Sometimes. At least they knocked!' Laglen smiled. 'Come, I think that's enough for tonight. Let's return to the cabin.'

As much as Girvyn wanted to continue learning, he was aware of his heart pounding in his chest, and the relief that came with the thought of home. 'If we have to,' Girvyn shrugged, keeping his relief to himself.

Seven

Elaya led Derrilyn, her conscientious, young apprentice, towards the main city gates. It was just before sunrise, and the dawn's luminance glinted in the droplets of the night's dew. At the city walls, the lookouts were changing shifts.

'Any tensions?' she asked them.

'Nothing yet,' one replied. 'A few groups have arrived, but we have separated them into different sections of the keep as you asked,' the watchtower guard said.

'Which groups were they?'

'A settlement on the Capels River, a small delegation from Klevis. Nothing big yet.'

'Take your break and return at dusk,' Elaya told them. 'Derrilyn and I will take over.'

'Right, you are.'

Elaya and Derrilyn climbed the ladder to the top of the gatehouse and gazed upon morning mist that caressed the distant horizon. The North Road originated at the castle gates, vanishing into the shadowed forest ahead, ultimately guiding travellers to Cundelly's primary entrance some hundred leagues away.

'Who are we expecting?' Derrilyn asked.

'Cundelly, Lale, Trefgwyn and Stoer are all sending emissaries. And all the rest: Foresters, Highlanders, desert tribes, who knows? It seems to have snowballed. I'm entrusting you to be on top of the undercurrents so you can spot the flashpoints, Derrilyn. Yes, you have the druid sense, but applying readings of emotions in this setting also needs political understanding and a grasp of facts. So read each group on arrival – who holds sway, what do they want, who stands in their way, how powerful are they? I will be testing you throughout the day.'

Derrilyn made a face. 'But I am not good at the political stuff.'

'One only needs to know the basic facts. I am not expecting you to know the history of each group. But where the conflicts are.'

A wind swept down the slopes of the mountains of the north, swaying trees into whispering dances. Derrilyn pulled his tunic close to his chest.

'Your druid senses are growing every day,' Elaya said. 'Anticipation, deduction, speed, these we have seen. But has awareness moments slowed down for you yet?'

'You mean, seeing things around me all at once?'

'Yes.'

'No, not really. Although, as you know, moments like that happened when I was a child.'

'I don't mean those incidences. Back then your druid abilities rose to protect you without you even knowing they were there. Now you are aware, your senses should heighten.'

'I've not noticed anything different in sword practice.'

'Perhaps we need a more challenging incident to awaken your skills!' she encouraged. 'When you pass the Chattara, you will be one of us. It will be clear to you then.'

'I feel pockets of clarity popping through sometimes.'

'You will. Consider today and how our druid skills can help us. Different delegations should be met in different ways; for some a display of force, for others a show of courtesy. Get it right, and that delegation behaves better, and we keep the peace. There may also be an element of some groups riding up fast or quietly to try and catch Rathnell slightly off guard. This could even be probing for weakness,' Elaya explained. 'Being a druid allows us to sense these things earlier than others, and therefore, be able to exactly prepare how to handle each group.'

'I understand,' Derrilyn replied, his face crunched up in concentration.

She gestured towards the horizon. 'Look ahead. What do you sense?'

'The wind has changed direction. There's something on the breeze,' he answered, his gaze searching the distance. 'Is it saddle oil?'

'Impressive,' she said, nodding. 'And what does that tell us?'

He concentrated again on where the road ran into the darkened trees. 'That we're about to see our first group arrive...?'

She kept looking at him. 'How many?'

'Fifty or so? Freshly oiled saddles: I'd say from the city rather than the outer districts.'

Elaya nodded. 'Plus, it's dawn, so they have been travelling all night. For there to be a hint on the breeze, I would conclude that they left the city yesterday. The oil would have evaporated if it was longer, which means we are about to see...'

'Trefgwyn,' Derrilyn said. 'They're from Trefgwyn. It's closest.'

'Good work!'

They heard the sounds before they saw them: a quiet clip of horse's hooves, echoes of conversations trailing through the dawn air. Unconstrained by the dense trees, the sounds grew louder as the procession entered the open road.

'Do you think they are going to hand over their weapons?' Elaya asked.

Derrilyn pondered the question, counting under his breath as he tallied the riders. His attention seemed to pass to each of them. Elaya knew he was following the signs she had taught him to calculate their strengths. 'Look at the third rider from the front,' he told her. 'Two swords, a dagger strapped to each thigh, and his fists are bruised from combat. They will not want to be disarmed.'

'Good. Keep your gaze sharp today, Derrilyn. We must ensure this remains peaceful.'

'So many men,' he commented.

'I feared this. Come on, let's get down and meet them.'

Elaya and Derrilyn joined the gate guards and took centre stage before the portcullis. As the line approached, a runner boy moved to the front and lifted a flagpole, displaying the House of Trefgwyn emblem. A second crest flapped further behind, but the insignia was concealed by the rippling wind.

'Two groups ride together?' Derrilyn observed. 'Not for protection, the road from Trefgwyn is safe. Is this because of an alliance?'

'Good, you are showing great deduction skills.'

Before the procession came to a dead stop, Elaya eyed that third rider again.

The man took the lead and dismounted, glaring at Elaya. 'We have ridden all night and require food and rest. Take our horses to the stables, wench.'

'Welcome to Rathnell,' Elaya replied, her smile dangerous.

'Take your *own* horses to the stables. And the kitchens are that way.' She stabbed a finger in the direction of the castle. 'But before you go, I will require all your weapons.'

'I see from your colour you are not from around here. Get me your commanding officer. Preferably a man!'

She planted a wide step. 'Your weapons.'

The man glanced at Elaya and took in her plain, loose clothing. 'We are here accompanying the great Lord Grisham from Trefgwyn, so get out of my way, woman.'

Elaya's expression remained blank. 'There are no weapons in the summit, so leave them or drop them off at the barracks. Either way, you are not walking into the castle armed.'

'Shouldn't you be cleaning our rooms?'

Derrilyn's hand dropped to his sword hilt. 'I'd watch your mouth.'

Elaya placed a hand on his shoulder and regarded the man. 'Shall we wait for Lord Grisham to join us?'

Finally, an older man in a flowing black cloak joined them, dismounted, and walked over to Elaya. 'What is going on here, Sward?'

'Lord Grisham, this woman is asking us to disarm.'

Lord Grisham welcomed Elaya with enthusiasm. 'Greetings, Queen's Protector!'

Elaya responded with a smile. 'Very nice to meet you again, Lord Grisham. Counsellor Stasnier is waiting for you inside the castle for a breakfast meeting.'

'This is Sward, younger son of the most notable Andergine family. His ferociousness has featured in several battles. The Andergine House has joined us in this journey here as we are considering an alliance. Hand the weapons over, Sward, before Queen's Protector gets angry.'

Sward stammered, flashing Elaya a glance. 'But, Lord Grisham, I don't think…'

'We all want this summit to go well, don't we, Sward? Let's not ruin that before we even step into the keep.'

Elaya signalled to a waiting soldier. 'One of my guards will escort you.'

Lord Grisham nodded. 'Thank you, Elaya. It's good to be back in your great city.'

'I will make sure the queen hears your kind words,' she replied.

Sward sheathed his sword, cheeks flushing as he unbuckled his belt and dropped it to the floor.

'And the knives,' Elaya added, voice even. 'That bow at your saddle and that punch ring in your right pocket. All your men's weapons, too.'

They handed them over, grunting and protesting.

'Good day,' Elaya swung around.

After they had left earshot, Derrilyn said, 'I don't understand. Grisham wants this to go smoothly, right? Why would he not come to the front and sign in with us first? Instead, he allows Sward to start provoking you and make a fool of himself.'

Elaya sighed wearily. 'There is a lot of politics going on here, some internal. Sward's powerful family are pushing him as a suitor for Grisham's daughter, but Grisham doesn't want him. Allowing him to publicly make a fool of himself helps Grisham reject his advances.'

Derrilyn puffed out his cheeks. 'It's going to be a long day.'

'Looks that way.'

They waited on the parapet, blowing into their fists, drinking mint tea, and eating hot bread brought to the gate by the kitchens. A few riders came out of the woods and approached the gates: merchants and city folk.

When mid-morning came, the sun had washed away the chill and golden shafts of light glistened on the city walls.

Elaya sensed their arrival before she saw it: the delegation from Stoer, accompanied by a formidable military presence, marching synchronously, their unit banners fluttering in the wind.

Derrilyn whistled. 'There must be over a hundred-fifty men.'

'Military displays deter potential opponents from hostile actions. But it can also intimidate and abate adversaries in diplomatic talks.'

Derrilyn frowned at her. 'What? For a show? But's it a summit, not a parade.'

'Most people collapse at the first sign of conflict. Pushing your chest out has its rewards, even at a summit. What else?'

'Okay, then I see a show of strength,' Derrilyn reflected. 'Also, a sense of pride, a recruitment tool for young people to enter the army.'

'There is more here than meets the eye. Tensions are high between Stoer and Cundelly. Casper wants to build a road to Stoer through disputed territory. Envoy Praleck might use this opportunity to gather support for this road at the summit. Arriving in such a way intimidates Cundelly, showing everyone what an illustrious, powerful kingdom Stoer is, with its special friendship with Hoppenell. Look!'

'What am I seeking?'

'Look above the men.'

Derrilyn caught his breath when he saw the Hoppenell's insignia further back in the procession. 'They travel together!'

'Seems that way to me. Their alliance may well become the greatest threat the continent has ever seen.'

'That armour! Why's it so reflective?'

'Indeed, it shines like light!' Elaya declared. 'It's made from a rare ore excavated from the mines of Hoppenell. It's rumoured to be unbreakable.'

'No,' Derrilyn muttered. 'That would make their knights invincible.'

'Hmmm, indeed,' she agreed. 'I think they perpetuate the stories to breed fear in others.'

'But we have the Peace Accord.'

'If Cundelly don't agree to let them build this road through this disputed territory, they may ramp up military action. That's the fear.' She glanced away. 'Maybe they think they could take us all on. Who knows.'

'Why don't we have this armour in our barracks?'

'Rathnell's blacksmiths are good, but Hoppenell has the only mine where this metal originates, and they have renowned metalworkers to forge their armoured plates.'

'Can't we buy it?'

'They won't sell it. Hoppenell has an exclusive trade agreement with Stoer. Stoer, in return, protects them and shares with them all the secrets and riches from their newfound ally, Amjad.'

Derrilyn gasped. 'Amjad, from across the sea?'

'Yes. So, who knows what treats they have stowed in those trunks? Spices, rice, silk, tobacco?'

'What are they?'

She shrugged. 'Delights from The East.'

'I still don't understand why that makes them powerful? I don't get why a city from across the sea is so important to our continent. Is it because they have this armour?'

'That's only part of it. Let's take our maps,' she said, explaining. 'There are many uncharted territories in the Deserts of the South and in the northern peninsula, but they do not reveal great cities of treasure. Whereas Amjad is a powerful city and a gateway to exotic imports. Stoer also has a map of the east, which we do not have.'

'What, the maps are not shared?'

'No, there is no universal map. And our map just shows our continent. Theirs will show much more. Those on the coastline that have found new territories can either keep that to themselves, sell some secrets, or sell the resources. Stoer is doing all three.'

Derrilyn nodded. 'I understand now.'

Two high-ranking officials broke formation and rode toward the gate, their shields adorned with the crests of Stoer and Hoppenell gleaming in the sunlight. They unfastened a clasp at the side of their bascinets, raising the visors to reveal their bronze visages.

Praleck, a stout man dressed in a black tunic with ornate stitching and yellow buttons, wiped a hair from his face. 'Hail, Elaya Faith!' he cried out with warmth in his voice. 'I see you're playing diplomacy.'

'Envoy Praleck, welcome to Rathnell,' Elaya replied. 'I see you are too. Though you bring a small army?'

'It has been two seasons since I drew my sword in anger, but we come in strength as these are dark times indeed.' Praleck's eyes glimmered. 'Shall we meet for a friendly duel before the summit?'

Elaya chuckled. 'Alas, there is no time.'

Praleck shrugged. 'May I introduce Envoy Sevada from Hoppenell, a young and astute politician destined for a bright future.'

Elaya looked at Sevada, who removed his helmet. A feat that, with Rathnell's armour, would have taken more time. There was a murmur of disbelief from the watchtower guards. Sevada shook his head, allowing his golden mane to cascade down to his shoulders. He then fastened the helmet to a saddle leash, showcasing another Hoppenell innovation.

'Greetings, Elaya Faith,' he said, eyes glancing across the ramparts.

'Welcome to Rathnell.'

The rest of the armoured parade came to a halt; flags flapping in the breeze.

Praleck smiled. 'Give this woman a package,' he said, gesturing to a runner boy.

Elaya received the hessian pouch from the assistant. 'I will still need all your weapons,' she told them. When Praleck signalled his agreement, she granted passage to the riders, offering a nod of recognition to those who met her stare.

Praleck waited until he was the last to ride through. 'A gift from Stoer,' he told her, then headed into the city.

Elaya called after him. 'My men will collect the weapons – all of them – and store them at the barracks.'

Praleck, without looking back, raised a right arm in acknowledgement.

'What's in the bag?' Derrilyn asked Elaya, once they were gone.

Elaya opened the pouch and popped something in her mouth. She offered him the purse. 'A sweet.'

'Well, he's not buying my loyalty!' Derrilyn declared, but still taking one. 'And I hope he changes outfit for the feast.'

'Indeed. I would have to give him two spaces at the table with that armour.' Elaya patted his shoulder. 'Glad to have you with me!' Elaya's face darkened. 'I'm dismayed by how many soldiers are arriving with each group.'

Derrilyn considered this. 'Because everyone is posturing, and posturing preludes conflict?'

'Good. But also, while the delegates and their support staff may have quarters in the castle, these soldiers will have to camp in the grounds and outside the walls. Rathnell becomes a powder keg of small armies with differences and grudges. Have a think about where their camps can be placed to minimise conflict and inform the City Guard Master.'

'What? You want me to decide?'

'Yes.'

'Can I run it by you first?'

Elaya smiled. 'Of course.'

A short time later, the Cundelly representatives approached the gates. While eighty or so had made the seven-day ride to Rathnell, they arrived with less pomp and regalia than Stoer.

Elaya felt the presence of Counsellor Stasnier, waiting surreptitiously in the ramparts above to greet Envoy Seskin.

'Envoy Seskin, so wonderful to see you!' Stasnier called, announcing himself and making his way down.

Elaya stepped aside to let the Counsellor schmooze.

Seskin glanced triumphantly at his entourage, then looked back at Stasnier. 'Stasnier Glencast, how grateful I am to have such a "special relationship" with Rathnell that the Head of the Privy Council comes to personally welcome me.'

'We have much to talk about,' Stasnier said, though his voice had noticeably lowered. 'Perhaps, once you're settled, we could meet?'

Seskin's eyes darted around for a moment. 'Indeed, we do. Is Stoer here?'

Elaya replied, 'Yes. We've ensured your quarters are on the opposite side of the castle from Praleck's.'

Seskin nodded, satisfied. 'I will see you presently, Stasnier.'

Stasnier smiled, though the smile's creases didn't reach his eyes.

Derrilyn groaned after Cundelly soldiers had finally handed over their weapons and left them in peace. 'Combat practice is much easier than this.'

'That's why I wanted you down here at the gate with me. We still have the Foresters and Highlanders to come!'

Elaya tensed, gazing ahead to where the north road disappeared into the dense, ancient trees. A shiver of anticipation coursed through her. Amidst the whispering leaves and dappled sunlight, there was an undeniable presence, an unquestionable connection to a druid!

'Do you sense it?' she asked Derrilyn in a hushed tone.

Derrilyn's youthful face was etched with lines beyond his age. 'A druid's coming! When I was young, I used to think the feeling was recognition. That I knew that person from somewhere I couldn't recall.'

'It's the same for all of us,' Elaya agreed. 'At least a druid won't ever sneak up on you! But, as you know from first-hand experience, while we can sense each other, not all druids are good. Here, though, I believe we are about to see a friend!'

As if in response to their shared anticipation, a figure emerged from the treeline. Lady Adara rode gracefully on horseback, a man by her side. Elaya could feel the distinctive aura of druidic power emanating from them both.

Lady Adara beamed when she saw Elaya. She urged her horse forward, galloping the remaining distance.

'Elaya!' she hailed.

'Lady Adara! Welcome back to Rathnell,' Elaya said, smiling at the esteemed druidic leader. 'I trust you are well.'

'As well as can be in these mysterious times, Elaya.' Her smiled faded. 'It is not just babies and communities that are missing. We must talk later.'

'I will be at the feast this evening, so let's talk then,' Elaya replied. 'Your quarters are ready. Follow one of my trusted men. I am afraid they will ask for your weapons.'

'We don't need them!' She introduced her companion. 'This is Jaden from the Druid Guild.'

'I have heard much about you, Elaya Faith,' Jaden said. 'You are often referred to in the druid circle.'

'The pleasure is mine, Jaden,' Elaya responded. 'Welcome to Rathnell. I am sorry your visit comes during such grave times.'

'If we rally together,' Jaden said, 'we can face whatever befalls our land.'

For the next two hours Elaya and Derrilyn waited on the ramparts, eating quietly, talking seldom, happy to remain in the silence of their thoughts while the westering sun lowered. The gate guards and those who roamed the battlement called out when a rider appeared, mostly residents and traders returning to the city. Envoy Jakub from Casper arrived, followed by Envoy Nark from Lale, each bringing over a hundred men. They passed through without incident, but the swelling ranks of soldiers milled outside the keep, while Derrilyn planned their camp locations.

Elaya sent out scouts to roam the folds of the land in expectation of the Highlanders and Forester's arrival. When one such scout returned, galloping down the final straight of the North Road towards them, Elaya rose, ready to meet the next group.

Not long later, six mountain folk arrived through the trees, draped in mottled fleeces and with daggers and sword scabbards fastened to wide leather belts.

Elaya looked down at the parchment by the gate office and checked the group list and leader names.

'Envoy Maltip,' she greeted as they arrived. 'Welcome to Rathnell.'

'Envoy? I do not know this term,' Maltip replied, a hint of confusion in his voice. 'I command my tribe, so I have come here to tell you all what we know.'

Elaya extended her hand. 'Then it's Commander Maltip. Queen Amelia looks forward to welcoming the Highlanders into her queendom. My team will take you to your quarters.'

'Keep us away from the Foresters,' he replied gruffly.

'We fully intend to,' Elaya assured him. 'We appreciate your appearance despite their presence.'

Maltip's gaze sharpened. 'Are they here?'

Elaya shook her head. 'Not yet.'

'Good, then we will go now. Who do we tell of the missing babies and the killings?' Maltip said.

'That comes tomorrow at the summit. Tonight is a feast to welcome all the guests. Also, every bow, knife, stick gets handed in before you enter the castle. My men will take them.'

Maltip grunted. 'As long as it's everyone.'

'It is,' Elaya replied. 'And you will have them back when you leave.'

Maltip let out a grunt and led his men inside.

For the next twenty minutes, the gate remained silent, and the path leading into the dense woods was devoid of any activity.

Then, Elaya's keen senses detected the scout the moment before he emerged from the forest and charged down the road towards them. Elaya pointed. 'What do you sense, Derrilyn?'

Derrilyn's eyes narrowed as he peered into the trees. 'Our gate lookouts are flustered. They can see from high, so this is big!'

The scout arrived, but Elaya signalled with a hushed gesture for him to maintain silence, allowing her apprentice to determine the identity of the mystery arrival.

Derrilyn looked into the sky. 'Wood. Pulled into…bows, of course! The birds fear the bows. Foresters then?!'

'I suspect so, and among them, the girl everyone has come to hear. Do you feel the protective formation without the normal arrogance of rank at its centre?'

Derrilyn looked abashed. 'No. Such things are still a blur, really.'

Elaya patted his back. 'That will come in time,' she encouraged. 'Come, our honoured guest is arriving. Let us approach this calmly. They are unaccustomed to stone and walls. And we might find their ways strange.' Elaya barked an order at the gate guards. 'Make sure the Highlanders are disarmed. I will delay the Foresters at the gate if I must.'

'They're out of sight, Elaya, and already at the bailey wall.'

Elaya whispered to Derrilyn. 'Follow my lead.'

'Will the Highlanders give us any problems?'

'Not if we keep them separated from the Foresters. The route from The Highlands to The Orran Forest is not a short journey; the clashes were always orchestrated meets, and they have not fought for two decades. But old grudges may rise. This girl has lost her family and her entire tribe and is being escorted to us by a different tribe. There may well be elders who believe the Highlanders were responsible for the massacre of the Foresters. This summit will hopefully persuade them that it is a common enemy instead. Our main objective is to keep them apart and allow this woman to speak.'

'Poor woman.'

Not long later, the Foresters emerged from the woodland onto the final straight to the main gate. Longbows strapped around their shoulders jutted into the air high above their heads. A guard called from the watchtower. 'I see five men and a girl.'

The men, gruff-looking with short beards and shifting eyes, began spreading out when they saw the great towering walls and the guarded main gates. They edged closer to the city, arrows nocked to cheeks.

'Impressive!' Derrilyn breathed.

They wore ragged animal hides, fur at their ankles, necklaces of beads and flushes of orange feathers. The girl walked at the rear. A brown hooded cloak hid her face.

Elaya came forward, arms held high in a peaceful approach.

A slim, dark-featured man with feathers among his unkempt locks approached Elaya. He stabbed a finger at the air before her nose. 'Longhorn! Longhorn!'

'Longhorn! Longhorn!' The other men grunted, shouting unintelligible instructions to one another.

Elaya addressed the gate guards. 'Drop your weapons.' Elaya unsheathed hers and instructed Derrilyn to do the same. She knew some of their traditions; showing a visual willingness to avoid conflict was appreciated by the Forester folk. 'Peace, Foresters, peace. We greet with peace on the wind,' Elaya said.

The girl came forward, pushed back her hood, and shook free her auburn hair. 'A *Piliki* wind?' she asked, seeking clarification. Her emerald eyes met Elaya's.

Elaya frowned, trying to remember what that word meant. 'Yes, a *Piliki* wind. Soft and peaceful.'

'I am Hazel and have come to speak at the summit,' she read from a piece of paper. 'Take me to Elaya Faith to register.'

One of the Foresters shot Hazel a glare; she stopped speaking and lowered her head in compliance. He lifted a multicoloured tooth necklace and brandished it. 'I am chieftain. You speak when you are invited to. I am sure your great, late father would agree with such rules,' he said.

'Sorry, Chieftain Gleffton.' Hazel's gaze flicked to the guards along the city wall, then returned to Elaya.

Elaya wanted to take Hazel away and talk to her. Woman to woman. Something in her eyes spoke of a life of constraints and traditions. She was the sole survivor of a tribal massacre, yet Elaya saw a hidden fearlessness.

It reminded Elaya of the day she, herself, had arrived in Rathnell as a refugee.

Chieftain Glefforn measured Elaya. '*I* was told to register at the gate.' Emphasising his leadership in this matter.

'I am Elaya Faith. Welcome to Rathnell. Hazel is the fifth speaker.' She glanced at Hazel, then back at Glefforn.

'Take me and my kind to our trees and show me where the summit is.'

'All will be revealed.' Elaya gestured to an usher by the gate. 'Go with this man. He will show you to your quarters.'

'We have requested to sleep in the trees.'

'That is not possible, Chieftain Glefforn.'

Glefforn stared through the city gates at the managed coppice. 'What have you done? Why are your trees so trimmed? It is not natural.'

'Ah. Indeed. But that's how we like them.'

Glefforn said something in the old tongue, and a conversation ensued. 'We accept your hospitality; please show us the rooms.'

'May we have your weapons first? No weapons are allowed within the walls.'

'You may,' he said, and they started handing over bows, quiver packs, and hunting knives. 'Are the Highlanders unarmed?'

'Of course.'

'Check that; they are lying murderers,' Glefforn snarled.

In a gruff, deep voice, one of the other men added, 'Keep us away from them.'

'We will,' Elaya replied through a gritted smile, catching Hazel's gaze as they passed into the keep.

Elaya waited until they were out of earshot. 'That went better than I had hoped.'

'At least they gave up their weapons,' Derrilyn replied. He thought for a moment. 'So, we separate Cundelly from Stoer, Trefgwyn from Casper, Foresters from Highlanders, and watch for other grudges and pledges?' He passed her a parchment with scribbles of encampment locations.

She looked at it and gave it back, face unreadable. 'Make sure you tell the Guard Master what you have decided so we can get these groups separated.'

Derrilyn glanced away, and Elaya sensed his pleasure. 'What did you make of the Forester girl?' he said.

'I think she is waiting to let her testament burst out.'

'Yes,' Derrilyn agreed. 'I could feel it in her chest.'

'Did you see a colour yet?' Elaya asked.

'Yes, a sort of orange haze.'

'Good. For me, orange is apprehension, sometimes a defensive impulse: a prelude to fight or flight.'

Derrilyn digested this. 'Will you be in the summit?'

'Yes. I want you outside, as I need my best guarding the door.'

'Of course.' Derrilyn fought back a smile.

Elaya was pleased her praise encouraged him. 'But with so many tensions between groups, we must do our utmost to separate sparring communities tonight. It's an insane idea. An open hall! And I warned the committee. But they think of pleasantries and policies.' Elaya's eyes snapped to the horizon. 'Do you sense it? Another...?'

'A druid! I sense ... wait...two?'

'It's him,' she said distastefully. 'Can you feel his aura?'

'I think so. Is it red...?'

'Yes, that's a fight mode. So stay behind me.'

'As always, Master.'

Two riders approached the gates, riding side by side, scarlet cloaks flowing off broad shoulders.

'Baron Kerrick Shadstone approaching keep!' a gate guard called from the lookout platform above them. 'With Finlack Shadstone.'

'What's he doing here?' Derrilyn murmured.

Their great mares reined up at the gates. Elaya watched Kerrick dismount. That pristine tunic gilded with fanciful patterns. A thickset, shiny bald head, fluctuating fake expressions of interest. She could feel their druid spirit pulsating through them, rippling with their undulating arrogance.

'Ah, Elaya Faith,' Baron Kerrick Shadstone made a face as if tasting bad wine. 'Doing gate duties?'

'Can I help you, Kerrick? The barons are not invited to the summit. The Privy Council does not require your attendance.'

Kerrick sent her a sneer. 'I hear your nomadic brethren are joining tonight? Does it not make you nostalgic for the sands of the South? Perhaps you should return, tell old wives' tales to the children and cook snake.'

'You can't come in. The summit is a private invitation.'

'But dear gatekeeper, I am here for a meeting with Lord Haysham. The summit is tomorrow, when I will be back at my estate.'

Elaya inclined her head reluctantly. 'Very well, but if you are going into the castle, I want your weapons.'

Kerrick raised a thick eyebrow. 'Now, that will never happen unless you want to duel again, old friend. This time shall we say to the death?'

Her attention flashed to Finlack, his companion, his son. 'Go on, Father, you can beat her with a sword or words!' Finlack snarled, coming forward, hand on his sword hilt.

Elaya shook her head. 'Last time we did that our tutor broke it up. Who is going to save you this time?'

Kerrick didn't seem bothered by the reminder; his grin widened. 'He was an awful teacher and a woeful mentor. And that is why he is dead.'

Elaya felt Derrilyn tense beside her. She knew her apprentice sensed her burning rage and was ready to leap into whatever happened next. 'At ease, Derrilyn.'

A group of noblemen appeared at the gate, and Kerrick had already turned his attention to them. 'Lord Kendell,' he said smoothly. 'I trust since your stallions have resided in my estate, you have seen improvements in their security and performance?'

'Baron Shadstone,' Lord Kendell replied. 'Indeed, being in your stables is well worth the levy and the honour.'

Derrilyn shook his head as they moved away. 'How do you keep from getting angry?' he muttered to Elaya.

'What? Noblemen, or Kerrick?' Elaya replied quietly.

Derrilyn watched their pompous amity and snorted. 'Both.'

'What, have my emotions rule my abilities?' she smirked. 'What a mess I would be!'

'How do you mean?' Derrilyn's brow was creased with worry.

Elaya gazed at him, remembering that time before Chattara when the future had been blurred and frightening for her. 'Okay...when you come into your powers, you'll understand why they're not something to be used lightly, but let me give you an example: do you see that boy?'

'Which one? The urchin loitering behind that crowd of minor nobles trying to look important?'

'Yes. Twice already I've sensed his intentions. Peoples' auras can be in the form of frequencies, tones, or colours, as you know. Sometimes, all three radiate. For most of us it's colours, which is enough to read a person. I don't see his thoughts; I feel his motivations. The boy is looking to pickpocket one of the nobles. The thing is, he's doing it because he's hungry, which is a strong desire that keeps returning as his belly rumbles. He's just spotted another chance. Watch him.'

Derrilyn watched, and sure enough, the boy, careful to look everywhere else, was sidling alongside a foppish lordling who was busy applying a laced handkerchief to his nose against the smell of horse dung.

'He's at the point of reaching out, and when he does, I will intervene.'

As expected, the boy, hand extended, slid towards the nobleman.

'Boy!' Elaya called out. 'Can I help you? Are you waiting for someone?'

The boy gave a sudden yelp, causing the lordling to turn, spot him, and move disgustedly away.

Elaya's voice dropped to a whisper. 'What we do is a journey that lasts a lifetime and that I still find myself unsure of. The law protects the lordling's purse, and I don't wish to see the boy whipped or worse, but I've also prolonged his hunger, which in some ways should be an affront to all humanity.' She sighed. 'And some days I wish I wasn't a druid and didn't see any of this. Does that help?'

Derrilyn, clearly awed by this demonstration, managed to give her a muted nod. 'I was hoping for something less bleak.'

'As I know you do too, I remember that boy's loneliness and hunger from years as an outcast. That's one reason I have such confidence in your sense of perspective and responsibility. We have an extra sense, and as you learn to read the colours and tune into it, you will see the shifting tones and learn the nuances of state...'

'My pouch! Stop! Thief!'

A gate guard lunged at the boy, but the boy leapt away, darting one way and another. More men tried to catch him, but he skipped and weaved past, causing them to bump into each other and hindering Elaya, who was seconds behind. She thought he would make a valuable aide or messenger with some discipline and training. Maybe even get to trainee guard.

Suddenly, Kerrick was there and blocked his path. Once again, the boy sidestepped and feinted, but Kerrick anticipated and grabbed hold of his clothing. He threw him to the ground, brought up a boot and stamped on his neck. Bones snapped, and the boy quivered and lay still.

'No!' Elaya yelled.

An amused smirk twitched Kerrick's lips. He drew the nobleman's pouch from the dead boy's pocket. 'Don't worry,' he said casually. 'He won't be going anywhere now.'

Elaya knelt by the boy and closed his eyes. Her words hissed through clenched teeth. 'You will pay for this.'

'Why? This is an embarrassing incident for the city protector. You are guarding the gate this fine day. You had better write a report,' he waved her away. 'And stealing from a noble is punishable by death. It was a quick arbitration.' Kerrick threw the pouch to the nobleman, who caught it and returned a grateful nod.

'Damn you, Kerrick Shadstone!'

'Elaya Faith, I was damned long ago.'

∽

An hour later, Elaya and Derrilyn stood in the barracks, shrouded in a sombre silence that clung to them. Elaya gazed at the lifeless boy, now prone on the floor. She had dispatched men to spread the word throughout the city, hoping to locate any relatives, though she harboured little optimism that any kin would emerge. His body would be consigned to destruction, devoid of a proper service or words. Another tragic casualty of Kerrick's actions.

'I can't get my head around it. Kerrick must have sensed the urchin, too, at the same time you did?' Derrilyn said to Elaya.

'I fear I brought his death,' Elaya said, her voice so low it nearly vanished into the air.

'What do you mean?'

'If I had ignored the boy, would Kerrick have intervened? He may have left the boy to swipe a coin. But the moment he heard me throw a warning to distract the boy, he saw I cared and assessed the situation in a totally different way.' She wavered, stiffening. 'And killed him to make a point to me.'

'These skills, they are disturbing and complex,' Derrilyn fell silent. 'It worries me,' he said distractedly. Elaya didn't reply; just waited for him to continue. 'Which direction my focus will take?' he finished. 'I don't want to end up like Kerrick.'

'You will not turn out like Kerrick. Of that I am sure,' she said, turning back to look at him. 'Neither must it be good or bad, light or dark. There are always grey areas in between that will make up your druid identity.'

'But what if I come out different and don't like myself?'

'You mean after the Chattara?'

'Yes,' he said quietly.

'A druid's Chattara is the strands of their identity coalescing into a unified whole. That whole will not know doubt or dislike of itself, so however you are forged will seem fair to you.'

Derrilyn snorted. 'Is that supposed to be reassuring?'

She shrugged. 'The problem is your past. The Chattara

will take you to your deepest, most vulnerable place: your abandonment.'

'I didn't ask to be an orphan.'

Elaya's voice softened. 'There you go. You have not dealt with it. It's still an issue.'

Derrilyn blinked. 'Is it that obvious?' He topped up his mint tea from the stove to his left and let fresh peals of vapour warm his lips.

'The negativity about it, yes. You haven't accepted it. I have trained you for two years, so maybe we could say I know you.'

'Elaya, I have always wondered: of all those girls and boys who lined up in front of you four years ago I was the least adept, the least accomplished. I mean, I was a ragged urchin, like that boy over there, hanging around looking for a chance to beg or steal a coin. Why did you pick me?'

Elaya considered him. 'True, they were more formed than you, but I perceived in you the greater potential. As well as this you had lived alone in the wild, persecuted by bandits. You had to fend for yourself and think on your feet to survive. Those are valuable skills in our role, Derrilyn. And may I add that I never, not once, regretted my choice that day.'

He nodded gratefully, but his face was still filled with concern. 'How long before the Chattara takes effect?'

'Weeks.'

She clapped his shoulder. 'I'm sure it will pass quickly.'

Derrilyn gave her a thin smile. 'You never talk about your experience. Will you tell me about it?'

She shrugged. 'It was quick, over in a day or two. Although I was told that I was on the penumbra, the edge of the shadow, until I found my way.'

Derrilyn spilled tea down his front. 'Shadow?' He wiped the wet patch.

She chuckled. 'Don't worry, Cronmere was there to guide me, and I am here to guide you.'

'What was he like?' Derrilyn asked her. 'You rarely talk about him. Was he as legend says?'

'Well, yes, he was strict and powerful and feared. The greatest knight that ever lived. In his time, forty years ago, you would get lynched for being a druid. So he kept his true identity hidden. They all did. But as a man, a mentor, someone whom I loved as a father, he was kind and wise.' She fell silent for a moment. 'I miss him.'

'Thanks for telling me that. I'm not ready for this!'

Her voice took on a formal tone, that deep, rich accent coming out again. 'Training you for the Queen's Guard is definite. But I think you could make Queen's Protector one day.'

'What?' he seemed astonished.

'I have been training guards my whole life, so yes, really.'

'I can't do what you do. It's how you act in public: your manner, your way. I watch what you do and can't see myself doing it.'

Elaya laughed. 'That takes time, and you'll learn through practice.' She pursed her lips. 'I'm not that good at the politics. I react, where my impulse takes me.'

He shrugged. 'From where I stand, it always seems the right choice.'

She stared at him. 'I didn't do it right today.'

'Don't blame yourself for this. It's Kerrick's fault.'

There was an awkward silence.

'I sense you wish to know why Kerrick and I hate each other so...?'

'Are you doing a druid mind read?' he said with a wink.

Elaya's voice dropped to a hush. 'Be careful what you say, even in jest. Even when you think we are alone, we might not be. Druids are more accepted than they once were, but we keep our aura-reading abilities hidden for good reason. Those lynch mobs would rise again if all our skills were public knowledge.'

Derrilyn's cheeks coloured. 'I'm sorry. I won't joke about it again.'

She softened her voice. 'If people think we can read minds, they will never trust us. And we would be hunted for something that's not true.' She slapped his shoulder. 'But I don't need to be a druid to tell you are itching to know more about my past with Kerrick?'

'I'd never presume to ask.'

'And yet you have my confidence, and I would answer you, Derrilyn. After my tribe was destroyed by raiders, I headed north and came to Rathnell. Kerrick and I met on the streets and became friends. A history between us there is. Both of us orphans, we were drawn to each other because of this shared experience. We were street kids and stole what food we could. Necessity, competition, and survival built a bond, but when I look back, I wonder if it was a real friendship of care and respect.' She lingered, staring with distant imaginings. 'Cronmere saw in us what I see in you, Derrilyn.'

Derrilyn listened diligently, then said, 'Being a street kid, how did you learn to speak so well?'

'In the royal court one learns to adapt.' She took a deep breath. 'Kerrick and I grew apart when he came to prominence, gaining land and status. Many matters are unresolved between us. The death of Cronmere was one of them. I felt his death was suspicious, but Kerrick didn't care. All he cared about was power and wealth. He used Cronmere and me to take him to the next step. When we held no further use, he discarded us. That's what he does.'

'How did he turn into a baron, then? If he was a street kid, he can't have noble blood.'

'There are some things I do not wish to remember, and this is one of them. Suffice to say he used his druid powers to fight his way to that honour.'

'Like a gladiator?'

Elaya averted her gaze. A numbness settled over her as she recalled those memories. The transformation from a child to an adult, from a nomad to a druid, and to the role of the Queen's Protector, all intertwined with the years she had experienced with Kerrick Shadstone.

Derrilyn assessed her. 'Could you beat him?'

'He is the finest opponent you would ever meet. So focused on his druid skill he is. Show him one hesitation, one wrong move, and he takes the opening. Ruthless and deadly.'

'You didn't answer my question.'

'Of that, I cannot say. Others may focus their druid's skill on medicine, tracking opponents through marshes, or even working the lands. Some of the best farmers are druids, their skills focused on nature. Mine is defence and protection. Kerrick's is attack. Were we ever to fight without restraint I do not know who would prevail.'

Derrilyn's jaw clenched.

'I sense your anxiety. So many possibilities from the unknown. But I will guide you,' Elaya said.

'But what if you can't?'

'I have guided you this far. I fear far less for you than Kerrick's son.'

'What, that brute Finlack?'

'Yes. And you rightly call him a brute, but is that just because he has been schooled in brutality? I don't know him well, but with a guide like Kerrick, could he avoid going to a similar place of self-interest and lack of morality?'

Derrilyn contemplated her words.

Elaya continued, 'You are the finest in your class,

Derrilyn.' She brought him closer, her voice lowering. 'But where you end up in your moral compass is unclear until you pass the...' her words tailed off; she didn't want to say the C word anymore.

He sent her a thin smile. 'Yes, I know,' he muttered. 'But, if I become a nightmare, will you replace me?'

'Oh, definitely!'

He smiled and fell silent.

'We need to prepare for tonight,' she said. 'Let's visit the castle and scope out the spaces our lovely committee have allocated for the feast. I will meet you there soon; I need to check on something first.'

∽

Elaya arrived at Laglen's hut a short time later. It was near sunset, and bands of coloured clouds dispersed into a dull grey night. She was surprised to find Tarith stationed outside. 'I was expecting you to have eyes on the boy? Everything okay?'

'Oh, yes, I just prefer the chill on my cheeks. No one is coming in or out, I assure you.'

'When was the last time you saw them?'

'A few hours ago.'

'You didn't think about checking in on them?'

'No need, Elaya. They said they were sleeping.'

Elaya searched ahead, using her druid scan, but found nothing. No presence, no emotional auras at all. But then she didn't expect to if they were asleep. This did make sense, though. At least Girvyn was safe and under Laglen's tutelage.

She opened the door, to check on them anyway.

'Hello? Laglen? Girvyn?'

Tarith went to join her, hand on hilt, but Elaya held him back and entered.

She scanned again. Nothing. Then she found them. Toes sticking out of covers at the ends of their beds. She considered cleaning up; with both of them in the Realm, the hut was messy again. But she laughed out loud at the idea. The feast was tonight, and she still had much to do.

Back outside, she said to Tarith, 'Can you keep watch until midnight? I will get Sargon to relieve you until the early morning hours. Then come back before dawn. By tomorrow evening, we should be done.'

'Of course, Elaya, anything you ask.'

Elaya nodded and left for the banquet.

Eight

Girvyn stood in his uncle's Atrium, excitement rushing through him. Not far from the two of them, the assistant waited respectfully while Laglen continued. 'I have created a simulation space where you can practice as if it's your own structure, but with some limits.'

'Why can't I practice in my structure?'

'It's rare but possible to hurt yourself when you are learning without having mastered the flow of The Pull. Also, you could hurt me.'

'Okay, I see. What happens next?'

'Hold your hands out.'

A second later, a book appeared on his outstretched palms. 'What's this?'

'This is a ten-step beginner's guide to Dream Travelling, written by Kalamayn. I always thought you would start with this.'

Girvyn passed him an incredulous shake of his head. 'So you're not actually going to train me, Kalamayn is?'

'I'm not good with the detail. Kalamayn has put together a

thorough step-by-step guide for beginners. Perfect for your attention to detail. Why don't you try it?'

'What, now?'

'Yes, think of a chair, sit in it, and start reading. Kalamayn has penned examples you can try out as you learn.'

Without planning it, chairs began popping into view. One, two, then half a dozen, in different styles and colours.

'Wait!' Laglen laughed. 'You have a bit of me in you, always charging ahead, eager for the bigger picture. Control your thoughts. Clear it all away. You just need one chair. The Pull is creating everything you are thinking. There is a way to allow it to just hear the thoughts you want it to hear.'

'How do I do that? Do I say its name, like "Pull, do this..."?'

'No, it's just the tone of your thoughts.'

Girvyn scowled. 'Uncle, thoughts don't have tones, do they? They don't make sounds.'

'Read Kal's book; there is a way to demarcate your thoughts. It comes with practice. As you get used to the way the tingle swirls through your mind, you can keep thoughts to yourself.'

Girvyn stared incredulously. 'Thoughts *are* kept to oneself.'

Laglen rolled his eyes. 'Yes, yes, very true. Always precise and rational.' He raised his hand before Girvyn could speak. Then clicked his fingers, more for drama than anything else. The chairs cleared away. 'This guide is going to be great for you.' A new desk and chair appeared. 'Start reading. I will return in three hours to see how you are progressing.'

'What? You're leaving?'

'I'm not going far. I will just be in another structure, that's all.' Two palm-sized discs appeared on the desk. Laglen picked one up and put it in his pocket. 'If you get anxious, press the centre. It will vibrate my one, and I'll come straight back.'

'Where are you going?'

'I need to do some racing.'

'But, Uncle, you promised.'

'Look, Girvyn, I need to clear my head and get my thoughts in order, and racing is the best way I know to do that. It's harmless, and it's just while you study. It's not like you are in the Waking tidying up while I am asleep. Those days are gone.'

'Okay, fair enough. Three hours then?'

'Three hours.' Laglen paused.

A window showing the racecourse scene appeared, and Laglen pointed at it. 'I will be in there. Just read.'

Then, in a blink, he was gone.

Girvyn sighed, put the book on the desk, and sat in the chair. He opened the cover and read the inside page.

A 10-Step Guide to Dream Travelling.

1. Mastering Breath.
2. Clearing the mind.
3. What is the Difference Between The Pull and The Source.
4. Controlling Thought Flows.
5. Understanding Time Differentials in the Realm.
6. How to pull from The Pull
7. What to Create and Why.
8. Ethics: Are Creations Real?
9. Learning to Control Addiction.
10. The 32-hour Rule

Girvyn turned the first parchment, then began browsing back and forth between each chapter, eyes flicking across the text. The workbook contained drawings, explanations, examples, and a worksheet he could follow.

For the next fifteen minutes, he scanned through the book. When he finished, he closed it and leaned back in the chair.

'You are not doing it right. Follow each step and do the exercises.'

Girvyn gave a start. 'Oh, hello. Are you not with Laglen in his race?' he said to his uncle's assistant, who had just appeared beside him.

'I can be in multiple structures at the same time. I am a creation of Laglen's mind after all.'

Girvyn considered this. 'How does that work? If you are in multiple places at once, which one of you is the original, and do you all share your experiences afterwards so you are all up to date?'

'No, we continually synchronise. Right now, Laglen is in the race construct.'

Girvyn nodded. 'When did my uncle create you?'

'Twenty-three years ago. I can give you the exact date, hour and second if required.

'And you have his mind?'

'Yes.'

'But you are so organised.'

'Ah,' the assistant raised a finger. 'I took his memories and character, but he added a new quality. Organisation!'

Girvyn smiled, then stopped. 'But what happens to your life? Do you become something different from my uncle?'

'I do indeed. The moment he created me, we took separate trajectories.'

'I would be keen to try that out.'

'You should follow Kalamayn's beginner's guide first and focus on breathing.'

'I have read everything. I would have changed the guide order to make it more meaningful.'

'What!? How could you have read it all? It's only been fifteen minutes!'

'I can speed read. I can look at a page and can remember all the words. By the way, I would have structured the chapters in this order: 2, 1, 7, 4, 5, 3, 9, 6, 8.'

'You missed out 10.'

'10's irrelevant. According to Kalamayn, the longest sleep was recorded at 32 hours. One doesn't need to read about that in a beginner's guide. They can experience that in practice.'

'How can you assimilate all that so fast?'

'That's the thing, I can come back to it later and digest it, since I have memorised it all.'

'Very impressive. That is certainly a skill that will help in here.'

'How?'

'Memory and detail. It's about engagement. It will make your structures more realistic. Remember the racetrack?'

'Yes.'

'Did you notice anything unfinished about it?'

'Lots of things. The stone was blurry up close, and people were dressed identically. How does that work, because I thought once they'd been created, they all evolved?"

'A good question! They only evolve if you want them to. Making a real person is actually very hard. You have to set a lot of parameters to make it work. A quick win is doing what Laglen does. Kalamayn loves details. But his structures are painstakingly slow to make for your uncle's liking.'

The large spectator stand from his uncle's race materialised above them, distinguished by its two levels and the curved roof.

'What are you doing?' the assistant cautioned.

Girvyn stepped closer for a clearer view. He populated the scene with figures, ensuring a more diverse selection of clothing than his uncle had used. However, the figures stood still, as if awaiting activation.

'They stay like that until you enter instructions. Do they eat? Do they speak? How clever are they? Is there a class system? Do they love and protect their young? What type of society do they advocate? How old do they grow? Like I said, doing people takes practice.' He pointed. 'Look at the stone though; you have added detail. Their clothes are all different. The faces are all different. That is very, very impressive to do that so fast.'

'I wasn't even aware that I did it.'

'That's why you should concentrate on the basics. You will find much more reward in thinking high and low levels simultaneously, and may have a skill for both! But your uncle is right; follow the guide first.'

Girvyn removed the stand with a flick of his hand and sat back down at the desk. 'Okay, I will digest the book some more.'

~

Before starting the race, Laglen paused everything.

'What's the matter?' the assistant asked him.

'I need to find the others.'

'Oh, you just lied to Girvyn. So, you are not racing?'

'No, I'm not.'

The assistant shrugged. 'How will you even find your kindred? There is no meet agreement. It's been years.'

'I will look through windows.'

'You mean enter!' The assistant looked worried. 'For the first time in years, I think you SHOULD race!'

'I didn't want to worry him. If I told him I was entering other structures, which is decidedly dangerous, he would get worked up.'

'Why don't you send a message by bird tomorrow?'

'Then wait for a reply, set up a meet? That could take days and the summit is tomorrow.'

The assistant rolled his eyes and cleared away the race scene; they stood in the Atrium, floating windows everywhere.

'Clear away my structures.' Laglen studied the clutter, which had been reduced by about 30%. 'Get rid of Orts' signatures.'

That still left over five hundred scenes. Laglen felt The Pull throbbing through the Travellers' windows. 'Spread them out so I can see them individually.'

'You know this is quite random,' the assistant said. 'You are looking at public windows, and we are seeing what they want us to see. And who is Travelling at this moment.'

'Yes, I do know that!'

'Look at this one,' the assistant pointed to a battle scene. 'Do you really want to knock on that door?'

'I am going to have to enter them, not knock,' Laglen grumbled. 'These posted pictures could be fake. Or they could be coded invites. I remember my father told me, as an invite design for a dinner party he posted a burning castle, with people screaming and on fire.'

'This is crazy,' the assistant said.

'Look, most of these people are either waiting for someone or looking for someone.'

'Or they forgot to make the structure private, like you did!'

'Which is why I have to enter; if we knock, they may vanish. We are looking for Tasmin, Kalamayn or Mora. Let's start with Tasmin. Can you see any water features?'

'I'm not seeing water structures, just bodies of water,' the assistant answered.

Laglen walked through a maze of hanging windows, resembling an immersive installation, each pane a corridor into a dream.

'What about this one?' the assistant said.

Laglen saw a woman standing at a cliff edge.

'You found some sea,' the assistant commented.

'Is she preparing to jump?'

'Looks that way, or could be a calling card.'

'I'm going in.'

'Be careful.'

An instant later, Laglen materialised on the cliff not far from the woman. He felt The Pull flowing through her, felt his own reduced connection to it.

She sensed Laglen straight away and shot a wary glance at him.

'Hello!' Laglen greeted, cautiously moving closer.

'Stay back! Don't try and stop me!'

'I just wanted to talk.'

'Who are you? What do you want?'

'Are you sure about this?'

'Of course I'm sure.'

'Look, it's not my place, but if you are unhappy in the Waking, just live in the Dream Realm.'

'You don't know what's coming. He will find me on either side.'

'Who's coming? Is there no one you can talk to?'

'What do you want?' the woman demanded again.

'I am looking for some friends on the awake side: Tasmin.

Or Kalamayn or Mora, do you know them?'

'Never heard of them. Now go to hell.'

Concerned, Laglen took a step closer. 'Why don't you try and talk to…'

She disappeared over the edge of the cliff.

Laglen was thrown back into his Atrium.

'Any luck?' the assistant asked.

Grappling with his disbelief, Laglen shook his head. 'She took her own life.'

After a stunned silence, the assistant spoke, his voice tinged with unease. 'Okay,' he said, taking a deep breath. 'What about this one? It seems peaceful.'

Laglen pondered the new scene: a tranquil lake under the spell of a setting sun, a sky painted in hues of red, with a silhouette of trees casting shadows over a water's surface.

As soon as Laglen entered the structure, his reservation mounted. There was no lake, no peaceful sunset. It was night time. A path led towards a manor house. Candlelight flickered inside windows. Dogs barked in the distance.

It was an unnerving, realistic setting.

Interesting, Laglen thought, watching his breath dissipate in the chill air; the detail, the sense of a sprawling estate, it felt like something real. He pondered whether an actual location inspired this creation.

He could sense The Pull flowing through the construct, swirling around a powerful presence; despite this, he found himself unable to pinpoint the exact location of this potent source.

'You are late,' a voice grumbled, confronting him. A shape appeared. 'What's with this form?' the voice hissed. The shape moved closer, revealing a face. A scowling, unshaven visage that filled Laglen's field of view.

'Listen, Son, this business don't forgive mistakes. Follow

what I say, and I'll make sure you get your cut. Did you do what I asked?'

Laglen hesitated. 'What?'

'I'm in position near the back of the estate. Just make sure everyone stays in the kitchen so I can get to the drawing room and that safe. Got it?'

'Actually, erm, I was hoping,' he faltered, searching for the right words. His gaze drifted to the ground, then back to the person. 'I was hoping you could help me with something. It's a bit... out of the ordinary. I am looking for three friends.' He let out a nervous chuckle, trying to gauge the reaction of his listener, whose features were furrowing.

'Where's Elim?' the other hissed. 'What have you done with him?'

Laglen's chest constricted. Struggling to speak, he lost control of his windpipe. Eyes bulging, skin stretching taut, his body rose off the ground.

'Where is my son?! What have you done with him?'

'I'mmmm oooking orrrrr!'

Laglen felt his life force slipping away, waited for The Pull to leak out of him, for the moment of certain death.

A new voice urgently called out, 'Father! Don't do it!'

Laglen's body thudded onto the ground, and the air eased through his lungs, and he spoke again, 'I mean you no harm; I am just looking for someone.'

'How dare you!' the man hollered. 'What did you hear?!'

'Nothing. This is a total mistake by me, please accept my...'

'If I ever see you again, I will tear you apart limb from limb.'

Laglen found himself in his Atrium with his assistant. 'In night's name! That was close.' Laglen gestured at the windowpane. 'I don't want to see that one again. Get rid of it.'

'This is reckless,' the assistant groaned, staring at him. 'What happened?'

Laglen told him.

'You don't know what you are dealing with out there. Crazy Caspernites, Lale fanatics, Hoppenell mentals. They say the water in the west makes you mad.'

Laglen scowled. 'No, they don't.' He then brought his attention to another window. 'What about that one? They seem pleasant.'

He was drawn to the image of a young man and woman in an Atrium, engaged in an animated conversation marked by gestures and pacing. The moving images of them seemed like a live feed, not a loop or a window display image.

His assistant warned, 'You really want to try another one? Why not visit Girvyn? His study is going well; you might be impressed!'

But Laglen barely heard him; his focus remained fixed on the window. Despite his recent experience, there was something about these two individuals, perhaps it was their bright and earnest eyes, that struck a chord of familiarity in him.

As Laglen entered their structure, the occupants rounded on him. Laglen dropped to one knee. 'Wait!' he exclaimed. 'I am looking for someone this side,' he added quickly. 'You don't have to tell me who you are or where you live.'

'Stay back!' the young man warned, taking a defensive posture. He raised his arm over his head, positioning it like a scorpion's tail poised to unleash the power of The Pull. 'We're also searching for someone. Let's exchange names on the count of three,' he proposed.

Laglen gestured for him to proceed.

In unison, they counted, 'One, two, three...'

'Tasmin,' they said simultaneously.

They stepped back from one another. The man lowered his arm. Laglen slammed shut his gaping mouth.

'I remember you,' the woman said, coming forward. 'Laglen? You used to read me stories when I was a little girl.'

'Yes, I'm Laglen,' he said, still in shock. Something in her aristocratic manner jolted a memory. He looked at the man. Though he was now taller, and his black beard trimmed, there was a familiar softness in his dark eyes. Mora's little boy? 'Dremell?' Laglen queried, looking at him. Then, turning back to the woman, his gaze settled on her, recognition dawning. 'Nadine?'

'What are you doing here, Laglen?' Dremell asked. 'My mother said you are in Rathnell with baby Girvyn. Is that where you still are?

'Yes.' Laglen rubbed his brow with his fingertips, thinking. 'What are you doing with your structure public like this?' he cautioned. 'It's dangerous.'

'For the last few months, we have been looking for Tasmin in the Waking and the Realm,' Dremell replied.

'Have you been to her home?'

Nadine nodded. 'Father did a while back, but it was covered in dust and cobwebs. Then more recently, he went again, and another family had claimed her property.'

'What?' Laglen frowned.

'She disappeared years ago,' Dremell said. 'But oddly, since then Kalamayn has been receiving letters from her once a year, and my mother now thinks they are fake.'

'Fake? How?'

'A different handwriting, no returning address, saying nothing personal in the messages that link her to our past.'

'Mora always had an eye for script,' Laglen agreed and frowned. 'When was the last time anyone saw Tasmin?'

'The letters stopped last year, but seeing her – fifteen years.'

'That's the same as me,' Laglen muttered.

'We think she is a hostage somewhere, and her kidnappers are trying to make it look like she is alive,' Nadine said.

'But why?' Laglen managed.

Dremell looked down. 'Crane, we think he may have done something to her.'

'Tas was very angry after he killed Rosein, that's the last time I saw her.'

'Why are you looking for Tasmin?' Nadine asked.

'I'm looking for any of you. Tas was always the easiest to find, because of her water features.' He drew a thin smile. 'I similarly fear Crane is up to no good. Have you heard about the Rathnell summit?'

'About the missing babies and these lost tribes and such? Yes, who hasn't?'

'There is an account from a Forester girl who claims to have seen monsters.'

Laglen told them what he knew of the rumoured testimony, and about Girvyn's dream, and they listened in astonishment.

'We are near Trefgwyn. We can be with you tomorrow,' Dremell offered. 'We can help.'

'I was going to send a bird to Kal and Mora next; are they still in Cundelly?'

'Yes, Father still has the antique shop,' Nadine said.

'And Mum lives in the west district,' Dremell told him. 'She will be thrilled to hear we met you.'

A rush of memories flooded Laglen's mind, of monthly get-togethers, of innocent, reckless abandon, daring ventures, and deep regrets.

'First, we need to know more from this Forester girl. We

all know the saying: what we create in the Realm, stays in the Realm. But I am starting to wonder...'

'You can't be serious?' Nadine said. 'How could Crane connect the Realm to the Waking?'

Dremell let out a gasp. 'You must speak with Mother and Kalamayn. We hold daily sunset meets with our parents,' Dremell told him. 'Look for the window with flying pigeons, that's our structure call sign.'

'Sunset, that's a good idea.' Laglen said. 'Let's meet tomorrow after the summit. I can update you then. Stay safe,' Laglen concluded, then vanished.

∿

Girvyn set down Kalamayn's "A 10-Step Guide to Dream Travelling" on the desk, closing it with a soft click. 'Can we switch to something else?' he asked. 'I've read it six times.' He tried not to sound unappreciative, but his voice couldn't hide his sense of boredom.

'Would you like to change your form again?'

'No, I have done that plenty.' Girvyn laced his fingers behind his neck and leaned back in his chair. 'Can I see my mother's structures?'

The assistant moved to sit beside him, taking a breath before speaking. 'Once a Traveller dies, we don't know what happens to their dreams. I can't transfer you to her Atrium. Even when she was alive, we could only step into her public windows. When a Traveller passes, their windows disappear.'

Girvyn looked down for a moment, trying to find the words. It seemed the Realm could offer so much possibility, such endless creative invention, but why was there no trace of the author's work after they were gone? In the Waking world, an architect's castle remains as a legacy after their death. Yet here, when material reality was just a thought away, it faded with death; why did no one save versions of themselves in other people's constructs? It wasn't about escaping or achieving freedom, that was unattainable, but about the desire to be remembered. To leave a mark that echoed the universal yearning for remembrance, in the unique way each person hoped to.

'I just want to see her. I just wanted to get to know her,' Girvyn said.

'Death is death, that's inevitable.'

'Is it though...'

The assistant spoke in a hushed tone. 'What's brought this on, Girvyn?'

'I want to visit Mother as she truly was but I can't, I just have Uncle's version of her. Hear me out... Uncle has made this structure so I can train and create things here. What if I created a version of me? That would still be here when I am dead, saved in Uncle's structure, right? So why don't people do that for their loved ones? It seems like a missed opportunity not to be able to keep visiting the ones you love in their original essence, even after they die. Not just through the eye of the beholder, through their memories, but as they saw themselves.'

'I have never seen anyone make themselves wind or turn themselves into dust like you have,' the assistant said. 'No one thinks like this. And it's a very good suggestion.' The assistant dithered in contemplation. 'Much of what Travellers do here is self-absorbed. Your mother used to think a bit like you.'

'That's why I want to meet her. But her version not Uncle's.'

The assistant glanced sideways at Girvyn. 'All you have got is Laglen's version. Want to see?'

'Uncle invited me to do this. I said I wasn't ready...'

The assistant frowned. 'She is my sister too. When your uncle created me, we were identical and therefore we share the same memories of her. This Rosein he made is, in many ways, like her.'

Girvyn let out a lengthy, relieved breath. 'That's good to know. But she is still your version. But okay, fair enough, show me.'

∼

A short while later, the assistant guided Girvyn through a picturesque village nestled in the heart of a breathtaking rural valley. A sparkling river meandered along the basin, winding beneath rolling hills adorned in shades of green and amber, interspersed with the glimmering foliage of alder trees. The serene beauty of the landscape wove a tranquil scene.

'What is this place?' Girvyn asked the assistant.

'It's taken from a painting Laglen likes.'

'I thought I recognised it.' Girvyn searched for a moment. 'Beillbin, right? He is famous for these idyllic depictions.'

The assistant gave him a faint smile. 'Beillbin paints with brush and ink, but Laglen paints with thought and realism. I am quite proud of him for this place. He put a lot of effort into making it look real.'

Girvyn harboured doubts, spotting clear signs of a rushed stage design. 'Has the lighting always been this way? Is it a continuous sunset?' he inquired.

'Afraid so.'

'And there are only six shapes to the trees.'

The assistant smirked. 'That's more than his usual one.'

They proceeded up a path leading to a gated village named *Pleasant Tree,* marked by a blue and yellow wooden plaque. Inside, a mix of thatched buildings, some resembling workshops and others appearing more residential, were scattered across a gentle hill.

Girvyn caught a whiff of woodsmoke in the air. 'It's impressive,' he remarked, observing the villagers' daily routines. Some waved as they walked by, while blacksmiths pounded away at their tasks. 'Doesn't anyone question that it's perpetually sundown?' Girvyn asked the assistant.

'No, everyone accepts this reality.' He smiled. 'Come on. It's this way; your mother lives at the top, with a panoramic view over the vale.'

'Why did Uncle go to all this trouble?'

'Your mother loved country walks, and she liked Beillbin's art, too, so Laglen thought it would be a nice idea to place her here.'

'I thought we would find her in a room or something?'

'A room? That sounds like a cell. No, Laglen wants his memory of her to feel happy and contented,' the assistant told him.

'Her memory would be satisfied in a room, right, if my uncle had made her to not question the room.'

'True. But he has guilt about many things. That's why he went to great lengths to create this place. He felt happier giving her this life.'

'Is this place for her or him?'

The assistant stopped and pointed at a wide building at the top of the hill. 'She is in there. I am not going any further.'

Girvyn stared at the single dwelling, low-pitched hut. Smoke snaked out of a chimney. 'Why are you not coming?'

'I don't want to overcomplicate things. She will think I am Laglen. Oh, one more thing, don't mention you are Girvyn.'

'What?'

The assistant made a face. 'Just say you are a friend of

Laglen's, and he suggested you drop in to say hello.' He looked down momentarily. 'She thinks you left to cross the sea.'

'What do you mean? When did I leave for the sea?'

'It's patchy, Girvyn. You were a baby when she died. Laglen gave her memories of your birth and changed the story.'

Girvyn shook his head in disbelief.

'And she doesn't know she is in a structure,' the assistant muttered.

'How does that work?' Girvyn complained. 'Part of her life has changed?'

'Of course it has. The rural landscape stretches only five miles, but she shows no interest in travelling beyond it. In her Waking life she was adventurous. But many things remain the same: her empathy, her strength. She loved art in life, and she loves art in Laglen's memory.' He glanced away. 'She's content and happy not knowing she is in the Realm. Just go in and speak to her.'

Girvyn walked towards the door and turned, realising what the assistant had just said. 'What? She doesn't know she is a Dream Traveller?' he hissed. 'Let's leave it, she is too altered.'

The assistant raised his hands. 'She does know. But she thinks she is in the Waking. In her life now, she has retired. You wanted to meet her, so go in.' The assistant walked away.

Girvyn took a breath, faced the door, and tapped it.

A moment later, he heard Rosein's voice from the other side of the door.

'Who is it?'

Now that he was here, he didn't know what to say. He released his hand from the bronze doorknocker and brought his arm to his side. 'Err, my name is Fedrick.' It was the first name that popped into his mind. He chased away thoughts of the annoying market trader and waited.

'Fedrick, from...?' Rosein's voice trailed off, and the door opened.

Girvyn stared at his mother's wide smile, then met her sharp, dark eyes.

She was shorter than he was by about five inches, dressed in a baggy hessian dress smeared with paint marks.

'From where?' she continued.

'From Rathnell,' he said.

'So how can I help you, Fedrick from Rathnell?' she replied.

Girvyn closed his mouth, opened it again, felt his pulse quicken, his cheek twitch. 'Laglen sent me, I mean, suggested that I visit. I was passing by,' he stammered.

'Oh! Why didn't you say?!' She stepped back into the hut, offering him a curtsey and an invitation to enter.

Girvyn moved forward, heard wood creak from below his foot, smelt log smoke and roasted oats lingering in the warm air of her home. He couldn't help but marvel at all the detail his uncle had put into this.

'How do you know Laglen?' she asked him.

'He is a friend,' Girvyn said, clearing his throat.

Her eyes narrowed. 'You seem a little young to be his friend.'

'My parents died when I was young. Laglen looked out for me; he's been like my father.' It felt easier telling her something truthful.

She stared at him for a moment. 'I am so sorry to hear that, Fedrick. Come,' she said, leading him through to the kitchen. 'I have leaf brewing. Do you like fennel?'

'I love fennel!' Girvyn felt a sudden sense of pleasure. Were some of his ways her ways?

She passed him a cup. 'Let's sit in the lounge by the fire.'

Girvyn smiled and followed her into the next room. 'I didn't know you painted!'

Rosein frowned. 'Why would you know?' She gestured at the array of easels and finished paintings resting against the walls, mostly landscapes and river views.

Girvyn flapped. 'Laglen said some things about you but he didn't mention you were an artist.'

She blushed. 'I'm not; it's a hobby. Please, take a seat.' They sat next to each other on a sofa facing the fire.

'Who is that?' Girvyn asked, indicating a painting of a baby above the mantelpiece.

'That's my son Girvyn.'

Girvyn stifled a gasp and nodded. 'Yes, Laglen said you had a son. What is he like?'

'Girvyn?' Her words trailed off. 'Studious. A little blunt at times. He finds making friends difficult, but loves the library.'

Girvyn glanced away while he gathered his thoughts. Was this a twisted reality or a logical outcome of Laglen's creation? His mother had never witnessed his upbringing and would have no knowledge of Girvyn's traits. Yet, she needed some memory, so why not base it on the real Girvyn?

'He seems like he was a deskbound type,' he said, finally. 'Was it strange that he wanted to travel?'

She considered him through a dissecting squint. 'No.'

Girvyn glanced down. 'Laglen said you were a Traveller?'

'You know about that?' she said, an eyebrow hoicked. 'Surely you don't Travel? You're too young.'

Girvyn stammered, 'Err, yes, I am just learning.'

'Be wary of it, Fedrick. It feeds off false wants.'

Girvyn sat forward. 'What do you mean?'

'It's so seductive. Before you know it, your Waking life has faded away, replaced by fantasies you can make-believe. But genuine existence is in accepting what you can't change and coming to terms with the unknown. So don't run from real life; live it. I stopped Travelling years ago.'

'That's a very wise insight,' Girvyn said after a while.

'Don't you feel the Realm is alive?' She gripped his wrist for a second, eyes intense. 'I'm telling you, it's not what it seems.'

'The Realm? I feel it too,' he lied; it was too early in his training to identify with her warning, but he wanted her to continue.

'Have you ever contemplated what lies beneath these Realm appearances when we create autonomous beings?' she hissed.

'Yes, I have wondered,' Girvyn encouraged, nodding at her. 'What is underneath?'

Her face turned blank. 'I can't tell you.' She then relaxed and leaned back.

Girvyn sat back in his seat, too, pondering. Was this because she didn't know, or because Laglen didn't know. Or because she didn't want to tell him?

Again, he kept thinking. Who was this for? Was this world for Laglen or Rosein? Was this a guilt-built construct? Some perverse fantasy where this happy made-up sister could absolve his regret and not get killed by Crane.

Just then, Girvyn heard the front door open, heard the sound of scraping shoes, and waited for further resonances of who this might be.

Rosein looked up. 'Dearest, is that you?'

'Darling? I heard another voice. Are you okay?'

'Quin, come in; I am with Lag's friend, Fedrick.'

Quinlan. His father! No one had mentioned he existed in the structure too. Girvyn gripped his own leg, trying to calm down. Quinlan, an Ort, had died after Rosein. From the stories Laglen had recounted he knew all about the Realm, and, for the sake of their marriage, had urged Rosein to abstain from Travelling.

Quinlan came into the room and extended a hand to Girvyn. 'How is Laglen?' he asked. 'He hasn't visited for years.'

'Years?' Girvyn repeated, sounding surprised. He wondered if there was a time differential in play, and if not, why Laglen would create all this and not visit?

'Tell him we are quite content, aren't we, darling?' Quinlan said and dropped into an armchair to Girvyn's left side. Girvyn glanced at him, smiling.

'Yes,' Rosein commented. 'We love to walk; I love to paint.'

'It's a lovely set up,' Girvyn observed.

'Set up?' Quinlan's eyes narrowed.

'I mean life,' Girvyn corrected.

Girvyn couldn't help but notice his strong resemblance to his father; even the way Quinlan's leg was jerking was an impulse that Girvyn had thought was uniquely his.

'Quinlan helped me see that living was in the Waking, didn't you, dearest?' Rosein said, sending him a puckered air kiss.

'And it keeps you away from that sadistic maniac Crane.'

At the mention of Crane, Girvyn stood up and brushed down his tunic, feeling flustered all of a sudden. 'I think I should get going.'

'No, don't go.' Rosein implored.

'Would you like to stay for dinner, Fedrick?' Quinlan added.

Girvyn's vision began to blur, and he stumbled towards the door, feeling overwhelmed.

A short time later, Girvyn found himself looking for the support of a tree to provide a moment of assurance, but he found nothing, so he leaned into the breeze, feeling its coolness brush away the heat from his face and his dancing thoughts.

How did he get here? How did he get outside? He didn't even remember saying goodbye to her.

'Are you okay?' the assistant said, appearing beside him.

'Can we go back?' was all he managed to say. 'I want to clear my head.'

∼

Laglen returned to his Atrium and found his assistant waiting with a smile. 'Good news,' Laglen said, recounting his conversation with Nadine and Dremell.

The assistant still beamed even after Laglen had finished.

'What are you still smiling about?' Laglen asked him.

'I have news, too. Girvyn's class went well. He is quite unique isn't he? He has created many things,' the assistant said, then hesitated before adding, 'He also visited his parents.'

'What?' Laglen was taken aback.

'You suggested it,' the assistant reminded him, signalling for him not to interrupt. 'It was Girvyn's decision to go, and it turned out positively.'

'Positively? She thinks Girvyn left for the sea!' Laglen started searching through his windows for where he had left Girvyn.

'Wait. Before you go, there's more,' the assistant interjected.

'More?' Laglen cursed. 'What more?'

'He's been reading the book repeatedly and experimenting. Just be prepared,' the assistant warned.

Laglen scoffed and stepped into the structure.

There, he saw two figures and something else in conversation: Girvyn, the other assistant, and a life-sized wooden carving, a hybrid of a bat and a fox, one of Girvyn's creations.

'What in night's name is this?' Laglen exclaimed.

'Uncle, I finished the book and got bored,' Girvyn said.

'You couldn't have,' Laglen replied in disbelief.

'Finished the book or got bored?' Girvyn asked.

'Both!'

The assistant grinned. 'He needs more thought control. Things kept appearing unexpectedly. He has your talent but with a keen eye for detail.'

'And this is?' Laglen asked, pointing at the wooden figure.

'Hi, Uncle, I'm Eden. How did the race go?' the carving spoke.

Stunned, Laglen could only utter, 'What?'

'I gave him my identity,' Girvyn explained.

'How? You're too inexperienced to be doing this,' Laglen protested.

The assistant gave a sheepish shrug. 'I couldn't stop him.'

'And all this in three hours?'

'Nine, actually. I altered the time flow,' Girvyn admitted.

'And you didn't think to tell me?' Laglen snapped at the assistant.

Girvyn intervened. 'Uncle, you were busy.'

Eden suggested, 'Maybe it's just bad communication from everyone?'

Laglen raised his hand for silence. 'Thank you, Eden. Girvyn, we need to talk.'

'Of course, Uncle,' both Girvyn and Eden said in unison.

'Everyone else, leave. Girvyn and I need a moment,' Laglen ordered.

Girvyn blinked in surprise. 'What?'

The assistant made an awkward face. 'Laglen's upset.'

'Where should I go?' Eden asked.

'I'll take care of that,' Laglen said, making Eden disappear.

'Uncle, wait!' Girvyn protested. 'Can't we keep him?'

'You don't save creations in your first lesson. It's not about creating; it's about control and ethics,' Laglen explained.

Girvyn sighed. 'I understand, Uncle.'

'I had years of training before I entered the Realm. You're still a child,' Laglen reminded him.

'I just got carried away,' Girvyn admitted. 'I met my parents.'

'I know.' Laglen sighed, and patted Girvyn's shoulder. 'Are you okay, Girvyn? My construct of Rosein is a painful reminder of how I've been too absent too often.'

'It was amazing but sad,' Girvyn said. 'But she doesn't know she's a construct of your memory?'

Laglen looked away. 'In this version, they stay together, that's more important.'

'What do you mean?' Girvyn asked.

'I have many sorrows,' Laglen confessed but couldn't say more.

'I am glad I did it but was shocked and sad about how you made them think I had migrated.' He sighed. 'But I see the complexity.' He nodded thoughtfully. 'We can make up for lost time, Uncle. We can explore the Realm, and maybe go and visit them together?'

'I would like that. So you like this? What you, what we are?'

'Oh yes. Strangely I feel my whole life has been about preparing for this, but I never realised it. I want to do more. Try more. Push the limits and discover.'

Laglen laughed. 'Calm down! Now you know why I slept so much! But now you're here there'll be no hot soup waiting for us when we wake. I have to admit I will miss that!!

Girvyn returned a laugh. 'It's a shame we can't bring Sedgwick with us.'

'Sedgwick?'

'Your assistant.'

'But I never gave him a name.' Appreciating Girvyn's childlike innocence, Laglen smiled. 'It's a nice name. Just don't like him more than me. That would be another annoyance I have with him.'

Nine

Elaya led the first visitors into the royal assembly hall, feeling her pulse quicken as they scattered about. At this stage, it was only the small delegation from Lale led by Envoy Nark. Before Elaya had arrived, Derrilyn had placed guards inside and outside each entrance.

'The hall will get crowded quickly, so you might want to stay in your group when the queen arrives to greet you,' Elaya told Nark. She motioned to her guards at the door, 'Make sure everyone gets the same instruction.'

Derrilyn watched Nark quietly. Elaya could tell he was scanning him for any ill intent. She had already done that. If there were a skirmish in the hall, it would come later, when it was full; when belligerent factions and settlements confronted each other for the first time. And not from Nark. Nark would slither and wind, but not spring.

'Clever,' Derrilyn said to her. 'Encouraging everyone to stay separate.'

'There will be over sixty delegates and representatives here tonight, so let's hope we can keep it that way.' Her voice quietened. 'Nark and Jakub are the only ones at the summit representing the cloth. As you know, Lale is home to dozens of basilicas and is the capital of faith. I am sure religion resides not far from Nark's thinking.'

'Do you want me to keep an eye on him?'

'I think any fracas will come from elsewhere tonight.'

'Envoy Seskin from Cundelly,' the master of ceremonies announced.

Seskin, flanked by two Cundelly officials, entered the room, stroking his impeccably groomed, silvery beard.

'The House of Trefgwyn,' the master of ceremonies announced next.

With the gait of a royal knight, Lord Grisham entered, accompanied by four resolute-looking men who seemed more suited to the battlefield than court. An entourage of helpers tried to enter but were held back by guards. 'I am sorry, Lord Grisham,' Elaya told him. 'Only delegates have an invitation for the feast and the summit tomorrow. Your entourage must stay in their quarters and wait.'

Lord Grisham nodded without complaint.

'Is Sward not joining us?' Elaya asked.

'He'll be joining shortly in his own House.'

Stasnier entered next with second advisor, Berenger. Surprisingly, they moved to greet Elaya.

'So far, so good?' Stasnier asked her.

'It's early days, gentlemen.'

'Well, I am sure your fear will settle once the wine flows.'

Elaya clipped her urge to argue with him. She didn't fear anyone; she treated each moment with the same healthy readiness. 'We have to work together on this, so please inform me if you sense any tensions.'

'Of course, Elaya,' Stasnier said.

Elaya could sense a bobbing Seskin, keen to interrupt.

'Envoy Seskin,' she greeted him.

Without delay, Seskin homed in on Stasnier. 'I trust Cundelly has your vote against this road?'

Stasnier's voice dropped to a hush. 'Rathnell shares your concerns about the shifting power dynamics in the region. If Stoer and Casper turn on us, backed as they are by Hoppenell steel, we need an alliance greater than the two of us to strike back. So, I cannot support you publicly, Seskin,' he threw a wide smile at Lord Grisham across the room, 'until I know we have a wider support from those in the room,' he finished through his grin. 'But let's not discuss this any further just now.'

'Lord Sward from The House of Andergine.'

Sward, who had confronted Elaya at the gate, charged straight past them with his head held high in a show of pomposity.

Elaya chuckled, dropping her voice for Derrilyn. 'See how Sward wants his own entrance?'

'How do put up with that, Elaya? You've got more restraint than I.'

'I have had much worse treatment than that in my life! I embarrassed him at the gate so now he can't look me in the eye.'

'I think he embarrassed himself.'

Pleasantries began murmuring through the chamber. 'I hear Sward fights with determination in battle,' Elaya continued. 'But here, he struts like a peacock. Do you see his aura colour?'

Derrilyn squinted, and then his eyebrows lifted. 'Yes, yellow?'

'Indeed, I think this kind of setting causes concern in his aura, hence his belligerent attitude!'

'Isn't he a cowardly churl!'

'Now you are getting it.'

Berenger appeared and leaned into Elaya's eyeline. 'I trust we still welcome the queen when the room is full?'

'That is right. Give me the nod when everything's ready, and I will fetch her.'

Berenger took a goblet of wine from a tray and drank a sip. 'I am sure such a time will speak for itself.'

'Envoy Praleck from Stoer,' the master of ceremonies pronounced, louder than before as the room was getting noisy. 'Envoy Sevada from Hoppenell.'

Praleck strode in, his golden cloak billowing behind him. Sevada seemed to share his same sense of distinction. A murmur rose to greet them.

'What colour do you see around Praleck?'

'Cold blue!'

'Exactly. So why?'

Derrilyn hesitated. 'I don't know' he said.

'He is the most powerful man in the room, and he knows it. He is backed by Hoppenell and has the key to Amjad, with Lale and Casper at his feet. Look at him,' they watched as he passed out packages of gifts. 'He used to be a general, but now he is almost as slippery as Stasnier.'

There were hearty cheers as people unwrapped parcels and opened tied pouches.

'Silk!'

'Tobacco!' someone declared in amazement.

Elaya shrugged, unimpressed. 'The Elders used to inhale something similar in the deserts. If it's anything like that, the delegates will be out for days.'

Praleck raised his hands for silence and came forward, his cloak swirling as he cast his gaze around. 'Lords, Ladies, esteemed guests. I share a few gifts from The East.' His colleagues began handing out more gifts. 'Fear not, fear not, for those that miss a treat, we have more treasures in our trunks. Protected by Hoppenell Steel and brought to you via Stoer, the gateway to Amjad! Please make an appointment with my staff to learn about these exports.'

Elaya whispered, 'The arrogance of the man to make an unscheduled speech, trying to push trade deals.'

'They're all doing it,' Derrilyn grumbled, watching dozens of lips moving in excited scheming. He shook his head in disgust. 'They're supposed to be here to discuss the missing, not to plot.'

'Welcome to politics.'

'I prefer a street fight. At least you know who you're facing.'

'So do I. So do I.'

'The House of Aladre. The port settlement of lower Capels, and the city of Casper!!' pealed the announcer.

Three more groups entered the hall. Hearty greetings and various bits of chatter echoed off the dome ceiling.

'Jakub,' Praleck shouted at the Casper Envoy. 'Come and join us for drinks!'

All smiles, Jakub made sure his slow, straight gait almost emphasised the road they longed to build.

Seskin, who looked ill, sought support from Stasnier, but the Privy Counsellor had already shifted his attention to interact with Nark of Lale.

Elaya whispered to Derrilyn, 'This Casper to Stoer road is causing quite a division. Keep your focus on colours.'

'Lady Herya of Hallwich.' Her entrance elicited a cheer.

'The House of Stone!' A woman in a dress and elaborate head coverings entered and started chatting with the first person she met.

'The Highlanders of the Riddon Slope!' the announcer boomed. Every eye shot towards the entrance, and a sudden hush fell as three mountain dwellers made their way in, draped in thick sheepskin cloaks layered over fur garments.

Derrilyn deflated his puffed cheeks. 'There are so many colours in here. I'm not sure where to focus my attention.'

'I expect a scuffle between Highlanders and Foresters, but there are numerous disputes throughout the room to look out for.' Elaya's head snapped around then. 'What do you make of Lale?'

'You mean Envoy Nark?'

'Yes?'

'Now you mention it,' Derrilyn hesitated, thinking, searching. 'I'm feeling something. Hostility!' he declared finally.

'Yes, but to whom?'

Derrilyn gasped. 'It's towards us!'

'But why?' Elaya kept her face expressionless. 'Have you insulted him? Upset his wife, perhaps?'

'Of course not! I haven't even spoken to…ah! Is it because we are druids?'

'It seems that way.'

'But that was decades ago! It's over with now! There were the Reconciliation Trials, the introduction of The Druid Guild…'

'That doesn't mean we are not feared or despised among some sections of society.'

'I know the stories from the past, but I thought druids were accepted now?'

'Still not by all.' She smiled. 'Well done. You read his aura and used your deduction techniques. Now see what I see: Counsellor Berenger is talking to Grisham, and Stasnier is talking to the Cundelly ambassador. They seem engaged, true?'

With so much noise in the room and so many animated

people, Derrilyn searched this way and that. 'Actually, no, they're scanning around the room. What are they looking for?'

'A good Royal Advisor sees pressure and possible conflict before it happens,' Elaya said, 'and it pains me to admit it, but those two are the best. This is not a crowded tavern. No one is armed, but many scheming and bubbling animosities may flare beyond the pleasantries. In military terms, this is reconnaissance.' She lowered her voice even though she didn't need to. 'Have you heard them yet?' she asked.

'Heard who?' Derrilyn replied, confused.

'All of them. Strain...'

Derrilyn looked puzzled. 'It's so noisy. Who should I be listening to?'

'Anyone you choose. Your druid powers lie in your hearing as well as your sight. The nearer you are to Chattara, the more you'll understand. But try to listen carefully and tell me what you hear.'

'Strain?' Derrilyn repeated her word, went to speak, but then his expression changed to one of astonishment.

Elaya smiled encouragingly. 'Tell me what you hear.'

After blinking a few times, Derrilyn began repeating the various voices he could hear.

'Why should we pledge against some collective enemy when we don't know who that is – Sward.

I will not sweat blood nor money for a common alliance if Cundelly is in it – Envoy Jakub.

This could work to our advantage, sire; there is an opportunity to raise support for the Calpan Bay dispute – Lale Viceroy and third-in-line to the Throne, Crill Vrevan.

Indeed. Peace talks are nigh-on impossible. History knows the Highlanders have suffered, but it's a dispute long-standing without any respite – Envoy Sevada.

Is it true the nomads are coming? I hear they have never seen grass! – Lady Herya.'

Elaya was beaming at Derrilyn. 'Well done! Welcome to the noise!'

Derrilyn shook his head in amazement. 'How do I turn it off?' He smirked, looking at the wine tray and raising an eyebrow. 'Will that help?'

She flashed him a grin. 'That will make it worse.'

Elaya sensed the Foresters moments before they appeared at the entrance. She grabbed Derrilyn's arm. 'Get in position.'

'Chieftain Glefforn from the Forest Tribe of Elm, escorting Hazel from Sycamore,' the announcement echoed through the room.

Glefforn took the lead, followed by his tribesmen. Their weathered beards and serious expressions didn't invite warm greetings from those present. Nevertheless, all attention was drawn to Hazel. Whispers circulated throughout the room as she arrived, her bob swaying as she surveyed the faces in the crowd.

'What is she going to say?' someone whispered.

'Tell us, Forester, what is your testimony?' Nark's voice rang out. 'We've travelled a long way to hear this.'

Elaya sensed the tension building in the room, the collective curiosity. Hazel was the sole witness to the killings and theft of babies, and her account had been shrouded in secrecy, stage-managed by Stasnier to give import to the conference and, therefore, Rathnell's importance on the geopolitical stage. Differences had been set aside, tongues clipped, to be here; everyone had gathered to hear this young girl speak.

'Tell us what you saw, girl?' Sward swore. 'I am arse sore and tired.'

'Was it wolves?' Jakub shouted. 'We found many animal tracks near the sites of our missing.'

'We've lost people too. Why did you survive?! What forest witchery is this?' Maltip questioned. 'We have suffered greatly on our slopes.'

'Silence, you highland scum!' Glefforn retorted.

Elaya raised her voice to restore order. 'Enough! Save your questions for the hearing tomorrow!'

'Agreed!' Praleck announced. He swept into the circle like some court performer, his golden cloak following. He knelt and took Hazel's hand and kissed it, then rose, his voice loud and smug. 'Let this Forester girl have her eve of orientation before we ask her such questions. Come, child, and bring your brethren; you must collect your gift package: the honeyed taste of Amjad sweets.'

Elaya intervened, taking Hazel away from Praleck. 'Thank you, Lord Praleck. Let's leave Hazel with her own kind until her testimony ends.'

Praleck grunted and was about to voice his objection when Stasnier appeared. 'I'm sure, Lord Praleck, you would agree that everyone should hear together what she saw?' Stasnier modulated his voice to avoid embarrassment. 'You wouldn't want another delegate to exchange gifts and have private discussions with her.'

Praleck seemed unfazed. 'Counsellor Stasnier Glencast,' His voice rang. 'I would have thought by now you would have retired.' He sniffed the air. 'Has it not been at least two decades since you took your post?'

'Despite the politically challenging times reflected in the grey at my temples, don't be deceived. I started young.'

In a rare moment of unification, Berenger vouched, 'That he did.' Coming beside Stasnier, arms folded, he added,

'Stasnier, the queen is due to enter shortly. She has requested you.'

As they left, Elaya heard Stasnier say, 'Good timing. I was going to spit in his wine and ruin years of schmoozing.'

As the room filled again with noise, a runner boy rushed up to Elaya. 'The desert tribe is at the gate, My Lady!'

Elaya tutted. 'They are late. What do you expect me to do? I am here for the queen.'

'The gate manager sent me to get you.'

'Tell him to use the usher I left at the gate and to bring them here. First, run to the library and get Alwad, the translator.'

The runner bowed and left.

'Lady Adara and her associate Jaden, from the Druid Guild!' came the announcement.

Lady Adara came towards them, seeming to glide, her silvery locks reaching to her waist.

Elaya greeted her with a smile.

Jaden, dressed in loose black clothing, mopped a brown strand from his brow, and extended his hand to Derrilyn. Elaya could sense Derrilyn was reading Jaden's cool blue aura. Jaden's warm oak eyes glimmered briefly; it seemed he could sense their scans too.

'How is it going this evening?' Jaden asked him, his friendly smile still lingering.

'It shows signs of becoming eventful,' Derrilyn muttered.

'And rather noisy,' Lady Adara noted. The pleasantries passed, and Adara's face grew serious. 'Elaya, did you know some of our kind have gone missing?'

She flashed a look at Derrilyn. 'No, I didn't. When did this happen?'

'Over the last two years. About a dozen druids have vanished.'

'You think it's the old animosity coming back? We sensed hostility from Nark.'

'No, I don't. That is just his religious response. I think this is more serious and mixed up with the missing. Have you heard anything?'

Elaya contemplated mentioning Laglen, Crane, and Girvyn falling into Crane's hell. But how would she even tell it convincingly? They needed to hear the reports from the other communities first. That's what the summit was for: to piece together the stories, compare and match. She had her suspicions, but they needed more information.

Suddenly, Elaya's nostrils flared, and from the far side of the room she sensed trouble.

Foresters and Highlanders faced each other, pushing and jostling.

An insult was muttered, and Chieftain Glefforn spluttered in surprise. 'Say that again? My forefathers should have castrated your ancestors to prevent your spawn!'

Elaya tried to push through the crowds, listening to the insults fly.

Rowen, Maltip's son, pointed his finger. 'Don't speak to my father like that. You are deadwood!'

'Are the feeble Highlanders sending their children to fight now?' Glefforn taunted.

'Outside. Let's settle this,' Maltip shouted. 'To the death.'

Before Elaya could get there, Sward came to the Highlanders' side in support of them, arms folded. 'I have said this before and say it again: do you expect this girl's testimony to unite us all? How do we put aside our warring disputes and agree on a common enemy that only this Forester girl has seen in the night? Pah!'

Glefforn uttered an oath, squaring up to Sward. 'Are you saying she has come here to lie?'

'Gentlemen, please!' Lord Grisham cried, arriving.

Elaya was almost there, and her senses began to pick up something.

'Stay out of this, Sward, you know better.' Grisham went to pull Sward away from the confrontation. A punch was thrown.

'I will cut your eyes out and feed them to the birds,' Glefforn's lips twisted into a snarl.

Hazel's voice lifted over the noise. 'Please, put this warring aside! We face a horror, and we must face it together!'

'Aye, classic trick,' Sward said. 'Set up a pretty girl with a wild story and the look of a sorceress to have Andergine warriors pledged to Rathnell Lords and die on their front lines.'

'Get out of my way!' Elaya hissed. Two more people to go. That nagging feeling got stronger.

As she came into the middle, her senses exploded into sudden stillness. She sensed it. A weapon. That druid clarity, that lucidity, flowed through her. She watched a drop of sweat fall to the ground, saw the grinding crunch of a clenched jaw. Then, in that moment of stillness, saw the hand moving into the inside of a jacket. The knife came free. People yelled and backed away, shoving, but she gave it no thought, her focus now on his curved sneer and that glinting slither of steel. The knife rushed across her front. Slicing through the air. Worried expressions flashed in her peripheral vision.

She brought her arm up and blocked the next swing and saw that perfect rump of a throat, sitting open, staying exposed. She smashed her fist into it, and he staggered back, dropped the knife, toppled. The sounds came back. The movement resumed to normal speed. She saw Derrilyn pick up the knife and slip it into his belt. Two of her guards yanked up the Highlander and held him in a lock hold.

'Put him in the dungeons until the summit is over,' Elaya said with disgust.

Many of the delegates took the opportunity to glare at the Highlanders.

'May I remind everyone that this is a serious and peaceful gathering. We have brought you here to share information to determine the true extent of the baby theft problem. You will be asked to leave if you can't put aside your differences,' Elaya announced frostily.

Some delegates co-operatively nodded in mutual agreement. The tension eased, and a more emphatic chatter continued.

Stasnier came to Elaya's side, his arrogant smirk twitching at the sides of his mouth. 'A potentially embarrassing incident. I expect a report in the morning with the Privy Council on how your guards missed a knife at the hall entrance.'

Elaya cursed, swung away from him, and found Hazel staring at her. Hazel tried to speak but was choked with tears.

'Are you okay?' Elaya asked her.

'This feud has been longstanding,' she managed. 'Yet still they cradle distrust like a baby. Many have said I was blind that night, and it was no more than a Highlander attack! There has not been a clash in forests or mountains in decades! I know what I saw!'

Elaya caught Chieftain Glefforn's hostile glances, but he dared not come over now that he had witnessed Elaya's effective governance. 'Sometimes time is not enough to heal smouldering hearts.' Elaya squeezed her arm. 'The main thing is you have your story to tell. So, tell it loud and proud.' Her voice hushed. 'You should go back to your group before Chieftain Glefforn throws a punch at me!'

'He thinks of me as a wild cat. It's harder for them than for me being here. The elders are out of their comfort with your stone walls and your formalities. We have a name for a rigid wind in the forest: a *Doliki*. That's what he is.'

'A rigid wind?' Elaya thought it over. 'Do you mean harsh or stubborn?'

'Yes, I do, though Glefforn means well. I'll obey his instructions, but I'd also like to explore the castle tonight,' she said. She cast a sidelong glance at Glefforn, who continued to observe them. 'Perhaps on my own, so I can avoid the stubborn wind!'

'A *Doliki* or not, there will be no wandering tonight. I can give you a tour during recess tomorrow?'

'I prefer to roam like a cat across your stone walls this eve. I ask such a boon only because I need to move and feel the air to organise my thoughts and prepare my testimony for tomorrow.'

'I do apologise, but I can't let you leave the compound the night before the summit. It's dark and dangerous at night. You don't know where you are going and could end up in the east district. Once you have delivered your testimony, roam away.'

'I would love to see this famous room of dead trees.'

Elaya frowned, and then her creases softened. 'It's on the west side of the castle. We call it a library.' She patted Hazel's wrist. 'Roam away tomorrow!'

'Elaya.' A familiar voice rang in her right ear. 'It's time the queen made an appearance.'

Elaya ignored Berenger, but swung on her heels to fetch the queen.

A short time later, she escorted Queen Amelia into the room. The monarch wore a cream cloak encrusted with gems and gold sovereigns. A slender gilded crown perched perfectly on her head.

'Her Majesty, Queen Amelia of Rathnell,' the master of ceremonies boomed.

The room hushed.

Amelia entered a space formed by parting delegates, Elaya at her side.

'I welcome you all to Rathnell Castle this evening. For many, this is your first visit; for others, old friends from over the hill. Your presence always reminds us of the close amity between Rathnell and your communities, whether they are provinces and settlements, Houses or sovereign states. All are welcome. I hope over the next day we will have a fruitful discussion on these terrible tidings that befall us, foster old relationships, and develop new ones.'

The room filled with noise again, and a line of ambassadors queued patiently to greet her. The aroma of roasting meat began to permeate the room. The twenty-minute call for dinner rang, and the doors to the banquet room opened, revealing three straight tables lined with opulent floral arrangements. Waiters stood behind every chair.

Elaya groaned to herself. The seating plan was the biggest damned headache of them all. She had seen it earlier that day and made some changes. No one should feel slighted by their seating position or food arrangements. The lavish splendour of the flowers projected the queen's power and strategically blocked any opposing glares from across the tables.

Elaya became aware of a churning in her stomach. What was that? Nerves. It wasn't fear. Elaya felt the presence of her kindred before they entered the hall. Seeing her kind had been years in the making. While some city folk shared her skin colour, most were Rathnalites, as the Privy Council liked to call them. Migrants or merchants integrated into the receiving society through trade, but they were few.

The calm, authoritative voice of the translator, Alwad, cut through the din. 'Queen Amelia, may I present Donjul of the Tologon tribe.' The Tologon hailed from the heart of the desert sands. Unlike Elaya's exilic existence of in-betweenness they were outsiders here. Outside of language, culture and custom.

Alwad gave Elaya a brief nod of recognition. He himself had left the desert far earlier than she, and had since become a valued scholar at the library, known for his expertise on desert-related knowledge.

'Pleased to meet you, Donjul,' Amelia said. 'Welcome to Rathnell. I wish your visit could have come under happier circumstances. I am thrilled to have this early occasion to welcome such distinguished guests for the first time.'

Alwad translated what the queen said. Donjul listened, then responded, looking at Elaya.

It had been some twenty-five years since she had left the deserts, but to Elaya's surprise, she could follow the words.

'Our kind rarely leaves the sand. For many years, we have suffered attacks that have taken our young. Only now that it hurts your city do you take care to notice.'

'Then,' Amelia gave him a trained, agreeable smile after hearing the translation, 'we need to maintain a sustainable set of diplomatic channels from now on.'

Donjul blinked at Queen Amelia. 'Zorlakto jintra vu'nar, blorim ho zor zorlo firim thorn.'

Alwad looked embarrassed. 'He said: many of your kind come to see the sands, but the sun hurts their pale skin.'

'This is going to be eventful.' Amelia said under her breath, glancing away.

'Let's call it a thrilling challenge,' muttered Stasnier, who had come to her side to take her to dinner.

Elaya was left with the translator and Donjul, who scrutinised her through a creased glower. 'The weak sun of the north has softened your skin,' Alwad said.

Donjul spoke to Elaya in the mother tongue. 'Krantha zilka jintra vu'nar.'

Elaya shrugged at the translator. 'Is that a statement or an accusation?'

He shrugged back. 'I suggest both.'

'Tell him it was a long time ago. I don't remember my clan's name. They were my family, my community, that's all I remember.' Elaya hesitated at the next question. 'They are gone, all of them. So I came here.'

Donjul seemed satisfied with the answer and took his colleagues into the banquet room, with Alwad close behind. The reception room was almost empty; just a few delegates remained, finishing their conversations.

Elaya and Derrilyn stood by the banquet hall door for the rest of the night. Relieved as they were that further scuffles had been averted, they found themselves swamped by the stressful, unwanted memories from the evening. And this was just the conference's first day. Tomorrow would see Hazel testify, and tensions rise.

Ten

Laglen woke before dawn, blinking in the room's cold darkness. He dressed and slipped out of the hut, careful not to wake Girvyn so early. As he ventured into the thick morning mist, a silhouette emerged from the swirling vapours.

It was Tarith. 'Morning,' he said to Laglen quietly.

'Have you been here all night?' Laglen replied, keeping his voice low.

'I have just started my shift.'

'You can wait inside if you prefer. Put some logs on the fire.'

Tarith rubbed his hands. 'I like the cold and quiet.'

Laglen slipped into the misty morning. Some distant voices came from the east wall, where the market was. He guessed early risers, getting ready for trade. A few carts rattled through the foggy surroundings.

The walk to the castle was slow, and he had to keep turning and straining through the haze to see which direction he was going in. As the ground became firm, he left the coppice and reached the first inner wall. He followed it westwards towards the castle. A few patrolling guards passed by, just voices in the fog.

Once inside the castle compound, blocked by looming walls and courtyards, the mist faded away, and he came to the kitchens. He heard voices inside. Clattering pots and chopping noises. More staff than usual. He'd expected that. It was the morning of the summit; breakfast would be prepared before the opening plenary.

He entered the corridor, ignored the door to the kitchens and kept going. Halfway down, he stopped, checking left and then right. Then he pushed the innocuous brick, and the wall opened up.

Brennen stood there waiting for him. He pressed a finger to his lips and led Laglen down an adjacent passage.

'Keep your voice down,' Brennen whispered. 'Up ahead are the royal quarters on the other side of that wall.'

They passed it. Then Brennen halted. 'Take that passage until it stops. It's too small for both of us. It will bring you to the top of the dome, where you can see and hear the summit. Keep hidden in the duct, Lag. There is no grate or anything, and it's an open channel, so stay back from the edge.'

Laglen nodded.

'When you are finished, take this passage down to the bottom, which will bring you out in the same corridor you started in, next to the kitchen.'

'Got it.'

'Be careful; it gets narrow at the top. I don't want you getting stuck in my corridors. You'll create a stink.'

'Nice that you care more about your passages than me.'

Brennen chuckled in the dark. 'After a decade in solitude, I have actually named them.'

They clasped briefly. Laglen tightened his tunic and climbed the final passage to his hiding place.

∾

Girvyn sat up, swung his feet out of bed, and stretched. Outside, the decking creaked. He heard a throat clear. 'Tarith, is that you?' Girvyn shouted, voice laced with worry.

'Aye, fear not, Master Girvyn. It is I.'

'Did you want to come in?'

The door opened and he heard the sound of boots on the mat.

'I will put the kettle on, young Girvyn. Mint tea?' Tarith said.

'I prefer fennel,' Girvyn replied and began dressing.

Tarith made a sound of disgust. 'Got any mint?'

'You will find it all in the left cupboard.'

A short while later, Girvyn found Tarith tending to two saucepans of water over the hearth. 'How long have you been here?' he asked him.

'A few hours.'

'Aren't you tired?'

Tarith chuckled. 'I get tired at the end of the day, not the start.' He handed Girvyn a cup of fennel tea, pulling a face. 'Revolting stuff.'

Girvyn smiled and took a sip.

'What do you want to do today?' he asked Girvyn. 'Library again?'

'Yes, please. It's my safe place.'

'Fine with me. Elaya said three days, so tomorrow we will see what happens.'

'You mean you might not be protecting me?'

'I might not be.'

'That's a shame; I like having you around.'

Tarith faced him. Girvyn thought he would say something, pat his shoulder like his uncle sometimes did, sealing off a pleasant exchange. But Tarith did neither.

'Get your bag. Let's make our way.'

They departed from the cabin a couple of hours after Laglen had left, but the mist had grown denser, transforming into a shroud of fog that clung to the trees and the ground, enveloping everything like a suffocating veil.

Shoulder to shoulder, they made their way through the coppice, passing dim outlines of trees as silent as the haze.

Suddenly, a blue light shone through the fog. Tarith stopped and glanced at it.

Girvyn fell to his knees. 'My head!' he hissed through clenched teeth.

Tarith drew his sword and swung left and right. 'What's wrong?'

'My head... it's throbbing.' He managed to rise and point a shaking finger through the mist. 'What's that?'

Tarith brought a finger to his lips. He seemed torn between caring for Girvyn and scouting the mysterious light.

The light didn't resemble a typical campfire; it burned in a rectangular shape above the ground. Like a flaming entrance. Something about it tugged at Girvyn's memory, but the pain in his skull was too intense to let him focus.

'Tarith...' Girvyn pleaded, gripping his wrist. 'We need to go.'

'I need to check this out. Can you run?'

'No, don't,' Girvyn protested, his head throbbing in agony. Nausea surged through him. 'Must... leave... now.'

A shape passed across the light, blocking it momentarily, a towering figure with fog drifting around it; taller than any man, any knight. A giant in red armour.

Tarith gripped his shoulder. 'Girvyn, I want you to run.

Don't look back. Run as fast as you can to the library. Get there and stay put. I will meet you there.'

'I know what this...don't try and...' Girvyn stopped, the pain making it too hard to speak. He'd remembered now, but how could he explain that what they were seeing resembled the door in Crane's Realm; from a dream? He nodded mutely and ran, his brain crushing with pressure. As he got clear of the fog, the city walls rising through the dawning light, he stole a glance backwards at Tarith, who was vanishing like a spectral figure retreating into the ethereal netherworld.

∼

At the east side of the castle, the delegates loitered in the lobby before the Royal Audience Chamber. Elaya and Derrilyn, with four extra guards, stood by the main entrance to the assembly hall, fully kitted out, searching each attendee before letting them through.

Due to the previous day's altercation, Elaya had changed the entry procedure, implementing allocated time slots for arrivals into the hall and a painstakingly thought-through seating plan.

The Highlanders arrived first and were placed at the far side of the room, where two of her guards remained positioned in the isle beside their seats.

The other cities: Lale, Cundelly, Stoer, Hoppenell, Casper, Trefgwyn and Rathnell, were seated more informally around the hall. The desert people sat at the back. This was their first time leaving the sands, and despite their unreadable, windswept countenances, their attention flicked to the glinting, stained glass windows and the genteel figurative statues scattered around the edges of the Royal Audience Chamber.

The other attendees, from scattered settlements and

smaller houses, entered and were led to seats. A few tried to engage Elaya in small talk, but she was as curt as diplomacy allowed, jaw rigid, hoping they would disappear.

'Please take your seats,' she kept saying.

The Foresters entered the hall and there was a ripple of quiet when Hazel appeared. It took about ten minutes to settle everyone in the hall so that the eighty or so delegates faced a raised wooden podium, a lectern for speakers positioned in the middle of the stage.

Berenger, the summit presiding officer today, came to the raised platform. He took to the podium and called for a hush.

'Her Majesty, Queen Amelia of Rathnell.' He stepped back. Elaya helped the queen onto the stage, then stood beside Berenger.

Amelia looked out across the assembly. 'Lords and Ladies, I welcome you to the Rathnell Summit opening.' Around the room, translators muttered what was being said into the ears of those who needed it. 'It is a great pleasure to see everyone and open these proceedings. Also, welcome to the Highlanders and Foresters, and we wish to place on record our gratitude towards the desert tribe for joining us. This is a historic occasion, and I hope this day will be fruitful on many levels.' She paused, choosing her words carefully. 'I realise distrust exists between some kingdoms but let us remember why we are here. There is a great threat we must address. Unlike past summits about trade and land disputes, this threat affects all of us. For years there have been terrible rumours about attacks, possibly by raiders. Fortunately, we finally have a survivor who can provide eyewitness testimony. Let us work together, set aside historical differences, and decide on a collective response. We are in this together.' Some murmurs of agreement and nods followed. 'What comes next is in our hands. It is time to listen, reflect, and act.' The queen wobbled slightly as she finished. Elaya helped her to the front seat.

Berenger came back to the lectern. He banged a hammer on the wooden plate. 'At this critical moment, we are gathered to exchange accounts of the troubles that have struck us. These attacks are an affront to our humanity and our way of life. As yet no group has come forward to claim responsibility.' He considered each delegation, letting his gaze linger for a comparatively long while. 'But we hope over the next day of talks to narrow down possibilities and identify the culprits.' He raised his fist in a dramatic gesture. 'It does seem these attacks are across our entire continent, but without an openness to share facts, figures and dates, we cannot address these atrocities effectively, nor find our missing children.'

'Get on with it!' someone shouted.

'Order! Order!' Berenger banged the hammer again. 'May I remind the House of Alergon that when it is their time to speak, they will have ample opportunity to do so.'

'What about the babies!' someone shouted. 'We want answers.'

'Let the Forester girl speak!'

Berenger shook his head. 'We all want answers. And I know feelings are heated. But this must be conducted in a calm and organised way. Hazel's testimony will arrive in due course. I invite our good friend, Envoy Seskin from Cundelly, to address the assembly.'

Seskin took the stage, looking self-important. 'Over the last three years, we have seen sporadic incidences that we didn't link up until now. At first, babies were taken from their cots in broad daylight, from the marketplace, parades, parks, and even people's homes. They were reported to the council. We thought these infants were taken for slavery or by grieving, jealous parents who had lost their young. Cundelly is flanked by fishing villages that flow east and west from the capital. These settlements became ghost ports. The reason is a mystery. How can we know our enemy when we didn't know we had one? Then we began to see evidence of attacks. It was like they enjoyed the killing or wanted to leave signs for us to see. Burning buildings, body parts chopped and discarded. None were ever left alive.' Seskin swallowed and took a breath. 'In Yarnik, a tiny fishing village at the mouth of the mighty Capels River, our tax collector arrived one day to find all twenty-three souls dead. This time, evidence was left for us to see. We know not how many babies were in the village, but our soldiers found four cots. There were no bodies of the little ones, though. No trace of them left.'

There was a murmuring ripple of concerned voices. 'The same in Gathscar,' shouted Lord Grisham from Trefgwyn.

Elaya cursed under her breath. This was what she hated about politicians. Everyone wanted to hear Hazel's testimony, but to salve egos, a sequence of old men, officials, and honoured guests must be allowed to posture and pontificate first.

'I invite Commander Maltip to address the assembly,' Berenger announced.

Maltip, not so used to formal proceedings or public speaking, smashed right into it. 'We have seen communities go missing, wiped off our slopes. The young have been taken from our Highlands, under our noses for twenty years.' He wavered, reviewing their gazes. 'We are hunters and we know the tracks of every creature that crosses our land. The footprints we found at our destroyed village were not human nor animal. They were not of this world.'

A racket erupted in the chamber.

'Heresy!' someone shouted.

'He is delirious!'

'Monsters exist!'

'So does the tooth fairy!'

There was more jeering.

Berenger banged the hammer again. 'Order! Let him speak.'

Maltip continued, giving specific details of times, places, missing scouts and destroyed mountain settlements that went back, according to him, for decades. 'We've seen our tribes wiped off the map. Now we live in fear. We know who has done this. He lives on the east slope, protected by wolves.'

'Nonsense, this can't be one man,' someone dismissed. Not loud enough to bring the bang of the hammer. However, many listening shared that view and were nodding.

Lady Adara came to the stage. Many had seen her, but not many had spoken to her. Elaya felt her druid aura shine as bright sunlight. 'My name is Adara. I represent the Druid Guild. This may be connected. It may not...' She gazed at Elaya, who didn't blink, then returned to the congregation. 'For over a decade, our kind has gone missing. No trace. No evidence. Just gone. Killing a druid would be hard for many. The mass hysteria against the druids has ended, so we do not suspect the lynch mobs of the past. A druid could kill a druid, but if that is the case, then why? Have any of you seen druids go missing from your communities?'

When no one answered, Berenger spoke, 'Thank you, Lady Adara. You may be seated.'

Lady Adara raised an eyebrow and left the stage.

Donjul, the desert leader, who had, up to now, been listening through Alwad, stood and started speaking. Alwad stood with him, seeming somewhat hesitant translating his words to the assembly out of turn. 'We have seen a blue light that brings shapes on the sands that leave no trace. Scores of footprints simply go into the desert and then vanish. And with it go our young. No one listened when we told others, nor came to aid us. They come at night. Always attacking isolated groups and leaving no survivors. Only now it hurts you, do you listen.' Donjul and Alwad sat back down.

Berenger made a face as if he was wrestling with chastising Donjul for speaking outside of his allowed slot, but instead, he moved on, introducing Praleck of Stoer, who stepped onto the stage wearing a perfectly-shaped frown. 'My friends, we all share the same story. Let's not waste any more time with formalities. We are gathered here because we have heard that a survivor has emerged from the devastation we have only witnessed in ruins. We need her testimony, and I suggest we give her the podium immediately. Is there any objection?'

Berenger, puzzled, asked Praleck, 'Are you surrendering your right to speak?'

Praleck, looking pleased, responded, 'Stoer's story is not important in comparison.'

Elaya wondered if this was a political strategy, where the most influential party relinquishes its turn, and if so what Praleck hoped to gain by it.

A silence fell over the room as Hazel took the stage to address the crowd. Elaya sensed the audience's anticipation and looked up towards the dome, feeling a presence above her. She briefly glanced at the queen, who seemed unaware, then surveyed the delegates before returning her gaze to the roof. She continued her search until she finally stopped, fighting back a smile that threatened to spread across her face. It was Laglen, listening from an air duct.

Hazel came quietly to the front, seeming to take an age. A quality about her brought the room to silence. 'I witnessed one of these attacks.' She blinked away tears. 'I come to you today as the sole survivor of a tribal massacre two months ago in The Orran Forest I have come here to testify to what I saw.' She shuddered for a second, then swallowed. 'It happened very fast. I was on watch that night. At first, I saw a shape in the dark.' There was a murmur through the assembly hall, and she shot it down. 'Not an animal. It was too big for that, and too fast, with yellow eyes. I found my father, the chieftain,' she stammered, averted her gaze, then continued. 'He was with other watchmen, and I reached them just before the attack. When it happened, it was violent, deadly and organised. My kindred were pulled into the night, and I saw them: big heads, talons, and fangs. A tocsin rang out, so I knew it was widespread.'

'Tocsin?' Praleck asked.

Berenger waved for her to answer, casting his gaze across the room. 'Please raise your hand if you wish to speak.'

'A horn. The lookouts carry one, as do many others in the tribe. I rushed to the Mothers' hut where our babies and children sleep.' She shuddered before continuing. 'It was hard to see what was happening in the darkness. They moved so quickly. People were screaming. Fire erupted in the trees. So many of those cries were cut off. The dead were dragged away. People were chopped into two by monsters. I saw one up close, a towering monster in red armour; it took our young.'

'Armour?' Sevada quizzed. 'What kind of armour?'

There was a buzz of voices, several outraged.

'Is she blaming a knight?!' Jakub cried.

Berenger was frowning at her. 'Please explain, especially if there were any pennant colours.'

'There were no insignia. It wore a helmet that outlined its ugly features. It was not of normal size. Its movements were sudden, with so much strength and determination.'

Seskin shouted out contemptuously. 'You were in shock

and seeing things, attacked by no more than a gang with hounds. No-one has armour that colour. It was probably the Highlanders in disguise.'

There was a brief outcry of disapproving voices directed at Seskin.

Hazel's sudden rise in tone brought a hush. 'No! It was not the Highlanders. They were demons, I tell you. I saw them up close. Twisted faces, many arms, ugly mouths with teeth as sharp as arrowheads.'

Nark stood up. 'Demons you say?' He looked around at his fellow representatives. 'Then this is a demonic invasion, and the church must take control of all the armies.'

'Would you see us bathe our arrows in Holy Water, Envoy Nark?' Praleck remained intentionally still, his expression and voice unreadable.

'Do you mock Lale? Hmmm, Envoy Praleck?'

'Not at all, but faith can sometimes take a narrow view of things.'

Nark's face reddened with anger. 'This is heresy! Stoer has pledged support to Lale for multiple home-based basilicas and the building of this road. Would they support you challenging Lale now?'

'This proposed road, yes. But we are here to deem whether…'

'Gentleman, this is not the time to discuss border relations,' Berenger intervened.

'Exactly my point,' Praleck continued, his voice level. 'Stoer passed up the stage to let this girl speak. Yet she is being belittled. She must be allowed the space to tell us what she saw.'

A hand went up and Berenger hurriedly accepted the next question.

'Hazel, did you try and fight these creatures?'

Hazel collected herself, glancing between Nark and Praleck, then considered the new speaker. 'I watched others do this, and they fell. Those that fought died first.'

'How can you say this for sure? You said it was dark.'

'There was some moonlight.'

'It was wild dogs,' Seskin muttered.

'Agreed,' Sward said. 'You say you were on guard duty? A girl? Well of course you would fall victim to fears of the night and imagination. Women have not the resilience for such duties. Your chief should be ashamed, but this nonsense of armoured demons should also end right now.'

Elaya growled, ready to confront Sward once again, but Lady Adara intervened. 'I assume, Lord Sward, you believe that a woman's place is in the kitchen. Well, you're right. Let me grab a knife.'

'Order!' Berenger snapped, glaring across the assembly.

Hazel cut across the laughter. 'Listen to me! One of those things took our young! When the thing in armour came for the babies, it...' she faltered, 'it smashed through the Mothers' hut, then jumped from the tree. A leap like that is not possible for a human.'

An arm went up. 'How did you survive then?' Jakub asked. 'I share doubt as the honourable Nark does.'

'I hid in the store pits with the wheat and fruit.'

'Thank you, Hazel. You may sit down.' Berenger said.

'No! There is more.' She gripped the lectern ledge. 'A man was there. Directing the monsters. He was wearing purple robes. They vanished in a blue light.'

Maltip stood up, his expression serious. 'This is the man I spoke of. The one who resides on the protected east slope, guarded by wolves.'

'Then I wasn't imagining things!' Hazel smiled gratefully, appreciating the unlikely support from the Highlander.

Donjul's resonant voice boomed, and a moment later, Alwad hurriedly translated, 'We have also encountered this figure. At night, his blue light is visible along the sandy straits.'

'I believe her,' Praleck said. He was perched at the edge of his chair, deliberating on the proceedings with still precision.'

There was a murmur of agreement from some.

'So do I,' young Sevada from Hoppenell said. 'Tell us more about this armour, Hazel.'

Berenger motioned for silence. 'There will be ample time for questions later. We thank Hazel for her testimony. We have now heard what we came here for, so we will take a recess to consider. It will then be incumbent upon us to assess and clarify what this child has reported and to arrive at a considered response. Therefore, for our next meeting, it will be only the senior delegates.'

As Hazel left the stage, she whispered to Elaya: 'Do they mean to exclude me from here onwards, the only witness to this?'

Elaya sighed. 'Such are the ways of politics, I am afraid. You will not be readmitted and so should stay in your room.'

Hazel was breathing heavily, but Elaya wasn't someone you argued with. 'Foresters don't hide in rooms. Might I at least go into the castle gardens and this manicured coppice you are so proud of?'

Elaya shook her head. 'As I promised, you may roam like a cat inside where the castle is guarded. You wanted to see the dead trees? So go to the library.'

∼

As the delegates began leaving their seats, Cargya approached Berenger, who was still on the stage, talking with Stasnier.

'Gentleman, may I have a quiet word?'

Stasnier considered her for a moment. 'Might I enquire…'

'A Privy matter, and Ellis should join us.'

A few moments later they all stood in a private chamber. 'I have called this impromptu meeting to discuss some interesting findings I observed during the summit,' she said.

Stasnier waved at her. 'Go on.'

'We have an emerging division around Hazel's testimony that doesn't follow the regional alliances we have seen in recent years.'

Ellis nodded. 'You mean Stoer challenging Lale?'

'I took notes of who supported Hazel and who didn't, and it makes for an unexpected outcome.' She continued. 'Of the nine representatives that questioned her, only Grisham of Trefgwyn has not shown his hand.'

Berenger shrugged. 'Well, he is a balanced leader and the highest-ranking noble here, save for the queen.'

'Of the eight that quarrelled, we are evenly split. Delegates that supported her story have claimed witness sightings, namely the Highlanders and the Nomads. Stoer and Hoppenell openly support Hazel. Seskin, who has publicly lobbied against Casper and Lale for their proposed road to Stoer, have joined forces with them to denounce Hazel. Sward – who arrived with Grisham and has proven to be an obnoxious sexist irritant – supports the "no" camp. We are seeing a new alliance mount before our eyes.'

'Hmmm,' Stasnier said, pursing his lips. 'And where do we stand?'

∽

Elaya led the delegates into the royal courtyard, where light refreshments were lined along a narrow counter. Late morning sunshine shone over the broad top ramparts, glancing off ashlar masonry, leaving dazzling, shifting patches of light and shadow.

The delegates huddled in small clusters, whispering in animated conversations about what they had heard. When the Foresters arrived, Elaya moved them to the far side of the courtyard, away from the Highlanders. Though this time, the glares had softened to a quiet look of understanding.

Twenty minutes passed, when Berenger appeared and came straight to Elaya. 'Lots to consider. I think we will finish the morning session deciding questions for Hazel before calling her back for answers. Then, this afternoon, hear any remaining stories and try to work out what to do about all this.'

Elaya shrugged.

'What do you think?'

Elaya blinked in surprise at his question, taken aback by his interest in her opinion on the summit so far. Everything she had heard led to Crane. But she had neither met nor could describe him and knew little of the Realm, as it had remained Laglen's secret. And Laglen had always maintained one could not bring anything through from the Realm. One had to sleep to enter it. Their minds crossed, nothing more. So, how could it be him? One man on a mountainside.

Elaya shrugged again. 'I think we all need more guards.'

Berenger nodded pensively. 'Are you troubled by the story of missing druids?' he asked her.

'I am always troubled by any likely murder,' she said.

From the battlements, ravens kraa-ed, but with an unusual alarm for the stoic and cynical birds. Elaya managed to sense a fleeting aura in one of them, but then the raven was on the wing, and she lost the connection. All that was left was her sense of sheer naked terror. She caught sight of a figure in red. It had to be a mistake, though. She cast her scan across the battlements, searching. How could an armoured figure be on the roofs? They had been thoroughly checked and were accessible only via staircases that Elaya had confirmed were all heavily guarded.

Lady Adara appeared, expression grave. 'Something is amiss.'

A dreadful, sickening feeling curdled Elaya's stomach. She watched it pass along the battlement; flashes of red light glinted off its armour.

Elaya began motioning to her guards to exit everyone.

Sensing something too, Derrilyn came over, looking up. 'What's that up there?'

Elaya shaded her gaze, squinting; she had never felt so shaken before.

High up in the parapet, behind the crenellations, the shape passed behind the embrasure. 'To the right. There!' Derrilyn hissed. 'What is it?'

'I have never sensed anything like it. I sense part druid, part...' she faltered, looking for the right word.

'Death?' Derrilyn finished.

'We need to get up there,' Elaya declared, motioning to Adara. 'Get Jaden and meet us inside the castle. Derrilyn and I will go up and investigate.'

Suddenly, shouts erupted from the parapet. The midday patrol had arrived on the rampart. Elaya caught sight of a few silhouettes of her guards, a desperate yelp, and the brief sound of swords clashing.

One by one, the guards plummeted from the battlement, their cries of terror hushed as their bodies met the cold stone floor with dull thuds.

Eleven

Girvyn wondered where Tarith was. It had been three hours since he had got to the library, and his protector had still not arrived. The act of reading served as a welcome distraction from his mounting anxiety, though worries would still creep into his thoughts. Thankfully, his earlier headache had subsided during his journey through the mist, and by the time he'd reached the library, his mind was clear. He tried to approach the situation with a calm, logical perspective, much like his uncle would have done.

Yes, Tarith had been concerned, and the pounding heart in Girvyn's chest had felt like it would explode by the time he reached the library, but what had they actually seen? A light in the fog, a passing shape. It could have been wind in the trees. That glow no more than some refracted flare in the tendrils of mist. He had seen it sometimes. Especially at sunset, when the reddening light seemed hotter on his face. Yes, the light and mist must simply have distorted what they saw.

Glancing around the library, the raised voices of a few scholars brought his thoughts to the present. He watched

Zinnia, a young librarian, standing by the reference section, her blond hair swishing as her head turned towards the shelves.

Girvyn, cheeks flushing, focused on his book, re-reading the same line as if the letters had reformed into new words, which now made no sense. It had been weeks since she had started in the library, and they had not had a conversation beyond discussing referencing codes for shelved items. The fact that she was the daughter of the head librarian, beautiful to watch, and decidedly autocratic made her more intimidating.

'Hello, Girvyn.'

Girvyn placed his finger at the end of the sentence as if deep in study. 'Hello, Zinnia.'

'What are you reading?'

'It's called, Cultivating Flowers for Every Season.'

'Who authorised another copy of that? We already have two copies signed out.'

'Danko did.'

'Why is father over-ordering? Where are we supposed to store them all?'

Girvyn shrugged. His mouth felt dry all of a sudden. 'Did you know that the name Zinnia is a flower, part of the daisy family?'

She nodded. 'I was born in a daisy meadow.'

Desperate to impress her, he soldiered on. 'It is a common flower.'

'Excuse me?'

'Do you like bread?'

She frowned at him. 'Why? Are you going to tell me a bread yarn?'

'Um, no. There are lots of different kinds, you know.'

'Yeah, I know.'

'Which do you like?'

'What?' She glanced away, her hair swishing in a dismissive flick.

'Bread, you said you liked bread.'

'I'll leave you to your reading, Girvyn.'

Girvyn's finger remained unmoving on the page, still unable to make sense of the words, even after Zinnia moved away.

'That was painful to watch.'

The newcomer's voice was light, with a hint of an unplaceable accent.

'It was more painful to be in it.'

'I can imagine. At least I'm not the only one having a dispiriting morning of complete failure.'

Girvyn's mouth flapped open. 'She was interested about the flowers.'

'I'm not sure. I think you might have lost her at "Hello Zinnia".' She winced. 'I'm sorry, that wasn't nice of me to say. It's all these macabre things made from tortured wood everywhere, these books. I'm Hazel. And I already know I'm named after a tree, just in case you were planning to tell me.'

Girvyn finally released his finger. 'Hi, I'm Girvyn. I haven't seen you in the library before?'

'This is my first time.' She glanced around. 'It's big, so high.'

'Here,' Girvyn swivelled the book around so she could see it. 'Let me show you; this is called a book.'

'Don't start insulting me next. I know what a book is.'

Girvyn closed it, looking sheepishly away, wondering what to say next.

'And this impresses you?' She measured him, so strong it made him recoil. 'All these books impress you, yes?'

Girvyn gave a small nod. 'I like reading. And you?'

'No, I prefer oral storytelling, not written words.' Her expression didn't change, but there was disgust in her voice. 'Science is great, but must you cut down trees to record everything? How many of these books add to knowledge? There is memory of hundreds of years preserved and told in story and song in my community.'

'Story by song can change, but write it down, and it stays fixed.'

'You call this a library. I call it a graveyard.'

Girvyn remained quiet for a moment. 'I have never thought of it in that way. It's a fascinating perspective.'

'There is an infinite knowledge in nature we will never understand, yet you city folk think knowledge is written on the remains of dead trees.'

Girvyn pushed the book away as if he had found an insect in his dinner. 'I certainly will think about how we can record knowledge on non-paper surfaces. I like nuts. Do you like nuts?'

'You are like the Piliki wind.' She smiled, which dispelled any tension he felt. 'Yes, I like nuts.'

'Are you a Forester?' Girvyn asked her.

'Have you met my kind before? Is it my accent? My garb?'

'No, there is a badge on your dress, which says 'Forester' on it.'

She peered down at it. 'Oh.' She pursed her lips, frowning at him; her big green eyes quickened his pulse. 'You have a Forester quality about you.'

'Do I?'

'Yes, a skinniness like the boys in my tribe.'

Girvyn felt disappointed. There we go again. Boy. Too old to be a child and too young to be taken seriously. At least by her in the way he wanted. 'At the market, they call me the weed in twill.'

Hazel stared at him, expression blank.

He caught his breath; this must be the Forester girl who survived the raid. He exhaled slowly. 'Is that why you came over to speak to me?' he asked her. 'Because I look like a Forester?'

'Sorry, I should not have bothered you.'

'No, don't go,' Girvyn insisted, then adjusted his desperate sounding voice. 'Please stay.'

She smiled. 'Longhorn people worship dead trees. So I came here because I wanted to see the graveyard, to understand it.'

'Who are Longhorn people?'

'Those who live in stone. Named after the Longhorn Beetle, a pest of trees.'

Girvyn laughed. 'I have gone from a boy to a beetle.'

Hazel smiled, her eyes glistening as she considered him. 'You are a funny one.'

Girvyn shrugged. 'I don't try to be.'

'We have a name for that in our tongue.'

'A name for what?'

'Polothi means a charming wind.'

'Is that better than a Piliki wind, like you called me earlier?'

'That just means a peaceful wind.'

Girvyn frowned, trying to make sense of it. *So, I am peaceful and charming.* 'Polothi, Piliki, you need to sort your language out. You know wind is wind. It's warm, cold, soft or hard. That's it.'

'There are thirty-three types of wind, Girvyn. I can teach you them if you like.'

'I have a name for that in my tongue. It's called Ridiki.'

Hazel laughed.

Girvyn lowered his gaze. 'I am sorry about what happened to your tribe.'

'You know?'

'Everyone knows.'

Her lips tightened. 'I cannot tell you what was said.'

'I'm not asking.'

She considered him, then shrugged. 'I needed to have a different conversation. Thank you for the chat.'

She went to leave, but Girvyn quickly asked another question to stop her. 'What do you think of Rathnell?'

'I have never seen such high walls before, never mind a stone city. To meet for the first time the Highlanders who persecuted our people has been fearful on top of everything else.'

Girvyn frowned. 'But I thought the Foresters attacked the Highlanders?'

'No,' she said, voice fierce. 'They left the forest for the mountain, destroying all tribes they met on their way. They attacked us!'

'That's not what I have read. There is information in the library; this is the platform for human progress. You can learn the truth about anything from the information here.'

Hazel seemed sceptical. 'What, so the dead tree knows what really happened between the Foresters and the Highlanders eighty years ago?'

'Yes, look,' said Girvyn, flicking through the index cards on his desk. He took her to a shelf and pulled out a book. 'Erimell's Concise History. He's well-researched and balanced, so you can trust this.' He proceeded to read to her about the Highlanders splitting and the Foresters seeking vengeance on them for it.'

'No! They attacked us; the Elders would never lie!' Hazel exclaimed, her voice filled with disbelief.

Girvyn made a grimace. 'I'm sorry to tell you, but in times of conflict memories often become distorted and disputed.'

Hazel interrupted him, raising her hand to silence him, not because of his words but because she sensed something else. She brought her attention to the library door, concern etched on her face.

Girvyn followed her gaze and realised that he, too, could hear warning cries. Everyone in the library was looking up, their faces filled with alarm.

An anxious guard rushed past the doorway, and it took a moment for Girvyn to comprehend what was happening. The realisation sank in. From deep within the castle, screams echoed through the air.

Twelve

Elaya shouted at the guards. 'Get the delegates inside the Royal Audience chamber, and keep that door locked! Derrilyn, you're with me.'

She sped across the courtyard and up the steps towards the rampart ledge where the armoured figure had stood moments before.

'What about the queen?' Derrilyn asked her, breath shallow; Elaya felt his druid senses heighten as his adrenalin flowed. Searching ahead, the battlement was clear.

Elaya was standing on the top of the parapet; she glanced down at the courtyard to where the men had fallen and seemed preoccupied for a moment. 'The queen is safe; that thing is heading to the castle's west side.'

'What's that way?' Derrilyn asked her, pointing at the stairwell the creature had gone through.

'That's the question: the library, some private quarters, offices.' She drew the two blades from the double back scabbard, motioning Derrilyn to draw his sword and follow. 'Come on, keep up.'

They ran down the corridor, scanning each room they

passed, finding nothing. They came out into a hall where soft drapes and furnishings lined the walls. In the next room, again, nothing. Then they found two dead guards, single wounds through their hearts.

Up ahead they heard raised voices and a brief clash of swords. Chasing after the sound, they saw more dead guards and a frightened chambermaid pointing down the corridor. 'It went that way, me Lady.'

Elaya grabbed her arm. 'What did it look like?'

'It was a giant,' she said, voice trembling. 'I tell you. It cut through the guards like a knife through butter.'

It was straight out of Hazel's witness account, something from a dream Girvyn had seen. Laglen was adamant that this was not possible, but here and now, from this chambermaid, came a third account telling something different.

'Shut the door and don't come out.'

Elaya swept down the corridor, her senses collecting pockets of presences: anxiety, fear, and something more powerful: dread.

'It's up ahead. This is it,' she said, adjusting her grip.

'I sense it,' Derrilyn said, frowning.

'It is a druid!' Elaya gasped. 'But the power it has is frightening.' She paused, probing. 'I sense no free will...it follows a command.'

As they entered the gallery, they beheld a shocking sight at the far end of the chamber. The monstrous figure was engaged in a fierce battle with three guards who were valiantly defending a doorway. Elaya found herself staring in sheer disbelief at the creature before her. It was massive, a grotesque giant whose helmet conformed to the contours of its twisted face. But it moved with a lightness, despite the heavy armour in which Elaya could see no weak point yet.

Elaya shouted at a runner boy who was hiding under a

table. 'Get up! Run to the barracks and get more men! Get everyone!' She yelled at the men. 'Stay in defence.'

One guard tried to deflect its thrust and come inside, but his sword was ripped from his grip, and the creature's blade went through his neck. The other two men, blocking the onslaught with gritted teeth, backed into the adjoining room.

Elaya leapt in, coming at it from behind. It met her attack. The strength of its arm sent a shockwave through her elbow and shoulder.

Derrilyn swung at it from the left. His sword smashed into its armour. What would have knocked any ordinary man off their feet had no effect. The creature picked up a second sword and attacked Elaya and Derrilyn simultaneously. It was as if its blades had a mind of their own. Elaya and Derrilyn, feeling the strength in their arms ebbing, leapt back. But instead of taking advantage, the tall, armoured figure moved towards the next room.

'Where's it going?' Derrilyn shouted.

'It's just the library and a few offices,' she replied, running after it. The cold hand of fear gripped her: the library! Tarith had reported going there. Surely it would be empty now, though. Tarith would have swept Girvyn away at the first sign of trouble, and she had seen library staff running in all directions. In a sudden revelation, it dawned on her. Hazel, the sole survivor of one of its massacres. Hazel, who she had foolishly allowed to go off alone exploring the castle. This red giant was here to exact retribution for her testimony.

'Come on. Face me, Realm demon!'

It stopped and turned, finally giving Elaya its full attention. In a flash it hurled its sword at her. Twisting desperately, she felt the tip pass across her chest, cutting the buttons of her tunic. Derrilyn leapt to her side, and they fought it shoulder to shoulder, blades a blur.

Elaya felt Derrilyn's druid's senses keeping him alive and in the fight. Even with her fully-formed mastery of that same, time-stretching ability, she struggled to keep up with its speed and strength. Its blade went from hers to Derrilyn's, taking on both, showing no gaps, giving her no space to come inside or around, anticipating everything, regardless of how hard she tried to draw it one way then another. Her arm began to weaken. Joints jarring with every bone-quaking clash.

Then more soldiers were there. Dozens piled into the room, joining the fight. Swords slashing, axes swinging, arms jolting, metal ringing. Crossbow bolts glanced off the giant's armour, skating off the stone walls.

With thirty or so guards in the room, now the world was a frenzy of swinging swords, arcing axes and clenched faces, all mixed into an ear-crushing racket. At such close range the assault should have propelled the figure back or taken it down, but the strength of its footing held it firm, and the strikes just bounced off it.

'Draw back to the walls. Hold the room!' Elaya told her men. 'We have it trapped.'

All around, the soldiers pulled back to the hall's perimeter, shields raised. The thing drove into them, smashing the men into the stonework. A screeching clamour of steel on steel, cries of pain and fear from those crushed by its great weight and strength.

Raging like a cornered bull, it thrashed around, wild but still cunning, picking off its foes at every opening. Knowing, as she watched her men drop one by one, that she had to be the one to face it, Elaya stepped into the middle of the room again and ushered it towards her.

'Come on,' she said. Sweat poured down her cheeks.

But the thing just kept trying to break out of the room. So intent was it on continuing.

'Use the ropes!' Elaya told her men. They threw loops over the creature, and more soldiers joined in, pulling from each corner of the room as the creature struggled against the bonds now holding it still. It let out a great roar of rage.

In the overlap between the gorget and the helmet was a strip of metal held together by evenly spaced rivets. 'The neck!' Elaya told Derrilyn. 'There's a weak spot. If we can get to its skin, we might have a chance.'

Elaya and Derrilyn attacked the creature from opposite sides, causing it to become even more frenzied. A rivet flew into the air, but its skin remained covered by the plate. Then, the creature yanked at the rope around its wrist, pulling the soldiers towards it until the group fell to the ground with a sudden jolt. It was free again.

Brave men charged at it, but it seemed to know from which directions the attacks would come and brushed them aside, broad sweeps of its arm sending soldiers far across the room, where they fell motionless.

'Strengthen the door barricade!' Elaya cried in warning.

Four men jammed into the exit, planting a rear leg back to re-enforce the entrance, shields up.

Elaya kept slashing at its neck. Derrilyn, targeted the other side, left then right, right then left, alternating and randomising the swings.

It smashed through the wall of guards blocking the door, and swept on. It met more soldiers but they couldn't stop it. A trail of blood led from one room to the next. The sounds of running, clanking armour and shouting resonated beyond it, and when it reached the next room, the guards were there, waiting. Two of them leapt at it, hanging onto its sword-arm, using their body weight to prevent it from using its blade. Two more guards pushed it from behind, while another, valiant man crouched before its feet so it toppled over him and crashed onto its front. The men piled on top of it, trying to hold it down with their collective weight. One brave soldier yanked at its helmet, but the creature threw a backward head butt, leaving the man's chin hanging off his face. The thing rose to one knee, thrashed, then began throwing the battle-ready soldiers like they were no more than rag dolls.

Elaya brought an axe down onto its head, which hardly even jarred it. She ignored the numbness in her arm, and struck again, this time at that neckline. Another rivet flew free from the join. Back on its feet, it let out a deep, primitive growl and leapt towards the corridor, smashing through two brave-faced guards. Elaya and Derrilyn raced after it.

Up ahead, Elaya sensed a presence. Hazel! So, this was it. It was after her. If Hazel dies, the answers to the delegates' questions die with her, and there is less chance of everyone working together to defeat this threat.

The creature hurried on as if sensing its prey ahead. As they came to the corridor end, a large lobby preceded the great library doors. She saw some chairs, lavish tapestries, and a registration desk. All empty.

Elaya felt another aura inside the library. No, it can't be! A familiar mix of innocence and profound fear. Girvyn! Why had Tarith not taken Girvyn to safety? The last thing she needed was for him to get caught up in this.

'Girvyn, hide!' she shouted down the corridor.

The creature came to the entrance, almost as high as the twelve-foot door.

'That's the thing that attacked my tribe!' Hazel warned from inside, staring in disbelief.

Elaya and Derrilyn came in behind it and found Hazel and Girvyn beneath a writing desk. A few monks and other library staff, white as sheets, trembled in the shadows of the great bookcases.

The thing took a step towards them.

'Elaya,' Girvyn whimpered, pointing. 'This is the monster from my dream.'

Elaya shouted at him. 'Girvyn, stay down.' A thought struck her. 'Hazel, move away from the desk.'

'I don't have a weapon,' she said, lips trembling. 'I know what it can do; we should stick together.'

'I have seen what it can do; I need to know who its after. Move away from Girvyn,' she hesitated, watching: the thing moved closer towards Girvyn, helmet tilted fractionally downwards, pointing at where he was hiding.

Girvyn was quivering. 'Please don't leave me alone,' he pleaded to Hazel, who was edging away from him. 'Elaya...'

'Do what I say, Hazel!' Elaya ordered. 'Keep moving away from Girvyn. I'm sorry, Girvyn. We need to know.'

Hazel reached the left side wall, and the giant didn't even look at her.

Elaya jumped onto the thing's back. She felt the hardened armour slick against its skin, shaping an outline of muscles and distended edges along its back and shoulder. It swung around and threw her off, and she slammed into a wall, winded.

From within the helmet's narrow slit, two pitiless black eyes scoured the area and locked onto its target once more. Then, the giant extended its arm to the desk, flinging it aside, and with a swift motion, it reached down and grabbed Girvyn.

Thirteen

Girvyn watched Derrilyn's sword strike the creature's neck, producing a resounding ring. In response, the creature thrust out its hand and seized Derrilyn's tunic, hoisting him off his feet. Meanwhile, the creature's other hand continued to grip Girvyn's arm, causing him to sob in agony. It threw Derrilyn across the room, while Hazel forcefully struck the corner of a book against the creature's gloved hand that held Girvyn's wrist. She continued striking it, trying to get its attention.

'Run, Hazel!' Elaya yelled.

But Hazel kept hitting its hand.

It let go of Girvyn and pushed Hazel and she careened into a desk, which gave Elaya just enough time to pull Girvyn away.

It loomed over Elaya.

'Stay behind me, Girvyn!' She twirled a pair of short swords in a defensive pattern. 'What kind of warped druid are you?' she hissed.

All the hairs on Girvyn's body stood on end. His world reduced to a drum beat in his chest.

Boom. Boom.

Somewhere in his mind flashed a memory of this thing. Pushing a Forester to its fate.

Was there once a human face beneath the helmet? Changed into something horrible, like what had happened to the Forester.

Boom. Boom.

Shifting, sniffing suckers and reaching tentacles. A transformation. Wriggling worms on the outside of its skin.

Girvyn looked around and saw shouting faces. Saw saliva cast from wide, moving jaws. But no sounds reached him. Elaya pulled down a bookcase, crashing it on top of the giant, momentarily burying it under books and shelving. But then it started to rise again, pushing everything off.

Hazel yelled at Girvyn to run, but his legs were planted in the ground. He studied Hazel for a quiet abstracted moment but none of the shouts that left her mouth made sense. All he could hear was that pounding boom boom in his ears. He screamed at himself to run, every part of him beseeching his body to tune in and flee. But it wouldn't.

'Girvyn, look at me.' The voice cut through the chaos, and this time Girvyn recognised it.

Elaya, he could hear Elaya. 'Girvyn, feel your feet,' she urged, her words like an anchor. 'Take a deep breath and take back control.'

He looked at her, still stunned and speechless, but her commands began to steady him amidst the turmoil. He took a deep breath, feeling the sensation of his feet on the ground, and gradually regained control of himself.

'When I say run, run!' She gripped his arm. Those gentle, concerned eyes held his. 'Okay?'

Girvyn nodded mutely.

Everything sped up, or did it just jump back to normal

speed? He couldn't tell, but the silence around him blasted into chaos.

Elaya grabbed an oil lamp from a desk and threw it as the creature got to its feet. 'Run!'

The flames didn't do anything to hurt it, but the thing hesitated, fumbling at the visor, irritated by the flames that clung to its helmet.

His entire body wound tight, Girvyn sprinted at full pelt. But there wasn't enough time for him to reach the open door. The giant leapt with the agility of a flea, a smouldering vastness that knocked him to the ground. It picked him up by his clothes, threw him over its shoulder, and marched towards the door.

Hazel smashed a chair into its legs, and its knees buckled. With one arm holding a terrified Girvyn, it lunged its sword. There was a clash of steel. Elaya's blade jarred. Derrilyn followed up with another chair which brought it to one knee. 'It's not weakening! Get the boy!' he said.

Hazel tried to grab Girvyn off its shoulder but couldn't. 'Kick, fight!' she told him.

Girvyn tried to shout out, but as he was hurled about, the words that came out of his mouth were, 'Imm nngth.'

Derrilyn stabbed his blade into the creature's neck. Another rivet flew away, revealing a tiny gap in the plate. Glistening, bulging larvae moved on the surface of its skin.

Elaya stabbed her knife into the narrow target, and for the first time the blade broke through to cut into flesh. The creature roared and lashed out. It reared up and dropped Girvyn, whirling, emitting a sound that was a mix of pain and rage. All its smouldering fury was directed at Elaya like some ancient evil.

'Run!' Elaya shouted at Girvyn, fanning her two swords in a shielding pattern. 'Come on! Fight me!'

For a few moments protector and monster fought, blades clanging and screeching. Then, as Hazel and Girvyn leapt into the corridor, it refocused on its target and its relentless, unwavering pursuit of Girvyn kicked in again. It slammed into the doorframe, careering after them, leaving a cloud of stone fragments in its wake. Elaya and Derrilyn charged up the corridor behind it, yelling instructions to Girvyn and Hazel.

'Left corridor! At the end, take a right!'

They sped through the passages and rooms, booting open the doors and sending up dust as the thing chased after them. It slowed as one of its feet became entangled in a tapestry torn from the wall, causing it to stumble and a momentary delay as it thrashed and struggled to free itself.

'Keep running!' Elaya shouted. 'We need to get it outside into the open and get distance between it and Girvyn. Next left!'

They skidded through a sharp turn and were into a sitting room with grand oak bookcases, lavish golden tables and heavy swag curtains. They sped through the furniture, darting this way and that. They heard the giant coming, charging in a straight line, smashing through everything, casting debris outwards in a tremendous clatter.

At the end of the room was an open window to a small courtyard one floor below.

'Jump out of the window!' Elaya yelled to Girvyn and Hazel. 'Land with bent knees!'

Girvyn slowed for a second, hesitating, but Hazel kept him going. Taking his hand, they leapt together. They landed. Hazel rolled to the left, but Girvyn cried out in pain as he hit the ground. A few seconds later, the side of the castle wall blew outwards and the giant smashed through the window, taking the top and bottom of the frame with it. As it fell,

Girvyn noticed it holding its ears, like it was in pain or distracted. It dropped heavily, misjudging the weight of its armour on the way to the ground, and crashed front-first, momentarily stunned.

Elaya and Derrilyn dropped behind it, rolling to disperse the impact and soften the fall. Elaya came straight back up, her sword clanging against armour. The creature rose slowly, injured, but still powered by some unrelenting determination.

Two new people joined the group: a stoic looking woman with flowing silver hair and a man who raised his sword tip. They didn't appear to be castle guards, yet Elaya gave them a brief nod of acknowledgement. To Girvyn, who was scrambling away on his backside with a stinging ankle, it felt like the end. However, these four individuals, displaying fearlessness or at least the courage to confront the creature until their deaths, attempted to encircle it. Elaya released a sigh of relieved tension. 'Lady Adara!'

'Hold the circle,' Lady Adara instructed. 'We will distract it. Jaden,' she said to her companion, 'you attack its left side.'

Jaden caught his breath. 'I sense a druid,' he said grimly.

Girvyn noticed their lips moving, quietly chanting some words which he could hear strange power in. The creature seemed to stagger in response, again trying to cover its ears. Four druids against one, they circled it, anticipating its movement. Powerful as it was, its strikes now swung in the air.

Girvyn realised the incantation must be some druid unity invocation. Somehow, they had become one, foreseeing the giant's actions, responding with a singularity of purpose.

Elaya nodded at them. 'On my count, we attack its neckline.'

'Three, two, one!' The four of them swung together, hacking at the plate. A timed succession of attacks.

Whack whack whack whack.

The helmet moved. Whack whack whack whack. It lifted.

The creature lumbered in the direction of Lady Adara, drowsy like it was drunk. Despite its lumbering movement, one swing could chop any of its attackers in two.

Then they did it. The final rivet sprang free, and the helmet came off, revealing its hideous face: an extended jaw jutted outwards, two wide, high cheek bones, a mouth twisted like a tear in a bedsheet, all encrusted with glistening, moving worms.

'Here! Here!' Lady Adara urged, distracting it.

Jaden swept its feet from under it, and it crashed onto its back.

Elaya followed up. Two firm swipes, like an axe splitting a log, was all it took to take its head from its neck. The head rolled away from its armoured body. A black gloop poured out of the opening, and those shiny worms, wiggling at the severed ends of its neck became still.

Fourteen

Laglen crawled back along the air duct until he reached the passage with its door back into the castle corridor. His mind was whirling with thoughts and impressions.

Over the years repeated rumours of attacks had been brushed aside as minor conflicts and clashes between various races and factions, but Hazel's account as a survivor suggested that monsters were indeed involved in these incidents. Girvyn had noticed something in Crane's dream that appeared to align with the conclusion of Hazel's narrative. Yet the question remained: how could her version of events be plausible?

Crane's transformation into a twisted individual was deeply rooted in his tragic childhood. Orphaned at six and left to navigate the Realm without guidance, he faced abandonment and grief, which fuelled his anger and darkness. Despite Laglen's parents' attempts to help, offering him a place in their family, Crane's fierce independence led him to reject any form of charity or advice.

As he grew, Crane's dark tendencies emerged, subtly at

first, through casual mentions of enjoying torture within the Realm, before escalating to the creation of horrific dungeons of torture. Although he argued his actions caused no real harm, claiming his victims were merely figments of his imagination, this justification revealed his ethical ambiguity and deteriorating mindset.

The community, including Crane's childhood acquaintances and their parents, gradually distanced themselves from him, alarmed by his sadistic inclinations. Only Laglen remained hopeful of finding goodness in Crane, even as Crane's fascination with the colour purple –inspired by his gruesome pleasure in extracting the spleen from his victims – became a symbol of his detachment from humanity.

Had Crane somehow found a way to connect the two worlds? The implications of such power were staggering. This revelation, coupled with Hazel's testimony and Girvyn's dream, suggested Crane had managed it. Indeed, as teens, they had often fantasised about what it would be like: gods in both the Realm and the Waking. Crane, always more ambitious and driven, had apparently achieved the impossible. Meanwhile, Laglen had spent the last fifteen years running from his emotions and responsibilities. And the harsh truth was that, just as in the murder of Rosein that had started that malaise and made reconciliation impossible, Crane had outmatched him.

Something yanked his attention to the present: a sound. What was that? Shouting voices within the castle. Was there an argument in the kitchens, he wondered? The door opened near the staff corridors. He heard running and yelling, waited until it faded, and stepped out.

The first thing he saw in the corridor was blood-stained walls. A bloody smear slid along the corridor until it reached the door; a single crimson hand print on the wooden entryway to the larder. He followed it, his stomach sinking.

Hearing voices from within, he opened the door and saw two injured kitchen staff. Several other onlookers stood nearby, in states of shock. Wrin, the castle chef, was cleaning a gash on the arm of one of her waitresses.

'What happened?' Laglen asked.

'It attacked me,' the terrified woman said.

Wrin comforted her. 'Laglen, this is Seldra. Hear what she has to say. Tell us, Seldra. Tell us again.'

'I was in the corridor, carrying a tray of goblets back to the kitchens. It burst out of a side door at the castle's east side. It rushed into me.'

'What was it?' Laglen said.

'It was horrifying.

Laglen came closer, his nose almost touching hers. 'What was it, Selda?'

'A monster.'

'Describe it.'

Laglen listened. Not believing his ears. 'Selda, it's vital I understand what you saw. Are you certain it wasn't a man??'

'No man is that tall.'

'And where was it going?'

'Into the castle. But not towards the court rooms and the royal chambers. The other way. The library.'

Mind reeling and feet barely working under him, Laglen pushed open the larder door and ran down the corridor. 'No-no-no! Girvyn! I must find Girvyn!'

He couldn't believe that what this monster was doing could be related to his nephew, but he had to find him. Up until now, the attacks had been covert, targeting small communities and abducting infants. What possible purpose could an open attack within the castle serve?

His legs carried him as fast as he could go. He pushed on through the pain. Chest bursting, stitch tightening in his abdomen, breath shortening. He ignored the creeping nausea that seemed to rise from his stomach to his head and almost caused him to fall. He cursed; too much time in the Realm had made him unfit!

He hurried past more blood-smeared walls. Going deeper into the castle. He found two dead soldiers, their bodies twisted as if the spines had been ripped out.

More voices came from the next room. Five dead guards were strewn about the floor, plus one more, wounded and propped up against the wall, groaning. Two chambermaids were helping him.

'Which way?' Laglen said to him, his voice barely audible above a breathy hiss.

The man lifted a limp arm and pointed a finger into the castle. Laglen followed it, taking a corridor along the castle's west side. He came to more people. Frightened chambermaids and court officials standing over dead men. He continued past broken stonework and fallen paintings.

Monks came towards him, warning him to turn back.

Laglen stopped them. 'What happened?'

'A monster, Lag, loose in the castle.'

'Where is it?'

'The library!'

It was the exact fear he'd been trying to dismiss. He felt his skin go ice-cold. He wanted to fold in on himself and disappear, but he pushed on, unsure where the strength came to keep going. His legs were wobbly now. He couldn't even remember the last time he had run. But something deep within kept him going. Beyond what he thought was possible. Was it fear? The angst would not ease until he knew that Girvyn was safe.

He heard raised voices ahead again. A commotion. More blood. More dead soldiers everywhere. Furniture scattered and broken. He was nearly there now. Just one more passage, and he was at the library.

A scholar charged towards him. 'Your boy! Your boy! It went for your boy!'

'No!' The word screamed through his clouded mind. How could this be coming to pass? It was as though the sudden realisation that Girvyn's life was in jeopardy had condensed into a harrowing moment of truth. Laglen berated himself for not heeding Elaya's concerns.

'Why didn't I train Girvyn earlier when my instincts whispered to do so?' he hissed through clenched teeth. He had promised Rosein, but year eighteen was always so late to learn.

Why had he doubted Crane's ability to bring his creations from the Realm? His scepticism, apathy, and analytical nature had obscured the clue.

If Girvyn lay dead it would be all his fault. A regret and responsibility he would never recover from or forgive. He craved to see his nephew's face. To have one more chance to put this all right.

He skidded to a stop at the library entrance. There was no one there. Just broken tables, fallen bookcases, and smashed chairs. The destruction ran like a path. He followed it, his vision blurred with sweat and tears. He came to a far wall, where a curtain hung from one hook.

With his heart pounding, he approached the broken window and saw Elaya standing over the fallen giant in the courtyard below. He tried to call out, but his voice deserted him. Sensing his presence, she looked up.

Laglen blinked at her, unable to speak.

'Girvyn is safe,' she uttered, expression troubled.

Laglen stared at her wordlessly, then made his way downstairs. When he reached the courtyard, a few other guards were there, but remained at a distance, as if the corpse could issue some curse.

He looked at the red figure, but not for long because of his nausea. Scattered, still worms lay a few inches away from its severed neck, as if in the last moments of existence they had tried to crawl away.

'It came for Girvyn,' Elaya said, her voice flat. 'I lost many men trying to stop it.'

'I'm sorry, I should have listened to you,' was all he managed to say.

'Laglen, I had to summon the druid unanimity chant to fight it as one. It was the only way to kill it.'

Suddenly, Elaya was holding him in an embrace. He felt her sink into him – was this for him or her? He didn't question further; both clinging onto each other in desperate comfort.

'But I thought that only worked with three or more druids?' It felt an odd question, a displaced academic enquiry.

He stayed in her hold, waiting for his pulse to slow, for the sweat to drip from his stinging eyes.

'I fought beside my apprentice Derrilyn. Lady Adara and Jaden from the Guild.'

They parted, but continued to face each other. Laglen released a relieved breath. 'Where is Girvyn now?'

'I have hidden him in the south stables,' she said. 'It had his scent. It's the only place I could think of where his trace might be concealed. Derrilyn, Lady Adara, and Jaden are protecting him.' She grimaced. 'I found this on the creature, tucked into its glove.'

Laglen gasped. 'That's Girvyn's sock.'

'Your house had been ransacked, Lag. Tarith is dead. I

brought some of Girvyn's clothing; I thought we could put it in the north tower, in a locked turret as a decoy.'

Laglen shook his head. 'Night's skies,' was all he could say.

Elaya's expression darkened. 'The stables will hide him for now, but we need to get Girvyn out of the city. Whatever came for him, it was not of this world.'

'Crane has found a way to bridge the dimensions. It's the only explanation.'

Elaya's voice lowered. 'Lag, you must tell the summit your secret. They have a right to know the truth.'

Laglen made a face, feeling his anxiety grow. 'That's not my decision to make. It would put all the Dream Travellers in danger. And who would believe me anyway? I can't prove it to them.'

'Hazel's testimony and now this. That is the proof.' She looked away. 'It's a druid. Crane must be hunting them for his army.'

Laglen didn't respond. He felt the burden of the decision to reveal his secret weighing on him. But he lacked the authority to reveal their truth; he would put all Travellers in danger. He needed time to think rather than rush into making revelations that he might later regret. 'You know better than anyone what the druids went through, the oppression Cronmere faced after the world discovered the truth. Would you put yourself through persecution if you had a chance not to?'

Elaya remained resolute. 'If it helped the greater good, yes.'

Laglen sighed. 'They won't believe me.'

'It's too late for doubt. They need to know what Crane is and the truth about the Dream Travellers.'

'I am going to check on Girvyn first, and then I will speak

with the other Dream Travellers at sunset. We will discuss. It must be a collective decision.'

Somewhere deep down, though, Laglen knew she was right.

Fifteen

Laglen staggered to the stables. He couldn't have run if he wanted to. Now that his lungs were filling with deep breaths of air, it felt worse. All he wanted to do was stop and calm his pulse, but there was time for that later. He couldn't get that thing out of his mind. Its helmet hinted at what was beneath. A stretched head, cheeks that were more like steps. No nose. A wide and distended chin leading to a point.

He spotted Derrilyn conversing with Lady Adara near the stables. A man clad in black, presumably Jaden, stood nearby with a couple of other guards, gathered by the entrance appearing as if they were engaged in an informal discussion. Laglen couldn't help but think, 'Clever, Elaya. Of course, keep it innocuous, not guarded.'

Derrilyn sent him a concerned look. Laglen didn't know Elaya's apprentice that well. Enough, though, to know he had much potential. They let him inside, saying nothing as he passed them. The light grew dim, the air thick with hay and manure smells that almost made him dizzy again.

About fifteen pens faced each other. As he passed down

the middle, horses whinnied, while some extended their noses over their enclosure doors, their tails swishing.

At the far wall he saw a shape, sitting on hay bales, that stood up.

Girvyn ran and sank into Laglen's arms.

'Are you okay?'

'It was awful, Uncle. It came for me. That's all it wanted to do.'

'Tell me what happened?'

Laglen listened to the whole story, shaking his head in disbelief. 'So, it had you over its shoulder at one point?'

'Yes, but Elaya knocked it down. So did Hazel; she was amazing.'

'The Forester girl? What was she doing in the library?'

'She said the summit recessed. Uncle, she hates books. Who hates books?'

Laglen smiled. It was one of those moments when Girvyn shared fleeting thoughts that didn't require a response but were delightful to hear.

Girvyn gripped Laglen's wrist. 'Hazel said it was the same thing that attacked her village.'

Laglen averted his gaze, his cheek twitching. 'It could have killed you. It killed so many men. Maybe it was trying to capture you.'

'Why?'

'I don't know.'

'Maybe to turn me into one of those things?'

'What do you mean?'

'Uncle, the monster that attacked me; it was there that night, leading the Forester to his fate. The Forester was badly wounded. I saw him changed into that thing by some horrible tentacle monster, then he was covered in armour.' Girvyn recounted again what he had seen that night in gruesome detail. 'That thing was a person once!'

'Are you sure?'

'Uncle, I remember details. There were so many more of them. Spider creatures, ape-like monsters, all those glass cages, so many different faces peering at me! Thousands of them.'

'I am so sorry; when you first told me this I dismissed it as something Crane was doing in the Realm. Something fixed to that side. That is how it has always been. I am sorry I didn't pay more attention. I should have heeded Elaya's advice and taken you out of the city.'

'There's more. When I walked to the library this morning, we saw a blue light in the coppice. I have seen it before in the Realm. That's what the Foresters were brought through. Flames in the shape of a door frame. Tarith went to check it out.'

'Tarith is dead.'

Girvyn dropped his head, unable to speak.

'I am sorry, Girvyn.'

'Why me?' Tears dripped down his cheeks.

Laglen wiped them away and held his face. 'I don't know. But we will find out, and we will protect you. We need to get you out of the city. I will never let this happen again.'

'You were not to know, Uncle.'

They remained in quiet reserve, content to linger in ever-changing thoughts. They ate food supplied by the kitchens. It was generous and flavoursome. Laglen made a mental note to thank Wrin next time he saw her.

After the meal, Laglen became aware of the fading light. 'Girvyn, it's almost sunset, and I agreed to meet the others in the Realm to tell them what happened at the summit. I have to cross for about an hour.'

'Uncle, take me with you. Don't leave me here alone.'

Laglen regarded him. 'It does make sense to bring you, so you can tell them what happened.'

'Thank the sky for that. It stinks in here!'

∼

Laglen addressed his old friends, Mora and Kalamayn, now beside their adult children, Dremell and Nadine. 'I am sorry it's been so long, but we don't have time for pleasantries.'

'It's okay, Lag,' Mora said. 'Tell us what you know.'

Laglen took a breath and started from the beginning, from before the summit to the current attack, including what had happened in the conference. They all listened in astonishment, throwing troubled, surprised stares at each other during his retelling of Hazel's testimony. When he came to the bit about what he encountered after leaving the secret passage, he stopped and let Girvyn take over.

They all watched Girvyn as he shifted uncomfortably, but he ploughed on through the story of the attack. Laglen could see Girvyn was trying his best to keep his thoughts ordered, giving a calm, relevant description of a traumatic experience. Girvyn finished with the Realm dream from two months ago, and they listened to the story of Crane's monster-making hell. To Laglen, Girvyn seemed to have moved beyond the years of awkward or painful interactions: his communication was logical and ordered despite the stressful setting. It was impressive and convinced the other Travellers better than Laglen could have managed himself.

After a collective shudder passed through them, Mora spoke. 'How is this possible?'

'He has some doorway,' Girvyn told them. 'I have seen it on both sides now.'

Kalamayn whistled in disbelief. 'We have all fantasised about a day when our minds could bring anything to the Waking. Gods in both places we would be.'

Girvyn frowned at Kalamayn. 'Are you the library reference man?'

Kalamayn laughed. 'I guess you could call me that.'

'It's amazing what you have done.'

'It's amazing what *you* have done,' Mora said to Girvyn. 'And all underage and without any training on either side.'

'Are you all right?' Dremell asked Girvyn, interrupting his mother. He seemed careful to not disrespect her, but he clearly felt it was the right question to ask next.

Girvyn hesitated. 'I'm scared.'

'Understandable,' Nadine said. 'I am sorry this has happened to you, Girvyn.' Her jaw tightened. 'We will train you, make you as strong as possible.'

'It was terrifying, and it's all overwhelming. I just found out about the Realm. And now I've had a monster that's half-Realm, half-man come after me. Crane is taking people from the Waking and turning them into a demon army.'

It hit them by surprise. Mouths opened, then came soft, abrupt whistles of breath at something Girvyn had worked out that the others were yet to see.

'He has moved so far beyond our understanding,' Kalamayn muttered. Laglen respected Kalamayn. He was always offering sound, sage advice. 'Pure speculation, but perhaps Realm-based forms are weaker, but when mixed with Waking people they are stronger. We need more information.'

Laglen let his head drop. 'Well, I agree with that.'

Mora's cheeks flushed with rage. 'He needs to be stopped. That's all that matters right now. Not why. Not how. Not if it's all because of his past.' Mora sent Laglen a sour look, and he knew that point was for him. 'Not if this is the consequence of his abandonment, however much we might want to sympathise. We have to stop him doing this.'

Laglen couldn't let the retort pass. 'I have merely defended Crane in the past because he had a terrible upbringing. I didn't know these details...'

'There are plenty of people with terrible upbringings who don't turn out to be a mass murderer,' Mora countered.

'I couldn't have known Crane would turn out that way. I was trying to help him.'

Mora snorted. 'He killed your sister, Laglen, and you knew enough. He used to show us, give us tours. Do you remember?'

'How can I forget.' Laglen replied in a low voice. 'But they were structures. *His* creation to determine. We were young, and I was in awe of his technique. Yes, Crane was sick, yes, but his methods were revolutionary and inventive. Do you remember when he tricked us?'

Kalamayn shook his head. 'He tricked you; we were not there.'

Mora took a cloth from her pocket and cleaned a globule of sweat from her forehead, which was a strange action, given that this likeness was her Realm creation and didn't need to sweat. 'You know how I feel about this, Laglen.' He noticed she didn't use his warmer nickname. 'You might create structures for entertainment, but I consider my creations as alive as me. Crane held a million souls in a sea of blood which slowly dissolved their skin. Thousands of demonic birds pecked at faces, and just at the decisive point of death, he would heal the wounds, and it would start all over. A million eternal cries for mercy.'

'That's beyond sick!' Dremell exclaimed.

Mora sent Laglen a piercing glare. 'And still you defended him. You got it badly wrong.'

Laglen dropped his head, unable to find the words for a moment. 'I know,' was all he managed.

'Crane needs to be stopped,' Dremell hissed through clenched teeth.

'I agree with Dremell,' Nadine murmured. 'We need to take his miserable life away.'

'But how?' Laglen asked.

'He still needs to sleep. We attack him while he is in the Realm,' Dremell answered.

Kalamayn looked confused. 'How do we sync that up, and where does Crane sleep?'

'His stronghold in the mountain is the obvious lair where he would rest his body to cross. My mother draws him into the Realm,' Dremell glanced at Mora, waiting for her reaction; when she acknowledged, he continued. 'Once he enters her structure, we know he is asleep. Then I enter his room and kill him while he is vulnerable.'

Mora was musing. 'There are ways to draw his attention. That could work, but Kal is right, we'd need to synchronise this precisely. I won't be able to tell you he is with me if you are in the Waking.'

'It would need to be timed to the second,' Laglen agreed. 'Dremell could travel to near where Crane is sleeping. He gets into position, crosses to the Realm, and waits with Mora until Crane appears. Then he wakes and kills Crane's sleeping body.'

'It would be dangerous,' Nadine said. 'Crane will have creatures protecting him. I will journey with Dremell to his mountain to watch over him.'

Laglen sighed. 'But that won't be enough. We need to tell the Orts,' he muttered. 'About us. What we are. We need more support, and they could provide it. Yes, we feel responsible, but they have suffered. They have a right to know.'

'No! You can't trust Orts!' Nadine hissed.

'Daughter,' Kalamayn said. 'I know you lost trust in them because of your mother, but you may have to put that aside.'

'This has nothing to do with her, Father.'

'But Nadine is right,' Mora said. 'They will hunt us down for being different.'

'But our kind now hunts Orts. Should we not ally now to stop the threat of Crane?' Laglen implored.

'I agree with Laglen,' Kalamayn muttered.

'And I agree with Nadine,' Mora said. 'We have a tie.'

They all looked at Dremell. 'Then the deciding vote lies with you, Son,' Mora said to him.

'I want to eliminate Crane, and enlisting the assistance of the Orts to reach the mountain will aid in that goal. Therefore, I vote that we disclose our true nature to the Orts,' Dremell declared.

'Then it is decided,' Laglen said.

'A correct decision, that is. Now is the time to fight together, not stew in factionalism.'

They all jumped at the new voice.

Mora, who governed this Atrium, reacted first. 'Who are you?' She rose into a giant version of herself, ready to attack.

'Wait! He is a friend. He saved me from Crane's hell.' Girvyn blurted. The figure came forward and greeted them one by one. He moved like a hulking man of fire.

'Greetings, Master Girvyn,' he said, his voice soft.

Mora pointed her finger, ready to unleash her power onto the thing. 'This is my structure, and you were not invited, nor did you alert me. What kind of friend are you that hides his face? Show yourself.'

'Girvyn, who is this person?' Laglen demanded.

'Like I just said, he helped me escape Crane's Realm. He was there that night.'

Laglen's pinprick gaze flicked between Girvyn and this new apparition. 'That does better explain how you escaped Crane's hell. A feat I couldn't fathom.'

'What are you?' Mora asked it. She brought her size back to normal.

'I am beyond what you would call a Traveller. I am part of the Realm.'

'What is your name?' Girvyn asked him.

He addressed Girvyn. Seeming to give him more attention than the others. 'I don't have a name. You can give me one if you wish.'

'He's like a bit of fire from the sun, so let's call him Sunfire!' Girvyn suggested excitedly.

'Then call me Sunfire,' he said.

Kalamayn raised a bushy eyebrow. 'Are you The Source?'

Sunfire came forward, his form flickering like flames, and answered the question, 'The Source binds all things in the Realm; it hears your thoughts through The Pull and turns them into something tangible.'

Laglen's eyes narrowed to a pinprick. 'We know that. But is it alive?'

'It is conscious, if that is what you mean,' Sunfire said.

'You haven't answered. Are you The Source?' Mora persisted.

'I am a part of it. Think of me as a Realm Guardian. I exist in the dream substrates. Between where dreams are made and stored.'

'What is this glow around you?' Laglen questioned further, frowning.

'I am permanently connected to the Realm; I come to you now as the Waking is at risk. Crane has found a way to take Realm creations into the Waking. Let me show you what he has done...' Behind him, a fiery blue frame erupted. Crackling and humming, spitting sparks and heat.

Girvyn gasped at it. 'That's the door!'

'It's a portal which bridges our worlds. Crane has one that listens to his mind. This one,' he said, turning to Girvyn, 'is for you.'

'No!' Laglen objected.

Sunfire raised his arms. The golden vapour that followed him moved, adding to his divine likeness. 'Everything that was told at the summit was true. It's all Crane. He takes something pure from your world and combines demiurgic wickedness. Our dimensions must stay divided as they have always been.' He clenched his fist and lifted it into the air, and golden particles sprinkled towards the ground and faded away.'

'I don't want it. Give it to Uncle,' Girvyn moaned.

'You can't do this, Sunfire!' Laglen protested vehemently, his anger flaring suddenly. 'He's just a boy; pass this responsibility to one of us instead.'

'It must be Girvyn.'

'Why? What are you not telling us? Why did Crane single Girvyn out?'

'He has the mind needed to defeat him.'

'Why? Because I am clever?' Girvyn said. 'Look, they also read and are older and more experienced than me. Give it to my uncle; he was the one that got me into reading. Give it to Kalamayn; he is the catalogue man!'

'It must be you, Girvyn.'

'How do we know that you are a friend?' Kalamayn dismissed, waggling his hand at Sunfire. 'This could be all a trick. Anyone could enter another structure and change their form.'

'But he saved me,' Girvyn insisted. 'I saw Sunfire and

Crane together. Why would he save me from Crane's hell if he worked for Crane? Crane was shocked to see him.' He paused, frowning. 'But Sunfire, you have the power to defeat Crane. I watched you sweep his monsters away with a snap of your fingers. You should face him, not me.'

'I cannot. It must be you, Girvyn.' Sunfire regarded Kalamayn, 'You are right, of course, to doubt me, and I understand your reservation and welcome it.' He motioned for them to come closer. 'Here, let me show you something Crane doesn't know about you. Nor something a Traveller could show you.'

Two new windows popped into existence. Laglen could tell these were not live dreams, nor did they belong to Mora. But how had they appeared inside her Atrium like this? Even more troubling, he recognised one of the windows.

'What is this?' Kalamayn said in shock. 'This is a dream I made as a child. I deleted this years ago.'

Laglen attempted to conceal the window he recognised, frantically waving his arms in front of it to prevent the others from seeing its contents. Curiosity piqued, the others crowded around him to see. 'No, step back!' he urged.

But it was too late: they saw an image of a semi-naked woman swinging inside a birdcage. That woman he had created long ago. His hidden indulgence. Sequestered within a construct to return to as he chose. Yet, here she was, vividly displayed. A testament to his disgrace.

'Oh, Laglen, please!' Mora disapproved.

'Close this window!' Laglen rounded on Sunfire. 'You've made your point!'

The windows vanished. 'Indeed, have I proven my omniscient status to you? Come, there is more to show.' Sunfire gestured to the portal, where a new view was presented in the aperture.

They all gasped.

'What?' Kalamayn said. 'How have you done this?'

Through the portal lay a clearing where three modest shacks nestled beneath some trees, forming a small woodland settlement. Laglen's heart quickened – it wasn't just any settlement.

For a moment, everyone stood still, struck by the odd sight of a woodland entrance amidst the empty expanse. It was as though a fragment of that place had been severed and now lay here, isolated in the whiteness of Mora's domain. Laglen circled the portal, observing the scene from the opposite side, only to find the same landscape, its solitary presence stark against the surrounding void.

Girvyn pointed at it. 'Where is that?'

Nadine was mesmerised. 'I remember this from when I was a little girl. It's my grandparents' home.'

'It's all our parents' homes. It's their community, where they all live together,' Kalamayn told Girvyn.

'If Crane knew of where they lived would he not have vented his hatred by attacking them?' Sunfire asked. 'Go, step through... and see.'

Laglen noticed Girvyn glaring at him. 'Thanks, Uncle. You said no more secrets. Were you going to tell me your parents were alive?'

'They don't speak to us.'

'They don't speak to any of us,' Mora said quietly. 'They exiled themselves from us.'

'Can people see us from their side?' Dremell pushed his hand through the aperture of the portal, and Waking air coagulated around it.

'Yes, one can see through the portal from both sides,' Sunfire said.

A dog approached, yapping, darting back and forth. Mora

shooed it away, but it clearly had no intention of venturing into her Atrium.

Laglen was glaring at Sunfire. 'But how did you know where they live?'

'I know what you know. Crane does not know what you know.'

'Hold on,' Kalamayn said, working something out. 'How can we pass through? Our bodies are already in the Waking, back where we left them when our consciousness passed to the Realm. Asleep!'

'As long as the forms you take now return here, you can return to your sleeping bodies. A few moments in the same dimension won't hurt.'

'I'm doing it,' Mora said and stepped through. She glanced back, smiling. 'I can smell the forest.' She laughed with glee, shaking her head. 'I have lost connection to The Pull.'

'That will return when you step back.'

'Wait, Mother,' Dremell followed, taking her hand.

One by one, the others walked into the Waking.

'Not you, Girvyn,' Sunfire instructed, guiding Girvyn to remain in the doorway. 'Stand at the portal's threshold and share what you sense.'

Laglen hung back, close to the portal, ensuring he could hear what was said. He didn't trust this Sunfire one little bit. The notion of a Realm Guardian sounded like fiction to him; surely, if such a figure existed, there would be historical records in their lineage. Moreover, bestowing such potent abilities on Girvyn so swiftly struck him as both manipulative and foolhardy.

'Nothing. I don't feel anything,' Girvyn admitted.

'Wait a bit,' Sunfire encouraged.

Nadine, kneeling at the base of a tree, squealed in delight.

'I carved my name in the bark when I was a little girl; it's still here,' she declared.

'This is amazing,' Dremell said, crouching beside her. He touched the mud and smelt his fingers. 'This is the Waking.'

Girvyn took a breath. 'What is the portal doing?'

'It's bonding with you, becoming a part of you. You can sense each other,' Sunfire explained.

'Stop it!' Laglen interjected sharply, directing his frustration at Sunfire. 'This is happening too quickly. It's reckless and ill-considered.'

Realm side, Sunfire turned his hulking glow away from Girvyn and faced him. 'It's complete, Laglen. The pairing is done. Now, Girvyn needs to learn how to harness it wisely, and you're going to assist him in that.'

'But I don't know how,' Girvyn confessed anxiously.

'You see? You're overwhelming him. It was never your place to bestow such potentially catastrophic power...' Laglen argued.

However, Sunfire didn't let him finish.

'Girvyn, concentrate on a spot in front of you. Think of the energy of the sun. Imagine it as individual particles of heat and split them. One particle stays where you are, and the other moves towards where you want to go. Keep building, and perpetuation will evolve into an opening between the two points you have projected.'

Girvyn sighed. 'I don't understand.'

'You just need more practice; it's easier to use than explain. Never open it over water or too high up, or you could fall and die. Likewise, inside a tree might prove hard to step out of. Also, you can only go to places you have already been to or can see, as you need the memory to have an image of it in your mind.'

Laglen cast a disgruntled glance back at the portal. 'That

restricts its usefulness. Girvyn hasn't travelled beyond Rathnell's borders.'

'Yes, I have,' Girvyn countered, his expression wounded. 'I've visited the nearby mountains, a few farms, and the city's woods.'

'Alright, fine,' Laglen conceded, not wanting to belittle his nephew's experiences. Yet, he remained deeply troubled, and he couldn't shake the feeling.

Sunfire couldn't enter the Waking; his upper form projected out of the portal while his lower body remained submerged inside. He beckoned them back and urged, 'It's time to go. Everyone inside the Realm.'

However, a new voice interjected, 'No, you don't! What do you want?' An elderly woman appeared with a pitchfork, followed by a dishevelled man who was clutching a broom.

Laglen whispered, 'Father... Mother...!' He looked back at Girvyn, still standing in the portal doorway. 'This is your grandmother and grandfather.'

For a moment, their countenance softened. 'Baby Girvyn,' Laglen's mother murmured, then it was gone, replaced with stabbing stares.

Laglen's father hissed. 'Laglen, we told you not to come here.'

'What do you want?' came another voice. Four more people came into the clearing, clutching walking sticks.

'We told you we desired nothing to do with you all, and you come back, with this?!' Laglen recognised Mora's mother straight away despite her frail form. 'What is this?' she growled, pointing at the portal.

'Mother, Crane has found a way to breach Realm and Waking,' Mora said. 'Will you help us defeat him?'

'Be gone,' Kalamayn's mother said, refusing to look at her son.

Laglen regarded Tasmin's mother. 'Tasmin has gone missing.'

'You have all gone missing, as far as we are concerned,' she replied. 'My daughter died years ago. You didn't listen to us then; why would you listen to us now.'

Laglen's mother turned away from them and declared, 'We're leaving the compound. When we come back in five minutes, I expect all of you to be off our property!'

Laglen observed their departure, his head shaking in disbelief. First, the revelation of the hidden woman, and now this. Sunfire had demonstrated abilities beyond what any Traveller could achieve, leaving them all without words. 'Well, that was definitely real,' Laglen finally muttered. 'Crane couldn't have done that; he hasn't seen my parents since childhood and didn't know they lived here.'

Kalamayn shrugged. 'That was exactly what they were like last time we saw them.' He puffed out his cheeks. 'Brutal.'

'That was no trick,' Sunfire assured. 'As soon as Girvyn uses the portal, you will know this is a gift, not an illusion. Come, let us return to the Realm.'

Once back in Mora's Atrium, the portal closed, and they were left facing each other in shock.

'What was that all about?' Girvyn asked them.

No one replied at first; distracted expressions betraying painful memories.

'They disapproved of the Realm when Crane killed Rosein, and asked us to abstain,' Kalamayn said. 'And we didn't.'

'They gave us a choice: them or the Realm,' Laglen said; he couldn't look at Girvyn.

'Where is Sunfire?' Girvyn asked.

'He disappeared,' Dremell told them. 'He was here, and then he wasn't.'

'What just happened?' Nadine asked. 'Did we really just cross to the Waking?'

'We did,' Mora muttered. 'But now we have Girvyn's portal, and we need to change the plan. We have options.'

Laglen growled. 'Girvyn is not some parlour toy or court jester.'

'I am okay, everyone. I don't feel any different. Maybe it didn't work,' Girvyn said.

Laglen cursed silently. After the summit attack, they needed to run, not take Girvyn onto the front line. It would be like giving a child control of an army. But worse, if what Sunfire had said was true, then Girvyn could bring through anything he thought of: flying bookshelves, giant hybrid wooden figurines to stomp through the city, smashing everything in their path. Laglen refused to put Girvyn in harm's way. He had promised him. He had been given another chance to do the right thing, and intended to stick to his promise.

'He is just a boy,' Laglen continued. 'He needs training. Having this portal levels the playing field.' He paused. 'Yes, I agree with that. But what it can do is beyond anything we have ever seen. He is not ready. Whatever we do, Girvyn is not an option.'

'No one disagrees with that, Lag. But what does Girvyn think?' Mora regarded him. 'Girvyn?'

'What do I think about what?' Girvyn snapped.

Laglen watched Girvyn's frightened gaze glimpse about. He smiled to himself. *That's it*, he thought. *That familiar terse way of interacting. Show them.*

'It's the most absurd idea, sending me out there to face him,' Girvyn said, his voice cutting.

'No one is suggesting that. We can direct what you do with this portal,' Mora replied softly.

'No, I don't want this. I wish I didn't have it. I wish you had it. I want to read in the library, and now I can't even do that!'

Dremell came up to Girvyn and patted his shoulder. 'It's okay.' He crossed his arms. 'We stick to our plan: attack Crane while he sleeps. It's our best option.'

They all looked at each other and nodded in agreement.

Girvyn let out a held breath. 'Thank you.'

Laglen rubbed his hands. 'Well, it's decided then. Girvyn, time for us to return to the stables.'

'It was nice to meet you all,' Girvyn said, glancing around at the others, who acknowledged him with agreeing smiles. He gave his uncle a nod. 'See you in a second,' he added, before vanishing from the construct.

Laglen lingered a moment, casting a final look over his old friends. But as he was about to leave, Mora stopped him with a sharp gesture.

She made a face, explaining, 'I've slowed the structure, Lag, so Girvyn won't notice your delay. Before you go to him, there are things we need to discuss.'

Laglen's eyes narrowed. 'What is it, Mora?' he said, voice terse.

'The Realm fulfils our dream desires. That's it. So I don't trust what just happened. A Realm Guardian?' Mora snorted. 'Pah! That's nonsense. The Realm has never spoken directly to any of us before – or our ancestors – and it chooses Girvyn over all of us? We all know what happens in the Realm, stays in the Realm. Yet, somehow, Crane defies our ancient rule, and a boy can match his power. Just like that? Doesn't that seem strange to anyone? Did Sunfire give this power to Crane years ago as well? Is he trying to start a war in the Waking, so we end up destroying ourselves?'

Laglen paused, considering her for a moment. 'I agree, it's

unprecedented and incongruous, but I'd rather Girvyn have the power than none of us,' he replied eventually, glancing at Kalamayn for support. 'At least now we have a way to counter Crane.'

Kalamayn nodded in agreement. 'But Girvyn needs training. Crane has a big head start on us.'

Mora's expression didn't waver. 'Yes , on that. There is something about that boy that unsettles me, Lag. He has confidence beyond his years, but he is totally unworldly.'

'He has spent most of his life in a book,' Laglen sighed exasperatedly. 'That might explain it.'

'He may be well read, but he is badly lived.'

Laglen felt his hackles rise. 'He doesn't follow social norms, Mora. He suffers from anxiety mainly caused by new situations. He says what he thinks, and a lot of the time, it's interesting and correct.'

Mora's expression remained still. 'We are doomed; a know-it-all has all that power.'

'He is a child, Mother,' Dremell muttered, defending Girvyn. Dremell shrugged. 'I found him charming. But what should we expect from a boy?'

'So then it's worse, a child know-it-all has all that power,' exclaimed Mora.

'I think what Mora is saying,' Kalamayn said, glancing between them. 'Is that this Sunfire is asking us to trust a boy with the same power as Crane. A portal between Realm and Waking, a transportation door? This is the stuff of futuristic constructs. It's catastrophic that Girvyn should have this power.'

'I agree,' Laglen protested, folding his arms. 'Sure, he may seem peculiar to some, but Girvyn is no know-it-all; he listens, he learns, and he has the kindest heart. Maybe Sunfire looked at all of us and found us lacking.' He shot a glare across the group. 'Have any of you considered that?'

'Who has been his maternal figure, Lag? Has it been Elaya?' Mora asked, sending back a raised eyebrow.

Laglen glanced away, feeling his cheeks flush. 'Elaya has been a constant, but she is not the most affectionate type. She watched over him and kept him safe. He was never really held as a baby.'

'What? Not even by you?' Mora disapproved. 'What happened when he needed a cuddle?'

'Well, I would sit him on my knee and read him a book.'

Mora shook her head. 'Rosein would turn in her grave, Lag.'

'Don't judge me! Rosein wouldn't!' Laglen felt his lips draw back. 'I did my best.' He raised a hand to stop her from speaking. 'I know I could have done better. I had my own demons to face. Often, I would send him to the library while I raced. It was his safe place and where he was happiest.'

'In a place he can control? Books don't answer back, Lag. They are just tomes of information. Consistent and unchanging. No wonder he is scared of the unknown. There is a deficit there, like Crane. A kind of neglect....'

'Are you saying his weaknesses are my fault, Mora?' Laglen felt anger flare. 'And don't you dare compare him to Crane. Girvyn turns his failings onto himself. He's a self-reproachful soul. While Crane attacks others!'

'There is no doubting his academic ability,' Kalamayn muttered, trying to dampen reactions.

'No one is perfect, Mora,' Laglen continued, 'and you are harsh on him. True, he can be rash and brazen. He likes routines to regulate himself, but it covers up a deep insecurity inside him. Just leave the boy be.'

'That's my point,' Mora persisted. 'How did he end up with this power?'

'Well, he has it now,' Nadine interrupted. She glanced at Dremell, looking for support. 'And we must all guide him.'

'Mother,' Dremell added calmly, his voice carrying a weight of reprieve. 'Can we try and support Girvyn? We all have a part to play.'

Laglen nodded appreciatively at Nadine, then Dremell. 'Exactly! The young are showing sense! Right, it's been a pleasure.' He smiled disingenuously. 'I think we are done.'

Nadine raised her hand suddenly. 'One last question nagging about Crane I have is, could he be working with others?' she asked Laglen. 'Crane can't be doing this alone.'

'Nah,' Laglen replied, looking away. 'He would never go into partnership. Crane was always a loner.'

Sixteen

Baron Kerrick Shadstone waited for Crane at the end of the jetty, looking out across his private lake. He didn't want to stand on the bank as he never knew where the portal would materialise and didn't want to be too close when it opened. It was that intense heat when it arrived; it was almost unbearable. Crane seemed to revel in unnerving him or causing sudden consternation, and Kerrick hated showing weakness. But Crane would never open it over water in case he missed his landing spot, so waiting at the jetty end narrowed down the possibility of surprises.

In the distance came the sound of barking. The dogs were out on their evening run, although it would be some time before the groundskeepers came to this part of the estate. The sun had set, but a luminescent sky remained in the west as if the last remnant of the day was reluctant to leave.

Then it came. Near the water's edge, a hum at first, a crackling of leaves curling in the heat, that smell of ozone, then the dazzling doorframe of blue light pulsated in the twilight, illuminating the whole lake line. The door remained dark, a glistening, rippling surface, and then it revealed a citadel on the other side.

Crane stood back from the doorway for crass dramatic reasons, showing off his power in the Realm. Loath as Kerrick was to admit the fact, it was impressive. Winged monsters – huge fire-breathing bats – swirled in the sky. Below them rose a vast, jagged fortress around which swarmed brutish creatures. Fearsomely armoured and twice as large as a man, they would make terrifying foot soldiers, all the more so for the lack of intelligence in their glazed red eyes. Commanding them stood a demon, which now came closer. Kerrick almost recoiled at the sight of the two-footed creature before him. It had a broad and powerful physique, reminiscent of a bear, and a prevailing wolf-like snout.

Head bowed, Crane came forward, filling the aperture of the doorway. His usual robe was adorned with long heavy stoles embroidered with fanciful gold designs, draped over each shoulder like some religious emissary.

The portal vanished, and Crane stood in the low light at the water's edge.

'You're late,' Kerrick said, striving to appear unimpressed.

'Walk with me, will you,' Crane replied.

After a while of doing this in silence, Kerrick cleared his throat. 'What is it?'

'How long have you been in this estate now?'

Kerrick glanced sideways at the drooped, shaded cowl. After all these years, he still hadn't seen his face. 'I earned the honour of baron, and the estate, nearly twenty years ago. When you came to me, I had just been titled.' Kerrick was quick to correct himself. 'Of course, my estate has grown since then with your help.'

'Your wife and son? How are they?'

Kerrick stopped him. 'What is going on?'

'How much do they know of me?'

'My wife knows nothing. My son, Finlack, believes you are an acquaintance from Cundelly for whom we do some work.'

'Fitting. Most fitting.' Crane nodded for him to continue moving. 'It's time to move into the final moment. It will come with great sacrifice.'

'I have never shirked any responsibility. You wanted druids; I brought you them. I have been your eyes and ears in Rathnell from the beginning.'

'Indeed. Indeed. You have served me well over the years, my greatest ally in the Waking. Now I make my biggest demand. I need to use your estate in readiness for Extinction Day.'

'Extinction Day?' Kerrick glanced through the trees, thankful nightfall concealed his surprise. 'What happened to The Day of Taking?'

'Extinction Day is a far more fitting explanation of what is coming. And it has a better ring, don't you think?'

Maybe it did, but where did Kerrick and all he possessed fit into the word extinction? He had always assumed the Day of Taking referred to multiple levels of acquisition. Gains for both. Crane had already helped him gain power, land, and influence, as well as clear the road of any court blockages. It was easy to accomplish using a portal that could transport him to a competing estate. There, he could clear a path to power, return to public court on the same day, and deny responsibility.

'Don't worry, your route to the throne will remain clear as ever. And no harm will come to you when the dying begins.'

'And my wife and son?'

'If you truly hold them dear they will be unharmed.'

Kerrick did. But not in the way he had seen some simple

farming folk do, seeming happy in the banal bosom of family existence. As if that alone could ever lead to fulfilment or contentment. His family were useful, for sure. His wife presented a certain message to anyone looking in from the outside. It was the proper thing to do. But she was a prop, a stepping stone to a greater destination. There were feelings for Finlack, his son; he could rear him in his own image. One less loyal guard to train.

'Well, it has already started, hasn't it,' Kerrick said. 'The dying, I mean. You have their attention. Whether you intended it or not. They are discussing you today at the summit.'

'Indeed. We will come back to that.'

Kerrick's thoughts drifted back to a previous point. 'My estate? You want to use it?'

'Did I arrange this estate for you just so you could tend its gardens? It was for my purposes too. Its size and privacy, so proximate to Rathnell, serves well...'

'What do you want to do?' Kerrick interrupted. As the hood tilted a fraction towards him, he felt a flash of foolishness for cutting off Crane, but damn it his blood was up, and he'd been left uninformed for that whole library assault by that thing of Crane's.

'I want to give you some of my minions.'

'You're not serious? Demons? But the estate, it's full of staff.'

'Get rid of them.'

Kerrick stopped in his tracks. 'I am not killing them!'

'Your staff?' Crane flicked his hand. 'Sack them if you prefer. Is there anywhere your wife could go for a while? Family?'

'I can arrange it.'

'Good, do it. I trust your son will be on board with this?'

Kerrick gritted his teeth. 'He will.' He gazed around; it was dark now, and he hadn't even noticed the final light fade. 'My staff are needed to maintain my estate.'

'When Extinction Day comes an overgrown garden will be the least of your worries.'

Barking sounded to the north, towards the house. It was louder than expected. Kerrick raised his hand and stopped him. 'My dogs are coming. You'd better go. Call your portal.'

'Come with me.'

'What? Really?'

'This is what you wanted. All these years. To visit the Dream Realm and make use of what I can offer. Come then.'

The gateway burst into life. Kerrick felt the heat on his cheeks, the smell, that blinding light.

They were gone in a step, passing from night to light.

'What is this place?'

'It's where we create. Name something.'

Kerrick blinked. 'What?'

'Think of something. Anything.'

'Gold.'

'Gold?' Crane waved a cursory hand, and as far back as Kerrick could see, there were mounds of gold bars strewn in every direction. 'So boring.' The disappointment was evident in Crane's voice, and the white space was empty again.

Ever since learning about the Realm, Kerrick had sought this moment. To be able to create anything he wanted. Bring it through to his estate. The portal wasn't just a gateway to cross the land. That had its purposes, for sure, but it was what lay inside. A treasure of possibilities. Now that he was here, his spine tingled with excitement.

Kerrick eyed Crane quietly, sensing the challenge. 'Okay, what about a winged horse?'

'Finally. Some imagination.'

Crane's lips curled for a moment, and a second later a majestic winged-mare appeared before them, its velvety coat glistening.

Kerrick tried to determine if it was real or an illusion. He reached out his hand, felt its powerful neck, and stroked its back. 'It's real.'

'Of course.'

But Crane made it vanish. 'How about this?' Crane continued. Standing in front of Kerrick was his wife, but twenty years younger.

'Hello dear,' she said. 'When are you coming back to the manor?' She raised an eyebrow and started to unbutton her blouse.

'Enough. This is not her.'

It was hard for Kerrick to see, for the recess of the cowl shaded all features, but he was sure Crane was smiling at him in amusement. 'So be it,' Crane said, and she vanished. 'How about something a little more relevant?'

Kerrick's pulse raced in his ears as he imagined it all. The riches. The power. He had only to keep Crane happy and all this could be his. The enormity of it swelled in him and he half-wished to have a wench – an anonymous one, not his wife – appear so he could ravish her on the spot. He'd had dreams of acquisition his whole life, but this went beyond them a hundredfold.

'I believe I shall choose today's gifts. I have something subtle that will blend into their surroundings and be of great use for our campaign. I have prepared it earlier, it's much stronger than these quick creations. I give you changelings. They will appear as whoever or whatever you want them to look like, and are quite exceptionally talented at spying.'

Crane took him through a window to meet them. Two faceless human forms waited inside the structure.

'Show him,' Crane said.

Then, across their smooth, blank, stretched face, their features formed into a person, then another, constantly changing appearance. Again. Again. Again. Shifting somehow across all the people Kerrick knew, almost quicker than he could distinguish. Friends, associates, loved ones, enemies, and even people he had killed.

'Stop it! Stop it!'

'They are reading your mind, becoming the people you know, or have known. Concentrate on an identity, and they will become that. Try it with one of them.'

Kerrick thought of a young boy he had killed many years ago on the battlefield, and there he was, standing there.

'If anyone enquires, new staff are working for you.'

Kerrick raised an eyebrow. 'Can they become anything?'

'Feel free to play around later when you are back in the Waking,' Crane suggested, spreading his arms wide as if unveiling a grand surprise. From the vast expanse of empty whiteness, shapes began to draw nearer. 'A few more gifts...' Crane paused, noticing Kerrick's growing excitement. 'I envy you your avarice. The childish joy of possession left me many years ago. Here...' At that moment, a stallion approached them. 'This one may not have wings, but it will be the fastest horse you've ever ridden.'

Kerrick's eyes glimmered. 'How fast can it run?'

'As quick as the wind!'

Kerrick smiled. 'And, what do these two ugly things do?' Kerrick said, noticing more gifts arrive.

They smiled simultaneously and said, in unison, 'We will help you stay in touch with others.'

'One final gift,' Crane motioned into the white. At first, it was hard to see, as it was so far away. But as it drew closer, Kerrick saw it was a red armoured giant on a black horse.

'What is this?' Kerrick frowned. 'I sense a druid! Ah! Is this what you have been making with the captives I acquired for you?

'Yes. This is the strongest yet, and I found this one myself. Straight out of the forest; he put up quite a fight. Now he is mixed with objects of the Realm. You have something rather special at your disposal: obedient, loyal, relentless. The one I sent to Rathnell today required finesse with its direction. So we try again. I call it a Drone Druid.'

'You want me to go to Rathnell? Take another one of these things there after the mess the last one made in the castle?'

'Yes.'

'I came back three hours ago! You should have come to me first! Now you want me to return and finish a job you couldn't do?'

'It lacked precision and coordination. It was too doggedly fixated on Girvyn's scent. We need a veiner rather than a hammer, which you can bring to the table.'

'I can't return to Rathnell. Elaya will be all over it. I need another plan.'

'Then make one.' Crane waved a dismissive hand. 'Tomorrow, no later. Do what you have to.'

Kerrick had endured twenty years of being ordered around by Crane, resenting every moment. But, yet again, he acquiesced with a nod.

'Come, it's time to return to your estate.' As these words were spoken, the portal burst into existence before them, emitting a blue glow that illuminated the copse now visible through the opening.

Kerrick stepped through the portal, followed closely by his newly assembled team crafted within the Realm.

Crane, lingering in the doorway, made his final demand. 'I want the boy. I want him alive. I don't care how much carnage is caused by getting him. Do this, and you can have whatever your imagination desires.'

As these words hung in the air, they were left in the night, leaving Kerrick on his lawn. Careful not to show his surprise or any weakness, he considered the changelings. 'Show me more.'

They began altering, switching between the identities of people he knew. They were drawing from the edges of his awareness, but as he honed in he was able to steer it. Perfect likenesses of guards, chambermaids and lovers stood before him. He barely caught the more useful faces: royal court officials.

Kerrick clapped in glee. 'Change. More. Again. And again.'

Sometimes the people paused and said something glib, each time in a different accent and distinct personality, seeming like the true selves they represented. Kerrick roared in laughter.

Then they stopped. In the pale moonlight, back in faceless form, one leaned against a tree, looking at its nails. 'You do know this is untold tedium for us?'

'Father,' the other one said, in the form of Finlack. 'Shall we retire for dinner?'

Now Kerrick himself was there. A perfect reproduction. Even that arrogant tone. He dropped a hand on Finlack's shoulder, and they both snarled at the real Kerrick. 'We could kill you now, take your identity, and no one would ever know. Not even Crane.'

'Oh, can we Father, please?'

'Very funny.' Kerrick's hand went to his sword. 'What kind of demon makes jokes all the time?'

'But we are not joking.'

Kerrick stared incredulously at the mirror of himself.

The copy of Kerrick shrugged, its grin widening. 'Crane has made us this way so you might find us more familiar. We can do clipped sentences and talk about the end of the world if you prefer?'

'No banter required, thank you,' Kerrick's voice grew serious. 'How did you take on their personalities and aspect?'

'We draw that from you. Your druidic perception gives us a lot to work with, by the way.'

As much as he resented the intrusion, it made sense. They needed every detail to be convincing in the forms they took. Possibilities bounced around his mind like a trapped fly.

'How does it work when you become someone I don't know?' he asked.

'Then we need to touch the person to get their full body details,' the copy Kerrick said.

'Not as easy when we become the people we touch,' the Finlack copy added.

'It's all about blending. We draw from a fluctuating spectrum of personalities. Ah, alas, who is the true changeling?'

'Beats me,' the other one said.

'Only demon philosophers can speculate.'

'I said no more jokes,' Kerrick snarled. 'You do what I say when I say it, and just give me straightforward information.'

'Of course, if that is what you want?' they both said.

'I would chop anyone on my staff's head off for mucking about like that. Act however you want in the Realm, but not here.' Kerrick was thinking it all through. 'When you touch someone, do you acquire their memories?'

'We are changelings, not mind readers. So, no.'

'No sarcasm either. How do you become someone else if you know nothing about them?'

'Acting. As long as we know a little bit about the person we are becoming, it's all improvisation after that. It's amazing what you can get away with.' The changeling hid a rising grin behind his hand. 'If in doubt, play dumb, pretend you are ill, or have a hangover. We have to make sure we get rid of the original. We can't have two of the same person hanging around.'

'Makes sense,' Kerrick said.

'That's about it. You have us pegged now. Rue the life of a changeling demon.'

Kerrick was excited to bring them into the estate, show his son, and start brainstorming how they could capture Girvyn. He just had to remove his staff and get his wife to leave first. 'You must stay in the estate grounds until the house is clear. I will have everyone gone by the morning.'

'We will manage.'

'I might become a farm boy while we wait,' the other changeling said.

The young lad that morphed into being wasn't one Kerrick had ever met. 'Do you have your own archive of identities as well?'

'Crane has collected human specimens which we access for our collection. We have enough to give you a generic range of people.'

Kerrick gazed at the mother and child now standing before him.

'Oh, please help us; we have been hurt in an accident and need assistance,' the mother begged.

'That one always draws them in,' quipped the child, throwing a thumb. 'Never fails.'

Kerrick's eyes narrowed as he noticed something. 'Hold on; I am not sensing any emotion from you both. It's a giveaway.'

The changelings shrugged.

'This will not work on a druid. We can sense people's

emotions,' Kerrick said. 'Although it's only broad sensations through a mix of body language, voice and feelings that give off an aura. Your standard method won't trick a druid. Not in close quarters, anyway. You'd just be blank, empty spaces.'

'But what about now?' the mother said, straightening up to be scanned.

'What is that? Happiness? Excitement? I want fear.'

'That was fear. Look, it's hard for us to be scared. You try being us; you would feel excited.'

'I said no more jokes,' Kerrick hissed. 'Try again and make it better.' Kerrick paused, contemplating the new aura. 'Yes, okay. That's more convincing. Just do that. A constant feeling of anxiety works for most people.'

'Please, sir, I have hurt my foot. Will you help me stand?'

The little boy threw a thumb at his mother. 'That's right before she smashes the unsuspecting victim's head in.'

Kerrick smiled. 'Now we are on to something. That mother and child routine works. I think I have an idea how we can use that. Can I get more changelings?'

'We can ask Crane,' one said. 'I don't see why not.'

Kerrick nodded, satisfied. He went to leave, then remembered the two identical demons that Crane had gifted him. They stood stock still, blinking at him. 'And, what do you two do?' he demanded.

'We are the perfect communication device,' they answered in synchronicity. Mouths moving, body shifting in perfect harmony. 'We link live conversations across huge distances. We can show you?'

'I will be back in the morning; show me then.' Kerrick headed into the dark. 'And you,' he called over his shoulder, addressing the Drone Druid, who had remained in perfect, obedient readiness the whole time. 'I can sense death off you a mile away. But I have a plan for you too.'

Seventeen

Elaya woke Girvyn with a touch of her hand. It was just after dawn, and golden light cast shadows across the stable ceiling. Girvyn peered into her face. 'Wake, Girvyn,' she said, with a dash of urgency. 'The delegates are here and want to speak with you.'

Girvyn's body shook with tremors that began to subside under Laglen's comforting touch. 'Take deep breaths, Girvyn,' he advised soothingly.

The line of delegates seemed more focused on where they stepped, lifting their robes and holding their noses. Despite a breeze that brushed through small open windows, it was close and stuffy.

The queen, supported by Stasnier, seemed oblivious to the smell and horse manure, and came straight up to them.

'I remember you,' the queen said to Laglen. 'You were friends with Cronmere.'

'Your Majesty,' Laglen spluttered. Unsure of royal protocols, he bowed. 'Yes, I was.'

'Are you citizens of Rathnell?'

'I work in the library.' He rested a hand on Girvyn's shoulder. 'Girvyn is my nephew.'

She gave them an assessing stare. 'Hmmm, a most unusual pair you are.' She swivelled to face Girvyn. 'Do you know why this creature attacked you?'

Girvyn stammered. 'I don't know anything.'

Elaya reassured him. 'Don't be alarmed, Girvyn.' She regarded Laglen with eyes that implored. 'Tell them everything, Lag,' she urged.

Stasnier looked Girvyn up and down, and with a hint of disbelief and displeasure, said, 'We want to know why this creature hunted you.'

'I don't know why it came for me, sir.'

'He is just a boy! This is absurd,' Seskin muttered.

'I was there with him,' Hazel said passionately. 'It is like I have told you. That thing in the library, that was what attacked my village.'

'It's true,' Girvyn blurted. 'I saw it in a dream.'

There was a din of disbelieving voices.

'Quiet!' Cargya shouted. 'No more squabbles.'

Lord Grisham swept his cloak in a dramatic gesture that caught all their attention. 'Let the boy speak,' he hissed.

Girvyn shrugged and stammered, trying to find the right words.

Seskin scoffed. 'This boy is a witless fool. It is a ruse or a nonsense. What could anyone want with him?'

Elaya heard Jakub the Casper Envoy's acidic laugh cut the silence. 'This is clearly an orchestrated event to galvanise support to some Rathnell-driven agenda.'

'We know Rathnell offers back door support for Cundelly,' grumbled Nark. 'What better way to delay our road proposal than to create a decoy crisis? These settlement attacks are no more than organised gangs.'

'Be careful what you accuse us of,' Stasnier replied.

'I vouch for Laglen. It's best that what you hear next comes from him.' Elaya nodded encouragingly. 'Hazel and I have recounted what happened in the library. But *you* have something to tell the queen, don't you... Tell them, Lag...'

'I can provide the answers you seek, but it will sound strange to your ears...'

'Tell us what you know, Laglen,' the queen said.

His features tensed up as he wrestled with what to say. 'Your Royal Highness, members of the Court.'

'At ease, Laglen. Just tell us.'

'There is a Realm of imagination some of us can go to. I believe the thing that attacked Girvyn was made in this place and brought here.'

Sward laughed. 'Have the fumes of the manure gone to your head?'

Ignoring him, Laglen continued, 'The suffering that your cities and communities have endured has come from one man called Crane, not a gang of robed figures; a man who has the power to move across...'

'One man?! Don't be stupid,' Seskin shouted. 'You are as witless as the boy.'

Sward shook his head. 'What a waste of time this is.'

'What does this Crane want with your nephew?' the queen asked Laglen.

'Girvyn possesses the same power as Crane, and we believe he poses a threat to him,' Laglen said, shifting his feet uncomfortably. 'Let me clarify. My nephew, myself, and others – including Crane – are descendants of individuals capable of traversing to the sleep dimension through our minds.'

'Sleep dimension! What?!' Seskin spluttered.

Laglen shook his head and continued. 'We've lived among

you with this secret for generations. We cannot take those who cannot Travel with us, nor show the fruits of our creations on the Dream side. So why share a secret that has no bearing on your life or society? We also remember what happened to the druids; many would hunt us down for our ability.'

Nark hissed like a snake. 'And rightly so if what you say is true.'

Shaking his head, Laglen continued. 'Our ability has always been in another Realm. We could never take anything from there. Not until now. But Crane has a door between our worlds.'

Donjul, receiving whispered translation, gave a guttural shout. 'As I have told you all before, I have seen this door!' Alwad said. Donjul continued speaking. 'Monsters on our sands take our young. Why is no one listening to us?'

Sward stroked his wispy chin. 'Pah! All the delegates were herded into the hall during this supposed attack. I saw dead soldiers and broken walls, yes. Perhaps the only evil here is that you yourselves slaughtered and broke to stage this whole scene hoping to frighten us into committing our support to you. Shame on you!'

Elaya stepped in front of him. 'Sward, are you accusing me, Elaya Faith, Queen's Protector, of being complicit in the deaths of my own men?'

Sward looked her in the eye. 'I smell a rat. This has all been a farce. Conjuring tricks and scare tactics to make us hand real power to these crazies. Why, even the Forester girl's testimony could have been planted as part of it. The sole survivor? Well, isn't that convenient; no one to contradict her! And a slip of a girl lives when hardened warriors fall?'

The Foresters tensed up, and Elaya sensed an imminent skirmish. She drew her sword.

'No,' Hazel said, a fierceness in her eye. 'I watched that thing take my father.'

Grisham considered this. 'I do not share Sward's view that these people are trying to deceive us into gaining power. I believe there is some truth to the patterns of these destroyed settlements. But how are we supposed to believe this old man when he claims that it's all about a place we can never go to.'

Elaya re-sheathed her sword.

Seskin jumped in again. 'The creature that attacked today could be no more than a diseased man. It could be makeup, costume, or a parlour trick.'

Laglen stared at them. 'For what purpose?'

'You tell me, you crackpot,' Seskin said, waving a trivialising hand.

'What Laglen tells you is the truth,' Elaya said to the queen. 'Of that much I am sure.'

'How do you know if he can't prove it?' Stasnier said to Elaya, raising an eyebrow. 'He sounds like a mad fantasist. He should be locked up for wasting our time.'

Elaya fixed Stasnier with a look. 'This isn't about our differences.'

The queen contemplated Girvyn. 'It seems your uncle is claiming you are the most powerful of your kind. Can you explain that?'

Girvyn stammered, throat tightening with every word. 'This is also all new to me. I mean, literally; it's a revelation merely hours old. I am trying to digest it.'

'It's not food, boy,' Stasnier snapped. 'There is nothing to digest.'

'Ask my uncle the questions; he is better prepared to explain.'

Seskin laughed mockingly. 'He is not doing a very good job, boy. He is a crackpot.'

'My uncle is not a crackpot.'

'Leave the boy be,' Elaya said. 'I was there in the library. I saw what I saw.'

Girvyn went to speak, but his voice didn't work. He wobbled, gasping for breath. Elaya caught him before he hit the stone floor.

'Breathe, breathe,' Elaya said, trying to soothe him, orientate him. His eyes flickered, and she helped him stand up.

Sward tutted while they waited for Girvyn to gather himself. 'Show us this door, boy.'

Laglen growled. 'He cannot. I was going to train him when he came of age, but he discovered his abilities before I could. So right now, he needs protection. He can't use this door. He's not ready.'

There was a laugh.

'Take me to Cundelly, boy!' Seskin scorned. 'I want to see my family.'

'Please, leave me be,' Girvyn muttered.

'Send them to the dungeon!' Seskin hissed.

'No!' Something snapped in Girvyn.

Elaya saw in that moment, it was as if all his feelings; anxieties; deficiencies being laid bare; fears of being hunted; and now fury at his uncle being ridiculed, focused into a single moment of anger, and exploded into the room.

The portal ignited, causing everyone, including Laglen, to recoil in surprise. Glowing blue, it hummed and spat, vibrating with rising intensity, matching Girvyn's mood. The emanating heat and light forced everyone to retreat, while the strong scent of ozone filled the narrow space of the stables. Yet once the palpable ripple of shock and amazement had passed, all eyes fixed on the opening. Beyond it lay a mountain path, vivid as a view through a window.

'What is this?' the queen whispered, entranced.

Elaya, swords drawn, came in front of the queen. 'Nobody move.'

'Those,' Girvyn said smugly, pointing a finger at it, 'Are the mountains outside our city. If you don't believe me, step through and I will close the door behind you. You can walk back to Rathnell.'

'Enough,' Laglen's voice cut through the room. 'Girvyn, close it.'

But Girvyn didn't. He glared at Envoy Seskin, who, remarkably, threw a dismissive hand in the air. 'This is not possible. More tricks. You have a better chance of training a rabid dog.'

Elaya stepped closer to the portal, her breath catching. 'Everyone stay back!' she warned.

Something was at the entrance. Something not from the mountain path, but something new. Its shape filled the lower part of the door, black and shimmering at the swirling threshold.

There was a deep guttural growl, two glinting eyes, then it was through. At first it looked like a dog, but its back legs and tail were that of a giant fox.

'Nobody move!' Elaya hissed.

The dog-fox, thick trails of spittle dripping from its fanged-filled snarl, fixed its icy stare on Envoy Seskin. Its lips peeled back behind pearly white teeth, and it sprang.

Seskin fell back. The thing on his chest snarled, preparing to bite.

'Girvyn, put it back in the Realm!'

'I don't know what I did, Uncle!'

Then the creature yelped as a blade came through its neck, and it went limp. Elaya kicked it off Seskin's chest.

Sward helped Seskin up. He was white as a sheet, staring in disbelief at the dead creature.

Stasnier cleared his throat. 'Who knows about this?'

'Just us,' Laglen said. 'And the other Travellers.'

'How many?'

'Four.'

'Can they be trusted?' Stasnier asked him.

'Yes.'

'Hmmm, well, then there is no need to create a panic or tell others what this boy can do. If his power got into the wrong hands, disaster could ensue.'

Laglen looked bothered. 'It is in the wrong hands.'

The queen sighed, her face full of weariness and understanding. 'This boy is not ready.'

Laglen bowed thankfully. 'Which is what I have been saying,'

Seskin brushed himself down. He went over to the dog and nudged it with his foot. Then he pressed his palm to its neck. 'It's still warm.' He considered Girvyn with suspicion and fury, though his words were directed at Queen Amelia. 'Your Majesty, I'm sure I speak for us all today when I express shock. However, I am perturbed that this Laglen apparently knew of this danger and yet did nothing, warned no one... unless Rathnell deliberately kept Cundelly in the dark?'

Amelia shook her head. 'Envoy Seskin, we knew nothing of this either.'

'Of course, Your Majesty. That does rather reinforce my point, though: if this young man is as powerful as he seems, then should his training and his safety really be left to his negligent uncle who only now, when there is royal interest, sees fit to consider his duty to his sovereign and country.'

'What do you suggest?'

'In fact, I propose that the place for this boy is under the tutelage of the renowned hierarchs at Cundelly's High Temple?'

'What?' Laglen blurted. 'I am the one who should train him. Me and the other Travellers who know him.' Laglen put his hand on Girvyn's shoulder, which was trembling.

'Uncle, please, I want to stay with you.'

Seskin hesitated, and it looked like he might concede, but he didn't. 'The Cundelly High Temple will ensure this boy receives instruction in the observance of good moral character, which he seems, right now, to be lacking. Through our wise teachings...'

'I see what you are doing, Seskin. But this boy belongs in our city,' Stasnier pressed. 'He is the property of the crown. His particular skill set would be useful to us, Your Majesty. I am sure the monks here will make sure he receives calm and disciplined training. It is renowned as highly as the esteemed Cundelly High Temple, and here we can keep an eye on his progress. It seems clear,' Stasnier continued, ignoring the protests, 'that the revelation of this power unites us all in common cause. As a citizen of Rathnell, Girvyn's place is under our rule, but we will ensure reasonable access to him for all interested parties.'

'We need to get Girvyn out of the city,' Elaya disagreed. 'Crane has already come for him once. He needs to train in hiding.'

'This is a protection issue, and Elaya always offers the most cogent advice,' the queen said. 'Elaya, what would you do?'

'I would take him somewhere only a few of us know about. Somewhere high, protected by walls and water. With a flat plain so one might stand at the gate and see for miles around, ensuring any dangers will be easily spotted.'

'Sounds like a castle on a hill,' Amelia mused. 'There are many we could consider.'

Stasnier interjected; that sly, soft voice mollifying and

worming. 'As to the combined force that we must assemble to defend against the new threat from this Crane, it is nothing more than good sense that it must also be based in Rathnell, and therefore under her majesty's command...'

Jakub interjected, 'But it seems you are asking for the keys to all our kingdoms, Stasnier. Will you also ask the good Nark here to cede control of the church to your secular government?'

'Blasphemy! Never!' spluttered Nark.

'Indeed,' continued Jakub smoothly.

'Your Majesty,' Elaya warned. 'More posturing...'

'Silence!' rattled the queen's frail voice. She moved to stand in front of Girvyn and contemplated him. 'So young and yet such a great responsibility sits upon your shoulders. I, better than any here, know that weight, Girvyn. I believe that you may well, as your uncle claims, be key to our very survival. If we are to require your aid, then it behoves us to provide you with assistance and comfort as we can. We will plan for you to train with your uncle in hiding.'

'Thank you,' Girvyn gushed. 'And Uncle has a plan for how we can beat Crane.'

But his voice was drowned out as everyone began offering their own solutions on how to defeat Crane.

Seskin's jibe rose above the rest. 'And now we are supposed to listen to a proposal from a man who could have helped us prevent many deaths? We don't need his strategy; we have the boy.'

Cargya called for silence.

'Tell us this idea, Laglen,' the queen said.

Laglen began detailing Dremell's plot to lure Crane into the Realm while he slept. The more he described the plan, the more Elaya found it convincing. Crane's weakness was the Waking body, without which his Realm mind would die.

And they knew it lay in his cabin on the mountainside, albeit heavily guarded. However, as long as the team sent there was well-equipped and prepared, they could succeed. While Crane would have sentinels and dark creatures from hell watching over him while he slept, they could neutralise the defences and strike him at his most vulnerable. There were, of course, risks involved, as there always were, but it was all about minimising them. It wasn't so much that this plan would keep Girvyn out of the direct line of danger, more that she knew he would fail if placed there, taking the hopes of everyone down with him. She couldn't stand that, and it was immeasurable relief to hear Laglen lay out a better solution.

The queen reflected, and the others did the same, some nodding in agreement. Only Seskin was shaking his head. 'I recommend a three-month solitude of study at The Cundelly High Temple, then we get Girvyn to build us an army of soldiers. Hundreds of thousands of them, and we wipe this Crane and his minions off the map.'

Praleck, who had remained quiet up to now, frowned. 'No, that is folly. Even if this boy could create an army, would they be trained, ready to fight, take orders, lead? Military strategy would advise that if a weapon is not yet ready to use you hide it away to continue development and attack with what forces are prepared. Laglen's proposal is sound, and it has the dual purpose of buying Girvyn time to mature and improve as a backup. It is the right strategy to pursue. It's focused and direct, which I like. An elite squad goes into the mountains. They reach the perimeter, scout the threats, remove the defences, and kill the target.'

'I agree,' Sevada said. 'And the Hoppenell men are protected by our armour. We will ride north with you.'

'We know where Crane's stronghold is and can lead you

there,' Maltip said. 'He has been a blight on our Riddon Slopes for over a decade.'

Lord Grisham nodded in agreement. 'Trefgwyn rides with you in this alliance.'

The queen looked at Elaya. 'In the last three days, Elaya, how many soldiers arrived at Rathnell?'

'Across all the delegations, over five hundred, Ma'am. The Barracks' Armour Master has the list of what weapons we took from each clan, including those camped outside the walls, so I cannot say the exact numbers off the top of my head, and whether they are all soldiers.

'We will ride with you,' Donjul said.

'And so will I,' Lady Adara said.

'As will I,' said Jaden.

'I lost over thirty men in the fight with that thing. Rathnell can offer only twenty men, as I need to retain a garrison to protect the keep,' Elaya said. Even with this support though, the numbers were too small. 'We need everyone to agree to this alliance.'

'We could ask the barons for their men,' the queen mused. 'It is what they are there for when I need them. Elaya, I want you with the boy.'

'But, Your Majesty, I need to be by your side.'

'My mind is made up, Elaya. This boy may be our only hope. By protecting him you protect me, protect us all. How can you get him away most safely?'

Elaya was unhappy, but did not question her queen's command. 'Large groups are too easy to track. We will travel fast and light, using woodland paths instead of the open road.'

'Then the Foresters will protect the boy with Elaya,' proclaimed Chieftain Glefforn.

'No!' the voice cut through the rising spirit of positivity.

'We will not pledge our forces to this unholy alliance,' Nark sneered. 'These Dreamers are an abomination that should be washed from our great land.'

'Nor will we offer support, for the same reason,' Jakub hissed.

'Andergine will not join this venture,' Sward said. 'It is folly.'

'Cundelly withholds support for this so-called mission,' Seskin hissed. 'Girvyn should create an army and we send them instead.'

Cargya screamed in frustration. 'This is insane. Your combined numbers make up nearly two-thirds of the five hundred stationed here!' Her glare hardened. 'You four have done nothing but rebut and oppose since you arrived! We need to talk this out!' she continued. 'One voice "For" and one voice "Against" this plan. A chaired, civil discussion in the Privy chamber.'

Stasnier smiled at her. 'It seems our former chair makes an outstanding suggestion. This squabbling must cease.'

'Then I will represent the "For" side,' Praleck declared. Lord Grisham and Sevada expressed their agreement with a brief nod.

Cargya crossed her arms, her voice icy. 'We will take a recess for one hour to allow time for all arguments to be prepared. Who will represent the "Against" side?'

'I am,' Nark hissed.

As the group dispersed, Envoy Nark lingered, turning to face Laglen. 'I have a question. Could we speak briefly before the meeting?'

Laglen's eyebrow arched in curiosity. 'A question, you say, not an accusation? Sure, why not.'

From a distance, Praleck called out, not looking back. 'When you're finished, Nark, I need to speak with him, too.'

Eighteen

Seskin, his face contorted with a blend of rage and desperation, argued, 'I should speak; we need to gain control over the boy. That's the stance we should take.'

'No,' countered Envoy Nark, sharing a look with Envoy Jakub, 'We need to eliminate all these Travellers. Lale and Casper are united on this issue, and together we command a significant portion of the troops they desire. Combined, we offer two hundred soldiers, overshadowing your mere eighty, Seskin. So I am representing the "Against".'

Seskin clenched his fists, feeling the real issue slipping away from them. 'Can't you see? With this boy's power, we have the means to control everyone. Make the plea for authority over him and his power would be ours to share.'

'Purged,' Nark hissed.

'Eradicated,' Jakub agreed. 'All ungodly forms, whether benign or wicked, must be expunged from our land.'

Sward, with a tone of discontent, added, 'I may have only twenty-five men, but I refuse to deploy them on a futile mission. This is a Rathnell scheme, fuelled by these lunatics, to usurp control of our forces. This whole proposal is absurd, resting on the testimony of some tree-hugging girl.'

Jakub frowned at Sward for a long moment. 'I'm taken aback by your zealous stance on this, Sward. By aligning with us, you're opposing Trefgwyn and forfeiting the chance to unite your House with Lord Grisham's.'

Sward responded with a shrug, 'When it comes to choosing between principle and alliance, principle always prevails.'

'Ten minutes,' Cargya's voice rang out and they stopped speaking, glancing at their opponents who were huddled in a corner on the far side of the Privy meeting chamber.

The queen presided over the table, surrounded by the Privy Council members poised for the meeting to start. In a separate corner, the Highlanders and Foresters huddled, engaging in solemn whispers. Elaya and Derrilyn watched these old enemies talk. What was this? Seskin wondered. Some pitiful armistice, born from a joint sense of victimhood. They could destroy each other for all he cared.

Seskin turned back to Nark and Jakub, and in the face of their unified front, he dropped his head.

∼

Hazel waited with bated breath while Maltip digested what Glefforn had said.

'We all have suffered at the hands of this Crane,' he responded, eventually. 'Why does your pain outweigh ours?'

'He destroyed our tribe!' Glefforn hissed, then lowered his voice. 'What do you have but stories of some missing slope lovers.'

'He has wiped away settlements!' He gestured at Hazel. 'And with us, he left no survivors.'

'Your fate is deserved.'

Some of the other Highlanders stiffened.

Maltip remained composed though. 'Then so is yours.'

Glefforn's nose flared. 'Shall we count the losses from when you turned against us?!'

One of the other Highlanders went to move forward, but Maltip held him back. 'Yes, we should.' He took a deep breath. 'The Foresters have suffered one single attack. Crane has tormented us for years. Creatures of the night take our young, burn our camps, remove the dead.'

'That's nothing compared to what we have suffered by your hand. What are you suggesting then? A truce because we now share a common enemy?' Glefforn looked away. 'I have not the authority to decide such an outcome.'

'We are here representing our communities. On this issue, on this mission, we do have the authority!' Hazel pleaded.

'Quiet, child. Let the adults discuss this,' Glefforn said, then returned his bitter stare to Maltip. 'You travel north, and we travel with the boy. And may the trails never meet.'

'Now is not the time to argue over our differences,' Hazel interrupted.

Glefforn waved this away. 'What are you suggesting here, Maltip, The Great Slope Licker?'

Hazel could see Maltip had lost his patience now. 'What I am suggesting,' Maltip hissed, through clenched teeth, 'Is that we have a chance to finally stop this Crane. While you protect this boy, we will slide the killing blade into his heart!'

Both men glared at each other, brows furrowed.

'You're in agreement! You realise that, don't you?' cried Hazel.

'No we're not!' the two shouted in unison.

'You are and you can be,' Hazel pleaded, glancing between them both. She placed a hand on both of their shoulders. 'You argue about our past, but history can be remembered differently. There is a book here that gives an impartial account of what happened between us.'

'A book!?' Glefforn reared towards Hazel. 'I told you to be quiet.'

Cedar, one of the Foresters in Hazel's group, and second in line to Chieftain, gripped Glefforn's wrist and brought him back, his voice slow and even. 'Now is not the time to throw deadwood on our ancient fire, Chieftain. Should we not agree on our position for the debate that is about to take place? The Foresters are with this plan, and so are the Highlanders. We are united with a common enemy and both ride their separate paths to help it succeed. If there is any distrust of what might happen unobserved, we could share one from each clan to go with the other? Indeed, we might even learn of our differences and history.'

'Yes,' Hazel said. 'We put aside our grievances for the duration of this crisis, to hear each other's accusations.'

'I am not doing that,' Glefforn rounded on Cedar. 'Who would submit to travelling alone amongst…'

'I will,' Cedar said. 'To represent the Foresters on this mission north and to hear the Highlanders' list of injustices.'

'Their list?!'

'Then I will send my son, Rowen, to ride with you and the boy,' Maltip said.

'Father, no! I don't agree to ride with them. After what they did to us…'

'That is why it should be you, Son. You know my stories but can tell them without the bitterness of first-hand memory.'

'My second-hand memory rages as fierce as yours.'

'Please, Rowen, do it,' Hazel asked. 'Only our generation can help our sides find peace.'

'One minute,' Cargya called across.

The two groups faced each other in sudden silence.

Then, finally, Rowen reluctantly nodded.

~

Elaya followed everyone into the Privy Council's meeting room, her scan moving slowly from one delegate to the next, assessing their motivations. There was heightened stress everywhere, shooting streaks of red and orange.

Cargya looked at the queen and then Stasnier, waiting for their slight nods, before speaking. 'We are here to discuss the plan to march to Crane's stronghold and end this. One person speaks from each side, and only in turn. Shall we place a strict hour on this deliberation?'

Nark and Praleck murmured their agreement.

Cargya looked at Stasnier. 'As presiding chair, would you like to oversee this?'

'This was your most excellent idea, Cargya, and as former chair of the Privy Council you are more than qualified to do this. Plus, I don't think my voice will cut across the rancorous squabbling like yours can.'

There were a few chuckles at this.

'What are the terms of this debate?' Praleck asked.

Nark sneered. 'Debate? I think not.'

Praleck went to speak, when Cargya cut across him. 'We will hear the "For" and then the "Against". The listening party may ask questions or reply to an argument, but must signal to request this, and do so on agreement from me. Then we consider the arguments at the end, and vote.'

'And if we remain divided,' Praleck asked, 'who makes the final decision?'

'Unilateral treaty.' Cargya said, her voice sharp. 'We all

must be in agreement. All sides that are providing troops, including the delegates not speaking, must agree. As it stands only Sward, Seskin, Jakub and Nark hold dissenting views of this plan. Our aim in this hour must be to find agreement.'

'Then why even waste that much time?' Jakub retorted, 'As Casper will not agree to this folly.'

'Neither will Andergine,' Sward added.

'You will not speak during this process until it ends,' Cargya replied tersely. 'If you cannot restrain your voice, you will be removed. Praleck, please begin.'

Praleck considered them all, and then returned his gaze to Cargya. 'Let me explain why I vote for this mission. We are all here because we have suffered profound evil. Up until now we have dealt with this in isolation and not known the culprit. The evil that we confront is not just an external threat, but a test of our collective resolve and humanity. These demons tear at the fabric of our communities. Their threat requires us to come together, not as isolated individuals, but as a cohesive force for good. This battle is not solely for the sake of those of us that remain, but is also for the ones we've lost. Our very survival might hinge on this unity. Therefore, I implore everyone to look beyond individual differences and to see the commonality of our shared human experience. It is only with a united front that we can overcome the darkness that threatens to engulf us.'

Nark raised his hand and waited for a signal to speak. 'I agree with you there. Just not on your single target.'

Praleck ignored him. 'Combined we have five hundred men. If you choose to not march, do the rest of us march alone? In just a seven-day ride to the mountains, we can rid this land of this horror.'

Praleck leaned forward. 'All of you know of the stories we

heard growing up, of creatures of the night that sleep during the day, protected by the hounds of darkness. *This* is not made up. We have heard what they did to Hazel's tribe. It won't be easy.'

Donjul interrupted. 'Fought them and seen them we have,' Alwad interpreted. Donjul continued vehemently, his face as course as the sands he came from. 'We must fight in the sun. In the night, they will prevail.'

'Why do they get to drone on in such detail about this lunacy?' Sward complained. 'This is unfair.'

'In order for you to agree or reject the plan, you must first hear it!' Cargya said sternly.

Sward dropped back heavily in his chair, then gave a small nod.

Cargya continued. 'Nark is representing your arguments against this mission, Sward. It is his choice to voice them or not.'

Sward glanced at Nark, who didn't meet his gaze.

'We get to this stronghold, get into position,' Praleck continued. 'Wait for the signal from the Dream Travellers that Crane is there, then kill him while he sleeps. The boy remains safe, in hiding. Training.'

Lord Grisham smiled in approval.

Seskin muttered in complaint.

The queen raised her finger. 'On that topic, after this creature attacked Girvyn, we sent messages by bird to estates in my queendom and my other family related holdings, warning them to close their keeps. One such message has already prompted a return from the Leverstock estate. It has all the criteria for a safe training place that you requested, Elaya.'

Elaya inclined her head slightly.

Stasnier raised his hand. 'Your Majesty, may I propose

twenty gold pieces to Leverstock as a token for their secrecy and hospitality in hosting our small gathering?'

'Agreed,' Amelia replied. 'See to it the treasurer releases this commission.'

Nark motioned to speak and Cargya agreed. He laughed. 'You all make it sound we have accepted both the plan of attack and the one for the boy, but we haven't.'

'I didn't hear a question. Praleck, please continue.'

'I questioned the boy's uncle more about their abilities in preparation for this discussion. If these Travellers can indeed communicate in sleep, from different places, then this could be a good military thing to do. Scouts could go forward with one of these Travellers, and the other one stays in camp with the rest of the army waiting for updates as we go. This will make our journey faster.'

'I see the military value of instant communication!' Stasnier said, then apologised for interrupting. 'I am just saying,' he sent the queen an imploring look, 'Rathnell should be the base of command. One of them should remain with us and relay instructions from here.'

Elaya raised her hand to speak. 'Stasnier, you are a politician not a military strategist, and all the military tacticians will be on this mission. No, it makes sense to send both to the north. One only needs to cross, but if they die or are knocked out we have a backup who can carry the message from Laglen's team that Crane is in the Realm and can be attacked in his sleep.'

Nark gestured to speak. 'This is ridiculous. Where is the chain of command? Who leads this proposed group? Do you plan that those who provide more than half the men be muzzled and usurped?'

'No. We assign a war council to draw up an attack plan

during the journey,' Praleck answered. 'I suggest that Adara and Jaden are on that committee. The two Dream Travellers that Laglen has told me about, Dremell and Nadine, should be on it too. Alongside them, one commanding officer from each community.'

Lord Grisham nodded in approval.

'What if there is resistance at his stronghold?' Hazel said.

Glefforn's furious glare swung to Hazel. 'You speak when you have not been given permission, child!'

'Ah at last, the Forester girl sees folly in this plan,' Sward muttered.

'She is the only one here who speaks when she wants to,' Amelia told Glefforn, her voice frail but the words shut him up. 'This young woman alone has faced the enemy we discuss. She has been through a lot. Far more than you, Chieftain Glefforn. She dared to stand up and tell her story when others mocked her and most did not believe her. I admire a woman with the resilience to stand up for what she believes in and who has strength in her voice among the company of men. So, she can speak.' She turned to Hazel. 'Tell us, Hazel.'

'I have seen what these demons can do. They are not like normal soldiers.'

'We will have five hundred strong, trained, battle-ready soldiers,' Praleck told her. 'And a hundred and fifty in Hoppenell armour. We will have the advantage of surprise.' He offered Hazel a thin smile. 'I mean this respectfully: you were a tribe with some lookouts, fighting with knives and arrows in the dark.'

Jaden raised his hand to speak. 'I have received word from the Druid Guild in Cundelly that the Guild can offer fifty druids to march with you, if this alliance goes ahead.'

There was a murmur of excitement at this.

Nark spat. 'The druids offer makes no difference. We fight a bigger evil than one person.'

Cargya glared at Nark, while her words were directed at Praleck. 'Is the "For" concluded, Praleck?'

Praleck glanced around at his comrades' faces, then said, 'We are done.'

'Envoy Nark. The table is yours.'

Nark cleared his throat. 'About time. This boy is an abomination!'

There was a sudden commotion and Cargya called for quiet. 'Let him speak.'

Nark's nose flared. 'You revel in this battle committee to kill one man…pah! When he is merely a minion of a greater threat that faces us. First, we should identify them, and then we stage a land-wide hunt. How do we find these Travellers? They sleep among us! They could be our wife, our friend, our colleague. The devil grows and worms in plain sight, and this Crane is just the tip of it!'

Praleck raised his hand. 'Envoy Nark, we appreciate your theological wisdom as a man of the cloth, but this is a state and military crisis which we must hold front and centre before we bring to bear any other forebodings, religious or otherwise.'

'Lale chose to send me, and we are a religious state. And so is Casper, who I also represent at this moment. Are we the only ones here that question the origins of their power? Only God has such power.'

Adara, who had remained quiet up to now, raised her hand to speak. 'I call for tolerance, not persecution, Envoy Nark.'

'I saw a door to some other place, as did all of you.' Nark growled. 'No mortal man should have such power. You want facts rather than prayer; well, consider that this Realm was the origin of the abominable attacks by demons that brought us all together here. Why, even the boy brought here a fusion monster. I tell you that this is the devil's work, and only evil will come from this. Realm, hell – they even sound alike! God teaches us to be vigilant for such gambits of his immortal foe, and to be ruthless in our caring for the world when such rise up like brambles in the cornfield. So yes, we are right to hunt down this Crane, but as part of cleansing all these Travellers. God is all-loving, all-knowing and would not give such power to His subjects. This must be the work of the devil.'

Lady Adara sat forward, her voice scathing. 'What are you suggesting? Lynch mobs, public executions? I have heard these arguments used before against the druids. You seem to agree on the need to concentrate on stopping Crane, so why not focus only on that?'

Donjul, who was listening via his whispering interpreter, began ranting. Alwad hurried to keep up. 'You call yourself a man of faith?' Donjul was glaring at Nark. 'Faith is belief without proof. This boy is more of a god than the God you worship. At least you can have a conversation with him.'

Nark lurched up. 'I have a conversation with God every day!'

'Be seated!' Cargya said swiftly. She glared around the room. 'No one speaks unless I say so. We have allowed the "For" to speak. Now it's Nark's turn.'

Nark lifted his chin, seething. 'Only Crane and this boy have this power. This is catastrophic and beyond comprehension – do we all agree?'

Stasnier shook his head at Nark. 'May I speak?' he asked Cargya.

'You may,' she said.

'If we can't stop Crane on his mountain, Girvyn is a key weapon in our fight against him.'

'You would say that, he is your property.' Nark lifted a fist. 'But what happens when he isn't? What happens when he decides to be his own property? None of us can stop him. Before he is trained, we must strike him down. And anyone else that crosses to this Realm place, thereby preventing any more of these devil spawn from gaining this sinful power.'

Elaya felt her blood boil. As she listened to Nark she felt their strategy slipping away. No consensus would be reached, neither on this matter nor any other. Though executing their plan with two hundred men was feasible, doubts lingered, especially considering Hazel's input. They had the advantage of surprise, and the extent of Crane's defences during his "sleep" remained unknown. Yet, the question of division persisted; why take the risk of proceeding with less than half the potential combined force?

Derrilyn was gazing at her intently, waiting silently by the door, waiting for her signal. She sent the nod, and he stepped outside. People stood, voices rose, Cargya fought to contain them. Anger flared, faces animated with fervent pledges and accusations. People looked at Elaya, frowning at her, willing her to intervene as tempers frayed. Nark stood up and Praleck followed, stabbing accusing fingers at one another. But she stayed oddly silent and waited.

Derrilyn came back through the door, and passed her a heavy sack. She leapt onto the Privy Council table, surprising everyone, and tipped out the severed head of the red-armoured giant, its hideousness now visible beneath the open visor of its helmet.

Its evil sat greater than any artist could have imagined: slimy, wormy skin, unfathomable black eyes, and a flat, black triangle-shaped nose.

'What in night's name?!' Jakub retched, looking away,

'It's vile!' proclaimed Sward.

'Look at each other!' Elaya commanded, stunning them all into silence. 'Maltip and Glefforn, you could pass as brothers. Seskin, would you attract a single stare if you visited Rathnell's market? Even Donjul or I do not seem out of place in this city. Nark, for all that not everyone worships as you would like, would you label your fellow man ungodly? Even those whose minds drift someplace else as they sleep? THIS is ungodly. This is hell on earth. Look upon this head, upon the destruction it wrought before thirty of my men died killing it. Does it not shine a light on the smallness of our differences? As Queen's Protector, I urge Her Majesty to declare that Rathnell stands against this and will fight it. Stasnier, does the Privy Council do likewise?'

Stasnier hesitated, as if tempted to try and modify Elaya's point or add a caveat as usual, but he did neither. 'Yes. This abomination must be fought.'

'I am with you,' Sward declared his loyalty.

'I am with you,' Seskin affirmed, his face twisted in a nauseated expression.

All gazes shifted to Nark and Jakub.

'Casper is with you,' Jakub announced turning his face away from the helmet so his eyes didn't see it one last time.

Praleck extended his hand across the table towards Nark, who grasped it firmly and shook it.

'Lale is with you!'

A wave of cheers filled the room as each person voiced their support.

'Five hundred men with the best specialists from the world will set out from Rathnell!' Praleck proclaimed, his smile broad.

'Then we march to victory, to cleanse this land of its scourge,' Nark agreed with a nod.

While everyone was transfixed on each other, smiling, congratulating, cheering their invincibility, Elaya noticed Sevada was preoccupied with the monster's helmet, his expression troubled. Overcoming revulsion, he picked it up for a moment and turned it over in his hands, examining the edging, the sheen on the thin plates. With a flick of his finger against the plate, he paused, listening to the metal's tone.

'Everything alright, Sevada?' Elaya asked.

Sevada looked up. 'Yes, sorry.' He put it down. 'Hoppenell is with you.'

∼

As the delegates rose to leave, Derrilyn came beside her, his youthful face full of concern. 'It's happening then?'

'I want to leave in the next couple of hours, so send someone to give word to Laglen to prepare. They may need a guard to collect more clothing from their home.'

Derrilyn nodded and left. When he came back their eyes locked, and Elaya gave him a deliberate look. 'I want my best on this mission.'

'What? Me, go north? But I'm not trained yet. My place is by your side.'

'Your place is where it most aids queen and country. And that is on the mountain mission. I need the eyes and ears of someone I can trust. Join the attack committee with the others and offer a balanced counsel like you can. I see that in you.'

'What about the Chattara if it arrives?'

'I promise you I will be by your side when it comes. You

will be back in two weeks. You have Lady Adara there if you need some druid wisdom.'

Derrilyn went to object again but closed his mouth. 'Okay,' He fell quiet. 'Elaya, but might I give you a bit of counsel?'

They walked together along the castle corridor. 'Yes, what is it?'

'When was the last time you left the city?'

'I don't know, maybe... why?'

He stopped and faced her. 'I don't mean this disrespectfully, but I've known you five years, and you haven't left the city walls.'

'So?'

'So, a journey like this, even three days, needs expertise.'

Elaya laughed incredulously. 'Are you saying I am not equipped for a trip?'

'I'm not saying that. You have told me stories of trips to Cundelly on royal visits, but how many have not been on the North Road in a long procession, escorting the queen protected by garrisons of men?'

Elaya scoffed. 'I can lead them through the woods.'

'Do you know how to track? Do you know how to hide tracks? Finding game along the way, fine, but what happens if there isn't any?'

'It's a three-day ride.'

'I lived in the wild for six years before I ended up here. Hiding from raiders and bandits every day. It takes a certain skill to...'

'Derrilyn, I must be with Girvyn and therefore you must be with the attack group. Perhaps you have a point about the suitability of my skills for this journey, but then what do you suggest?'

'You need a ranger...'

'What? No, I don't. Anyway, our best rangers will be needed in the other mission.'

'I'm not talking about someone who can just scout, scope out the space in front. We can all do that. They are not true rangers. It's a dying art, and most who have it want to remain hidden. You won't find them if you go looking for them. Unless, that is, you're prepared to buy those skills, which is why you should go to the east district.'

'Mercenaries?'

Derrilyn gave her an awkward look. 'The best ones are for hire. It's always been that way.'

'I will use my druid deduction. I can spot a change in the air, the land. I can work it out.'

'I know you can, but you can't do it all and be right by Girvyn's side to protect him at the same time.'

'If I needed anyone's help it certainly wouldn't be a ranger for hire. They can't be trusted.'

They came out of a castle door, and stood in a courtyard.

'It's not about trust, Elaya. I have never given you any advice before, ever. You should consider it. You must avoid the open road. A ranger can lead the group through the rough. Once you hit the first woodland strip, a few miles from Rathnell, it leads for twenty miles under cover. Elaya, you assure me you can act as a ranger, and I believe you, but tell me what is the ranger's role? To scout front and back, read tracks and hide our own. To see both what waits ahead and what follows behind. To know the land when you do not. And can you do this while also staying touching distance from Girvyn to guard him should Crane's portal appear from thin air and one of these demons come at you?'

'Oh.' Elaya blushed. 'You demonstrate well why I have such certainty in you, Derrilyn.'

'Would that we had more than one of you, Elaya. But we

do not, and the ranger performs the lesser role here. You must, therefore, find one, and the best is only for hire.'

They walked in uneasy silence for the next few minutes. Before getting to the barracks, Elaya stopped and gazed across the city towards the east.

'Okay,' she said. 'We will look and see. But if I don't like what we find, you drop it, okay?'

Derrilyn hid his smile and motioned her eastwards.

Nineteen

Elaya let Derrilyn push open the tavern door and she followed him, eyes glancing around, seeing a mix of troublemakers, louts, retired soldiers, and an assortment of unsavoury individuals. The scent of ale rose up to meet them while the sticky floor tried to wrench their steps.

She shook her head. 'This is a bad idea.'

'Let's start over there,' Derrilyn pointed to a group of men at a table in the corner. Elaya recognised one of them, a mean-looking man who had been in the courts once or twice for stealing.

The man stood up, hand on his sword. 'What do you two want?'

'Sit down. We're not here for trouble,' Derrilyn said.

He sat, though Derrilyn remained standing. He cast his gaze across the other men, all watching, waiting. 'Hands on table,' Derrilyn said.

They complied.

The first man snarled up at them. 'What are you here for then?'

'This is pointless; I told you this was a waste of time.' Elaya turned to go.

'We are looking for a hire,' Derrilyn said. 'A tracker, ranger. Someone who can...'

The man laughed. 'Is Queen's Protector getting too old? Lost your way to the sands?' He snarled. 'I will do it. It's sixty pieces, there and back.'

Elaya raised an eyebrow. 'You wouldn't know your arse from your elbow.'

The man stood up again, and Elaya pushed him back down, making a chair alongside him topple. The room fell silent. Fearing a bar fight, the barman began clearing empty glasses from the counter.

A second man at the table, pointed a finger. 'Ander can do it.'

Ander. She recognised the name. She followed the direction of the finger and saw a well-built, man, elbows on the table. Elaya shook her head. 'True, he might, but I am not working with him.'

'That was over two years ago,' Derrilyn replied.

'It doesn't matter; he can't take orders.'

The man pointed another finger, this time to the opposite side of the room. 'Well, if the Queen's Protector has the queen's treasury behind her you can always try Maude, if she's available and will hear you out. She's the best here, but she knows it and charges for the privilege.'

Maude was watching them. She sat alone, back against the wall, in a black cloak, hood drawn, but not too far forward to hide her shoulder-length brown hair sticking out the cowl like spider legs.

Elaya and Derrilyn came forward. As they approached where she sat Maude's feet snaked out and pulled the two free chairs firmly under the table. 'Speaking to you could harm my future commissions. I don't want anyone thinking I'm a spy, so make this quick, and you'd better make it damned good.'

Derrilyn went to speak. 'This is Elay...'

'Do you take me for an imbecile? I know who she is.' She rolled her eyes. 'This is too painful. Just sit and get on with it,' she said, then pushed the chairs towards them.

They sat. 'We need a ranger, a proper tracker,' Derrilyn continued. 'Not some novice.'

Elaya studied her. Her aura was composed. While the others in the room projected a mix of fear, anger, and distrust, hers was hard to read. There was something druid-like about it, but she wasn't one. Derrilyn eyed Elaya, then Maude. Elaya could tell he had sensed the same thing and was weighing her up.

'What's the cargo?

'People.'

'How many?'

'I can't say.'

'Ten, twenty, a hundred? How many people?'

'Somewhere between the first and second number.'

'Where are you going?'

Elaya shook her head. 'If you take the job, then all will be revealed. But after...'

'How can I agree to something I don't know anything about?'

'It's a month's work. You will get the details if you sign.'

'Sign?'

'Yes, sign. It's a royal directive.'

'Are you going?'

'I am,' Elaya said. She felt something. Surprise, was it? Excitement?

'You won't get scrambled eggs in the morning, but I will

get you and everyone else wherever we're going in one piece. But you do what I tell you.'

'I only take orders from the queen,' Elaya said.

'Forget it then. I am not going.'

That steely, collected aura again. She meant it. 'It depends on what the orders are,' Elaya said grudgingly.

Maude ground her jaw. 'How about we call it advice. But I expect my advice to be followed.'

Elaya eyed her, then gave a single nod. Next to her Derrilyn released an explosive breath laden with tension.

Maude smiled, the line of her perfect teeth catching the light below her hood. 'The legendary Elaya Faith walks in here looking for a tracker. Clearly this is dangerous, or so important that you don't think you can handle this on your own. Which surprises me, to be honest. And I can see you don't want to be in here. You must be desperate.'

'It's time-sensitive.'

'How time-sensitive?'

'We leave in three hours.'

Maude sat forward, an eyebrow hiked. 'So, no time for planning a route, little time to prepare supplies. No knowledge of what this expedition is about. You'll definitely have to listen to my advice.'

Elaya rolled her eyes. 'I can do that.'

Maude sat back and folded her arms. 'Be aware that I only care about your mission to the extent of earning my payment. And about staying alive. And a dead woman can't spend her money, now, can she?'

'I will ensure you get paid. How much?'

'One hundred gold pieces. And it if goes over a month, even by a day, it's two hundred.'

Elaya scoffed. 'That's a five-year salary, even for those that frequent the courts. Don't you have even a shred of honour, or loyalty to your crown?'

Maude's eyes blazed. 'Like you, you mean? With your abilities you could have been the richest woman in Rathnell, truly free and in control of your own life. Instead, you sleep in the barracks, own no house nor land, and do the bidding of someone whose greatest talent was being born into a title. Don't make the mistake of thinking I aspire to be just like you, Elaya Faith. I despise your kind as much as you despise mine.'

'You're disgusting,' Elaya seethed.

Maude shrugged. 'No, disgusting is the serrated blade the one-eyed man at that table to your right has hidden up his sleeve. Disgusting is also the open sewer that runs down Torbald Lane, which I can still smell on the both of you. Before that you took the castle thoroughfare to get to this quarter of town; the lime from it cakes your boots almost as much as that horse manure. But that's not from a street, so you rushed here directly from the royal stables, where whatever group you wish me to protect is already assembling. Supply and demand, Elaya; if you want to haggle about the price don't let anyone see how desperate you are.'

Elaya glared at her, then looked around the room before turning back. The room was noisy again. Gangsters, thugs and ex-royal guards. Not one batting an eyelid at them anymore. Maude was the best in here. Elaya admired her demeanour, which said something more than the bravado display she had seen from everyone else.

One last time, Elaya wondered if she could do this on her own. She seldom relied on the help of others, especially that of anyone outside her team. And a mercenary of all things. They were the lowest of the low.

Having the Foresters there was helpful, but Hazel seemed

the only sane one among them; and now they had this Rowen, the Highlander son of Maltip, with them, that would probably flare up more fires, which she would need to fight throughout the trip. And Derrilyn was right that she couldn't be both a ranger and next to Girvyn at all times. His safety was paramount.

'Are you going to just stare at me? Time is not on your side. If you want to delay the decision, my fee goes up another 20% for the inconvenience. Less prep time, more risk, more danger.'

Elaya blinked. 'I accept your price, but you don't involve yourself with the group. Nor question them, or ask what we are doing.'

'I don't care about your group. My product is my skills. Whether it's royalty, prisoners, or a cart of scrolls we are travelling with, I don't care. So, how many people?'

Elaya estimated the risk of giving her more information before the queen approved the fee. Girvyn was the most important subject that the crown had ever owned. She could smell everyone's greed like it was off milk. It stank out the stables; the possibilities of what riches Girvyn could bring through the portal. Elaya was sure Stasnier and Berenger were already drawing up a list of wants with the queen.

She heard Stasnier's slimy voice creep around her mind: so what if it cost one hundred gold pieces to ensure some protection? Girvyn could pay for it himself with one hundred gold pieces brought to the queen by a mere thought. They just needed to invest in him while he trained.

This would get agreed upon, so telling Maude the information to do her job now was prudent.

'There are nine of us. Five Foresters and one Highlander, heading to the Leverstock Estate.'

Maude pursed her lips in thought. 'Ten horses and one

pack horse then, and we go at its pace. It's about safety. And if we need to, we leave the packs and have the speed.'

'Agreed.'

'There's a storm coming from the east; bring hessian sheets for night-time to keep the rain off us. Also, make sure everyone eats well before we leave.'

'Very well. Although we would save time by eating as we travel.'

'No. Don't bring food; it will weigh us down and leaves a scent. I can find food on the way.'

Elaya nodded, a hint of apology in it. 'Anything else?' Begrudgingly, she saw Derrilyn's point, and just how useful Maude would be. She hadn't seen these things.

'Flints.'

'I've got flints.'

'We need a quiver pack per person.'

'We are travelling with Foresters; they have lots of arrows. Is that it?'

'I need ropes.'

'How many? How long?' Elaya asked.

'Stand, would you?'

Raising an eyebrow, Elaya complied.

Maude's gaze moved slowly up and down her body. 'Twice your height, three rolls. Do you have any traps in the barracks?'

'Game traps? No.'

'Fine, I will bring mine. Always useful if we need to set an ambush or slow any trackers on our tail.'

'Anything else?'

'Yes, I want a signed guarantee of payment from the queen. Give it to me at the front gate. My money would slow me down, so I will collect it on return to the city.' Maude stood up. 'See you in three hours.'

'Make it two and a half,' said Elaya, trying to gain some authority back. 'Main gates.'

Outside, Derrilyn seemed to be fighting back a smile. 'She seems thorough.'

'Get the supplies Maude asked for,' Elaya replied, not looking at him. 'The hessian sheets and flints are in the barracks. Tell the Foresters and Rowen we are leaving in three hours.'

'You told Maude two and a half.'

Elaya growled. 'She can wait at the gate. Brief the stable boys to prepare the horses. Tell the rest of my group to meet at the stables where Girvyn is. I am going to the queen to get a signed declaration. Then I want you to wait at the gate to welcome these Dream Travellers. They may need to eat and resupply before you leave. See to it, will you?'

'Consider it done.'

Elaya started to move away, then stopped so they could embrace. 'Be safe,' she said.

Derrilyn's face betrayed heavy thoughts. 'Be safe too, Elaya. I'll see you at the gates before you leave.'

Twenty

The door to the stable corridor closed, and Leon stepped in front of it, arms folded, in a no-nonsense, don't bother me, sort of communication. The other three men on guard duty with him sniggered and took a more relaxed attitude – blowing into hands and chatting amongst themselves. Leon knew that they teased him for his conscientiousness. Elaya had taught them all well. They were the best in their rank and had survived the druid monster attack by sheer will and strength. Leon just took a serious approach to everything he did. That made him dependable, but sometimes unpopular.

The stable door opened, then Girvyn's face crept into the gap.

'Stay back, Girvyn,' Leon said, softening his voice. 'What is it this time?' They had been running errands all afternoon for clothing, books, and other pointless possessions Girvyn kept asking for. Enough was enough.

'We have run out of water and need our pails for the trip. Can you get those as well, please? They are in a leather cover on the kitchen top shelf.'

'I'm not sure Elaya would want us making another trip. She will have thought of everything. If you are missing something, it's because you don't need it.'

'Just one more, please.' Girvyn said and went back inside.

Leon sighed and looked at his colleagues. 'One more trip to their home,' Leon said to them. 'You have the door.'

One of the other guard's cracked a twitching smile. 'We have the door, Leon. Don't you worry about it.'

They laughed.

Leon shook his head at them and left.

For the third time that day, Leon approached the hut, keeping an eye on the windows, listening to the rustle of the wind through the trees. Taking in as much detail as he could, just as Elaya had taught him.

The front step creaked as he stepped on it, as he knew it would. He reached forward, swung the door open, and stepped in, dagger in hand.

The hut felt cold. Furniture was upturned, drawers pulled out, their contents scattered across the floor. They had taken some of Girvyn's clothing to the north tower as a decoy scent, in case another monster came back, but nothing else had changed since the last time he was here.

He went to the kitchen, searched the top shelf, found the water pails and stuffed them in his rucksack. He shut the front door behind him, waited on the step, listening, looking into the trees, studying the shadows, making sure he was not being watched, then he made his way back to the stables. He took the long route, which Elaya had specified to shake off any spies. First going into the bailey, the barracks, an enclosed private quad, then across the west courtyard, through two adjoining enclosures and out by the south stables.

As he arrived at the stable door, he froze.

He felt a rush of blood and a surge of panic, and almost raised the alarm there and then. But the thought struck him: this is what they wanted him to do, to make a scene and embarrass himself. It was unprofessional of them to abandon their post, but barracks humour was never far from their interactions with him.

Assuming they were inside, Leon crept up to the stable door, expecting his co-workers would pounce on him if he rushed in.

He set his ear to the door and caught his breath. The voices from within were not familiar. He heard the rasp of a sword being drawn.

'No going back now, is there,' someone muttered.

'Remember the money. When we get it done, we will never need to work again.'

There was a pause and the sound of someone being dragged across the floor.

'We take the boy alive.'

'What about the old man?'

'No one dies, that was the order.'

'It's a bit late for that,' another voice mumbled.

'I'm not talking about the guards. I mean the targets. Just knock the old man out, like you did the boy.'

There was a muffled noise of protest and a thud.

'The boy is coming awake!' came another harsh voice.

'Then hit him. We all heard what this boy can do if he wakes up. We just deliver him to the customer, then we retire. In a few hours, this will be all over.'

Leon carefully drew his sword, heart hammering in his ears. He could blow his whistle. Go and get help. But waiting for others to come would waste vital time.

He kicked open the door and charged in. For a moment,

he was enveloped in darkness and dust, assaulted by the thick smell of hay and manure. Leon searched frantically, his eyes darting in all directions as he sought out the attackers. He spotted Girvyn's unconscious body and Laglen, tethered and gagged on the floor.

Leon felt and saw the attackers at the same moment. To his left side, the pen door squeaked open, a shape moved, then a glint of metal flashed below his nose. He went to speak but blood bubbled in his mouth, he touched his neck, felt a gaping wound, warm liquid oozing down his throat. Then everything faded to black.

∼

Twenty minutes later, Elaya arrived at the stable door and found the entrance unguarded. Hackles raised, she scanned beyond the door with her druid senses then kicked it open. The interior was shadowy and the air stuffy. No sound came from the pens, as all the horses had been moved to the north stables to avoid the staff finding Girvyn's hiding place.

'Laglen? Girvyn?' she called.

She scanned again, eyes moving from shadow to shadow.

Nothing came back; but then her druid senses didn't reach infinity. It always helped to have a focus and proximity. One, two, three. The seconds passed. Then she sensed something: an emotion. Fear. She hurried towards the back; sword drawn.

'Laglen? Girvyn?' she called again.

She heard a noise: a moan, a whimper. At the far side of the wall, hidden behind a pile of hay blocks, she caught a form of orange. She sensed a familiar character in it. That distinct signature and tone: Laglen.

Laglen's arms were tied and upstretched, hooked over a

wall spike. Elaya untied the tether, freed his arms then the gag. He had bruising to the cheek, but his distress engulfed her rather than any feeling of injury.

'They came in. Took Girvyn. They knew we were here,' he gasped.

'When did this happen?'

'I don't know how long I was out of it. I just came round.'

'I know your head will be heavy, but try and think, Lag! Collect your thoughts.'

Laglen stared unblinking. 'There was a fight.' He pointed at a pen door.

Elaya found nine dead men. Four of them were her guards.

Laglen's voice trembled. 'The blond lad who'd gone back to our house, he had no chance. He came into the stables and was ambushed.'

Elaya paused in disbelief. 'That would be Leon, he was a meticulous young man,' her voice was heavy. 'They all were loyal and valiant men.' Elaya scanned the carnage, taking in the wounds, reading their final moments. How many attackers were left?'

Laglen's lips trembled. 'Five.'

'So three killed five from ten in the melee. I will tell their families how courageous they were. Was there anything the kidnappers said? Anything they did that might help me understand this better?'

'They were dressed as soldiers, and had an order not to kill.'

'Have you seen these men before?'

'No. But I am not like you, I don't notice what you see. They knocked Girvyn out straight away, so he couldn't use the portal. They knew about his power.'

Elaya cursed. 'It's not Crane. This is something else.'

'How do you know that?' Laglen exclaimed. 'We know Crane wants Girvyn!'

'Calm down, Lag,' she said, her gaze searching this way and that. She worked her jaw while she thought. 'These men were for hire.'

'Then Crane could have hired them!'

'What, attack using a demon, then he goes into the east district to put on a bounty?'

'Crane could be working with an intermediary?'

'Yes, he might. But this attack was specifically directed at the stables. Only the delegates knew Girvyn was here. They've all suffered at the hands of Crane's attacks, so why would any of them support him? No, this is something else, another play. Right now, I need to track Girvyn down. When I catch them, I will find out more.'

'How will you find him?' Laglen's voice was filled with regret. 'Please find him.'

She patted his shoulder. 'You know I will. I know where to go. You don't kidnap the most powerful person known to man and then hide out, even in the east district. They have left the city. They must be moving in a carriage or something, because they can't pass the gates with an unconscious boy tied to a horse.' She sighed. 'Laglen, it is safe for you to leave the stables. Go to the gate, find the others – Chieftain Glefforn and his men, Hazel, Highlander Rowen – and tell them what has happened. We have a ranger arriving first named Maude. Tell her to wait at the main gates for news. Get word to the queen.'

'Be careful.'

They embraced, then Elaya parted.

'What the hell will the kidnappers do when Girvyn wakes up?' Laglen called after her.

Elaya heard Laglen's question but was already untying her

horse from the line outside the stables. The horse reared onto its hind legs, then was gone in a cloud of dust and galloping hooves.

Her senses pushed ahead. Glancing at walkers in the coppice. Sharp over the wind in her face, the sound of the rattling saddle and pounding hooves. Picking out every person she passed, scanning their tone and mood. The city walls came into view.

Derrilyn was at the main gate, guards and gate watchmen looking on.

'What is it, Elaya?' Derrilyn cried.

'Girvyn has been abducted! Who has passed through in the last thirty minutes?'

'Merchants, lords, a few people,' Derrilyn's expression strained. 'I don't know.'

Elaya's gaze flashed to the North Road, where a few lone travellers and small groups of riders were moving away from the city.

Derrilyn's eyes widened. 'An apple cart passed through not long ago. Five men went with it.'

'Five men escorting fruit! You didn't think that was odd? Think about what I have taught you.'

'I scanned them,' he said defensively. 'All were boisterous in their self-belief. That's all that came through to me.' Derrilyn blushed, and Elaya could see he felt chastened for not stopping the cart.

'It's fine. Girvyn was unconscious. You were not to know.'

'I'm coming with you!' Derrilyn announced, calling for a horse.

Elaya heeled her horse, which sprang into a gallop, leaving the shouts of gate guards lost in the sound of hammering hooves.

She pushed forward, her senses attuned to the space in

front of her. Her mind whirled with thoughts of past, present, and future. What could she have done differently to protect Girvyn? She had left four of her best men in front of the stable door. She hadn't wanted to make a show of force, so had kept the detail small. Had that been a mistake? She could have kept Girvyn in the barracks, or the north tower protected by twenty men. But she had seen what that druid monster had done and had opted for an agile, subtle hideout, concealing Girvyn's scent. If Crane knew Girvyn was in the stables, he would have sent in more demons, or just portal jumped in.

Only her loyal team and the delegates – around thirty people - knew Girvyn was in there, and she was certain not one would be in league with Crane.

This felt desperate and reactive, a hurried and ill-thought through plan. Laglen had been right to fret about what the kidnappers might do if Girvyn woke up. Given the chance, wouldn't he just portal back to the stables? So would they knock him out again? Would they just kill him if he was too much to handle? Was it an all-or-nothing strategy? If the person behind this couldn't have Girvyn for themselves, would no one have him? The possibilities flashed across her mind. Yet her determination and certainty endured.

She continued, encouraging the horse with repeated nudges of its flanks. On either side of the road the trees flashed past her vision. For a moment she wondered if she should take more account of the bankside; look for an opening or the tracks of a cart leading into the bush. But her instinct told her to keep going; the attackers would be slower if they went off road, and their priority would be to get as far away from the city as possible.

She stopped and reined up to listen to the wild. Her heart pounded in her ears. The horse shifted agitatedly. Excess energy peeled off it. Birds flew southwards, towards the keep. In the distance behind her, she heard the faint sound of hooves and looked back and saw Derrilyn.

'Yah!' With a sharp kick of her heels, she urged the horse forward at a gallop. It obliged.

She raced along the North Road for the next five minutes, leaning into the horse's neck to lower the wind resistance. Despite this, the wind blinded her vision, forcing her to turn her face sideways to clear the tears. More trees flashed by in the periphery of her sight. She kept pushing the horse as hard as she could. She felt in tune with it, so knew what it was capable of. She could feel its powerful body beneath her, the rhythm of its gallop neither weakening nor relenting.

She reached the opening of a valley, where a vale of green and red hills rose left and right of the road. Salt Lake River glistened off to one side, snaking leftwards into a hazy horizon. She paused, letting her eyes follow the contour of the vale: the road, the river, the hills and sky. And there, below a wedge of flying geese, was a dust trail from riders.

For the next few minutes, she gained on them. Four riders around the cart, which left one man riding it.

They noticed her, and the cart sped up, bouncing and pitching, while the other men faced her. Their warning auras began flaring: spikes of fear and strength.

The riders stopped, spreading across the road to block her path. She came closer, picked out individuals, detected minor signs of emotions. Their aspect signifiers, and shifting, changing colours seeped into her awareness. Put alongside other indicators – a clench of a jaw, downturned mouths, darting eyes, flicking, flinching grips on swords – it was like reading a book.

The cart was about to leave her line of sight as the road

curved into a bank of trees. She knew she could catch it. The obstacle were these men blocking her path.

She was at last at ease.

'Stop right there, Elaya Faith. You will not be passing today,' came a loud voice.

Elaya came to a stop. Two men had swords drawn, and two more had arrows nocked to cheeks.

'Give me Girvyn.'

'That's not going to happen.'

'It's over. Step aside.'

'No, you turn back.'

'Who paid you to do this?'

The man snorted. 'He said you might ask that.'

Elaya heard another horse approaching. It slowed to a trot further behind her, then the clip-clop came to a stop. She didn't look. She didn't need to. It was Derrilyn.

The man raised an eyebrow, unimpressed. 'Reinforcements?'

Elaya sensed his sureness, but he was more mouth than action. Two nocked arrows pointed at her, though. Could she move quicker than a flying arrow? She knew she couldn't, so she needed to take out the archers first. This man who spoke – confident, loud, cocky – he wasn't the strongest there.

'What are you going to do when Girvyn wakes?' Elaya mused. 'Have you thought about that yet?'

The man shrugged. The others chuckled. 'He's woken twice, and we put him out each time.'

'Third time lucky for Girvyn then.' Elaya gave a small shake of her head. 'Step aside.'

'You know we can't do that.'

She measured them again, sparing an instant of attention. 'Two, one, four and three.'

'What the hell is that about, bitch?'

Derrilyn's voice rose from behind her. 'See, from the left to the right, she's reckoning who she'll do in first. You, my friend, are last on her list.'

The bowman flinched. A micro-shift of uncertainty was enough for Elaya. She threw a dagger in a staggeringly fast movement. He fell from his horse, blade in his throat. Derrilyn's arrow whizzed past her head and dropped the second archer. The third man came at Elaya. Fast, as she knew he would. She met his sword, coming inside to thrust the tip of her blade through his neck. It almost caught her by surprise: that burst of blood from his mouth, those bulging eyes; then the dead weight dropped to the ground.

The last man, strong with words but weak in battle, came at her anyway. His horse crashed into her with a startling shudder. He came about, swinging his sword for dear life, which echoed as it met Elaya's blade, sending a sudden shock up her arm.

In combat, sometimes a person discovers a reservoir of strength within themselves that they never knew existed. She heard her own words, the wisdom she imparted to all her students when they began training.

She deflected the next attack, anticipating his move. His lips bent in a twisted sneer. Hair flying across his face, he lurched forwards, swivelling his body in the saddle and stabbing his blade down towards her abdomen. Elaya felt the blade pass across her front. They parted and came back around, facing each other once again.

'Give me a name of who ordered this and I will let you live.'

'And if I give you that name then its owner will hunt my loved ones down and feed them alive to his dogs. He already told me this and I believe him. You do not know the lengths he will go to to get what he wants. If I succeed, I'll earn ten lifetimes of soldiering for this boy. You cannot match his offer, Elaya, for you have not that evil in you. So, fight and may the best sword win.'

'Every act vibrates. Every word echoes beyond our actions. Think carefully about what you are doing.'

But he was too far gone for reasoning. His blade rose again.

She caught a glimpse of his face: sweat, fear, and rage, all coalescing in one final instant before she split it open with a thrust of her sword. The man fell, and for a second, she did nothing as her chest heaved and muscles burned. Lifeless bodies lay scattered on the road in front of her. Blood leaked into the hills.

'You alright?' Derrilyn said. He was beside her now, concern in his face.

Elaya glanced at the curve of the road, where the cart had gone.

'Come on,' she said. 'We need to catch Girvyn.'

They galloped for the next few minutes. The river continued beside them like some great shining light. When they came around the bend they reined up in shock and horror.

The fruit cart was upturned. An angry portal hovered not far from it. Girvyn stood beside it, an outstretched hand reaching upwards. The driver hung in the air a few feet away, eyes wide, face turning blue. He tried to speak but his throat constricted due to an invisible choke hold.

Elaya cried out. 'Girvyn, no! Stop it!'

Girvyn's arm came down, but too late; his fingers sending the final signal to the invisible force that squeezed the man's neck. It broke, and he fell to the ground, still and silent.

'I'm sorry. I'm sorry, Elaya,' Girvyn whined, his cheeks

dripping with tears. Confusion and repulsion mixed into an expression of horror.

Elaya went over and dismounted to check the man's pulse. She shook her head, then closed his half-open eyelids. 'It's okay; it's not your fault. You were defending yourself.'

Girvyn fell into her arms, his face buried into her neck. His body shuddered, following the rhythm of his sobs.

'I'm sorry. I was just trying to stop him.'

'I know you were.'

'They kept knocking me out. I was scared. So I pretended to be asleep. And then... and then... What did they want with me?'

Elaya didn't mean for her voice to be terse, but it was. 'We may never know. I wanted him alive so we could find out who did this to you.'

'It all happened so fast.'

'Girvyn, just close the portal now, okay?'

Girvyn whimpered in her arms, but did what he was told. Without him looking at it or doing anything, it just vanished.

'Look, Girvyn,' Elaya pulled away so she could face him. 'You have been given this power but must learn how to use it. Learn how to exercise restraint and control.'

'I thought they were going to kill me. I'm sorry, I messed up.'

'No, you didn't mess up. You were abducted, and you are fourteen, not a trained soldier. It must have been terrifying for you. They deserved it. I killed the other men. It's not the deaths that matter to me. It's the doing it without intent.'

'I didn't want this! It shouldn't have been me! Mora, my uncle, one of the others, should have this power. It's not my fault.' Girvyn began shaking.

'Derrilyn,' Elaya instructed, voice soft and firm. 'Go back to the city. Get the others and bring them here. We are not going back now. We will ride from here. I will wait here with Girvyn. Tell the queen what happened.'

Derrilyn nodded wordlessly, transfixed on Girvyn. 'Of course,' he said finally, and steered his horse away.

'Look.' Elaya led Girvyn away from the upturned cart and the body. 'Let's sit on the grass. Tell me about your favourite book.'

Twenty-One

From the passage, Brennen could hear every word in the Privy Council meeting through the inch-wide crack in the rock wall. He could recognise each voice in the Privy Council, but today the room was filled with delegates from the summit. The queen presided at the table's head, members and delegates along its length, while additional observers lined the walls. Near the catering entrance, servers stood at the ready, prepared to serve drinks upon request.

'I must inform you all that there was an attempt to abduct Girvyn. Fortunately, it was thwarted by Elaya Faith, but she has taken charge, and their new destination will be revealed to no one else.'

As the queen finished, an uproar rose in its place.

'This is unilateral action!' bleated Seskin. 'You have no right to keep their whereabouts hidden.'

'No. I would do the same,' Maltip muttered, nodding at the queen. 'The finger of suspicion is pointed at all in this room.'

'I wish to doubt no one here,' the queen said, 'but these

events mean Girvyn must be kept safe. Prudence must take precedence over courtesy.'

'Is he still going to Leverstock?' Seskin asked.

'As the queen has said,' Stasnier interrupted. 'We will not reveal his whereabouts.'

'Stasnier, may I remind you that we agreed an alliance; therefore, you should be sharing information.'

Stasnier answered again as more questions arose. 'I'm sorry, it's better for everyone this way.'

'I didn't tell anyone!' Seskin's beady eyes darted around the group. 'Did any of you tell anyone outside this room that the boy was in the stables?'

Faces glanced around furtively. Everyone remained silent.

'Girvyn is safe now,' the queen reassured 'But it does beg the question of who ordered this abduction? Only we knew about his powers and his hideout.'

'Well, I did not do it?' Lord Grisham sounded horrified.

'It wasn't us!' Nark snapped. 'I have been open about my intentions!'

'Emissary Nark,' Stasnier said, answering for the queen. 'There is no accusation from the queen directed at you or the sovereign of Lale, but, as she said, the question needs asking.'

Glances flashed around the table. Expressions that tried to pry and guard against suspicion.

Brennen shook his head in disbelief. He observed the people in the room, their flushed faces peeking out from their extravagant attire. Many would betray their own kin for political gain, but he acknowledged the queen's wisdom in refraining from accusing anyone outright. Laglen was depending on him to identify the trustworthy nobles and those who couldn't be trusted, though, so Brennen would remain vigilant.

'What about your chambermaids?' Seskin waved a hand. 'Your staff are everywhere. Hear everything. Could it be one of them? Looking for a quick commission! Information like this pays.'

One of the waiter boys caught his tray. He placed the cups and jug down on the table and left soundlessly.

Stasnier remained calm as ever. 'All of our staff are vetted and loyal.' He peered down at a sheet of parchment with some figures on it. 'There were eighty people at the summit. Twenty-nine saw Girvyn open his portal. Of those, fifteen saw the head of that monster.'

'And I hear even your own barons can't be controlled,' Seskin smirked.

The queen displayed a rare show of emotion in place of her customary diplomatic aspect. Stasnier blinked at Seskin. 'I assure you our barons are loyal to Queen Amelia. Where did you hear such a thing?'

'Your corridors leak gossip,' Seskin said. 'Don't you think it's odd that all your barons except for one have pledged soldiers to the crown in your hour of need?'

'The pigeon left yesterday. Baron Kerrick Shadstone is away from his estate, and we will be receiving word of his commitment in due course.'

'I hear you two are quite close.'

Stasnier glared at Seskin. 'The Privy retains close relationships with all our barons. This is just deflection tactics.'

'My point is people talk; it could be anyone who ordered the boy's kidnapping.'

Lady Adara was nodding. 'Whoever it was was desperate.'

The queen raised a weak arm as high as she could. 'It may be that information about Girvyn's location was passed unwittingly and no-one has behaved dishonourably here. If that is the case then I beseech whoever might have let this slip to share the details so that we might remedy the situation. Let us start with you, Praleck. Have you told anyone?' She glanced across the room of blinking faces.

Praleck's jaw tightened. 'No, Your Majesty, I told no one,' he answered and looked at Seskin. 'Stoer does not engage in loose gossip. And we may have disputes with Cundelly over various matters, but nor do we hide from a quarrel or send others to fight the battles we can fight ourselves.'

Donjul spoke, his voice rustling and deep. 'We have told no one of the boy,' Alwad said for him.

'Neither have we,' Sevada said, his expression stern. 'Hoppenell is loyal to this mission.'

Seskin lambasted, 'What nonsense! A proper investigation would take days to conduct, and what would we learn? That a chambermaid sold the information to mercenaries.'

'Let us ride to the mountains and stop Crane; enough discussions,' Maltip said fiercely.

'The boy is too powerful,' Nark said. 'That we know.' He took a breath, hesitating before speaking. 'Your Majesty, as you told us, he is your property, so it's your decision. But with respect, we should have all had a hand in his guidance and protection. And if we had, this wouldn't have happened.'

Stasnier spoke with firmness, 'The decision falls under the jurisdiction of the state, and it's been made by the queen. Our current priority is identifying the source of the leak.'

Cargya was fixed in place, only her eyes moved around the room, flickering to each person. 'We will begin our questions now. She held up a parchment with a list of names and times. Interviews begin at once. Maltip, you are first.'

Maltip nodded firmly. 'Then begin.'

Chairs pushed back, and voices grew louder as everyone rose to vacate the room. From where Brennen watched through the peephole, he saw Seskin look across at Nark.

They stood, then came together for a whispered exchange. Seskin drew him away from the table, a few steps back towards the wall where Brennen was positioned.

Brennen strained to hear. Through the mix of sounds – upraised voices and scattered conversation – he caught the last few words. '...speak in my quarters.'

Twenty-Two

Derrilyn waited at the main gates for the two Dream Travellers, Nadine and Dremell, to arrive, his thoughts spinning with all the memories of what had happened over the last two days. Leaving Elaya was his toughest challenge yet. Not that he didn't trust Girvyn; he seemed a sweet boy, and she had known him for years. But such raw unimaginable power at his fingertips. Would he open the portal and do something unthinkable by mistake? It had already happened; first, the fox-dog and now a chokehold levitation. Would everyone have to start stepping on eggs shells for fear of upsetting the boy? And how far would he go? Could he turn an entire region into a wasteland with a throwaway thought?

Having murderous thoughts was not a strange occurrence in Derrilyn's life. But going from thought to doing it took time, time in which a whole set of checkpoints came first to ensure it was the right course of action. He felt blessed it wasn't him with this power.

Amidst the noise and arguments among the delegates, he was relieved to embark on the mission to Crane's stronghold.

Something tangible and cooperative. And he would be outside as well, which was always nice.

He had spent so many years in the wild on his own, and from time to time he missed it. The single, simple quest for survival: food, shelter, warmth, self-preservation; goals unclouded by others, politics, and social change.

'Two riders approaching!' the watchtower guard announced.

Derrilyn peered over the battlement. A man and a woman were talking and smiling as they rode up to the gates. Was this them? He hoped so. As Laglen had said that Travellers didn't have druid abilities, he was relaxed about reaching out his awareness to study their auras. The man – Dremell – seemed resolute. Derrilyn already felt as if he knew him, and wondered again what it would be like when the Chattara extended his perception.

Then he switched his attention to Nadine, and suddenly his heart was racing. Hers was an unassailable presence. Returning to his own mind and eyes, he studied her. She wore a black cloak over russet-coloured garments. So beautiful, like a young queen in court. Ageless skin. A flawless face. Angular and striking. Black hair danced on her shoulders with the rhythm of the trot.

Awash in her confidence, he went down the bastion platform to meet her.

He scanned the man again, felt his reliable aura, felt warmth in his eyes, Was he her husband? He was dressed in black with a neat, soot-black beard.

Derrilyn waved a greeting.

'Greetings, I am Dremell, and this is Nadine,' he said, nodding. 'We are here to see Laglen.'

'I'm Derrilyn. Laglen has left, I'm afraid.'

'Ah, okay, so we are looking for Elaya.'

'Elaya has left with him.' Derrilyn came closer, aware that Nadine hardly noticed him. 'I've been expecting you.' His lowered his tone. 'You are the Dream Travellers?'

'I prefer it if you don't speak about us in public,' Nadine said, her chin lifted in dismissal.

Dremell made an awkward motion. 'An unprecedented situation has revealed our existence, but we would appreciate it if our abilities stayed as private as possible.'

'I assure you, your secret is safe with me. I am a druid, so I know what it is like to be different and feared.'

Nadine made a sound somewhere between a laugh and a hiss. 'Being a druid is nothing like being a Dream Traveller. You are just a notch up from an Ort.'

Derrilyn felt their changing auras. He saw colours. Nadine, smouldering red hot fire. Dremell, turquoise as a cool cavern pool.

Dremell's smile seemed forced, a gesture to maintain peace. 'We need to join the team going north, Derrilyn. Where are they?'

'The war committee are waiting for you at the barracks. I'm coming north, too.'

'We want to see this monster,' Nadine dismissed.

Derrilyn barely heard their questions, their words. His mind wouldn't leave her cutting remark. 'What's an Ort?'

Dremell's stare shifted between Nadine and Derrilyn. 'It's a word to describe those that don't Travel.'

'So, a negative term. I've never heard it before.'

'Why would you have?' she answered, her voice dripping with disdain.

Her fiery aura had calmed somewhat. A soft orange glow, with sparks of amber.

Derrilyn folded his arms. 'Why are you better than me?

Your adventures are only in your sleep.' He stopped: red again with hot yellow flashes.

Nadine clucked her tongue, brooding. 'I don't expect you to understand.'

'Try me.'

Finally, she spoke, 'The monster?'

He felt his heart hammering and her colour boiling. He tried not to break from her gaze, but the strength of his attraction to her was compelling him to look away. 'It's in the infirmary.'

She made a clicking sound, more for the horse this time, and trotted inside the grounds.

Derrilyn let her go, then turned back to Dremell, pointing a thumb at her. 'What's her problem?'

'I am sorry about my friend. When you get to know her, she is nice.'

'Sounds like she doesn't like ordinary people.'

Dremell sighed. 'You were…how best to say it? A little too visually appreciative, my friend! She looks the way she does, but she hates it when men let themselves get affected by it. To make matters more complicated, she doesn't trust Orts. But she will bring a lot to this mission!'

Derrilyn released a short puff. 'The infirmary is on the westerly bit of the castle. We leave in an hour from the main stables. There's food for you in the barracks.'

Dremell smiled. 'Thank you, Derrilyn.'

'My pleasure. See you later.'

Twenty-Three

Brennen had rushed through these passages before. Countless times, following the web of unseen corridors, switchbacks, and hidden doors. Yet today they seemed like strange dark corridors of night that he was surveying for the first time. He fell. Winced. Felt the pain rush from his knee to his thigh. Just go slower, he told himself, as he entered a narrower corridor, which also lowered in height, forcing him to crawl for a few minutes. He dropped into another switchback, felt around for the passage wall and took the opening in the darkness, now moving slower despite the racing beat in his chest. This was precisely why he had hidden in a loft: to avoid stress and danger. It caused paralysing anxiety. He tried not to think about that day when it first happened. The day he was tortured; the day Elaya had saved his life. Leaving the odd note for Elaya was nothing like this, especially when so much hinged on something so important as Girvyn. Could his prying lead to torture? No. It need not. As long as he stayed hidden, he could help anonymously. Blinking in the dark, he cleared away past memories.

Only a few more corridors to go; he just had to keep it

steady and calm. For Seskin it was but a short walk from the Privy Council meeting chamber to his quarters. Brennen wanted to hear all that was said, but if he fell and injured himself he might miss everything.

Voices began to leak through the wall to his right. There were nine private chambers on this side of the castle. Seskin's room was towards the end. He stopped, ear close to the wall, listening. Wrong room. He kept going. Next one. Wrong room. Running his hand along the stone's surface, he felt the next support pillar, then the subsequent flat wall. No sound. Then at the next exterior, he froze. Two voices.

Thin shafts of light arrowed through the partition. He found the largest gap in the stonework and pressed his ear to it.

'I think we see eye to eye on many things,' Seskin said. 'Although I do not agree with destroying this boy.'

'God does not give a select few the power to bring through demons and a rabid dog,' Nark disagreed. 'Even if he isn't already evil, the allure of power and greed will corrupt Girvyn in time.'

'He's the lesser of two evils, no?' Seskin said.

Brennen could hear the eagerness in Nark's voice: 'This Dream Realm leads us to an extinction risk. How do we stop that? By snuffing out the root cause. These Dream Travellers are a blight on our existence. A disease that needs eradicating. All our futures face this greatest danger.' There was a pause. 'There are many that believe as I do.'

'What do you mean?' Seskin said, a trace of worry in his voice.

'I do not stand alone. I have the backing of Lale and the basilicas.'

'Unified? The basilicas *and* the sovereign?'

'This alliance is quick to dismiss us and points to a separation of faith and sovereign. But not so in Lale and, dare our say, our sister capital Casper. The Casper authority may not agree with me, but the people do. We have thousands ready to march.'

'Are you saying what I think you are saying?'

'There is harmony within the faith, and men and women ready to rally against this evil, regardless of what regime they are subject of.'

There was a pause. Brennen couldn't see clearly, but he was sure Seskin seemed bothered. 'Are you talking about the rise of a cross-border religious army?'

'People look to us to explain world events. Poverty, injustice, war, famine have been the strife of our time. For all that our words in our sermons in our parishes have often suited the royal dynasties, religion is one unified voice that should transcend tribalism, states, Houses, and crowns. Now we meet this new storm. The kingdoms must adhere to religion's one voice. Fail to do so and we will see a fissure that will widen in this crisis,' Nark said.

'This is not a holy war.'

'What else can you call it? These demons prove the existence of God. How can there be hell without heaven? We must stand up and fight this hell on earth and all those concomitants with nefarious, incomprehensible underworlds. The Dream Realm is the hell, and all those going there are the dark lord's pawns.'

Seskin released a heavy breath.

Nark continued. 'Whoever tried to kidnap the boy was a step ahead. But you can't make a pact with the devil. They should have put a knife through his brain.'

What seemed like, at first, a customary lull in dialogue soon became something more. Brennen strained to listen. A gasp of surprise. Sharp whispering. He pulled back from the wall, looking for thicker daylight beams he could peer through. He ran his hand over the gaps, felt a draft from one of them, and lowered his eye to the hollow.

They were huddled in the middle of the room. Seskin had his back to Brennen. Their gestures were agitated. 'You... how... impossible risks... not serious...?' Nark said.

Seskin spoke, and his already hushed voice became even quieter.

Nark's mouth dropped open. 'To take him to the High Temple?' More unintelligible words. Nark's voice grew louder at the end. 'Why?'

Seskin shushed him. 'To train him,' Brennen couldn't catch the words until the end. '... greater good.'

Nark clapped, voice clear again. 'You dirty rat! It was you all along!'

'Shhhh,' Seskin said. He straightened, voice normal. 'Now we both know where we are coming from, can we help each other?'

Nark considered this and walked over to the window, looking at the rising castle walls and the gabled roof for a long moment before speaking. 'If this mission to kill Crane works, then the clear and present danger will be eliminated. In seven days, we will know for sure. Assuming it is, the need to preserve the boy as a weapon disappears. That leaves us free to answer the question of what to do with him and these other Travellers. I had a private conversation with this neglecting uncle of his. He reluctantly told me that any child of a Dream Traveller also becomes one. Clearly all need to be documented and eradicated. Would Cundelly ride with us?'

'I can send word to ask once we know the outcome of this mission north.'

Brennen waited while they finished the conversation – a

brief exchange of pleasantries about meeting later at dinner and a vow of secrecy – then Nark left.

The journey back to the attic was lost to time and place. Something he crawled through and had to pass over to bring him to daylight. To a thinking space.

As he opened the attic hatch and felt the light pour over him, felt the calmness of his safe place, he sensed the pain in his wrists and knees from the crawl. He sank into a chair, accepting his rapid breath. He closed his eyelids and ran through the conversation again, unpicking the words said and the words unheard until a considered conclusion settled in his mind. There was no one else to consult with. Laglen and Elaya were in transit and he hadn't spoken to anyone but them in years. He would not seek audience. There was no other option. He stood up and went to his desk. He laid out a sheet of parchment and dipped a quill nib into an ink pot.

Then, choosing his words carefully, he began writing.

∼

Brennen watched through the crack in the wall as Queen Amelia held up the parchment for them to see.

Stasnier squinted in thought, absorbing the content of the message she had just read aloud. 'Where did you say you found this?'

'It was on my dresser, in my changing chamber.'

'Who else has access to your room?'

Berenger interrupted with a loud throat-clearing sound, and the queen waved for him to continue. Stasnier glared at Berenger. He seemed loath to seek his counsel; to even look into that snobbish expression. Brennen knew Berenger was one step below Stasnier on the committee ranking, yet the queen sought both their opinions.

'Personal assistants, a senior dresser, chambermaids,' Berenger finally answered. Even Brennen knew that. Once again, offering nothing.

Stasnier kept his voice even and held up the note to re-examine it. 'This is not from the chamber team: it doesn't read like something they would have penned.'

'I agree. If it was one of my staff, why not come forward and present the discovery in person?' the queen mused. 'I think this is someone else.'

'I concur,' Berenger said to the queen, pursing his lips, as if offering great insight.

Stasnier suppressed an eyeroll, but they still cavorted slightly. 'Whoever left this note must be very close to you, Your Majesty, to leave it in your private dressing room. As we have already established, if not staff, then they are likely to be in your circle or have other proximity.'

'Proximity?' Amelia raised an eyebrow. 'Many years ago, when Elaya was investigating a plot to kill King Eadie and I, she came through a hidden passage to save us,' the queen stumbled at the memory, clearly still too strong to bear without stabbing pains.

Stasnier nodded, eyes glowing with recollection. 'So did the attackers, Your Majesty. They got hold of ancient master plans and used hidden passages to attempt a coup.'

'I believe I recognise this hand. This is not the first such note, and all previous ones have proven true and of immense use,' the queen said.

Stasnier scowled. 'And this has never been investigated? Elaya is remiss in her duties.'

'You discredit yourself, Stasnier. And I believe Elaya knows more about the source of these notes than she will say.'

'Then that amounts to treason, Your Majesty!'

'No, it does not. Not if I accept to trust her judgement in the matter, which I do, always. Anyway, no attacker has come through those passages in over fifteen years. Elaya secured all the building plans years ago.'

'I am not saying you are unsafe, Your Majesty, but that doesn't mean they are not being used.'

'You refer to this rumour of a hermit in the walls? Yes, I remember this person, a scholar from the library; he was with Elaya that day and was tortured by the assassin that plotted against us. If it is him in the walls, he is not a threat. Elaya would have flushed out any danger.'

With Laglen now Waking-engaged, his secret out, and flushed with the success of his eavesdropping in the tunnels, Brennen hadn't felt this alive in years. Two great minds like theirs were destined for more than hiding in attics and dreams. If there was a way to get news to Laglen of Seskin's involvement, they could plan the next step, like a master puppeteer controlling the players from the fly tower.

'But can we take this note seriously without knowing who gave it to you?' Berenger said.

'Why should we not take it seriously?' Stasnier said, voice annoyed. 'The warning note says what we already suspected: Seskin has been the most vocal opponent of our plans, especially the queen's decision to train the boy in hiding. He could have hired mercenaries to take Girvyn at an opportune moment while Elaya prepared for the mission and Girvyn's protection was most vulnerable. There was too much inside knowledge to accept his kidnapping as coincidental.'

'We need proof,' Berenger said, mulling it over. 'What if we put him on the rack?'

'What, torture him?' Amelia exclaimed.

Well, that was a suggestion outside the box, Brennen thought. At last, Berenger was doing some thinking.

'A very interesting proposal. It has worked in the past, Your Majesty,' Stasnier purred.

Amelia shook her head. 'Everyone knows confession by torture is unreliable.'

'Not if we torture them separately and their stories corroborate the note left in your dressing chamber,' Berenger suggested.

Stasnier hiked an eyebrow. 'You are brutal today.'

'This is not some forced confession of a corrupt merchant. Cundelly are our friends. Seskin is a sovereign representative. It would be an act of war,' the queen responded.

'Not if you say you didn't know anything about it, Your Majesty,' Stasnier answered. 'We could take the risk and responsibility. You can say you had no idea, and that we were acting outside of state directives. Should it ever come to it, we will confess to this. Therefore, we protect the crown and yourself.'

'You would be putting your careers and lives on the line; I might even be pressured to give you up to their sovereign states for a trial.' Amelia shook her head again. 'Anyway, we are not torturing Nark. For what? Having a fervent religious disposition? What did we expect from him? Many of us may disagree with his views about killing all Travellers, but many would ride if the Prelates asked them to. We cannot go against the force of the basilicas.'

'Very true, Your Majesty. Many within our ranks have devout faith and would be torn if we did and may rise against us.' Stasnier responded.

'But Seskin? Does that mean we can at least torture him?!' Berenger asked enthusiastically.

'Seskin, on the other hand, is an irritant,' Amelia agreed. 'Finding out if Seskin ordered this kidnapping will allow us to nip it in the bud at the source.'

Berenger nodded. 'I suggest we do some investigating first. We ask some questions in the old town. Show an artist's drawing of his face and see if anyone has seen him. If it comes up that he spoke to mercenaries, we put him on the rack and find out if he is acting alone, and if he has plans for further strikes.' He waved his hand nonchalantly, 'And, most importantly, whether the Cundelly High Council is involved.'

'Very risky if they are,' the queen muttered.

'Which is why I don't think likely, Your Majesty,' Stasnier added. 'If Seskin admits his guilt, I would imagine Cundelly would hang him out to dry and deny all knowledge, even if they knew about this.'

Berenger rubbed his hands. 'I will get a drawing made up and go to the old town. On my way back, I will speak to the jailers in the Tower and get a private room in the sub-levels.'

'I do not want to know the details,' Amelia said. 'Tell me what you find out when you are done.'

Twenty-Four

Five hours post-attack, their journey had advanced notably. Guided by Maude, they shifted from the open road to a secluded woodland path, forming a single file to conceal their tracks more effectively. Girvyn, their precious charge, was positioned centrally.

Silence had enveloped them. But in the gaps between heavy thoughts and whispering words were the thuds of shod hooves on the forest floor, dropping rhythmic thumping drumbeats.

Laglen rode up beside Girvyn. 'This is a new situation. How do you feel about it?'

Girvyn let Laglen's words trail into the late afternoon air. It was not that he didn't want to answer him. He didn't know how to. He didn't know what to say.

What was Laglen implying with his question? Each scenario felt unprecedented. He was caught in a cycle of processing new revelations, attacks, and decisions, barely catching his breath before the next onslaught. Compounded by a relentless pressure on his chest and recurring headaches, this had become his new normal – a relentless state devoid of any sanctuary. Yet, amidst this turmoil, he found it surprising how he was managing, considering he had taken a life with a mere thought.

Whether Laglen decided he wasn't going to get a conversation from his first question or just moved on wasn't clear. 'How is your ankle?'

Now that was a question he could handle. 'It's better.' Not that he had put much pressure on it since he'd jumped out of a window and sprained it. After the night in the stables and the immobility of being kidnapped and now riding a horse, it had healed. 'Just don't ask me to run from a monster again.'

'If another attack comes, let Elaya and the others protect you.'

'You mean don't open the portal again?'

'I mean, let Elaya do what she is good at.'

Girvyn averted his stare. 'Is our plan the right one? I am having doubts now. What if the Crown want to use my powers?' he muttered.

'Girvyn, you are not the plan. Derrilyn and the others leading the army to kill Crane is the plan.' Girvyn's nerves eased, slightly. He glanced back at his uncle. Laglen straightened his back, eyes straight ahead. 'The position you are in is very vulnerable. More attacks may come while you are raw and untutored. We must get to Wigginton as quickly as possible, lay low, and train.'

Girvyn listened, staying silent for a moment. 'Why would they attack me again?' He wasn't being arrogant, and he hated the way he'd lost control, but what did they expect him to do? Welcome them in? If one had the power to stop an abduction, wouldn't one use that power? They had it coming. A sudden feeling of guilt washed over him. 'What if that man had a family?' Girvyn mumbled.

'I am sure he did. I am sure the ones Elaya killed did, too.

They knew the risk when they became mercenaries. What about Elaya's men who died trying to stop the druid monster? Did they have families too? Most probably. These are harsh times, Girvyn. People die for causes, die for money, and die for nothing.'

Girvyn knew his uncle was trying to give him different perspectives, and he was thankful for that.

'The main thing is to get you into hiding,' Laglen paused. Finally, their eyes met.

Girvyn frowned. 'Wigginton? So, we are not going to Leverstock now?'

'The queen's cousin offered to help. Elaya says it's a good location. This has not been shared with the delegates, we've been told.'

Girvyn felt some relief at that.

Laglen took a breath. 'All of us are vulnerable, which is why I didn't want to reveal our abilities. Many decades ago, during the war with the druids, druids were persecuted in unthinkable circumstances.'

'They should have been revered, not hunted.'

'People thought the druids would rise up and take over.' He shrugged. 'Prejudice doesn't have to have a logical reason to do what it does. That's why it's irrational.'

Girvyn fell quiet again. 'I read about it. They were hunted down by states and sectarian groups. Most went into hiding, and some tried to hide in plain sight. Those caught were sentenced to public execution or sent to death camps.'

'There were some terrible atrocities unwritten. The druid hunters kidnapped children, tortured them, and threatened to kill their parents and siblings unless they helped them find other druids. Using that skill they all have for sensing each other. Imagine having to give up your own kind to save your family. An impossible situation and one a child should not have to endure. The hunters exploited their innocence and vulnerability. Of course, they killed them anyway when the child was of no further use. This was why parents abandoned their children and so many druids became orphans. But my point is when you are young, you are vulnerable. Yes, you might be able to perform a mid-air choke hold. But what if they kidnapped me and asked you to create things in the Realm – weapons, money, men – in exchange for my life. You would do it, right?'

Girvyn felt numb. 'I guess I would.'

'They could trap you, use you, exploit you. At least some factions that were at that conference will want to come for us like they did the druids. Of that, I am certain. And you are the biggest asset of all. We could have two wars, one with Crane and another with the fanatics.' Laglen sighed. 'You're a sensitive lad and I'm glad that you regret taking that abductor's life…but Girvyn, the war you've found yourself in may require you to take that life and others like it. Had that man lived, Crane might have visited him in the cells and learned what you're capable of. That information might have given him an advantage. Avoiding that possibility was, I'm afraid, worth the life you took. You made a horrible decision, but it was also the right one. Do you see?'

Girvyn did, but it was all he could do to not scream at his uncle that he hadn't made any of that analysis before he'd acted. That made it only a clever argument to justify what he'd done instinctively, and it only strengthened the fear that he was a monster. Looking to change the subject, he asked, 'How did the persecution of the druids end?'

'It went on for years. Cronmere hid among the hunters in plain sight, warning druids they were the next target. Over time, people stood up against these mobs. And died protecting them. There were key people in society: knights, noblemen, and royals, who finally came out and admitted they were druids too. It shocked the hunters and the haters. These were people they respected. When Cronmere came out, the tide changed. It was a tipping point, and an opposing movement to accept them grew.'

'What happened to the hunters? Were they put on trial?'

'No. The druids refused the opportunity for justice and swore they would not hunt them down. They said a trial would be like another witch hunt. Amazing, really. The Druid Guild was formed: a sanctuary and a voice for druids. And it also became an agency. The people that had been hunting them then began to hire them.'

'That is crazy.'

'Some still harboured resentment. A few extremists could never accept them: they called the druids supernatural beings or devil's spawn. I call them A Trace of The Pull.'

Girvyn reined his horse in, blinking a few times, processing what was said. 'What?'

Laglen reached out his hand and patted Girvyn's horse. 'Keep moving,' he told him. 'We don't want to bunch up the line.' He felt the horse buck and lurch forward, then smooth into a trot. Laglen cleared his throat. 'Many years ago, I noticed a dream structure authored by Elaya. I wondered if it was a one-off. So, in the following months, I waited, searched, and entered many more dream structures configured by Orts.' He faltered at the mention of Orts' dreams but ploughed on. 'Elaya kept coming back. She was creating structures without realising it, each construct partial and strange. Back in the Waking, when I spoke to her about my experiences, she asked questions as if she had never been there. Yet, in the Realm, she remembered me.'

Girvyn glanced back at Elaya. She'd moved just out of earshot to give him and Laglen privacy, but otherwise, she was staying close, ready to defend him just as she'd done the queen for so many years. Her dedication was awesome. And Hazel seemed to feel that too, riding just a little further back, gazing at the woman from the deserts as if she embodied new possibilities in the world.

For a moment, he cast his gaze across the group. Chieftain Glefforn and his men led the line. Rowen maintained a significant distance from them, his gaze fixed ahead.

Maude, in contrast, remained as enigmatic as she was mobile. Continually in motion, assessing, traversing the line, vanishing into the trees, to reappear further ahead, guiding the group in a new direction.

Girvyn brought his attention back to Laglen. 'Tell me more about this dream you saw Elaya in, but keep your voice down. She doesn't miss a thing.'

Laglen chuckled. 'Very true,' he whispered. 'I think Elaya has a connection with The Pull, and I assume this is the origin of her druidic power. Maybe there are variants in the population, with people having different degrees of connection to the Realm. Maybe the connection with The Pull determines peoples' relationship to it. Maybe druids have more advanced heredities than we do. After all, what we have is self-indulgent, a by-product of our imagination.'

'Not anymore; it's not imaginary since Sunfire gave me the portal. Ask that man I choked and pat that dog Elaya killed. Hardly imaginary.' Girvyn went quiet. 'I don't trust him.'

'Who?'

'Sunfire.' They held each other's stare for a long moment. 'Take both portals out of this situation; we don't have a crisis. Why has he given it to me?'

'I assume, firstly, because Crane has one, so we have a levelled battlefield. And secondly, I don't trust him either. There is more he isn't telling us. There is no such thing as a

Realm Guardian. It would have been recorded; someone would have seen him, or them, before. Are we meant to believe this is the first time they have needed to intervene?'

'Why can't Sunfire destroy Crane next time he crosses into the Realm?'

Laglen whistled. 'Good point, Girvyn, good point.'

Girvyn made a face. 'It should have been you or Mora or Kalamayn. Even Nadine or Dremell would have been better suited than me. Why give it to a boy?'

'I agree with you. Just keep it shut and let Elaya do the protecting.'

Girvyn nodded.

'As we all know far too well now, I neglected to train you as I should have, Girvyn. One thing I have always done, though, is talk to you like a rational adult, and I'm proud of the way you're analysing the situation here. Asking the questions you're asking is the first and most essential part of any training for the kind of power you hold.'

Girvyn nodded again. 'Thank you, Uncle.'

Laglen continued. 'We don't know enough about this portal. In the Waking, sleep has always separated us from the Realm. That is one of the beautiful things about both sides. They never touched each other, never met, so to speak. When I trained, I learnt how to control my thoughts and how The Pull reacts. And if I made a mistake, if I did something that hurt someone or destroyed something, it was all in a structure. No one on this side got hurt. Some might disagree and say that just deleting a structure is a sort of annihilation. Many debates among our sect exist about what is ethically appropriate to create. Each of us makes our way along this foggy road. But imagine that power on this side, imagine being able to blink everyone in Cundelly out of existence with a thought.'

'Is that possible?' Girvyn cried out, then lowered his voice. 'Could I do that?'

'In the Realm it's possible to give birth to a city and then blink it out of existence with another thought, but that's because we form the sole connection to The Pull. Elaya's dreams, and even those of Orts, are evidence that all Waking beings have some form of connection, so no, I don't think you could just will everything out of existence. But that doesn't mean your capabilities aren't terrifying.'

Girvyn felt a pang of fear. 'Uncle, I sensed it when I opened the portal.'

Laglen led his horse closer, almost to the point of touching. 'Go on.'

'That tingle, it's there, coming out of the portal. My fear and rage thoughts turned into actions. I wasn't even aware I considered I should choke that man in mid-air. It just happened!'

'Strange that I did not then. When you opened it in the stables, I felt nothing, not even a sliver. That portal must connect *you* to The Pull.'

His voice became subdued. 'See my fear now?'

'Girvyn, you can't blink people out of existence here as they are not made by the Realm. But you can use The Pull to do things to them. Blast fire into them. Throw people around with your mind. Make creatures as Crane has done and bring them through.'

Girvyn considered this. 'When the portal closed, the tingling went away.'

'Well, that stands to reason, as it's from the Realm. Close the door, close the connection,' Laglen said.

Girvyn recalled their earlier discussion about druids in the Realm, a topic that had piqued his interest. Like his uncle, he felt most at ease when analysing others or speculating on external matters. 'Are you suggesting that Elaya has brought a kind of residue of The Pull into the Waking with her, which is the source of her druidic power? If that's the case, why hasn't it affected you? Why don't you have druidic abilities?' he asked.

'I don't know if it is a residue; maybe she has just been touched by it differently to me. Without doing more research and seeing if more druids create structures without knowing it, it's just a theory.'

'But you said everyone goes there. The people who don't remember are called Orts. Isn't Elaya an Ort?'

'Firstly, I don't know if the entire population cross. That's impossible to determine. For me, it's about classifying memory. Orts don't remember in either dimension. We remember in both. Druids remember in the Realm. They create stuff but have no memory of it when they wake. Maybe druids sit somewhere between Orts and Travellers. What they do have that Travellers don't, though, is some element of Realm abilities but in the Waking. Travellers are just regular people here. But druids can do a little of what we do in the Realm here in the real world.'

Girvyn laughed at the hypothesis. 'Uncle, you have conducted a single case study! It's hardly undeniable empirical evidence.'

Laglen beamed. 'Corrected again. You are so annoying sometimes!'

'You sent me to philosophy and debate class at eight years old; what did you expect?'

'And Advanced Existentialism,' Laglen mused. 'I think you are the cleverest person I know.'

The question persisted: how could Elaya, who wasn't even a Dream Traveller, carry The Pull with her from her dreams? Determinedly, he tried to focus on each of his travelling companions, straining to tap into their thoughts and emotions. He believed that he, too, should possess this power. Yet, as he moved from one person to another, all he encountered were empty mental spaces. It was as though he were probing a void.

Then, finally, he brought his attention to Hazel, the one whose thoughts he wished to understand the most. With desperate determination, he attempted to read her mind, to be met once again with a profound nothing.

He let out a long sigh.

'You okay?' Laglen asked.

'Sorry, Uncle, I was just distracted by my thoughts.' That wasn't strictly untrue. Sometimes, the solitude of reflection intensified the pressure in his chest, making the cycle of catastrophic thinking more acute and unrelenting. But talking with his uncle had a grounding, calming effect that carried the stress away like flowing water. Girvyn smiled at Laglen. 'This has been a nice chat; it's helped me feel calm again.' His voice dropped. 'But have you seen the way the others look at me?'

Laglen paused to think about it. But Girvyn knew he must have. It was hard to miss it.

'They are just cautious, that's all,' Laglen answered.

'Hazel risked her life to save me in the library, but now she won't even look at me.'

A playful smile briefly lit up Laglen's face. 'Aha, I see! Well, Girvyn, have you considered that in the library you were nothing more than an unthreatening youth, but now you're more powerful than her entire tribe put together?'

Girvyn blinked momentarily, unsure how to process that. 'That's easy because they are all dead.'

Laglen shook his head, speechless for a long moment.

'Anyway,' he said. 'I think you are wrong; Hazel keeps looking at you.'

'Yes, for the wrong reason! With fear in her eyes.' Her avoidance of conversation added a depressing veneer to Laglen's words: she was afraid of him!

Laglen sent him a sympathetic look. 'Just talk to her.'

'How?'

'With your mouth.'

Yes, maybe that's it, he thought. Maybe he was expecting too much from her because she was older than him. When they had met in the library, Hazel had been the brazen one and had come over to speak to him. Perhaps he was expecting her to take that role again. There was no reason he couldn't become the bold one and talk to her. He told himself he would do it the next time they stopped for rest.

Girvyn paused, then smiled to himself. 'When can I do more?'

'More what?'

'Training.'

Laglen smirked. 'I think this whole conversation has been training. But you mean more Realm practical work, don't you? Well, we could start this evening, but I would rather wait until we reach Wigginton. Being on the move does not induce a stable setting. If we must leave at night, Elaya won't be able to wake us.'

'Did I hear my name mentioned?' Elaya's voice rose from behind. 'I am not carrying your sleeping bodies over a horse saddle.'

'Talking about sleeping...We may need to pop into the Realm for a quick catch-up as we go, though. It would be useful to hear from the others how the journey to Crane's stronghold is going.'

'I understand,' Elaya said. 'But make such meetings quick.'

~

Hazel spent most of the journey watching Girvyn. Partly because he was positioned in front of her as she rode, and partly because she couldn't tear her eyes away from him. She tried to be discreet about it, but ever since Girvyn had revealed his newfound powers, Hazel's thoughts had been in turmoil. He was so powerful, but his control over those powers was tenuous at best. Her conflicting feelings of hope and guilt waged an internal battle within her as her desires for revenge against Crane were pinned on this young and immature boy.

Maude, though, was easier to understand; she ghosted through the trees, swiftly patrolled their line, was intently focused, keeping her conversations quick and brief with Elaya.

Hazel guessed Maude was mapping sectors they had left and sectors they were passing into in widening circular patterns. It was not too unlike how tribe watchers would place themselves in a perimeter around the camp. But in this case, they were moving, so the perimeter moved with them. Having them in file made it easier to hide their tracks and pass through the dense forest. It all made practical sense.

She hadn't exchanged a word with Maude yet, and it seemed the ranger had no intention of initiating a conversation with anyone but Elaya.

The same could not be said of Rowen, who muttered whenever a Forester spoke. The Highlander brooded in the saddle, glaring at each person in the company, reserving an especially lingering look of contempt for each forest dweller.

It was rather a strange dynamic, Hazel thought. Her kindred, with whom she shared a cerebral, geographical, and cultural homeland, felt equally foreign to Rowen, who seemed to despise them.

She felt most comfortable riding behind Elaya, in a protracted silence where thoughts drifted freely, like seeds in the wind. Elaya retained an eye on Girvyn, looking above and around the gangly teen – who was now apparently the most important person in the world – as if she was expecting Crane's portal to heat the air at any moment.

Elaya dropped back a touch to exchange some words with her. 'You're very brave, Hazel. As much in speaking up at the conference as during the fight in the library.'

'I have always been that way. Quite unlike the other girls my age. But lately, I feel even more alienated. I don't mix with the traditionalists. I was young when I learnt the new tongue, and it changed me.'

'New tongue. You mean…?'

'The language of cities, of towns. The language we are speaking now.'

'You learnt well. When I arrived from the sands as a little girl, I only spoke the desert tongue,' she glanced away as if old thoughts pushed her stare into the wind. 'I learnt from the streets.'

Hazel nodded. 'We must adapt to a changing forest with outsiders arriving to make new settlements. At first we rejected this and kept to ourselves, but then we learned the benefit of trade. My father allowed me to settlement swap for six moons, so I stayed with Longhorns and learnt their ways and words.'

'Longhorn? I have heard your people say that term before. What does it mean?'

Hazel caught herself. 'I am sorry, I shouldn't have used

that word. I am still influenced by the old sayings. Longhorn beetles infest the trees and eat them from the inside out. Just, as the elders say, do those from the cities. Before you know it, you are invaded by them.'

Elaya laughed. 'The desert nomads call them the Digaya; it means rats of the stone.' She paused. 'In my experience, people are good and bad everywhere. Regardless of age, gender, race or place.'

Hazel's voice fell quieter. 'My people hate the Highlanders, of that you know. Yet the reasons to hate are generations old. I look at Rowen and see the same unthinking distrust and disgust my people have for his.'

'The hatred circles like dawn to dawn.'

'Unless someone can stop it,' Hazel said. 'And make others see the errors of their ways.'

She noticed Elaya was squinting at her. 'Why did you come along with us?' Elaya asked. 'You finished what you came for, and could have walked away.'

Hazel stared at Elaya. 'Revenge, redress, justice. To protect Girvyn.' She looked away. 'What if the plan to kill Crane doesn't work?'

'Of course the plan will work,' Elaya muttered. 'And if it doesn't, there will be other plans.'

The colour drained from Hazel's cheeks. 'When Girvyn killed that man, was it scary to watch?'

Elaya glanced at Girvyn, and Hazel was sure she was checking to ensure he was out of earshot.

'I don't look at Girvyn and feel dread,' Elaya said. 'I see a boy. So no, I was more worried about his welfare. Do you fear him?'

Hazel's lips pursed while she considered this. 'I don't know what to think. Crane came into my village with this portal and brought demons to kill my people.' She faltered.

'My father was taken through that door to another world. And now Girvyn has that door, too. So, I don't know what I feel. Worried, maybe.' She puffed out her cheeks. 'What's Girvyn like?'

Elaya's mouth opened and then closed.

'What is it? Just say.'

'Hiding in a tree trunk while everyone was killed or taken must have been so upsetting and left you guilt-ridden. If you feel you need to make amends for surviving, now you can.'

The words threw Hazel. She hadn't expected them. During the summit, she had been interrogated for proof, for substantiation. But she hadn't been asked what surviving felt like.

'I want to believe I survived for two reasons. One to tell the world what happened, and two to help stop Crane.' Thick lines of worry creased across her brow. 'But there is something I haven't told anyone. For fear they would think I was in league with him.'

'What is that?' Elaya said, her voice laced with urgency.

'That I think I was left for a reason. It wasn't an accident. They knew one was missing. It wouldn't have taken them long to find me. But they let me go.'

'Why?'

She didn't reply.

'Because of arrogance?' Elaya addressed her own question. 'Because they wanted you to tell? Because they wanted you to spread fear?'

'It is a question that worries me. But I will make them regret the day they spared me. My father saved me. He could have killed himself but he…' Hazel choked back a sob, but continued, '…he sacrificed himself to torment just to distract them from searching for me.'

Elaya gazed at her, mute understanding in her eyes.

Hazel continued. 'But in the last couple of days I've wondered if that made any difference at all. I fear Crane left me deliberately because he wanted me to provide that testimony. I think he believes himself invincible and wants to enjoy the spread of fear, and I was his vessel for that. Or worse, what if I have been used? The only survivor at the summit who then bears witness to the armoured thing in the library that attacked my tribe, the consequence of which has led to these two missions.'

'Your point?'

'I don't know, but why leave a witness?'

'Maybe you were just lucky. It's not your fault.' She paused. 'Your father sounds like a noble and loving man. And I didn't answer your question about Girvyn: I've known him all his life. Before all this, he was always correcting, choosing long words, being sometimes blunt and saying what he thought. But fragile too, with many moments of stress. And now I don't see any difference. Just more confusion, anxiety, and reluctance.' She chuckled. 'He wouldn't hurt a fly, that boy.' The smile widened. 'Just don't kidnap him and stuff him in an apple cart.'

Hazel's expression stayed serious. 'I am glad it's not me,' she said, lips tightening. 'With all that power. I am glad it's not me.'

'I am glad it's not me either,' Elaya muttered. Then, she reached down and checked her sword.

Twenty-Five

Envoy Seskin let out a harrowing, gurgling scream. His connection to the sound felt so detached from his thoughts that he couldn't be certain it had originated from his own mouth. Another agonising wail echoed through the dungeon, seeping through the cell's cracks, howling like trapped cats. The pain momentarily subsided, just long enough for him to utter some words.

'I will make you suffer for this! I will cook your balls and feed them to you.'

A snigger. A breath. A whisper. It was hard to tell them apart. So duplicitous they were. He would kill them both. But not before Cundelly invaded Rathnell, stripped it of its resources, dismantled the Crown, and buried alive the Privy Council.

'You'll make *us* suffer?' A laugh. 'I think we are in charge here.'

'We'll invade you!' Seskin hissed through clenched teeth.

'But Rathnell and Cundelly have been twin pillars of economic cooperation for decades, Why would you jeopardise our political and diplomatic relations? Do they even know you tried to kidnap the boy? Hmmm, Seskin?'

Seskin couldn't tell whose voice it was. Perhaps it was their whispers or was it the blood and sweat in his ears that stilled the sound.

They were risking everything; torturing him amounted to nothing less than a declaration of war. But the questions remained, what did they actually know and how had they found it out?

The silence seemed to greet him then, Stasnier and Berenger came around the bench and faced him.

'Tell us!' Berenger said, spittle bursting from his mouth. 'Again.'

Another click. His back seared with unthinkable agony. He screamed. Burbling, rippling peals of pain.

'We know you sent the mercenaries after Girvyn. Tell us who else is involved?'

The cog turned a notch more. That click on the rack, then that click in his back. Had it broken this time? Had someone just stabbed a burning spear into his spine?

'Release the tension,' he recognised Stasnier's voice this time.

The cog clicked, easing backwards. Loosening him. The pain lessened, and his body deflated onto the bench. Sweat and grit dripped into his eyes. 'Go to hell!'

A silence. A click. This time forwards.

'Arrrrrrr! Pleaaaaasssseeeeee stooooooooppp!!!'

'Is Envoy Nark involved?'

'I said go to hell!'

Stasnier spoke again. 'Rack Operator, release.' A short pause, then more words. 'I'm sure your motives were loyal to your crown, Seskin. Oh yes, I don't doubt that. Thing is, that weapon you wanted, Girvyn and his portal, already belongs to Rathnell. What on earth made you think we would give it up without a fight? Tut tut. But you made your foolish gambit, and now here we are. So let me be generous, Seskin, your actions here were not sanctioned by Cundelly. Tell us every detail of the plot to snatch Girvyn, and perhaps a number of state secrets to ensure your future loyalty to us, and this can end. Then you can return to your exalted role and comfortable life.'

Seskin took a moment to savour the cool breeze on his face.

'I'll boil your eyes and...'

'Rack Operator, two more notches if you would,' Berenger interrupted.

'Aaargh!!!!!!'

Then, again, the release. The pain ceased and another lull followed.

'Let me spell out the options for you,' Stasnier said. 'One choice you have is more of this until your body gives up its hold on life. Alternatively, you tell us everything and we have you forever. You see, Seskin, one way or another you are ours completely now.'

'You don't have any evidence of my involvement!' Seskin managed. 'This is just pressure to get me to confess when the real perpetrators are out there!'

'Then we will have to kill you and hide the body,' Berenger answered bluntly.

Stasnier's voice oozed, 'Wouldn't you prefer to align with us, earning favours from our courts? We will make sure that the road between Stoer and Casper is never built. Just tell us the truth. You could even exile here for safety, should Cundelly later discover your role in supplying us with intelligence.'

Seskin had no intention of confessing. He loved Cundelly

and would never betray her. The entire charade was a ploy to coerce him into talking. But the more it went on – the pain close to unendurable – the more he wondered about their latest threat. Would they indeed kill him? 'Go to hell you...'

The cog turned. The clamps on his ankles bit into his feet. The rope ties dug into his wrists. There was a deafening crack. His shoulder dislocated. His back erupted in agony.

This time, he couldn't speak. He remained in that agonising, outstretched position, almost as if levitating, with only the numb, paralysing pins of pain coursing through every inch of his body.

'A pause, Seskin?' Stasnier said. 'Before we break something for good? Consider how you got here for the next five minutes. Consider how you'd like this to end too. Gain your focus for when we resume.'

'Rack Operator, loosen a little.'

Seskin heard the door open and then close.

A breath left his chest and he sunk onto the torture table.

The kidnapping had been a carefully calculated gamble, he knew that, but with so many strong voices in the discussion, how had they worked out it was him? He had taken precautions to conceal his tracks, wearing a disguise in the east district, acting alone. Envoy Nark was unlikely to have betrayed him, given his desire to kill Girvyn. But would they keep going until he let out his last breath? Many of the inquisitors in Cundelly's dungeons would do the same. But he would hold out for now; he sensed their hedging.

The door opened. They came back in. A throat cleared.

'Look, we've been at this for three hours now. Let me recap, because it's time for decisions,' Stasnier said. 'Who else is involved? We know you plotted with Envoy Nark in your quarters.'

'We know you planned a partnership with Nark to take

things further than you already have,' Berenger added. 'Did you really think you could visit our home and plot against us? In our own backyard? We have spies everywhere.' A pause. 'Who else is involved?' Another silence, longer this time. 'Rack Operator!'

The pain exploded in his head. Strange, given that his spine, arms, and elbows were taking the strain; in fact, every joint in his body felt ripped and popped.

Faced with the choices – to confess, accept their offer, or perish without a word – it appeared his indecision inadvertently made the choice for him.

'Aaaargh!!!!!!!!'

'Wait!'

Which voice was that? Was it Stasnier? He couldn't tell. 'I need a word,' the voice said.

Footsteps. The door opened, and then closed again.

∽

Stasnier led Berenger away from the cell. They walked along the corridor, past two guards spaced equally apart, into an empty cell, then stopped by the back wall, keeping voices low.

'Are you sure about this?' Stasnier said. His usual calm bearing had been shaken by what he'd seen and heard. 'You seem to be enjoying it too much, Berenger.'

Berenger shrugged. 'Maybe I have an art for punishment. Maybe I get a thrill from it. Maybe I am just looking for the truth. Perhaps all three.'

'It's his word against ours. His resistance seems like that of the fanatic, but he's more a political operator and open to changing his position, is he not? So why is he holding out? Because he thinks we have nothing on him, and that is giving him belief. Your torture is not working. Maybe he would choose death, but that won't help us.'

'You care about his welfare? He is scum and had this coming.'

'I care about getting a signed confession and learning the truth. But we don't want a war with Cundelly. If this gets out...whatever you think about all this, it has blinded you to our true objectives. We agreed we would cause pain but not lasting damage, at least not until we get what we want. But now I think you would kill him to prove a point.'

'What do you propose we do then?'

'Give me an hour. I have an idea.'

∽

'Seskin. This is Stasnier. Contrary to what you might think, we are not enjoying this. We want this to end as much as you do. We know you went to the old town and paid for a team of...'

'Go to hell, Stasnier!'

'We know you then went to Nark and proposed an alliance. We just want to know if Cundelly was involved. Or, are you the tip of the sword, so to speak, and it starts and ends with you?'

Seskin's words hissed through clenched teeth. 'You have no evidence of anything.'

'If you don't admit it, Berenger will keep stretching you and you will die. And for what?'

'Stick it up your arse.'

'We know you hired a team. I don't blame you, I would have tried to capture Girvyn for myself as well. We just want to know more.' After a silence, he said, 'Bring him in.'

The door opened. A man hesitated at the entrance.

'Just come in,' Stasnier said encouragingly. 'Don't be afraid. Come round the table and face him. Just answer the question.'

The man did. He was nervous, eyes darting between Seskin, Stasnier, Berenger, and the rack operator.

'Is this him?' Stasnier asked the man.

'I can't tell. He wore a hood in my tavern. Could be.'

Berenger grabbed Seskin's cheeks and tilted his face upwards, away from the table, so the man could see. 'Is this HIM?'

'Like I said, hard to tell. Looks about right.' He shrugged. 'He came into my tavern and sat with a group of men. They talked, then they all left.'

Berenger's grip loosened, and Seskin's cheek slapped back down on the table. 'And your establishment is frequented by mercenaries?'

'All the time. It's their hub.'

'And these men, have you seen them since?'

'No, they've disappeared.'

Stasnier pulled back a sheet, revealing a severed head on a spike. 'Is this one of them?'

'In night's name! Yes.'

Seskin's whimper broke the silence as he stared, horrified, at the dead man's face, frozen in an expression of terror. 'What... what happened to him?' he stammered.

'Girvyn happened to him.'

'Okay, you can go now,' Stasnier said to the barman.

The man left. The door closed. Spittle arched from Berenger's snarl. 'Did you really think your ill-conceived, desperate plan would work? How did you even think the boy would willingly come with you, or follow your requests?' Berenger gestured at the rack operator. 'More!'

'Wait!' Stasnier interrupted, his voice softer than

Berenger's. 'We can help you get what you ultimately want here, Seskin.' Stasnier sighed and knelt so his face was level with Seskin's. 'Don't you want to get out of here? Have some meat and fruit? Let your body repair and be repatriated back to Cundelly? You can say your injuries were from a fall down some stairs and Rathnell has taken best care of you during your recuperation. Look, we have Girvyn; he is our weapon.' Stasnier's perfectly modulated voice oozed reasonableness. 'We might even be able to loan that weapon to help the great King Harald of Cundelly, from time to time. Perhaps push Stoer's military presence away from your border? You know, a fire from the skies burn them all? Just confess it was you who kidnapped Girvyn, and you will get everything you want.'

Seskin gauged his options carefully. There was still circumstantial evidence against him. The barman could not identify him. Yes, they could kill him, but he was sure they would not. He was not some petty thief or gang lord. Apart from stopping the torture, their offer of joining their side was unappealing. He would do the same thing as Stasnier in this position: offer Girvyn's services. As everyone knew, he wanted to wield the boy's power.

He was certain of the ruse they played. They were cut from the same cloth.

'I will not confess to anything. Kill me or let me go.'

Stasnier sighed. 'Oh well. I didn't want to involve Nark in this, but you have brought it on him.' Stasnier called for a guard. The door opened. 'Get Nark and start the rack.'

Berenger left the room. They waited for about five minutes. Muffled voices could be heard through the cell door.

'What is this nonsense?' Nark's voice demanded.

Berenger replied, 'We have some questions.'

'Then ask them, man! The Lale basilica will hear about this!'

'Get him in the cell and begin.'

A struggle, stifled yelling. A door slammed. A few minutes later came the gut-curdling wails. One after another with intermittent gaps.

'Noooooo!!!!! Pleaaaaasssee!' came lowered, warbling cries.

The screams continued for some time before Berenger came through the cell door.

'I have given him a break. Nark is much softer than our friend here,' Berenger reflected, almost with a look of disappointment. 'I think he is going to either die or crack in no time.'

Seskin's bloodshot eyes searched for Berenger's face.

But Berenger had already gone.

'Aaaaaarghhh!' continued the harrowing screams. 'It was Seskin!' came the gurgling voice of Nark. 'He did it He told me in his quarters!'

'I want a written confession, Nark, telling us everything!' Berenger's voice shouted.

A silence.

'Rack Operator!' shouted Berenger.

More screaming.

'Pleaaaaase stopppppp! Okaaaaaay!'

Several minutes later Berenger reappeared, a smear of blood on his grinning face. 'Signed and sealed! Stand aside now, Stasnier. We don't need this one any longer, but I may be able to extract some extra trivial details from him whilst I'm administering the final justice.'

'No!' Stasnier shouted, blocking Berenger's path to the table. 'He can be of use to us. If he cooperates, I will not permit you to kill him!' The Privy Counsellor turned, panicked. 'It's over, Seskin,' he gabbled. 'Just sign this confession, admitting you tried to kidnap Girvyn and tell us who else was involved. Do it man! I will keep you safe. Then the queen's doctor will click your joints back into place. In a couple of days, you will be ready to ride.'

He had gauged it wrong, guessed far too short on what they were prepared to do. Nark should have been untouchable, but they had dared. The realisation hurt as much as the rack. Through the pain in his joints, his back and his head, he searched for a reply, worthy of a king's envoy. 'I have always desired peace between Cundelly and Rathnell,' he said, voice barely audible. 'Why, the more I think about it the more I see that providing you the truth would be a noble act.'

Stasnier's face remained blank. 'I'm sure you could call it that, and it strengthens our friendship.'

'I want an agreement in writing, Stasnier. With the queen's signature, offering to let me go.'

'And if I get you one, will you comply?'

'Yes.'

Stasnier removed a folded parchment from his inside pocket. 'I have one prepared.'

Seskin looked it over, his bloody eyes just able to read it. 'Remove the restraints, so we can talk.'

Berenger growled, but submitted to Stasnier's gesture for the rack operator to comply.

As he was freed, Seskin tried to sit up but he couldn't, so he just lay there, barely able to work the pen as he signed Stasnier's document without even reading it first.

'Yes, I did it,' he began, hearing the words leave his mouth but not knowing if they were his own. 'A young man like Girvyn doesn't deserve this immense power, nor does he possess the wisdom to wield it responsibly. Gaining control over him would have settled decades of disputes. Cundelly would have become an instant superpower, ruling over all through fear. King Harald would have hailed me a hero, granting me a seat at the highest echelons of power. But you have miscalculated. Lale will not take kindly to Nark's torture. You attack the cloth today. Unless you kill us both, which would not go unnoticed. So you have started a war.'

'That's our problem to solve,' Stasnier said, going to the door. 'Move him to a cell with a hay bed and give him some food. Get the doctor down here, too.'

～

Outside in the corridor, Stasnier and Berenger met two other men. They were leaning against the wall, looking at their nails.

One looked up. 'How did it go?' he whispered.

Stasnier led them away from the door to a quiet end of the corridor.

The man who spoke first was dressed in outlandish clothing and performed a theatrical bow. 'Did it work?

'Let's just say the next time you perform for the queen, she will request impersonations.'

In an almost perfect Nark accent, the smiling actor said, 'I will let the basilica know of your appreciation.'

'What do we do about Seskin?' Berenger said.

Stasnier fixed a stern gaze on the two actors. 'We are done here,' he declared, tossing a gold coin to each. 'You're dismissed. Speak of this to no one.'

Once the actors had departed, Stasnier brought his attention back to Berenger. 'I've been pondering the same issue,' he mused. 'Once he realises Nark hasn't confessed, he might withdraw his own statement.'

'Can he do that?'

Stasnier shrugged. 'This is all new territory.'

'Hmmm, whatever happens, he creates a stink. Are we really letting him go?'

'Of course not. That whole offer was just a false carrot to draw him out of his burrow.'

'So…?'

Stasnier nodded, thinking. 'We'll fix him up and feed him, puff up his pride a little over some wine. Then we pump him for all the information we can get about Cundelly, and he never sees the light of dawn. Wait for Nark to leave for Lale. We then send the signed confession to King Harald to inform him of Seskin's betrayal, but tell them, considering our great relationship, we are letting Seskin return to his home kingdom. Then, when all the moving parts are aligned, we'll tell Cundelly he was killed in a bar fight in the mercenary section of town. Yes, a most dangerous plague we would love to stamp out, we will say, but whatever was he doing there all alone? We had assigned guards for his welfare, of course, but for reasons which elude us, he snuck out of the castle in disguise. Their response to that should be most entertaining. Would they even care?'

Berenger's eyes glimmered. 'Who is the brutal one now?'

Stasnier's reedy smile faded away. 'Like you said, he is scum and has it coming.'

Twenty-Six

The five-hundred-strong procession funnelled along the North Road, a mixture of wagons, weapon carts, pack horses, and riders clustered in the enclave of their Houses and clans. Derrilyn rode some way back from the lead riders. It was a hotch-potch of an army, and a slow, monotonous journey filled with furtive, distrustful glances across the divisions.

Derrilyn had secret doubts about the mission. But the process of getting there, to the mountain, was the issue. It was arduous and he was saddle-sore already, and they had only travelled one day. Without a general making decisions, every detail was being disputed by opposing authorities vying and jostling for power. Even within some groups factionalism dominated discussions.

The procession congested the narrow road, and any travellers coming the other way had difficulty passing. It took some minutes for the army to move disjointedly to one side, and even longer for them to reform ranks.

When night arrived there was nowhere to camp. About halfway up the convoy, Derrilyn saw a group of people on the road verge in discussion. He spotted Lady Adara, Lord Grisham, and other community leaders. As he came closer, he heard Donjul's interpreter speaking. 'We sleep on the sands; we can sleep on the mud.' He led his men into the trees to set up camp.

Lord Grisham shrugged. 'There are too many of us to lead to a clearing. Where we stop, we rest.'

Derrilyn recognised Sward, the younger son of the House of Andergine. He remembered him from the gate on the eve of the summit, where he had had an altercation with Elaya. Elaya had got the better of him that day, and his shame had been clear for all to see. Now, he strutted around like Lord of the North Road, hardly acknowledging anyone except his own soldiers. 'Gather our men; we feast tonight and ride at sunrise,' Sward roared.

For a moment, Derrilyn contemplated joining the Rathnell men for dinner, whom he knew from the barracks, but then Lady Adara's voice broke through the twilight. 'Derrilyn, would you care to join us?' She was with Jaden, who had aided their fight against the red-armoured monster. Derrilyn smiled, finding solace in the kindred spirit of druids.

Derrilyn settled beside the fire and held his palms towards the flames, watching smoke dance and spiral above a spit-roasted rabbit.

Dremell and Nadine appeared then, with Dremell seeming unsure whether to join them. Nadine's chin was raised to chime an unforgiving tone.

'Would you mind if we lay by the fire for a while?' Dremell asked them.

Lady Adara smiled. 'You mean to have us watch over you?'

'We don't need protectors,' Nadine snapped, folding her arms.

Derrilyn was strangely pleased she was rude to everyone. He didn't see the Travellers' colours this time, largely because he chose not to focus on that.

There was sniggering from the group of soldiers nearby. Then muttered comments: 'You might want protectin' from me darlin', specially if you don't know nuthin' about it.'

Dremell flashed the man an angry look. Keeping his voice low, he said to Adara, 'When we Dream Travel, our bodies cannot be woken.'

'Pritty little thing needs strokin' to sleep, ain't ya, I'll make sure she don't dream of demons!'

More sniggering erupted.

Observing these men around the fire, Derrilyn sensed the lecherous thoughts directed at Nadine. He had already sensed it among many in their army. She was beautiful. He strove to keep his own thoughts and reactions in check, relying on seeing her auras of conceit to normalise her. The constant, lustful scrutiny did give context to Nadine's aloofness, though. She faced objectification for her looks even as she was distrusted by those who feared the Dream Travellers. No wonder she raised a wall around her.

Derrilyn watched the men in the firelight, following the movements of their bodies, their interactions, listening to their jibes. He realised just by watching them he could discern their strengths and weaknesses. Was this a Chattara effect, blooming all his senses at once? He glanced back at Dremell and gestured to a well-screened spot by some bushes. 'Dremell, you and Nadine are crucial to the success of our shared mission. Please Travel without any fear for your bodies in the Waking. I will stand guard. Ask Laglen to say hello to Elaya, will you.'

He was determined to protect them while they slept, and

he knew that Lady Adara had already organised patrol shifts among the men to keep watch over the Dream Travellers.

Dremell tipped an imaginary hat. 'Thank you for that. We won't be long.'

A crude voice rose through the dark, 'Need that pretty little face tucking in? Dreamer scum.'

'Ignore them.' Lady Adara shot a furious glance toward the sniggering soldiers. Nadine, however, had already moved on, stretching out by bushes. Dremell lay beside her, becoming still. Derrilyn concentrated on them, finding no distinct colours in their auras. He brought his attention back to Adara, words hushed, 'I've got a proper worry about this mission.'

'We have division in our ranks, but we have a clear end goal at least,' Lady Adara said.

'Whatever that druid monster was, it was not of this world.' Jaden extended his hand, and Derrilyn shook it. 'You showed great courage in the battle with it.'

'Did I?'

'You have much potential.'

'You can sense that?' Derrilyn asked Jaden.

Jaden's eyes flicked briefly to Lady Adara. 'That I can! Elaya has picked you well.'

The fire snapped, catching their gazes. It seemed a sombre air cast over them. Lady Adara grumbled, 'A dark shadow hangs over the land.' She sent a narrowed glance to where the chauvinistic soldiers sat around a campfire; they had returned to talking amongst themselves and didn't notice her look. 'Regardless of creed, gender, or faith, hatred threatens us all.'

'Agreed,' Derrilyn said. 'Though not everyone sees eye to eye, unfortunately.' He smiled at Jaden. 'Good to have you with us.'

'As long as we are unified on the day of the attack, none of this matters,' Jaden offered.

Derrilyn let the words drift into the awaiting night.

Lady Adara interrupted the silence. 'Derrilyn, it's brave of Elaya to send you on such an important mission.'

'Do you think?'

'It shows how much she values you, that she would do this despite the Chattara being upon you.'

'You can sense that?' Derrilyn said in alarm. He hadn't considered that it left a scent. Was he like a dog on heat, he wondered.

'No, Elaya told me,' Lady Adara said, smiling.

Derrilyn laughed. 'I thought maybe that was a bit of a risk. I don't want to burden anyone.'

'We will deal with the situation if it arises.'

Derrilyn felt sheltered in Lady Adara's calm. It felt both maternal and enduring, not too unlike Elaya had been to him.

'I hear you had an unusual past?' Lady Adara asked.

Derrilyn raised an eyebrow. 'Elaya really has been confiding in you.'

'I am head of the Druid Guild, and not just there for my silver locks. I am often sought for counsel!'

'Elaya talks highly of you. What you've done for the druids has helped us all.'

'Thank you, Derrilyn. Elaya talks highly of you, too. You have come far.'

'It looks set to be a long night,' Jaden said smiling, 'and we need to be awake to guard these two Travellers. I would be interested to hear about your past, if you would consent to the sharing of it.'

Derrilyn took a breath. He saw his story as that: a told and retold narrative. As bizarre as it sounded to others, it was his past, his chronicle. And telling it did not cause distress or fester dark thoughts.

'Gladly. I was raised in a strict orphanage in Lale, never allowed out of the compound. I started sneaking out at night but got caught and got a hiding. So, I fled and hid in the city until the gangs had it in for me. I can't say my age, maybe eight or nine, but I hit the road and lived wild for six years before I ended up in Rathnell and crossed paths with Elaya. She's been training me for a couple of years now.'

'That is quite a story, fending for yourself at such a young age,' Lady Adara said softly.

'I didn't know it then, but my druid skills helped me keep away from them. I just knew the safe berries to eat and how to catch game.' He glanced away. 'Elaya helped me a lot. Not just with swordsmanship, but integrity, morals.'

'You owe her much,' Jaden acknowledged.

'I owe her everything. I would do anything for her. I am here because she asked me to be. Even though, as you observed, the Chattara is upon me.'

'What is this Chattara?' a new voice said from the dark.

Derrilyn watched Nadine and Dremell come closer to the fire. He wondered how much they had heard. Had they been listening to his entire story? Dremell gave him a kind look. His aura was cool blue, and so was Nadine's.

Derrilyn offered them some food, which they took, Dremell nodding in thanks for the both of them.

'The Chattara is a process that all druids undertake before they unlock their full potential,' Jaden told them. 'For each of us, it's different.'

Dremell stared at Jaden, seeming absorbed.

Derrilyn wanted to hear more, hear what other druids had to say about what he would soon go through, but Jaden did not elaborate.

Nadine patted a feigned yawn.

Derrilyn saw orange sparking spurs.

'How's Elaya getting' on?' Derrilyn asked Dremell, choosing not to look at her.

'Laglen and Girvyn weren't there,' Dremell replied. 'We just met Mother and Kalamayn, who are in Cundelly. Kalamayn is Nadine's father.'

Nadine said nothing; she just stared into the fire.

'I wouldn't read too much into them missing the meeting,' Derrilyn told them. 'Maybe Elaya didn't want to stop. She can be quite wilful.'

'We have six nights of sleep before we reach Crane's stronghold. As long as we organise our attack before then,' Dremell said, 'nothing else matters.'

'And of this attack,' Jaden asked, expression pinched into puzzlement. 'What if Crane is not asleep in his home? This is a lot of effort if he is not in.'

Nadine let out a frustrated sigh as though she were surrounded by children who couldn't grasp even the most basic instructions.

Dremell let Nadine finish her condescending gesture before speaking. 'Have you not wanted to raid your enemy's home? What stops you? Knowing that they might defend it successfully? But we can enter his home knowing he will be in the Realm, preoccupied and his body vulnerable. This is precisely why we can be so sure he will be there: that vulnerability. As we said, nothing wakes us when we are Travelling, not even the feeling of a blade against the throat. So why would he not be home when in that state? The single place he feels his recumbent body is safe?'

Derrilyn watched, listening. It seemed so reasonable and logical.

'Crane would never suspect in his wildest dreams that we

would have revealed ourselves to the world. The idea that we would be marching to his stronghold with the force of an Ort army would not enter his mind. We have both surprise and strength, which is why we cannot fail.'

∽

That evening, as the camp slumbered, Derrilyn lay restless, his thoughts running wild. What would the future hold? Would it sculpt him into a virtuous being like Elaya, or entice him down a perilous path mired in greed? He sensed his impending transformation. Everything was becoming clearer – his senses, the auras – and at times it was like an overwhelming noise that needed filtering. Without Elaya there, could he reach out to Lady Adara for advice on how to negotiate the changes he was feeling?

Amidst his reflections, a whisper, almost imperceptible, cleaved the night air, jolting Derrilyn from his thoughts. Another subtle rustle, a concealed voice, asking, answering, instructing. Something clandestine unfolded in the dark. His druidic senses detected four skulking figures drawing near through the night. His eyes snapped open, and his ears, as keen as on the evening of the pre-summit dinner, picked up sounds so hushed they belonged with the creeping insects.

Then it resolved into a clear picture, and Derrilyn leapt into action. His blade, gleaming in the firelight, materialised in his hand like an extension of his being. With remarkable speed, he surged towards the resting place of Nadine. His sword arced through the air in a breathtaking display of reflexes, interposing itself between her vulnerable form and the encroaching threat. A resounding clash reverberated through the night as steel met steel. Voices arose around him, and Derrilyn sensed three more shapes, each brandishing weapons. The first man, looming above Nadine, lunged at Derrilyn. The other three assailants closed in, poised to complete the task the first man had failed to accomplish, but now Lady Adara was there too.

Derrilyn blocked another swing meant for Nadine, his legs planted firmly over her.

'What is happening?' Nadine hissed in the dark, now awake and attempting to rise.

'Stay low!' Derrilyn declared. 'You're under attack!'

'Oi, clear the path,' came a coarse order. 'You dream sympathiser.'

In the cavorting flames, Derrilyn could now make out their faces. He recognised them from earlier: the soldiers encamped nearby, the same ones who had insulted Nadine. They attacked. Derrilyn parried, steadfast in his determination to hold his ground and defend the Dream Travellers.

'Step away, or we will slay ya too!' the first man demanded.

People around them were rising from sleep. Voices echoed from up and down the road. The call to arms resounded throughout the night.

Jaden stood over Dremell. He bestowed upon Derrilyn a look of kinship. 'We are with you!' he said.

'It's over. You are outnumbered,' Lady Adara said calmly to the attackers. 'Put down your weapons.'

'Keep yer nose out, druids. Mark me words, you'll be next in line, you will,' one of the aggressors snapped.

Dremell went to rise but Lady Adara stopped him.

'We can defend ourselves,' he said, dagger drawn.

'Stay down, Dremell friend, we have your back! Jaden remained between Dremell and the attacker and hissed through a clamped jaw: 'Only cowards attack the innocent in their sleep.'

'They ain't innocent! They are devils!' a voice came back from the dark.

The camp was awake now. Torches flickered in the darkness, casting eerie shadows upon the faces of the surrounding soldiers: the attackers were revealed as four burly middle-aged men.

Lord Grisham, Donjul, and Sward stepped forward, taking the forefront of the watchful circle.

'Lower your weapons!' Grisham shouted. 'As the highest-ranking noble and a general of House Trefgwyn, I demand you disarm.'

After what seemed like a comparatively long moment, the weapons clattered to the floor.

'Do yer bidding, but mind ya, we ain't beholden to the likes of you!' one spat.

'Lord Grisham,' Lady Adara explained. 'These men attempted to kill Dremell and Nadine. Derrilyn of Rathnell, came to their aid.'

Momentarily, Grisham's gaze shifted to Derrilyn, then down to the Dream Travellers. 'Are you unscathed?' he asked them.

They rose, dusting themselves off. 'We are fine,' Dremell answered, sending a nod of acknowledgement at Derrilyn.

Derrilyn noticed Nadine's gaze lingering on him, and she offered a faint smile. The gesture seemed as close to humility as he had ever witnessed from her. Their auras emanated a fizzing, vibrant orange.

Dremell then glared at their attackers. 'We stand united!' he told them.

'There ain't nothin between ya!' another scoffed. 'No saints here, just wretched souls, I tell ya!'

'Where are you stationed?' Lady Adara asked, her tone measured.

'Keep yer distance, druid. The Almighty didn't craft 'em. They're not of this land and need to be done away with, they do!'

'Forty years ago, you would have said the same of us. Now you aim your prejudice and hatred towards them. You have simply redirected your distrust and animosity.'

'They should be executed for such treachery!' Alwad translated.

Sward shook his head. 'I am not so sure. Look at their fervour and the risks they took to follow their beliefs. We need that kind of passion on the battlefield when we confront Crane. Such intensity cannot be taught,' Sward reflected. 'We tie them up and lead them to the mountain for battle!'

Donjul said more heated words, and they waited for the translation. 'No, the risks are too great. I have witnessed this before in tribal conflicts. Infighting has claimed countless lives. We must eliminate the infection before it spreads.'

Voices jeered and booed while others called for execution.

'No, release them,' Nadine's voice resonated above the rest. 'I do not agree to their deaths. No harm has befallen us.'

Once again, for a fleeting moment, her eyes met Derrilyn's.

'I concur,' Dremell added. 'We are the ones affected, and we should determine their fate.'

'Let them go free. Without weapons, they are harmless,' another voice suggested from the dark.

'We lack cages, and bringing prisoners into battle would divide our attention,' Lord Grisham declared.

Lady Adara surveyed the assailants again. 'Where are you from? What House, what kingdoms?' She brought her sword tip to the man's cheek. 'Tell me!' she spat.

'Lale!' he hissed.

'See!' Lady Adara winced. 'It's a religious attack from the Lale fanatics!'

'Casper!' the second man stated stoutly.

'Stoer!'

'Rathnell!'

At the mention of Rathnell there was a gasp.

Lady Adara's face snapped towards Derrilyn. 'Who leads the Rathnell troops?'

'Argon does.'

'I am here,' Argon said, stepping forward.

'Do you know this man?'

'Yes, I do.' He shook his head in confusion. 'He is loyal to Rathnell, loyal to Elaya.'

'I am loyal to faith above that!' the man said, spittle bursting from his mouth.

'You have betrayed your states, gone against the crown and this alliance,' Lady Adara declared.

'This is a most serious situation, Lady Adara,' Derrilyn explained, 'There are no basilicas in Rathnell.'

'We don't need a building to believe!' the attacker from Stoer said.

'This is graver than I realised.' Lady Adara was shaking her head. 'There is no compromise or agreeable settlement with hatred. Donjul is right; it needs snuffing out now before it grows in the camp.'

Another man, with ginger locks cascading over his broad shoulders, tightened his grip on an axe handle. His voice held a note of respectful dissent as he addressed Lady Adara, 'My Lady, it is wrong to condemn them. I know some of these men; they are good people. You do not have the right to make such a judgment.'

'Lady Adara, I do not want this. Keep them prisoner or let them go!' Nadine begged. 'You don't have to kill them.'

'This isn't your decision, Nadine. It's for the greater good, for the plan's sake,' Lady Adara retorted.

'Adara, are you sure?' Jaden asked her.

'Bring them to their knees!' Lady Adara muttered. 'Tie their hands behind their back.'

It took a few moments, then the men were forced down onto their knees.

Lord Grisham nodded, his face grim. 'The war council must stamp this out together,'

It was clear from Sward's face that he was wrestling with the same issues. Sward agreed reluctantly. 'We do this together then.'

Lady Adara gazed across the watching, blinking soldiers. 'If any among you harbour such hatred towards our dream-bound friends, then you will receive this very same fate.'

'No!' Nadine sobbed.

'In night's name,' Dremell muttered, looking away.

Sward, Donjul, Lord Grisham and Lady Adara, came behind each man.

'Wait!' Praleck said, coming to Sward's side. 'I know this man; it should be me that does it; he has betrayed Stoer's pledge to the alliance.'

Wordlessly, Sward passed him the knife.

With an effortless flick of the wrist, all four men lay lifeless on the grass.

Twenty-Seven

Chieftain Glefforn watched Rowen ride. He had watched him for the last hour. Now that they were on the journey, and all the bickering and blustering of the summit and what to do with Girvyn had concluded, he felt decidedly more composed. Being head of a tribe required balance, firmness, and fairness. He regretted and was embarrassed by how he'd come across in Rathnell. To be among equal leaders in a contested forum had been taxing, to say the least. In battle, he had always fired an arrow first and lifted a shield second, but he'd found the quick-talking, quick-thinking delegates, with their complex words and brainy manners, daunting and hard to keep up with. He'd resorted to a short-tempered mode out of desperation and intimidation. He yearned to put that all behind him and concentrate on the mission: get Girvyn to safety and protect him while he trains. Hopefully the considered leader that he knew himself to be could come through.

Hazel seemed content to ride with Elaya, though her eyes would often glance at Girvyn. Glefforn wondered at the reason, though Girvyn's doe-eyed glances back were far easier to read.

Rowen, on the other hand, was an unknown quantity, shooting stabbing stares at Glefforn and the other Foresters.

Glefforn decided to use the opportunity to ride beside him. See if he could reach some peaceful accord going forward.

Rowen glanced sideways as Glefforn came up to him. 'What do you want?'

'We are going to be together for at least a month. Can you and I agree a truce?'

'Why? You won't listen to what I have to say anyway.'

Abruptly, Glefforn felt a fury blossom in his chest. 'You agreed to come so we can hear each other speak. I am open to this.'

'I didn't agree, I was forced to come.'

'It's been twenty years since our last battle. But test my patience, and perhaps you'll find a blade to match that tongue of yours,' Glefforn said.

'Your reason for warring was our wish to leave the forest.'

'It's been eight decades since the great division,' Glefforn said.

'I'm well aware of the timeline,' Rowen retorted.

Glefforn suppressed his rising ire. 'We defended the trees against you.'

'We cherished those trees long before the allure of the mountain stone.'

'But you turned on our tribes, leaving destruction in your wake. It was our retaliation that drove you to the stone.'

Rowen's frustration bubbled over. 'That's not true! We left The Orran Forest in peace, and you chased us!' Exhaling in frustration, he repeated, 'My father gave me clear orders. I'm here to watch. Especially when you're near the boy, to make sure he hears both sides. He is the most powerful one, isn't he?'

'The Foresters have no plans to sway the boy. Please, I would like a temporary truce, given our mission and the possible dangers.'

Rowen was adamant. 'Your kind have always been the aggressors. Even as we left, the forest burned because of you. How can you ignore the truth when you were there to witness it?'

Glefforn's grip tightened around the rein, 'Corner a wild boar, and it won't respond kindly.' He regretted his words.

Rowen, inflamed, shot back, 'Perhaps a duel is what we need.'

'Enough!' Elaya's voice pierced the tension. 'Must I separate you two like squabbling children?'

As their horses inched closer, Rowen seethed, 'Those tales of atrocities were spun by your elders to shield you from the truth. The Foresters were the true monsters.'

Glefforn laughed mockingly. 'What stories?'

'You know of what I speak.'

'Maybe he doesn't,' Elaya cut in quickly, still watching them closely. 'We have a long ride ahead, so why not tell this Highlander history to help pass it?'

Rowen glared, but then began to speak of the Highlanders' persecution. As he told what was clearly a timeworn learning tale, Glefforn was stunned by a narrative completely contrary to all he knew. 'Are you serious?' he growled.

'Of course, I am serious. When do our people ever meet to talk? To hear each other's side? Is this the first conversation between our people in twenty years?'

After a prolonged silence, Glefforn admitted, 'As a child, I heard hushed conversations of discrepancies in tales, and witnessed the shameful eyes of the storytellers.'

'Those tales are true,' Rowen said. 'Did you know when

the Tribe of Oak first asked the elders to leave The Orran they were executed one by one. From a six-day-old baby to a ninety-two-year-old man.'

Glefforn's face turned ashen, and he couldn't speak for a long moment. When he did his voice was soft. 'I remember great warriors leaving for battle, then returning, not in celebration, but in sombre silence, telling the stories to the Elders in hushed secrecy. As a child, I was disturbed by these stories, because the one thing they never could tell was why they killed.'

'You are no longer a child. What does your mind tell you now?' Rowen said.

Glefforn gave Rowen a sideways glance, eyes narrowing. 'Your father would be proud of you.'

Rowen nodded, his voice quiet. 'When our current quest concludes, join us in the mountains. Listen to our stories firsthand. Maybe then, peace can return.'

Glefforn murmured, 'I regret the provocation. Instead of clashing swords, let's strive for harmony.'

Rowen spurred his horse forward, 'May today mark the start of that journey.'

∼

A short while later, Elaya halted the procession, her face creased with concern as she scanned the trees ahead. She raised her hand, listening. Maude flowed through the thick underbrush, effortlessly evading the branches and brambles. She came to a stop, her expression filled with foreboding.

Elaya reached for her sword. 'What's happening?' she demanded.

'There is something up ahead that you should see,' she

announced. This was the first time Maude had addressed the entire group.

'Go on,' Elaya urged. 'Tell me.'

'It will be easier if I just show you.'

'No, I need to stay with Girvyn. What's going on?'

'It's hard to explain. You need to see it. There is a road up ahead through the trees,' Maude said.

Elaya blinked at her. She had been impressed by Maude's abilities and seriousness throughout the journey, not to mention her steady demeanour. However, her emotional state now seemed agitated, with sparks of amber in her aura. 'Unless there is a very compelling reason to leave Girvyn's side, I won't.'

Maude's hands were trembling, and her words rushed together. 'I need your druid senses up ahead. There has been an accident.'

'What kind of accident?'

'There is an upturned carriage, and a mother and child injured on the bridge. I can't get close enough to see. I don't like the coincidence of it, and there is something else. Something unexplained, something I have never seen before.'

'What?'

'You need to see it for yourself.'

Elaya glanced at Glefforn, his men, Rowen, then Hazel. 'Stay here. Protection is your priority while we are gone.' Elaya kept her voice steady for Girvyn and Laglen. 'Stay calm, I will be back soon.'

A little while later, Elaya and Maude hurried towards a rising ridge. As they scrambled up the bank, the sound of running water came through the trees. Maude took Elaya's arm and held her back from entering the road. She placed a finger on her lips. 'Listen.'

Elaya concentrated. The sound of cries came from the left.

Help. Help. Please. Someone, help us.

'Can you sense anything?' Maude asked her.

Elaya gazed through the trees, trying to gauge. 'I can't lock on. At this distance, I need a clear line of sight to scan them. What can you tell me?'

'I crept closer so I could see. A mother and a child are injured. We need to take that bridge to get to Wigginton,' Maude reported. 'Something doesn't feel right, though. They have been like that for a while, calling out. As if they are waiting for something.'

'Or someone. It could be a trap. Is there another way for us across the river?'

'The next crossing is in a ford lower down in the valley, about thirty miles downstream.'

'That would take a day to reach,' Elaya mused. 'And, if these people are genuine and need help, we should go to them. I need to get closer to scan them.'

Maude's unguarded gaze digested all of Elaya in an abandoned pause. Then she shook away the moment. Elaya seemed to sense something: a sort of hunger, or fascination towards her, but it was gone as soon as it had arrived.

'Always thinking about everyone else, Queen's Protector.' Maude snorted. 'You hired me to get you to safety. My advice is we turn around and go downstream.'

'This other thing you wanted to show me, what was it?'

Maude caught her breath, as if merely mentioning it was a curse.

'What is it?' Elaya urged.

'You'll see in a moment,' Maude said. 'We must stay low as it passes.'

They huddled together, flat against the bank, peering at the road. For a moment, Elaya found herself irritated by

Maude's mysterious manner; but she knew this situation had unsettled the tracker.

Again, Maude pressed a finger to her lips and pointed with her other hand. Not left towards the bridge, where the incident was, but right, along the empty road. Elaya squinted. Through the trees, in the distance, she caught sight of a dust cloud moving towards them at an alarming rate. The full extent of its speed became visible as it passed them. It crossed their line of sight in a flash. Dust and noise billowed and blasted in an explosive moment, coming to an abrupt stop at the end of the bridge.

Elaya let out a breath. For a mere fraction of a moment, she saw a horse and rider, dust swirling around them. Then they vanished. Not even a lurch or a buck accompanied the disappearance. As it moved back past them spiral trails of dirt rushed into their faces, and they nearly got picked up and drawn by the slipstream.

Maude whispered, 'It comes and goes like that, like it is patrolling. I have seen it three times now.'

'What is that way?' Elaya asked, looking in the distance where it had vanished.

'The lower ford, where the other crossing is.' Maude's eyes remained fixed on her. 'Did you sense anything?'

'Nothing, it was too fast.'

'How long is the wait until it comes back?'

'Not long, five minutes.'

'If it's patrolling the two crossings, back and forth, that's sixty miles in five minutes.'

Maude murmured, 'I can't even imagine how fast that is.'

'Fast enough to pass in a blink of an eye and create a dust trail. I think it's a rider on a horse.'

'How is that possible?' Maude said.

'Anything and everything is now possible,' Elaya replied.

'I do not like this one bit.' She fell silent, wondering what to tell Maude. This was not of this world, so it must be Crane connected.

'What do you want to do?' Maude said, squinting down the track. She was calm again. Her aura simmering green.

'Go and get the others. Bring them to the bottom of the bank and stay back until I come. I want to watch this thing a few more times and see if I can sense anything. Then I will decide what we do next.'

As recurrent pauses went, this was interminable. The hush of nature back in place, a murmuring language, ancient and gradual, broke occasionally by helpless pleas. Waiting in the bush, her mind went over and over what she had seen. But whatever way she looked at it, she needed more information. The action was strange in itself. Was it some kind of patrol? Was it looking for something or guarding something? And who, or what, was the rider on that horse?

After what seemed an age, she saw the cloud again, speeding faster than the wind. This time, she was ready for it, and focused on the centre of the storm, and confirmed it.

It was a horse. A masked rider, a cloak flying. Its shape rigid in the saddle.

Then it passed. A crack of thunder followed it. Dust and dirt swept through her position. She blinked away the grit that stung her eyes and stared through the gap in the bramble bush. It came to a sudden stop. Was that even a second? Then it was gone again and past her in a wave of dust and roar. Within a few seconds it was over the horizon and out of sight. Again, it was too quick to lock on to with her druid senses.

She remained steadfast, unwilling to abandon her post until she witnessed it for the third time. A thrush called from the tree above. Elaya listened to its beautiful, strong phrases, repeating a few times.

She remained collected, calm and clear of distracting or questioning thoughts until the dust cloud returned. One consolation, as it came past a third time, was that whoever this was had not been able to sense Elaya either.

For a moment, Elaya entertained stepping out and confronting the rider or popping off an arrow in that second when it stood still. But the thought formed only as it was gone again in a trail of dust and noise.

She climbed down the bank towards the others. Scanning through the trees ahead, she heard their voices.

Laglen greeted her with intense worry lines. 'Maude told us what this is all about. What do you make of it?'

'It is very strange behaviour. Something from the Realm, I think. If we travel a day to the ford, we could still end up seeing it. I think it's patrolling; I am certain it is a trap of some kind, but what and by who, I cannot say.'

'If it helps,' Girvyn interrupted. 'I can keep the portal open in case we get into trouble.'

'No!' they all said together.

'I don't mean to choke hover anyone, but to use my portal as an escape door.'

'That's very kind,' Elaya said, her voice soft. 'But keep it shut.'

'This family?' Hazel asked. 'Do they seem genuine?'

'I haven't got close enough to tell. A scan would determine that, but they would be able to see me.'

Glefforn tutted disapprovingly. 'Foresters do not leave the weak or run away.' He brushed past Elaya, chest puffed out, and strode up the rise to the road above them.

As doubt and panic spread through everyone left behind, Elaya's mind raced. Chieftain Glefforn had displayed a penchant for dogmatism and impulsiveness in the past, but she had observed a recent change in his demeanour after the summit, a newfound reasonableness. Yet, that semblance of calmness had gone now, and he was as stubborn as ever. She had to decide what to do. And now. 'Everyone, head to the road! I'll conduct a scan on these fallen people and assess the situation.'

She rushed after Glefforn who was already at the top, staring at the mother and child, who were waving and calling out to him.

When they all got to the road Glefforn let out a puff. 'What do you sense?' he asked her. 'This does seem strange.'

The mother and child were sitting by an upturned carriage. His mother's head rested in his lap and he stroked her hair from time to time, assuring her. She grimaced; her ankle appeared to be broken. A loose horse waited patiently.

The upset boy waved at them some more. 'Hello, strangers!' he shouted. 'Can you please help my mother and me? An awful accident has befallen us and we need help to continue on our merry way.'

Elaya reached out. 'I do sense some concern coming from them,' she whispered. 'It appears genuine, at least from an emotional stance. They are in distress. But nothing is what it seems anymore,' she added.

'I believe this is a trick like those many Highlanders have seen on the Riddon Slopes, near where Crane lives,' Rowen insisted.

Glefforn grunted. 'I can see this is no illusion. If Elaya senses their distress, then that is good enough for me!'

'But what if it's a trap?' Rowen questioned.

Glefforn waved this away. 'My folk do not leave such unaided, and Forester bows will make light work of any treachery.'

'Please help us!' the boy cried out again. 'My mother can't

walk. Help me get her up and on our horse so we can ride away, please.'

Maude made a motion down the road where the dust had first appeared. 'Elaya, we don't have much time before the rider comes back. If we help them, we won't cross the bridge in time. We need to hide again!'

'It is not our way.' Glefforn interjected, his words seeming slower than normal. His chest thrust forward in front of her. 'I do not hide or leave the weak.'

'I am leading this mission,' Elaya snapped, seeming disconnected from herself. She made a decision: 'We hide in cover, wait till the rider comes then goes, and then we help them. That will give us time to cross.'

But her voice drifted away on the wind. Glefforn was already marching towards the bridge, the other three Foresters in his clan following him. Unsure whether to go too or remain, Hazel glanced between Glefforn and Girvyn.

'Stay with us,' Elaya urged. 'Nock an arrow and give them cover.'

Rowen went to follow the Foresters, but Hazel's voice cracked. 'Rowen, stay with us too! We need to protect Girvyn.'

Elaya could sense his conflict. He did not want to lose face in front of the Foresters. 'Remember what your father said. The priority is Girvyn.'

Rowen seemed satisfied and aimed his bow to cover the scene, where the boy was now standing, waiting for the Foresters.

'How good are you with that bow?' Elaya asked Hazel.

'I have obsessively practised archery in case I see that creature again.'

Elaya considered this, nodding. 'Have you shot anything but game?'

'No,' she replied, avoiding eye contact. 'I haven't.'

'Animals don't fire back.'

'Neither do a mother and a child,' Hazel replied.

Elaya drew her sword and looked back down the road. The horizon was still clear, but from the first sighting of dust it would be seconds until the rider arrived. Seconds to decide what to do, to ready a defence.

She watched Glefforn approach the boy. The boy waved him in. Something wasn't right. That feeling of distress. She felt nothing from them now, just a void.

She looked back. Dust. The cloud was coming.

Elaya shouted. 'Get out! Run! Everyone, run! It's a trap!'

On the bridge, everything seemed to move in slow motion. The mother stood. No longer suffering a broken ankle. A sneer twisted her mouth. The boy rushed at Glefforn.

Elaya Faith had never felt so petrified. Her stomach heaved, her skin, neck, brain – everything pulsated in a warning. Or was it something outside of her, coming closer, that made her chill so deep? Frost? Death? Those icy fingers were about to tear her apart and freeze her veins. That churning, curdling sensation in her stomach. She had felt it before, when the druid monster attacked Girvyn in the library.

The boy leapt into the air, delivering a knee strike to Glefforn's chin. That in itself was a fight-ender. But with strength far beyond his years and size, he carried on. The Forester fell back onto the road, unconscious. The boy jumped onto his chest, throwing hook punches from left, right, left, right. Glefforn's head smashed this way and that. Blood sprayed until a loud crack resounded from the bridge.

Hazel let an arrow fly, joining the first shaft she had fired, but it didn't stop him. The boy had another Forester on the ground, knee in his back, pummelling his head. Rowen let loose a shaft, which slammed into the mother. She plucked it out of her side and high-kicked the third Forester, sending him into the air, where he somersaulted before landing with a still thud. She removed a dagger from her neck, stuck there by the remaining Forester, who had now jumped onto her back. She spun around and around. He clung on for dear life until he was thrown off her back and over the bridge, where he disappeared into the dark waters of the roaring current below.

The dust cloud drifted around them, then the rider was there, pausing in the saddle. As the cloud settled, the man, now clearly visible on a great black horse. Beneath the helmet, Elaya recognised those piercing blue eyes and that undeniable gloating aura.

Then, another feeling: Death, thundering through the trees on a mare as dark as the night. Dust swirled around Death's horse. The blur of its super speed came to a halt by Kerrick. Death wore red armour, and the jagged, distorted helmet traced every inch and turn of its misshapen skull.

Death turned to Kerrick, and a dreadful quiet settled over them.

'Kerrick,' Elaya managed eventually.

Kerrick removed his helmet. 'The one and only. I must say, I know you headed southeast, but you have been hard to track. I have set traps everywhere from Dedisle Rise to Fates Keep.'

Just give me the boy, and I will let the rest of you go.'

Glefforn and his two men lay dead, bodies crumpled and folded in unnatural angles. Mother and son were walking towards them. Menacing grins widened their faces.

She tried to gather herself, buy some time while she calculated her options. 'What are you doing? What have you got yourself involved in? I know you love to win, but that druid monster is not you.'

Kerrick frowned. 'Druid monster? Oh,' he said, flicking a thumb at it. 'We call it a Drone Druid.'

So now I know your name, she thought, but Death all the same.

'Yeah, I was disgusted the first time I saw one. I did wonder what Crane was doing with all those druids I was bringing him. Only the best convert by the way. So much wastage, dying in agony…'

For a moment, Elaya was struck by what Kerrick had said. 'How could you sacrifice your own kind?'

Kerrick shrugged indifferently. 'Well… I don't really have a clan.'

'You will pay for this!'

Kerrick tutted, beckoning with his fingers. 'The boy, give him to me. I want his uncle too, for insurance.'

'No,' Elaya snorted.

Kerrick shook his head at her. 'You may think we are having a negotiation, but this isn't one. You saw what the Drone Druid did in the library. I am holding this one back out of respect for our past relationship, Elaya. And because I can't stand the sight of ripped-up torsos just before lunch.'

'When did you start working with Crane?'

He shrugged. 'Let's say it's been a long-standing partnership we are now happy to reveal.'

'You have picked the wrong side.'

'Do you all want to die? For what? Just give me the boy and no one else gets hurt.'

'That's not going to happen.'

'Oh, but it is,' Kerrick grinned. 'You're outmatched. I have two-super speed horses from Crane, a Drone Druid and,' he flicked a dismissive hand, 'that mother and child duo. You can't get away.' His voice held that cocky, controlled tone and got louder as he spoke. 'So let's be reasonable about this. What loyalty do you have to this boy?'

'What do you want with him?' She threw the random question out while her mind whirled through her choices. There weren't many. Even if she could take Kerrick out, which would be difficult enough, that still left the Drone Druid; and the one that attacked Girvyn in the library had smashed up the west side of the castle and killed thirty-three of her men. She just saw one option. One escape plan. It brought its own risks, but she had no choice and had to take it.

Kerrick's voice attuned to an even greater tone of smugness. 'This is getting rather tedious and, if I may comment on your situation, rather desperate.'

Elaya ignored his self-satisfied smirk. 'Girvyn, I am thinking a mountain path right now like the one you showed us in the stables.'

Girvyn nodded, seeming to come awake from his terror, understanding what she meant. He smiled. 'I can do better than that.'

Kerrick frowned. 'Huh?' Then his eyes widened, and he shouted at the mother and boy who were nearest to Girvyn. 'Knock Girvyn out!'

The smell of ozone came first, a rising temperature, a growing hum vibrating with heat. Kerrick sensed it too, for he reined backwards. The Drone Druid's horse reared onto its hind legs, leaping back from the door's raging fervour. A massive torrent of water surged through the portal, sweeping them away.

The mother and boy, who were behind Girvyn on the bridge, charged toward him with a desperate battle cry. With a flick of his power, Girvyn caught them both in a choke levitation. In an instant, their heads exploded, and their bodies collapsed to the ground.

'Shall we?' Girvyn said, motioning to the portal entrance.

Elaya let out a long, relieved breath, and looked back at the dead. 'This is by no means a moment of victory.' She gestured at the portal. 'Let's go.'

∼

Elaya stormed out of the portal and swung a kick at the mountain path, sending up a dust cloud. While she swore and paced, the others followed, glancing around the high ridge, saying nothing.

Laglen hadn't seen Elaya riled up like this for years. He remembered her fierce temper when she had arrived from the desert as a little girl, wild and fiery as the sun itself.

'Look, I'm sorry. I know this is a shock to you.'

'To me!? To us all, no? Lag, Kerrick is working with Crane!' She rounded on him. 'Did you know that?'

'Of course I didn't!' Laglen hissed, then calmed his voice. 'I had no idea. Crane is a solitary figure. He's always operated alone.'

'Well not anymore,' she said, scowling. 'I should have known Kerrick was involved somehow. That smug, self-important bully.'

Everyone else was looking away, lost in shock over what had happened. Everyone except for Girvyn, who was beaming. He pumped his fist in the air and joyfully hopped in place, his expression filled with excitement. 'Did you see that? I kept my composure! I saved the day! I got us out of there!' he exclaimed.

'Girvyn, please!' Elaya said, her voice heavy.

Laglen stared at Elaya, noticing how drained she looked.

He made a throat-clearing sound and waited for Girvyn's jubilation to subside. 'Now is not the time for celebration or for seeking recognition. Lives were lost.'

Girvyn appeared to realise how inappropriate his enjoyment was and stammered. 'I'm sorry, I didn't mean to...'

Laglen didn't blame Girvyn for being tactless. He was young, lacked emotional intelligence, had always struggled to read the room, and he was finding his way with new abilities to atone for his early misdemeanours when his powers had got out of control.

'I'm sorry, Uncle...' he said again, '...everyone. That was insensitive of me.' He offered a slender smile at Hazel. 'I am sorry you lost your kindred.'

Hazel stared into the middle distance. 'Glefforn did not deserve to die like that, killed by his own kindness. Enough of my people have been murdered by Crane and his servants.'

'We have just lost near half our company in the first attack,' Elaya growled. 'From now on, we cannot trust anyone, but we move on and trust each other.' Despite her bitterness, Elaya's words of encouragement, with that hint of a foreign accent, carried a reassuring tone. 'Do you all understand that?' She considered them in turn. 'Anyone we meet could be a spy, a thing from the Realm.'

Laglen's mind raced through Realm-based possibilities: travellers and soldiers across their route. Could Crane even send birds to scout for them?

Hazel looked around. 'Where are we? Where did you bring us, Girvyn?'

'I know where we are,' Maude replied. 'This is the Rathdangon slope, on the north side of the mountains above Rathnell.'

'Precisely!' Girvyn beamed. 'This is where I opened the portal in the stables, where Elaya asked me to take us.'

Elaya's cheeks flushed. 'I wasn't even sure the portal would work, but I ran out of options.'

'That's brought us backwards,' Maude told them, shaking her head in disbelief. 'We are two days in the wrong direction from where we were.'

'But are we safe?' Laglen asked Elaya.

Elaya gave a small nod.

Maude's pinprick stare remained transfixed on Girvyn. 'What was that door, Girvyn? What are you?'

'It's hard to explain,' Laglen interrupted. 'I will tell you later.'

'I want to know what's going on. Tell me.'

'What we face is an evil greater than we have ever seen. And this boy might be our salvation,' Elaya said.

Maude shook her head and looked away from Girvyn. 'You should have told me what he can do,' she muttered.

'Would you have believed me? You said you didn't want to know about the group anyway.'

'There is not knowing, and there is having relevant information to lead you all.'

Laglen considered Maude. 'Look, the less people know about him, the better.'

She sighed, shrugging. 'I want to know everything. What we face and what Girvyn can do.'

Elaya nodded. 'I will tell you it all when we camp.'

That seemed to satisfy Maude. Her voice softened. 'We should take a direction away from those bridges; north, then eastwards,' she told them all. 'Once we are down from this mountain. You all follow me.'

The company faced each other in troubled silence, broken by a mountain wind that rushed through the gaps between them.

Rowen, his face white as a sheet, shifted. 'Who is this Kerrick?'

Laglen considered his words. 'He is an unscrupulous baron. Elaya has a history with him.'

'And he is a Traveller?' Rowen stumbled as he said that word.

Elaya shook her head. 'No,' she shook it again as if trying to clear away unwelcome thoughts. 'No, definitely not. He is a druid like me.' She let out a heavy sigh. 'We need to get a message to the queen. The Privy Council must know Kerrick is involved.'

'But how? We are not going back to Rathnell,' Maude insisted, then hesitated. Was she about to ask for more money, Laglen wondered. Elaya had told him how hard the negotiation had been when they contracted her. 'I am leading you to Wigginton. Unless you think it's compromised.'

'I am considering this,' Elaya replied. 'But we proceed as planned. He seemed to not know where we were going.' Elaya's jaw twitched as a thought struck her. 'Don't worry, you will get your money.'

Maude flashed a glare at her. 'Good.'

Laglen wondered about their interaction. It was contradictory. On the one hand, Elaya seemed to place unusual trust in the ranger's advice regarding scouting. And indeed, she skilfully concealed their tracks and had detected Kerrick's trap well before they stumbled upon it, proving a valuable asset. But he had noticed on more than one occasion that Elaya would snap at her, and to make matters more confusing, Maude would cast long, observant gazes at Elaya in reply. Like she was trying to work her out or something. Perhaps Maude's unwavering manner was a welcome respite while Elaya remained distracted.

Elaya let out a long breath. 'When we get to Wigginton, I will send a pigeon to Amelia about Kerrick.'

'I can portal you to Rathnell,' Girvyn offered.

'No.' Elaya corrected the edge in her voice. 'No, Girvyn. Tempting as it is we have to keep your ability to move us like this a secret. Kerrick and his Drone Druid were too busy fighting the river to see that we escaped through the portal. Their not knowing is an advantage we have to keep. If I teleport into Rathnell and pass Amelia the message...well, even if no-one sees me, just the timing of it will tell Kerrick how it was done. We can't let him know your powers are growing.' Her voice softened. 'Girvyn, thank you for saving us. You did good. You also showed restraint and measure. Water was clever. It swept them away and kept any damage to the wildlife minimal.'

Laglen smiled. 'The wildlife was probably grateful. It's been a hot summer.'

'True, and I thought rain was coming,' Maude muttered.

'Good restraint?' Rowen cursed, cutting through their light chat. There was a surprising amount of passion in his eyes. 'You should have killed this baron.'

'I agree that the baron has it coming, for that and much worse,' Elaya said. 'But I don't want a fourteen-year-old boy killing people with thoughts.'

'He killed the mother and boy,' Rowen glared. 'Is that ok then?'

'Did they seem like a regular mother and child to you?' she chided.

Rowen's face flushed with anger, and he fell silent.

'I wouldn't kill you, Elaya.' Girvyn corrected, 'I mean anyone else.'

'Girvyn,' Laglen's voice was emptied of emotion. 'I think

you want to restate that. You don't mean to harm anyone, correct? Perhaps stop speaking for a while, okay?'

'Yes, Uncle. Sorry.'

Rowen sent Girvyn a narrowed stare. 'Why can't we just go through Girvyn's door to this Wigginton?'

'Girvyn needs to have seen the place before he can open his door to it,' Laglen answered him, annoyed by the suggestion.

Maude moved to the sloping ledge to look out. The sun was almost reaching the horizon, and the others could tell she was assessing the route. 'There is not much daylight left, maybe two hours. We must decide whether to camp here tonight or keep going until the dark stops us,' she announced.

Elaya considered this, joining her side. 'And if we go onwards today?'

Their voices lowered.

Laglen came up beside them to listen.

'The path gets steeper and narrower down the Rathdangon slope,' Maude continued. 'And I worry about the horses' footings. This whole thing is bad. We are on the apex of the mountain, and the horses could slip or freak out at any point, possibly getting a broken leg meaning that horse would have to die.'

They stood for a moment, not speaking.

Maude looked northwards. 'Stunning, isn't it,' she remarked, her eyes sweeping across the fields and flats in the valley below. 'The Plains of Deen.'

Elaya glanced across the settlements between where they stood and where they wanted to be. Smoke trails littered the landscape, announcing communities like wispy pointing fingers rising from the ground.

Elaya continued to stare ahead, a frown knotting her brow as she gazed at the villages dotted across the plains. 'Kerrick will have men out looking for us and will send messages to his spy networks, so when we go through the villages, we'll split into pairs and keep your hoods up at all times. If we are recognised, he will be on us again. He never gives up.'

Without warning, Girvyn opened his portal. The horses jumped back, and Elaya cursed, shepherding their mounts with gentle sounds so they didn't bolt.

'Girvyn! What are you doing?'

Girvyn hollered over the hum. 'Trying to get us out of here!' The portal moved along the slope, away from them and the horses. 'Sorry, that was a bit close; I apologise.'

'Girvyn, close it! You are scaring the horses and scaring us!' Elaya shouted.

It seemed in the light of the portal, Girvyn's confidence grew. 'Uncle, the portal can take us to places I know. But also to places I can see! Look!' He pointed at the portal, which showed a line of birch inside the doorframe. He then pointed to the bottom of the mountain, where the trees met the mountain base. And there it was, the same tree line.

Elaya leapt towards him to stop him. 'Girvyn, no!'

But Girvyn vanished, and so did the door. A second later, far below them, a speck of blue light flashed in front of the trees. Elaya peered down the mountain, shaking her head and cursing.

The portal bounced intermittently between the trees. On and off. On and off, flicking here and there as Girvyn experimented with it.

'I think I am getting the hang of it!' he said as it opened on the mountain trail below them. Then it disappeared again. 'I'm over here,' his voice came from the far side of the ridge.

'Girvyn, please stop now,' Laglen implored.

'It's okay, Uncle!'

The portal emitted snapping and buzzing sounds wherever it appeared.

Laglen shook his head. 'I don't know what to do, Elaya.'

'There is nothing we can do,' she muttered.

'He's there!' Hazel pointed at a flash of light on the horizon.

Maude tutted. 'He is like a child running loose in a market.'

'Oh yes, that was him,' Laglen said. 'A precocious child, don't you mean? He was always running off and getting lost, but now he doesn't want to hide in a book.'

Then, with a crackling hum, Girvyn reappeared and stopped.

Laglen wasn't happy that Girvyn had ignored their calls for calm and restraint, but he could see he was becoming more and more at home with his power.

Rowen frowned. 'If I shot an arrow into the portal, would it fly out at the point you chose it to go to?'

'I guess so,' Girvyn replied, smiling.

Rowen nodded for him to do so. 'Reveal that birch at the slope bottom.'

Girvyn seemed quite taken with the attention and the opportunity to experiment together. Laglen was happy to let this play out, and Elaya and Maude seemed intrigued to see what happened.

Rowen nocked an arrow and aimed it at the portal. He fired it into the doorway, and it flew through the door and thudded into the birch tree at the mountain's base far below.

Girvyn clapped his hands. 'When we get to the bottom of the mountain, you can pluck it out of the wood!'

'Let's use this doorway then and get off this mountain,' Hazel concluded. 'Can you take us all down there?'

'I don't see why not.'

'That would make it quicker and safer to get to the bottom,' Maude agreed, looking at Elaya for advice.

'Uncle, what do you think?' Girvyn asked him.

'You seem to be able to control it. But it's up to Elaya; she is in charge.'

Elaya's face had lost all its emotion. 'This is all very fun, and your unscheduled practising worked out in the end, but I promised the queen I would look after you, and you don't make that easy when you act individually.'

'I hear you, but I can make a difference. Almost half our group were lost in the first attack we faced and it was only my portal that saved the rest of us. So we don't have the capacity for passengers, and you also need my help, which I am happy to provide. So why not practice now, when it's safe? That way, next time there's danger I'll have this more under control.' Girvyn glanced at Laglen and Elaya. 'Please can I portal everyone to the bottom of the mountain? I want to help.'

Elaya raised an eyebrow, and Laglen could see she was surprised at Girvyn's directness. 'Okay, but you do exactly what I say.'

'Of course I will!'

Laglen smiled thinly. 'Elaya, you can lead the horses through that thing! If they kick out, they will knock me off the slope.'

∽

At the bottom of the mountain, at the birch line, Hazel made camp. Girvyn sat close by, watching Maude light a fire. Rowen, after retrieving his arrow from the tree trunk, tied the horses to trees and began wiping them down.

Laglen moved Elaya to where the others could not overhear. 'Elaya, we need to talk. Things are escalating.'

'I know, Lag. And there is another Drone Druid,' she cursed at having to even name it. 'It was worse this time. I had my men, and Derrilyn, Lady Adara, and Jaden with the druid invocation chant before. This time…if it hadn't been for Girvyn…' her words faltered, then became a whisper. 'I have never been so afraid, Lag.'

'This is my point, Elaya; we are out of control, out of our depth, underprepared.'

'What are you saying? That we change the plan?'

Laglen glanced over at the others. Rowen stood with his back to them, gazing at the sunset. Hazel continued building the campfire. Girvyn sat on a boulder, staring at the floor.

'Keep your voice down,' Laglen urged.

'He knows we are talking about him.'

Laglen blew into his hands. 'He is changing.'

'Yes. I didn't think it would be this quick.'

Laglen frowned. 'He is the same old Girvyn, but that power gives him confidence like he has found a place in the world.'

'I have lost so many men in the last few days. I need to protect him while you teach him.'

Laglen sensed her disappointment. 'Don't blame yourself for the Foresters, Elaya,' Laglen stopped and corrected himself. 'I am not saying you should blame yourself for the men that died in the library attack either. But they died doing their job. They died listening to you. Glefforn was under your command, but he acted unilaterally. You told him not to go, but he refused to listen.'

'I should have insisted.'

'You had seconds to decide whether to let him go or start a potentially destructive confrontation. You are used to people accepting your orders. Don't blame yourself.'

Elaya glanced away, then blew into cupped hands. 'A chill is coming. It will be a cold night.'

Laglen waited for her to continue. She didn't. He cleared his throat. 'This is what I wanted to talk to you about: because everything is happening so quickly, and there are so many moving parts, I believe we should utilise Girvyn's power. I am talking about travelling via the portal. He jumped us to the bottom of the mountain. We can cover many miles at a time this way.'

'I will not fight you over this,' she said. 'Besides, the queen entrusted you to train him and therefore to assess his capabilities.'

Laglen blinked a few times. 'I thought you would resist.'

'If we give him a bit of responsibility it might make him less rash. We must guide him, not treat him like a child.' Elaya looked down. 'He is too powerful to control even if we wanted to.'

'I will talk to him later.'

'But no creations coming out of the portal. You are talking about horizon jumps only, right?'

'I don't know what to call it. Yes, that's a good name. Horizon jumps, subject to you and Maude agreeing on the route. You can plot a course past the settlements you are worried about.'

'It's a good idea. Returning from the bridge to near Rathnell means we have gone from a three-day journey to a six-day journey. This will get us back to three days, maybe quicker than that, and prevent others from following us.'

'I want to take him to the Realm tonight.'

'If something happens I won't be able to wake you, Lag. Either of you.'

'I know. Look, I can change the time differential in the Realm so every hour is a minute here.'

'So in a single hour you'd do sixty hours of training? You can do that?' Elaya's voice lifted by several tones.

Laglen's cheeks flushed. 'I always do it. It gives me longer in the Realm. One sleep could be a lifetime if I wanted.'

Elaya shook her head. 'I am surprised you even know what's real anymore.'

'Indeed. Some of us have been known to have mental breakdowns in the past.' He pursed his lips. 'Look, sixty hours is too much; I don't want to overload him. But you get my point? We promised daily sunset meets with the other Travellers, but we haven't been able to enter the last two nights because of all the urgency. This is our first settled sunset. I will ensure we are in the Realm for no more than three hours on the Realm side and one hour on this side.'

Elaya nodded slowly. 'Do it.'

Twenty-Eight

Laglen and Girvyn finished their story and waited while the other Dream Travellers absorbed the news. The white expanse enveloped them, an infinite milkiness against which they exchanged solemn glances.

'This update,' Mora muttered, 'reveals a disturbing development. If Crane has forged alliances within the Waking, his sinister influence could stretch far beyond Baron Shadstone.'

'Indeed, this could be the mere beginning of something far worse to come,' Laglen said. 'These "super humans" from the Realm might very well live, disguised, among us in the Waking.'

'And Kerrick had another Drone Druid in red armour,' Girvyn added, explaining Kerrick's name for it. Girvyn found it remarkable that the Travellers stood together in his uncle's Atrium while their bodies lay in three different locations. It was such a clever way to communicate across long distances.

'We were worried when you didn't make the first two sunset meets.' Dremell glanced at Nadine. 'It makes our mission even more urgent. Kill Crane and snuff out the fire.'

'It seems like Laglen and Girvyn are not the only ones facing difficulties,' Kalamayn said in a concerned voice, turning to Dremell and Nadine. 'Are you both alright?'

'Yes, we are fine, Father,' Nadine said, brushing it away. 'It was just religious bluster.'

'Hardly,' Mora said. 'Thank the druids for us, will you.'

'Mother,' Dremell urged. 'Don't worry about us.'

Mora seemed concerned. 'Kalamayn and I are stuck in Cundelly waiting for you to reach the mountains. We are just worried and feel helpless here.'

'Mother, you have a massive part to play in keeping Crane busy once we ready our attack on his home,' Dremell assured her. 'Your danger is yet to come.'

Laglen cleared his throat. 'Now that we are seeing new causes for concern, let's expedite our plan.'

'What do you mean?' Kalamayn asked him.

'First, Girvyn is kidnapped from the stables, then Kerrick comes at us with Realm support. But both times Girvyn averts the danger using his portal.'

Girvyn felt a flash of pride at his uncle's praise. Then guilt, so he fought to keep his expression even. 'I just reacted instinctively,' he said. 'I didn't mean to kill that man.'

'Look, as we have discussed,' Laglen assured him. 'This is war, and you defended yourself. My point is we must start his training.'

Kalamayn's voice rumbled. 'We all have an interest in Girvyn's development, and I don't think your high-level classes are what he needs. He needs detail, careful consideration, historical context.'

'I do enjoy detail,' Girvyn said. 'I appreciated your 10-step guidebook.'

'See,' Kalamayn said proudly. 'Each generation of my

family have worked on that book, handed down for us to interpret and refine.'

'Some of your sections are repetitive, though,' continued Girvyn. 'And I would change the order of the chapters. The book should start with "Clearing the Mind", not "Mastering Breath". And where you say "how to pull from The Pull", I felt you were too impressed with your own play on words to properly explain it; the curiosity about thresholds, ethical and temporal, is inclined to produce provocation of a very lamentable sort.'

'What?' Kalamayn's mouth dropped open. 'How many times did you read it?'

'I lost count, but ask Laglen's assistant.' He beamed at Laglen. 'However, I was impressed with Uncle's race scene, too! It was so expansive and original.'

Laglen smiled. 'See. Detail is nothing without a grand stage.'

Dremell laughed. 'You two could argue all day about methodical versus whimsical or thorough versus inspired. I, on the other hand, could have him up to speed in one session. What Girvyn needs is a young, modern teacher. Someone who sits in the middle of you both, but with an eye for practice.'

Girvyn's face flushed, looking at Laglen and Kalamayn. 'I would appreciate that balanced take.'

'No!' they said in unison.

'Then we all do it,' Dremell suggested. 'We can each offer our own insights, and hopefully, he can learn from all of us.'

Girvyn glanced at each of them, his smile widening in hope.

∼

Beside scattered windows and a vast expanse of white, Girvyn listened as Laglen explained his approach. Girvyn was captivated by Laglen's ability to create things with speed. However, beneath his excitement lay a nervousness from witnessing the unintended consequences of hasty creations. When the dog had accidentally emerged from the portal, it had served its purpose by luck more than design, and Girvyn didn't want to inadvertently harm others due to his stronger connection to The Pull inside his Atrium.

Amongst Girvyn's saved structures and a stack of live dreams, was a waiting blank structure. Laglen gestured to enter it, and Girvyn readied to begin.

'Let's start with something familiar. Why don't you create Rathnell,' Laglen said.

Dremell sniggered behind his hand.

Kalamayn blurted. 'What? This is why I wanted to lead this session.' He raised his hands to halt Laglen's objections. 'If he is to create a sky, isn't it better he studies the formation of clouds first, so it is authentic?'

'I'm a quick learner. I think I could do a good cloud design.'

'I am sure you could, Girvyn. But you are not ready for high-level creation. You need to master thought control and learn why detail is important. Doing something quick and partial is easy but lacks integrity and depth. You will skip detail if we don't create properly.'

'What? You mean like me?' Laglen sounded defensive.

'How shall I put it? You have been known to jump straight into action.'

Laglen rolled his eyes. 'I agree with you about thought control, though.'

Girvyn was nodding. 'I am happy to take the long route.' He considered Kalamayn, feeling in awe of the great man. 'I am so impressed you brought library cataloguing to the Waking. Thank you for that.'

Kalamayn's cheeks reddened. 'I didn't invent it; I just copied a system I saw from a future construct. It made perfect sense.'

'But you found a way to contribute. That's what I want to do.' He faltered. 'And thought control is important to me too. Having read your guide, I agree it's the basis of everything.'

'Good, then keep practising the mind techniques I have outlined.'

'I do them every morning when I wake up. It helps clear my head.'

Kalamayn raised an eyebrow. 'Good. Good. Very good then.'

Laglen glowered at them, and Girvyn wondered if his uncle was feeling undermined or unappreciated. 'There is nothing wrong in being superficial if you plan it that way. There are great rewards from creating something quick, even if it's incomplete,' Laglen said.

Dremell threw a cursory glance at Girvyn. 'Gentlemen, it's about balance. I will have him creating detail in expansion soon enough if you let me take over.'

Kalamayn snapped. 'Dremell, we don't have much time. Elaya has lost half her team and is watching over them. Girvyn has a lot to learn. You and Nadine are in the north, asleep and vulnerable. Mora and I are in Cundelly, frustrated and wanting to help. Let me direct this.'

Dremell showed his palms. 'Please, proceed.'

Kalamayn clapped for silence. 'Girvyn should start with something simple, let's say a rock.'

'That does seem a little basic,' Girvyn admitted.

'I always start like this. It's how Nadine began, it's how I learned.'

A hand-sized rock appeared at Girvyn's feet.

'Good, make it bigger. Make it say, the size of your head.'

Girvyn enlarged it and shrugged. 'And now?'

'Make five hundred more, heading away from us in a line.'

They waited and watched.

'Good, about twenty feet from it, make a parallel line of rocks heading in the same direction.'

'Like the corresponding edges of a path?'

'All will be made clear. Add grass and extend it by about a hundred feet on either side of the rock lines.'

Girvyn stared at his work. It was an odd sight – two lines of rocks flanked by two extended sections of grass whilst everywhere else were sweeps of white.

'What you have here is almost an artist's drawing. But it lacks real-world dimension. I want you to imagine water in the blank gap between the rocks.'

'Ah, am I making a river?'

'Think of it as a stream,' Laglen intervened, huffing. He had obviously seen this lesson before.

'Got you.' Girvyn clicked his fingers. 'What do you think?'

'What do *you* think? Kalamayn said. 'What is missing?'

Girvyn frowned at it. Indeed, it didn't look right, but he couldn't pinpoint what it was. True, he hadn't seen the sea or the Capels River before, but he was sure this didn't cut it. Then, he realised. 'That's just an inch of water lying on the Atrium floor! It sits like rainwater on the street. It lacks depth.'

Suddenly it was deep. How deep was hard to say. He wanted to jump in and see. He couldn't swim, but could he just imagine himself out of the water? He noticed another thing. 'And the water is too clean. It needs to be murky!'

'Well done,' Dremell observed, impressed.

Kalamayn was brimming with pride. 'It's the subtleties

that make the difference. The Pull flows through your mind into the structure, and it can fill in detail sometimes, and often when you don't think about it. But it's harder when designing consciously. Your thought processes are easily blocked when you try and concentrate on constructing.'

'Yes, I remember creating Laglen's race stand when I was with his assistant; it had detail and depth, but I don't know why.'

'You must have thought it and The Pull listened, that's how it works,' Kalamayn said.

'Think of it as the differences between daydreaming and designing,' Dremell offered. 'A daydream is an impression but designing takes thought control.'

Kalamayn brought them closer to the stream. 'It's missing some things.'

'Character, purpose, colour, a point,' Laglen said sardonically.

Dremell laughed. 'Oomph, I felt that.'

'Please forgive my uncle's sarcastic manner,' Girvyn said, offering a wry smile. 'If you need a flying metal box, he is your man.'

Arms folded, po-faced, Laglen puffed out his chest. 'When it comes to high-level thinking, look no further.'

'And we won't,' Kalamayn said. 'There is no one better than you at grand, immediate creations. But let's not forget Jacarn. You can do detail too. It's one of your rare evolving structures, with much to be admired.'

'It was so draining, and it took years and hundreds of attempts,' Laglen complained.

Girvyn wasn't listening; he was staring at the stream. 'Of course, it's not moving!' he realised, punching an uppercut into the air. The water came to life, an effervescing mountain stream, but when it reached the end of the line, where the design finished, the liquid strained against nothing as if pushed up against an invisible wall.

'You have forgotten one thing. With movement comes...?'

'Sound!' And there it was, the babbling of the brook.

Dremell clapped Girvyn's shoulder. 'Well done.'

'Okay, you have taken an object, animated it, added depth, colour, tone, sound. Next for a big step. Create something alive,' Kalamayn said.

'Alive?'

'Something appropriate to the scene. A water vole at the riverside.'

A frog popped into existence. An otter jumped out of the water, a fish in its mouth.

'Slow it down. Control your thoughts. You are congesting the space. Where did you think these animals from?'

'From paintings and illustrations in the library. They are all related to water images, so I assume they are in their correct habitat?'

Kalamayn measured him, unblinking. 'Another lesson: you make the rules. It doesn't have to be exactly like the Waking. It depends on whether you want to mirror Waking realism. But creation, evolution: it's all up to you. I warn you, though, it's not easy!'

'I wasn't thinking about that, just river animals.'

'Well done,' Kalamayn said. 'But all at once is a little fast.'

'They are so detailed,' Dremell whistled in astonishment.

'Girvyn has a spectacular memory for details,' Laglen explained. 'I do appreciate why this lesson might be good for him,' he conceded.

Dremell clapped in applause. 'At last, Laglen is on board.'

Girvyn gaped at the product of his imagination. 'What are they made of?' He couldn't quite believe what he saw. There, in front of him, were beings he had invented. Moving, living creatures. Thought about, envisioned in his mind, created. It was remarkable. Staggering. Beyond comprehension. Yet natural, right. It felt like coming home. Despite an uprooted concept of reality, his sense of self dislocated, he felt faithful to this extraordinary journey.

It was much easier with the breathing techniques he had learned in the 10-step guide. The calming and focusing of his mind helped him let his thoughts flow into the tingling of The Pull. He sensed the energy responding to those thoughts, waiting for them, allowing him to control what passed through and, more importantly, what stayed in its psychic space. He could demarcate an area in his mind where thoughts remained his. The guide had taught him to do that, and he could see it working.

He wondered whether, if he was in a more intense, anxious setting, would he be so calm?

Girvyn's thoughts returned to the creatures he had created. 'If I cut them, will they bleed?'

'No one knows the answer to how The Pull understands our insides. It just does.'

'What if I don't know what an otter looks like? Will it fill in the gaps?'

'We think there is an imprint recorded somewhere in the Realm. The Pull has a memory of thousands of years, maybe more, and hundreds of thousands of structures.'

'How long has this been going on?'

'We don't know,' Kalamayn answered. 'Our ancestors left records that go back generations, with descriptions of structures, teachings and belief systems. But as far as we know, the structures vanish when a Traveller dies in the Waking.' Kalamayn looked back at the river, scrutinising the incomplete design. 'There is no origin or end. Extend the river to the horizon and fill the white space with nature. Do it.'

Dremell interjected, pointing up at the white ceiling. 'Look up, don't forget the sky!'

The landscape grew. The stream reached the horizon, the white space becoming fields and valleys in a blink. The sky turned a mottled patchwork of clouds and blue. They watched as a pale grey mountain range formed in the distance.

'Breathtaking,' Dremell said. 'That's quick and thorough. He is good.'

Kalamayn nodded in agreement. 'Very impressive, young Girvyn. You show a mix of both me and your uncle.'

Laglen was grinning. 'Thank goodness, I'm pleased some of my best bits have rubbed off.'

Girvyn was noticing his uncle's sensitivity throughout this whole session. Perhaps he still blamed himself for keeping the secret for so long and for all that sleeping.

'Uncle, many of your lovely qualities have rubbed off on me.'

Kalamayn was squinting at the scene. He gestured to it. 'Right, let's deal with time differentials. Speed up time so the time here is eighteen times faster.'

The clouds flew by as if pushed by super winds.

Dremell laughed at what he saw. 'No, you have speeded up the structure.'

Kalamayn flashed Dremell an irritated look and said reassuringly to Girvyn, 'Don't worry, it's your first time. Speeding up and slowing things in front of you sometimes is useful. It's on my list of lessons anyway. I'll tell you what: freeze it. Bring it all to a halt.'

They watched it stop, a haunting, eerie still of an instant. 'Take it back to normal speed. Good. I want you to create time here in relation to time in the Waking. Your sense of time defaults to the Waking. I want you to speed it up, but not in front of us, relative to the Waking. So that when we leave it and return later it will have aged faster.'

Girvyn had a strained expression while he tried to work it all out.

'Have you done it?'

'Not yet. I can feel the default sense of time I can measure from.'

'Good. As I said, that's the Waking default. It can be used in different ways. Crane's parents were addicted. They used to spend years in the Realm, taking their bodies to the thirty-two-hour limit. Then go back in. They weren't speeding things up like I am suggesting, but eking out every moment they could in here.'

Girvyn was concentrating on the maths. 'Okay, I have done it. Hold on.' He studied the spot before him and planted a young oak no more than twelve feet tall. 'I want to see how much this grows while we are away.'

'Good, close this structure then, and save it, running as you have set it.'

Girvyn did what Kalamayn told him. They returned to the Atrium, and the construct window they'd been in adorned a picture of a young oak.

Laglen frowned, pondering what to do next. 'Let's try another structure while we wait for it to cook. Something more complex, with people.'

'What about Rathnell market?' Girvyn suggested.

'Great idea!' Laglen breathed in relief. 'Some high-level creation!'

Kalamayn appeared dubious. 'I still think this is quite advanced for the pace of his teachings, but okay, let's see what he can do.'

A moment later, a new scene appeared as if they had teleported into it. A vast, overcrowded marketplace appeared.

The single difference was that where the market stalls ended there was that strange white haze of the construct, yet the sky continued onwards.

Dremell whistled in surprise as the usual murmuring hubbub of chatter filled the warm air.

Traders called out and offered deals; customers inspected produce from the numerous stalls, which provided everything from spices to ornaments. The loudest voice they could hear was somebody selling apples.

Laglen's mouth had dropped open, and it looked like it would stay that way for a long while. 'How have you done this?'

Kalamayn was shaking his head in wonder. 'Tell me your process?' Searching and measuring, he glanced across the market, soaking it all in.

'Girvyn, I knew you had a memory for detail, but this is fantastic.'

'Uncle, I have been to this market a thousand times.'

Kalamayn was squatting, studying the road. 'I am seeing space, light, layered facets. Smell, design, the people, the feel of a place. All so realistic.'

'But how did you pass all this info into The Pull so fast?' Dremell sounded shocked. 'I would have to test and assess, alter and try again – you did it on one go.'

'I just recalled it in my mind.'

'What, you can remember everything all at once?' Kalamayn caught Girvyn's puzzled expression and guided him towards an alleyway entrance. 'Look at how the shadows deepen further into the alleyway. The way light is used here is perfect.'

Dremell picked up on Kalamayn's point, adding, 'Most of our early structures lack depth or have incorrect perspective. Or everything is evenly lit wherever it is. To build this from nothing, to jump from the stream to this, is extraordinary.'

'Look,' Kalamayn brought them over to the stone wall and pointed at it. 'Look at this. The walls are thicker at the bottom, which is a tradition of all keeps to stop enemies tunnelling or smashing through it. And here.' He pointed to the wall. 'Look at the gap between the stone. The lime mortar has grain in its detail.'

'That's a good point.' Dremell's eyes widened in astonishment. 'How far down does the detail go? Are even the grains composed of smaller parts?'

'Is this not normal?' Girvyn asked them.

'No. Usually Travellers don't go into such detail. The Pull might keep a building upright because the author thinks of it that way, but the laws of how that works do not follow the same rules as in The Waking,' Kalamayn said.

'If Lag is an artist, creating smears and impressions,' Dremell said, 'then Kal is an oil painter with rigorous technique, fixed on making sure the lines and perspectives are exact. But what are you, Girvyn? I flattered myself that I sit in the middle and offer balance between detail and the high stage, but I don't. Not like this. What you have done is beyond my skill. Look...' Dremell followed the mortar line with his finger. 'Again, look at this grain! Normally here you might find a stripe of grey paint, like that from an artist's brush, which lies between the stone slabs, but nothing more.'

Girvyn remembered his uncle's track race. That grey floor. Stone but smooth. It was just a flat colour. He didn't want to mention it in case his uncle felt criticised. 'I have studied mortar in these alleyways in the Waking before. I guess that memory sat somewhere, and my core organisers put it together.'

'Core organisers?' Kalamayn asked him.

'Thinking, senses, emotions, movement, observation. That is what I drew from when I created it.' He tried to hide a smile that was bustling to reshape his mouth. 'Perhaps The Pull has appropriated this from an archive of detail I obviously have retained in my mind.'

'Perhaps it has,' Kalamayn said, shaking his head. 'Core organisers,' he said it again, smiling at him. 'You organise stimuli in your mind and draw from these layers when you create. Very commendable.'

'I can't tell you how impressive that is, Girvyn,' Laglen said. 'Especially from someone untrained. And you're right that it makes for a better, more realistic experience.' Laglen was beaming at him. 'I am so proud of you.'

Girvyn approached a market stand selling fruits and picked up an apple. The trader noticed this and glanced at him. 'I don't sell singles. It's one bronze piece for a tray.'

Girvyn held out his palm. One moment it was empty, the next a bronze piece sat on it. 'Take it. I just want one apple. Give the tray away to the next person who asks for one.'

'That's very generous of you, kind sir.' The man turned to a new customer at his stand.

'It's easy being generous when all you are spending is a thought,' murmured Kalamayn.

Girvyn tried to hide his expression, which he was sure would betray his feelings. Was Kalamayn insulting him? 'Very brutal, but true,' he muttered. He took a bite and made a face. 'It's bitter.'

Dremell was smiling. 'Food can be very realistic and often surprising.'

'Am I actually eating?'

'Here, yes. You could have an eight-course meal and feel replete. But in the Waking, no; you will wake up hungry.'

'The realism is frightening. Everything here fulfils your desires. How do you control your urges?' Girvyn said.

'It's very addictive. Be careful,' Laglen told him. 'You could create a world which seems the same as the Waking, but gives you everything you ever wanted without you realising you want it. You just exist successfully in it.'

There was no wind, but Dremell seemed to shiver. 'It's not easy,' was all he said.

Kalamayn nodded soberly. 'I know I snapped at Dremell for making jokes while those in the Waking are under extreme pressures – and our bodies lay waiting for us to wake – but that's the thing about the Realm: all stresses and pressures in the Waking fade away when you are here.'

Girvyn wasn't listening. His mind was whirring with possibilities. 'Imagine if I opened the portal in the market square back home; I could offer people the chance to shop in my market, where everything is free, and all the product is perfect.'

'Girvyn, this market is incredible, beyond what any of us can do already. There's another side though, and that's the question of why you created it and whether it was wise to do so? This, more than anything, is why our kind don't Travel until we reach eighteen,' Laglen said.

Kalamayn agreed. 'We teach the young to know the star lights, but not how to follow them to reach the Realm. We use those early years to reflect on these psycho-social, ethical, and philosophical issues first. Crane's parents didn't; they let him Travel as a child, and look at how he turned out. Yet, not only did you find a way to the Realm, Girvyn, you create in multicolour and realism.' Kalamayn's brow creased while he considered him. He patted his hand while he thought some more. 'This portal of yours is the key weapon in our armoury for the fight against Crane. If, and only if, the attack on his mountain fails, we may eventually need to use it. But you have had merely days to practice. Crane has had decades of research. I know you power that portal of yours, Girvyn. But it's something that we are all invested in. Forgive me for sounding harsh, but that portal is not for opening unless we say so.'

'I have been gifted it, and I just want to do good with it. Random ideas pop into my mind. It was just a suggestion on how I could help people, that's all,' Girvyn explained.

Laglen was contemplating him. Girvyn knew his uncle erred on the side of caution, and he'd thought he did that because he was overprotective, but now Kalamayn was echoing his wise, pragmatic words. Perhaps they had a point.

'You need to get it into your head that you don't have a God-given right to impose your power on anyone,' said Laglen.

'Okay, Uncle.'

'It might seem a magnanimous idea, but what about all the businesses in the Waking that would collapse if you started offering a door to a free market?' continued Kalamayn.

'And the mass hysteria if you arrived with this portal,' Dremell added.

Girvyn felt the young man aligning with the oldies and took note.

'Made-up worlds are something Travellers do. But it's never something anyone in the Waking can or should experience. You would be inundated with personal and official requests,' Dremell said.

'More like orders,' Laglen added. 'Look at what those kidnappers wanted: to use you! So, let's concentrate on thought control.'

'But I have used the portal sparingly, and it's helped us so far, Uncle,' Girvyn said.

'I know. And we are very grateful. But we need to run more tests on it.'

'I am not going to bring nasty things through. I just wanted to give people free fruit.'

'I know. But Kal is right, you have the key to something that can be the biggest weapon, and we want to help you use it correctly.'

'That's what we are here for, to help you tune your raw talent,' Dremell said.

Laglen lifted his voice and brought the conversation on. 'Come, let's go back and see how your other structure has developed.'

With the chastening moment over, they returned to the Atrium and regarded the window.

A rotating aperture displayed a picture of the structure: that blooming, hopeful oak. Girvyn felt his pulse quicken.

'Shall we?' he gestured at it, trying to hold back his excitement.

Dremell rubbed his hands. 'I always get curious to see how things turn out. The way The Pull evolves our creations is one area we can't control.'

Kalamayn frowned. 'What did you set the time differential at?'

'Every second in the structure's default time to a year.'

'What?' Kalamayn did the maths, estimating how long they had been away from the structure.

'That's 1800 years! I didn't mean that fast.'

'Sorry, I didn't realise. You said speed it up, so I did, I wanted to see what would happen.'

'Don't apologise, Girvyn,' Laglen said. 'Nothing bad has happened, and it makes for a more interesting exercise.'

It was confusing at first: the eeriness of the scorched brown landscape that stretched from the tree to the mountain. The river had dried up, there was no sign of any animals, and that blooming, hopeful oak was no more than a withered, decayed piece of lifeless wood.

'What's happened?' Girvyn complained. 'The tree never grew in size.'

Kalamayn sighed. 'Ah, in cooking terms, you might call it burnt.'

'It's dead, Girvyn,' Dremell said, with a trace of sympathy. 'The structure collapsed.'

'I don't understand. Why? I created life and it died!' Girvyn almost sobbed.

Laglen sighed. 'Don't be hard on yourself. We didn't know this would happen.'

'I did wonder,' Kalamayn said.

'What does he mean?' Girvyn asked his uncle.

'Hmmm,' Laglen mused, his voice considerate. 'Sustainable ecologies aren't that simple or easy. The Pull reacts to your thoughts and can only fill so many gaps. If you don't leave thought systems, things will die, decay, and starve.'

'But I don't understand how these things work. That's not fair.'

'It's not about fairness.' Kalamayn said. 'You needed to give it a framework. You could have set it up so nothing ever dies, but you didn't, so the life you created just fades away.'

'We were unsure what you had set up,' Laglen explained. 'As it's your relationship with The Pull it's invisible to us.'

Dremell pointed up. 'I suspect the sun baked the land. You were probably thinking about Waking natural systems when you designed the structure, so what you created expected to follow what you know, yet you didn't add rain, create food chain systems, ecology, even reproduction.'

'So it withered away,' Laglen shrugged. 'Take those people I made in the floating stands in my race structure. They don't need food or water. They won't die, they won't procreate; they just exist as props. Because I set it that way.'

'This is awful. All the animals are dead. And I killed them.'

'Sometimes we learn quicker with hard, painful lessons,' Laglen said, offering a sympathetic smile.

Twenty-Nine

'What you did was courageous. We will forever be in your debt,' Nadine looked at him. Since he had saved her life, Derrilyn had lost count of the number of eye-to-eye conversations they had had.

He smiled at her. 'Everyone involved in this mission plays a crucial role in its success. But both of you have an even more important role than others. Plus, I despise...' he dithered, searching for the right word.

'Prejudice?' she offered.

'Yes, that's it. Elaya has taught me integrity and rightness, but my words still sometimes fail me.'

'She sounds like a remarkable woman,' Nadine remarked.

'That she is.'

'Yesterday, she would have been proud of you,' Nadine said, surprising him with her kind words. Did it take such an extreme act as saving her life to elicit politeness?

'I couldn't help but overhear that you grew up in the wild,' she continued.

'It wasn't easy,' Derrilyn said.

'That must have been incredibly challenging,' she empathised.

'It was what it was.'

Nadine nodded. An awkward moment settled between them. 'Look, I apologise for being rude, as Dream Travellers, we sometimes develop an inflated sense of self-importance.'

'I've only talked a little to him during a night hiding in a stable, but Girvyn doesn't seem like that,' Derrilyn remarked before glancing away.

'And that's the point. Girvyn has lived his entire life unaware,' she explained.

'And that seems to be for the better.'

She sighed, struggling to continue. 'I don't trust Orts,' she confessed, not looking him in the eye. 'When we voted to reveal our secret, I did not agree with that decision.'

'Why?'

'Because we would be feared and hunted like the druids were. This was my main concern, and it has turned out to be correct! I also don't feel a split vote of our sect gives us authority to out all the other Travellers. How many have been put in a vulnerable position because we decided we needed to align with Orts to stop Crane? We could have gone on this mission ourselves, without any of you knowing. It would certainly have been less conspicuous!' She wavered. 'I also have a more personal reason, but it's something I would rather not share.'

Something about her intrigued Derrilyn; a depth. Her apology impressed him too. She acknowledged her shortcomings matter-of-factly, not reproachfully or lost in regret. As he got to know her more, he felt motivated to win her over.

'What sort of dreams do you make?' he asked her. The question had piqued his interest ever since he had found out about the Travellers, wondering in occasional moments about what he would do with such a gift.

She seemed reluctant to say. She shrugged. 'Dremell is more open. Ask him.'

'Are you two close?' he blurted the question out, saw her amused expression and instantly regretted it.

'He is my best friend,' she said smiling.

Derrilyn tried to keep his feelings from reaching his face. 'That's interesting,' was all he could say. He winced inside.

She continued, 'Dremell has collected a group of Travellers that visit his structures on a weekly basis. He likes to host adventures for them to enter his fantasies,' she said. 'Ask him about it.'

'Adventures?'

'He makes epic journeys for others to play. He is the host-master, and they take characters to uncover secrets and battle fearless foes.'

'What? Like what we're doing now?'

'Yes, though no one actually dies. They just get eliminated from the game.'

'Are you assuming some of us will die?'

'No, I am just saying.'

Derrilyn wondered what to say next. 'Do you play?'

She snorted. 'No, I find it boring, and the people are weird. They are almost as annoying as Orts.'

'I don't understand why you don't like Orts.'

'Mr. Derrilyn…' The contours of her cheeks dazzled him. He noticed a serene green aura. 'It's too difficult for you to comprehend.'

Their legs touched as the horses neared. A smile traced her lips. Could she sense his infatuation? He was at a loss for words. 'T-try me,' he managed to stammer.

'Try me?' she questioned.

'Explain it to me.'

'Explain what?' she asked.

'Why do you keep repeating what I'm saying?'

She winked.

'I think we got off to a bad foot,' he admitted. 'But since you have a life-debt to me, can you answer why you don't trust Orts?'

'You're not going to hold saving my life over me, are you?' Nadine teased.

He winked back. 'For now.'

'Anyway, I think the expression is 'bad start' or 'on the wrong foot,' she corrected.

'I stand corrected,' he answered, adding, '...on my bad foot.'

Nadine took a deep breath. 'Fair enough. My mother was an Ort, and she abandoned me when I was a baby.'

'That's dreadful. I'm so sorry,' Derrilyn replied. He wanted to inquire further, but he noticed her tightened jaw, prompting him to change the subject. 'You mentioned being a Dream Traveller gives you a sense of self-importance?'

'It's more about growing up knowing I was different. Unlike Girvyn, who had no awareness of it,' she clarified. 'With knowledge comes responsibility. We become akin to gods.'

'Gods in your imagination,' he mused.

'It's difficult for those who are not "in the know" to understand and for me to explain. Having this dark secret is quite burdensome. I can't be myself around Orts. I perceive them as the "other" people to avoid. I'm sorry.' She shrugged. 'I know it's unfair, but that's how I feel.'

Derrilyn frowned. 'But by shutting yourself off, you're ignoring an entire...'

'What if I make a slip-up?' she snapped. 'And accidentally

reveal my secret? Or worse, what if I fall in love with one of them, just as my father did?'

'In love?' Derrilyn's eyes averted to the ground as they continued riding. 'What, have you?'

Her voice became calm again. 'No, I've never been in love with an Ort.'

He asked tentatively, 'Have you ever been in love with…a Dream Traveller? What about Dremell?' he said, far too quickly than he wanted to. 'I know you said you were just friends, but could you not see yourself with him?'

A faint smile passed across her face. 'I have known Dremell my whole life, and I think you will find it's not girls that he likes.'

Derrilyn faltered. 'Ah, I see. Fair enough,' he said, finally, trying to conceal dual measures of shock and relief as he casually moved the conversation on. 'I, too, have undergone changes,' he confessed. 'I've made my own discoveries and harboured secrets.'

'Indeed you have. It's rather poetic.'

'Is it? In what way?' He pursed his lips with genuine interest. Had she been contemplating him?

'Girvyn's powers come from the Realm, while yours are here.'

'I believe Girvyn is a unique case.'

'Oh yes, I suppose he is!'

'In my case, I don't have power. It's more a heightened connection to this world,' Derrilyn explained.

She nodded in understanding. 'Now it's my turn to be corrected.'

A call from ahead signalled a pause, and the procession began stopping. Up and down the line, riders dismounted and groomed their horses.

'It was nice talking to you,' Derrilyn said, sensing their

conversation was concluded and wanting to be the first to acknowledge it.

She patted his cheek and left.

Derrilyn watched her go, seeing a glow of purple. Purple, he wondered, what does that mean?

∼

News of the grand procession spread far and wide, captivating the attention of distant settlements. As the days passed, children from scattered communities flocked to the roadside, awaiting the army's arrival. Occasionally, curious young men carrying swords or pitchforks would approach the group, filled with intrigue and a desire to join the cause. Each time, however, they were sent away, for the mission's true purpose remained shrouded in secrecy, known only to the war council and the summit.

Under the starlit sky, the leaders of each House and clan gathered around a snapping campfire, their faces illuminated by hopping flames. Derrilyn waited for the conversation to begin, preferring to remain silent, trying to keep his gaze from lingering on Nadine too much.

Lord Grisham fixed his stare upon Dremell. 'You spoke of encountering resistance, but what form will it take? Enlighten us.'

'I cannot say for sure,' Dremell answered.

Grisham persisted, 'But what manner of defence shall we encounter? Archers? Foot soldiers? Stone fortifications?'

'He has always used wolves as his guard animal,' Nadine replied. 'But according to Maltip these packs have increased in number. Laglen was the last to visit from our group, and that was fifteen years ago. Can you tell us anymore, Maltip?'

Maltip responded, 'Recently he launched attacks on our

communities along the Riddon Slope. I can vouch for that. Who knows what evil creatures serve him.'

Cedar cast a sympathetic glance at Maltip. Throughout their journey, Derrilyn had noticed the Forester and the Highlander riding together, frequently immersed in conversation. Elaya, wary of potential disputes, had requested that he monitor them, but to his relief, no such conflict had arisen; it seemed they might be on the path to a mutual understanding.

Maltip acknowledged Cedar's look with a nod before shifting his attention to Lady Adara as she started to speak.

'We understand the suffering you have endured on the treacherous Slopes of Riddon,' she said softly. 'A fact made evident by your impassioned testimony at the summit.'

Maltip took a deep breath. 'In the depths of night, mournful cries reverberate across the vast highlands, tormenting our young and unsettling our slumber. Crane harbours a darkness that does not belong to our world.'

'What form does this darkness take?' Praleck asked.

Sward, his scabbard laid across his knee, turned towards Maltip with keen interest. 'Tell us, mighty Highlander.'

'We have seen only its shadow, moving fast and from afar. I cannot describe the creature to you, only that its cry chilled our very bones.'

Nadine leant forward. 'This cry, how did it sound?'

Maltip's lips moved soundlessly, then he shook his head. 'Agral, come over here.'

A wiry Highlander who was one of Maltip's lieutenants walked quickly to his chief.

'You can imitate any animal's cry. Do the creature from the Riddon slope.'

Agral turned pale, but still obeyed. The noise he made was an elongated sound like "aaarkrooooyeawk", and it left an eerie silence in its wake.

'Dremell, surely he can't have?' Nadine was staring at her fellow Traveller. 'There's no way that could survive in the Waking.'

Dremell was shaking his head. 'No way we know of. But what don't we know? Oh, we have turned our eyes away from Crane for too long.'

'What is this creature?' Lady Adara said.

'One of his hybrid banewulfs. A terrifying Realm monster.'

In the silence that followed, they heard only Alwad's urgent tone, whispering in Donjul's ear. In that moment, their resolve grew stronger, and each member of the war council felt the weight of their responsibility.

Praleck lowered his gaze. He directed his question towards Dremell. 'Can you provide us with a description of his stronghold?'

Maltip took a deep breath, reflecting the memories of stories past. 'His stronghold is modest, a wooden hut.'

Dremell nodded. 'Crane spends his time in the Realm more than this side. He does not reside in a grand mansion. His humble wooden cabin serves as his abode and laboratory.'

Curiosity flickered in Lady Adara's face. 'Laboratory? What kind of experiments take place there?'

Dremell's words held a hint of revulsion. 'Decades ago, he used the cabin as a research shed and conducted chemical experiments. These volatile experiments were instruments of his sinister curiosity.'

Maltip, drawing upon his knowledge of the treacherous terrain, explained, 'As we ascend the ledge, the precipice widens, stretching before us. This much I can tell you. Once we reach the perilous Riddon Slope, I shall guide you there.'

'And of Baron Kerrick Shadstone?' Lady Adara said, glancing at Dremell, her expression creased with concern.

'The story you told us has disturbed us greatly. He has been bringing druids for Crane to turn into monsters such as this red knight. Will we see more?'

Dremell's voice dropped. 'As I have told you, they were ambushed on a bridge. Not just with this druid monster, but by false humans displaying extraordinary strength.'

'What happened to Elaya worries us too. There is much whispering and fear among the men,' Sward muttered. 'Word of where we are going and why is circulating among the men. There are many questions about the purpose of this mission.'

'We need to inform them all of what we face, but when we get closer,' Lord Grisham told him.

'Kerrick's treachery looms ever larger. There may be some that spy for him,' Lady Adara said.

'I still can't believe Kerrick would do this against his own people,' Praleck said in disbelief. 'But no man travels with pigeons. And those we have are locked and guarded. How could they get word to him?'

Donjul's voice rose louder as he addressed everyone. The committee waited for him to finish, engaging him with eye contact. The interpreter translated. 'We must stick to the plan and not deviate or welcome newcomers.'

Sward nodded. 'Baron Kerrick Shadstone has ears in the court; he could have told Crane of our mission before we left, and we could be walking into a trap.'

'It doesn't change anything,' Nadine told them. 'There are five hundred of us, and we will meet resistance anyway. His sleeping form will not rest innocently.'

'Tomorrow,' Jaden said. 'We embark on the final leg of our journey towards the mountain. We shall rendezvous with fifty druids stationed in Cundelly. Together, we shall ride forth to battle.'

There was a cheer.

'The druids are with us!' Praleck hailed.

At that moment, two runner boys arrived, carrying a tray of soups, which they distributed among the committee members. Lord Grisham picked up a spoon and tasted it, his face flushing as the flavours burst onto his palate. 'When we reach the base of the mountains,' he said. 'We must send scouts ahead to assess the situation on Crane's ledge. We need to gather as much information as possible before proceeding. Are we all in agreement with this course of action?'

Nods and murmurs of agreement rippled through the group.

Sward stood. 'Then let us sleep and recover from today's arduous journey. We have two nights' rest remaining before the final battle.'

The leaders dispersed, seeking solace in much-needed repose.

Thirty

A bell rang over the door, and Mora stepped into the cluttered foyer of the antique shop. She hesitated, not knowing where to place her next step for fear of bumping into a free-standing mirror or knocking over a vase from a shelf. At the back of the shop came a familiar voice. 'Steady there, wait for me. I will assist you.' The voice grew louder. 'It can get quite jumbled in here as I acquire new stock, but I assure you, everything has a place…Mora!'

Kalamayn's smile broadened from a collegial greeting to a warm surprise. He drew her into a hug. 'What are you doing here?'

'I wanted to talk to you about something, off the record from the others.'

'What's on your mind?'

She sent him a blank expression. Now that she was here, she didn't know how to say it.

Maybe he sensed her struggle, for he raised a finger. 'Wait, let me close up so we can talk privately.'

'No, you don't have to do that. What about your trade?'

'I am not wedded to the shop. It's my Waking hobby; it

helps me focus while not in the Realm. But this is more important. A friend in need prioritises everything.'

Mora was about to remind him that he combed the market for collectables and knick-knacks to restore and sell and excessively hoarded stock. It was hardly a hobby. But she didn't want to challenge him; she'd come to him for help.

'I am just going to say it: I am scared about facing Crane.'

Kalamayn bolted the door, flipped the sign over to closed, and led her through the shop, taking special care to show her where to walk so she didn't disturb any ornaments.

She was happy to be guided, lost momentarily in her thoughts. They sat down at the rear of the shop, and Kalamayn considered her. 'Tell me.'

'You have always said I was stronger, but what does that mean? If Crane can violate our ancient rule and bridge Realm and Waking, then even in my Atrium I might not be able to stop him.'

'First, let me explain that I don't think such an important task should be placed at the door of Nadine or Dremell, which leaves you, Lag and me. And what I mean when I say you are the stronger is that you are always faster in your thoughts under stress than us. You are the calmest, which is why you are best equipped out of all of us.'

'But it has been years since I have done anything like this. Any thrill-seeking worlds went with my youth.'

'It's just about having presence of mind. You are fearless. But remember that you don't have to defeat him, just delay him. We both know that there's no way to know what you will face, but we can decide the theory, narrow down a set of responses that might save crucial slivers of a second. Think of it as a chess game: we just must think through all the possible moves and counter moves.'

She screwed up her face. 'I feel uneasy about this.'

'Then why don't we practice?'

Mora blinked a few times at him. 'What? In the Realm?'

'Yes. I can play Crane, and you can get your creative juices flowing.'

~

A short time later, they stood in Kalamayn's structure. 'I have given you full access to The Pull in this simulation,' he told her. 'You can practice without fear of hurting me.'

Mora nodded, familiar with simulation models. Over the years, they had tried different power relations, making for more exciting collaborative experiences. Having an overpowered author sometimes didn't cut it, and could be dangerous for the visitor.

Kalamayn changed his form, facing her in a purple hooded robe. 'Shall we begin?'

She raised an eyebrow. 'Really?'

'You wanted to practice this. It makes sense to do a believable imitation,' he said in a Crane-like whisper. 'You draw me into your world, and now you stand here as a pathetic excuse of an equal.'

'That's uncanny!'

The hood jiggled. 'I, too, have been practising.'

'Well, practice this!' Mora said, lightning burst from her fingers.

Robes on fire, the Kalamayn-Crane was thrown back into the white, the smell of smoke and burnt skin bitter in the air.

A moment later, Kalamayn reappeared as himself, frowning. 'If we assume the timeworn rules apply, Crane will die in a second. Is this what we want?'

'If the opportunity presents, of course! We could save Dremell and Nadine having to attack his stronghold.'

'Even as arrogant as he is, I don't think he will enter if he knows you could kill him.' Kalamayn paused, contemplating the dissipating smoke and smell. 'So, you are adding real-world effects?'

'Makes sense to include drama; it makes it more foreboding.'

'Let's try again. If he is mad enough to come in using a weaker Pull connection, then there is no need to practice.' Kalamayn reappeared as Crane again. 'But,' he said, his voice hissing with contempt. 'I am going to fight you as your equal. So just keep me preoccupied.'

Mora took a breath and watched while Kalamayn glided through the air towards her.

Then Mora started shaking, her skin pulling in opposite directions. 'What is this?'

'Just unthink it!' Kalamayn told her, coming out of character.

She held up her palm, then pushed it at him, exerting a g-force. He shot backwards, then vanished, popping up behind her. She felt a shockwave hit her, her body somersaulting in flailing circles. She came around, determination etched upon her face, hovering in the air, considering him.

'Think about the weapons you have seen in your futuristic constructs,' Kalamayn, encouraged. 'You want to hit him with different earthly forces and different types of projectiles. It will delay his reaction.'

'This test is a stalemate. I can't win. I can't beat him.'

'You don't have to. Not by yourself,' Kalamayn urged. 'All you need to do is occupy him until Dremell and Nadine strike in the Waking. This is our advantage: community and family. Crane has only ever had himself.'

Thirty-One

Elaya's inscrutable stare didn't waver from the portal doorway. 'No,' she gripped Girvyn's arm. 'Not yet. Show me something closer.'

Girvyn picked a tree halfway between where they stood and the horizon, and then presented it through the door. 'What about there, then?'

Elaya could tell that Girvyn was making an effort to listen to instructions. She searched for any dust clouds, travellers, or campfire smoke. The scene seemed empty. 'Okay, we go together, just you and me, and I step through first.'

The others watched, mesmerised. It was a strange sight indeed. Another vista in the aperture of the door, disrupting the view, while the existing view continued when you walked around it.

She drew her sword and stepped through. Girvyn followed. She looked back and saw the others peering at her from the beyond the door. She waved them through. Hazel remained, waiting with the horses. Then, after some whickering and protesting at the dazzling light and distracting heat, she began leading them through one by one.

For the rest of the day, they continued horizon jumping, becoming more confident to make each leap as far as they could see. Maude now went first to scout each jump location, the others following when she declared it safe. By sunset they had reduced the remaining journey to Wigginton to half a day's traditional ride. Although the horses were not tired and could have made that journey during the early part of the night, Elaya didn't want to travel in darkness. Therefore, they decided to set up camp.

With little daylight left, Maude disappeared to hunt for game, leaving Hazel on bonfire duties. Rowen groomed the horses. While Elaya listened to Laglen explain how he had experimented with fusion teas, she couldn't help but notice Girvyn walk deliberately over to Hazel.

∽

Girvyn watched Hazel working the flames. Apart from an incongruous word once or twice, they had not had a private conversation since the journey had begun. He glanced at Elaya and his uncle to check their conversation status; it was lively but nothing serious, so he continued over to Hazel.

'Hello, Hazel. How are you?'

Hazel was blowing into the flames and didn't look up at first. 'Hello Girvyn,' she said finally.

There was an awkward moment. 'How is the fire going?'

'It needs more wood.'

Girvyn pointed into a bank of trees. 'There is loads in there.'

'I collect deadwood. I will not chop fingers off a tree to keep us warm.'

'Of course, I mean, I am sure there is lots of deadwood lying around.'

Girvyn fell silent, eyes rolling everywhere like a madman. So many times, on the journey, he had rehearsed what he was going to say to her. Why now, when it was happening, had he forgotten the words? Forgotten how to start a conversation.

Hazel raised an eyebrow. 'Are you going to tell a bread joke?'

Girvyn stared, feeling like he was moving slowly while she was in standard time. Bread joke? What was that? Of course, the library. She had overheard his painful conversation with Zinnia. How long ago was that? Four or five days? A week? It seemed like a lifetime.

She smiled at him, waiting for him to answer. Was a smile a good thing? He needed to say something.

'I didn't properly thank you for saving me in the library.'

Hazel's piercing green eyes held his wavering look. 'Oh, you did. And I was happy to protect you. That thing took my people's young. I will do anything I can to fight it.'

Another awkward moment.

'But I must thank you too, Girvyn, for saving us at the bridge.'

'I couldn't save your kin. I am sorry.'

She looked at him squarely. It was as if her reddish hair and perfect face held the sun's luminance, and even were the sun to set and never return to the eastern horizon, all light would stay in Hazel everlasting nonetheless.

Girvyn swallowed hard, pushing away such thoughts. He reached into an inside pocket and brought out the most perfect long-stemmed rose. 'This is for you,' he said and passed it to her, throat tightening until it felt like a stone had lodged in it.

'What is this?'

'A flower.'

'I can see that.' Hazel scowled, studying it. Was the scowl

good or bad, he wondered. 'It's beautiful. But where did you get it? And why are you giving it to me?'

She thinks it's beautiful! He almost punched the air, his chest on the verge of bursting. 'It's a gift. A special gift,' he corrected himself, confidence growing. 'Just for you. Because I think you are... special.' He cringed inside.

Hazel was frowning. 'Thank you, that's very sweet. But where did you get it? We haven't passed any rose bushes, and this looks freshly cut.' She glanced back down at it again. 'It's perfect in every way.'

'Thank you, like you.' He cringed again.

Whether Hazel ignored the last comment or was too caught up in the flower was hard to tell. 'Where did you get it, Girvyn?' she asked again, voice hesitant.

'Okay, look, I created it. I thought you would like it.'

'Does your uncle know you are bringing things through?'

'It's just a flower.'

'It's not right. Flowers grow here. They aren't made up in someone's mind and passed through some time portal. It's not natural.'

'It's not a time portal; it's an interdimensional doorway.'

She dropped the rose onto the fire and watched it burn.

'Are you scared of me?' Girvyn couldn't help himself. She had just burnt his gift. And it sizzled like his heart. The fact that Hazel was so bold and direct justified his straightforward manner. 'Why did you do that?'

She took a moment; voice a whisper. 'It's very kind of you to bring me a present and say nice things about me. But I don't trust the Realm. The Realm has brought devastation to so many of us.'

'Are you saying you don't trust me?'

She shook her head. 'I am saying I don't trust the power of

the Realm and what it might do to people with limitless control of it.'

Girvyn silently cursed. Limitless control? She doesn't trust me. Why? Because I am different? Because I have a portal? Because I killed a man who incidentally kidnapped me and was going to do untold things to me? What do I need to do to gain her trust?

'I just wanted to give you a present to express my feelings.'

'And that's very kind of you.'

'Because I like you.' Girvyn wished he had never said that. 'What do you think about me?' Was he losing his sight? Everything had narrowed to a pinpoint view.

She blinked a few times, considering him. 'Look, I understand what you are saying to me. But we need to concentrate on the journey and on protecting you. It's better not to confuse things.'

'I am not confused.'

It felt like he had stepped in mud and was stuck up to his knees.

'Even if things were different and we were not at war, even if I was not protecting you, and then, say, you were one of my kind, accustomed to my traditions, and we were in peacetime in the forest, we would still have one problem.' She bit her lip, then took a breath. 'I am in my twentieth year, Girvyn, and you are still a boy.'

Oh, he thought. So it's my age...

They stared at each other for what seemed like minutes. 'Look, I am not going to tell Laglen about the rose. But please don't bring me gifts again,' she corrected herself, 'or bring anything else through.'

'Not deadwood? I can help you with the fire.'

'No, Girvyn,' she stood up and faced him. 'Sorry, I should have done that at the start of our conversation. You deserve my full attention. I am very fond of you. You are a sweet and kind boy.'

There was that word again. Every time she said it he felt like he'd been struck in the side of the head.

'But we are friends and are staying that way. And I want to collect the deadwood myself.' She smoothed down the sides of her dress. 'I will go, before it gets too dark, and gather more firewood. Thank you for the conversation and for being so honest.' She smiled, leaned forward, and kissed his cheek.

Yes, Girvyn thought. She likes me!

He watched her walk into the trees, his mind still whirring, his feet stuck in the proverbial mud.

∼

A sickle moon cast a pale light upon the path. She picked up a frail branch, snapped it in two and carried both twigs. A larger log crumbled and was damp to touch so she left it. She didn't want to keep popping back and forth into the trees, trying to find firewood in the dark, so she picked up her pace and moved further into the woodland, scanning this way and that for any discarded pieces.

She was grateful for the quiet, and the dimness drew her thoughts into focus.

Girvyn was a sweet boy, quite unlike anyone she had ever met. There was much to be admired about him. Most of the men in her tribe would just pick a woman for mating. Dogmatic, true believers in themselves and their entitlement. Girvyn was different; respectful. He tried to articulate his feelings, albeit clumsily, and had asked what she felt, which hadn't gone unnoticed.

But the truth was she wasn't seeking a connection with

anyone. She felt relieved that her tribe elders hadn't mandated marriage for her. The Foresters' cultural traditions surrounding matrimony were stringent, and marrying an outsider was prohibited. Even though she often resisted the tribal customs and patriarchal dictates, she took solace in this particular rule. It could be her shield if Girvyn's fascination with her continued.

Not that Girvyn was implying marriage to her. He had a crush on her, that's all, she supposed. She should not have kissed him on the cheek, and she'd regretted it as soon as she had done it. But what's done is done, she thought. She could present clear boundaries going forward. She was sure he had got the point in a not-too-shaming message.

Without warning, there was a short blue blast of light through the trees to her right. She dropped to her knees and reached for her hunting knife. Frozen in fear, she held her breath; the smell of ozone wafted across her position. She heard steps on the forest floor, and then the portal closed. The footsteps continued, coming closer to her position. Heart hammering, she gripped the knife, blinking in the low light. Memories began flooding in, burning huts and shifting, looming demons.

Was this an attack? Not by a demon division anyway, nor towering insects. There was only the one set of footsteps. It was the shape of a man. Was it Crane himself? But he was not cloaked. No cowl. An assassin sent by Crane? Could be.

She needed to get back to camp and warn the others.

Hazel cursed quietly, unable to move without giving her position away. The shape hesitated, rotating in the dark as if lost. Then it took a step closer towards her. From her crouched position, she knew it hadn't seen her. This was her chance to come up on it in surprise.

As it passed her, she leapt up from the ground, knife glinting in the moonlight.

'No, wait! Don't be alarmed; it's me.'

The voice was familiar, the accent was – not the pitch, which was deeper. Hazel's blade thrust stopped an inch from his neck.

'Girvyn? Is that you?'

'Yes, it's me.'

'What's happened to you?' She lowered the knife and reached up with her other hand, then caught herself and drew it back. No shows of affection, she told herself.

'I could have killed you.'

'This is what you wanted.'

'Girvyn, what's happened to your voice?'

'It will be easier if I show you. Stand back.'

Hazel took a step back and waited.

'More. Another step.'

'Girvyn, you are scaring me.'

The portal opened a little behind where Girvyn stood, and Hazel realised he had asked her to move back to protect her from the light. In the blaze of the portal, it was hard to see him at first; his form was a silhouette. He came towards her and, with both hands, held her shoulders, steering her around so the portal lit his left side; then he tilted his face towards the light.

She gasped. 'Girvyn, what have you done!'

'Is this better? Do you like me now?'

Hazel fell silent for a long moment, her attention absorbed in studying his unshaven, manly jaw. She felt a strong desire to reach up and touch his stubble, to trace her finger along the contours of his age lines, but she pushed the urge aside.

He broke the silence. 'I don't know how much older I look; I wanted twenty, twenty-one, but I think I overcooked it.'

'This shouldn't be possible. Having the thought "I wish I was older" shouldn't be something you can act upon.'

'But do you like me now?'

Hazel wiped the corners of her eyes. 'Look, you can change your voice, change your face, but, but...' she faltered; she had given too much to him last time. Told him he was too youthful. If she added more reasons, would he react again, modify himself in the portal and keep trying? 'But, it's not real. Accept what you can't change rather than try and change it.'

'But you kissed me.' He dropped his head. The portal blinked away, leaving them in darkness, his voice lifeless. 'I feel so ashamed.'

'I'm sorry I kissed you, but it was on the cheek. And please don't feel embarrassed.' She wanted to hold him, protect him from himself, but she didn't dare. 'It's okay. I get it. But look, please, just change back; we will keep this between us, a secret,' she patted his arm. 'Agreed?'

Girvyn sighed. 'Agreed.'

But then he just stood there looking at her. He didn't change back.

Hazel studied him for a while. His voice had broken and gained maturity. His hair was rolled in a bun at the back of his head, not too unlike the officials in court she had seen at the summit. He had added a few inches to his height too, although he was tall anyway. He appeared weary; not battle weary, but understated. She was fascinated with how he had made this reference.

'I just don't think you should be using the Realm and

portal like this,' she said finally. 'I know you mean well, and my objection is not even fear that you will become corrupted by power; I don't think you will. I have known you briefly, and I can see a ...' she hesitated, careful not to use the word boy, '...a young man with the world at his feet. A considerate, sensitive soul, who detests violence and inequality.'

'I do! I do!' Girvyn declared. He seemed grateful that she understood him.

'But it's just that I don't trust the Realm or the portal. Even if you wield it, Girvyn. I watched my father get dragged into one of these and taken to some hell,' she glanced away, fighting back the memories of his last moments: on his knees, helpless, surrounded by demons, while she hid not five paces away in the trunk of a tree base. Her voice stiffened. 'My father fought bravely to protect the tribe and was the last man standing. Even with just one arm left, he wanted to fight,' she sobbed, 'but they took him from me.'

Girvyn gasped, a hint of recognition crossing his face. 'One arm, did you say?'

Hazel caught the flash of pain in Girvyn's eyes. 'What is it?' she urged.

'Was it his left one, missing from the shoulder?' he asked.

'Yes!'

'Was he wearing a coloured tooth necklace, like Glefforn did?'

All reservations about physical contact gone, she gripped him. 'Have you seen him? Where is he?'

'I am so sorry; I didn't know what I was seeing; I thought it was a dream. Crane and the demons brought the dead from the forest and took them away, but your father,' he stammered, 'he wasn't killed. He was taken for...he was...'

Girvyn's voice dried up.

'Taken for what?' she demanded.

'Alterations.' He paused, shifting from foot to foot. 'I couldn't stop it; I didn't know what to do.'

'Alteration into what?'

'Into something else.'

'Into what? How do you know? Are you sure you saw what you saw?'

'I remember everything I see.'

'Then tell me what Crane did to him.'

'I don't want to tell you Hazel. I don't want to hurt you.'

Hazel reached out and took his arm again. 'Girvyn, did I not just make it clear that I value truth above anything else? Please tell me.'

'I am so sorry, Hazel. He didn't die. He was transformed into one of those things in red armour.'

She let out a lone sob. 'The one we killed in the library?'

'No. That was there the night your father was taken. It brought him through the portal, and was carrying your tribe's babies,' his eyes locked onto hers. 'Your father became another demon in armour. The helmet had a slightly different form, which is how I can tell them apart. It...' He gasped as the realisation struck him. 'We saw it! Your father! He was the one on the bridge with Kerrick!'

She didn't hear the last part. Her head was dizzy and she was already falling to the ground. She didn't hit it. Instead, she felt her body being caught by Girvyn's arms. In the moonlight, she saw his kind, worried gaze upon her, and despite his youthful innocence, for a moment, she just wanted to stay held forever.

'I am so sorry,' he whispered. 'Each of us saw half of the event from different dimensions.'

'My father is still alive!'

'Your father is gone, that thing is not him.'

'I want to know everything,' she said to him. 'Tell me exactly what you saw.'

Girvyn did. She'd asked Girvyn for all the details, and she got it all.

It made her content to remain cradled in his arms while she tried to push away the images of the tentacle demon, a sucker attached to her father's mouth, his agonising transformation even as the slain members of her tribe were taken away into the dark by the spiders.

'Are you okay?' Girvyn asked her.

She didn't reply. She couldn't.

'One thing that sticks out, though, is that Elaya said she sensed a druid. Some twisted druid aura.'

'My father wasn't twisted. Strict, old fashioned, yes. A druid, I don't know.' She swallowed. 'He was very skilled. He was called a Ewen, a tree-diviner, one who senses the forest. So maybe he was. We don't work with the Druid Guild and get assessed.'

Girvyn remained quiet for a moment. 'Elaya would sense it in you. Maybe it skipped a generation.'

Only now was she aware her feet hung in the air. 'Girvyn, how aren't your arms killing you?'

'Oh, I added a strength thought.'

'What?' She sensed her feet being placed on the ground and moved back a clump of hair that had flopped in front of her cheek. 'How can strength be a thought?' She felt Girvyn read her bemused expression while he explained how things worked in the Realm. He could change himself and create anything he wanted. The portal was merely a conduit for bringing creations across; something which had never been possible before. But it sounded like the easy part was the creation; the hard part was developing the concept. She likened it in her head to the tribe lookout positions: overlapping, multiple viewpoints that covered every inch of their territory. The easy part was climbing the tree, and the hard part was coming up with the map of who goes where.

Suddenly voices were calling.

Hazel hissed quietly. 'It's Elaya. Change back!'

'We are over here,' Girvyn called out to her dutifully.

'Girvyn!' Hazel breathed. 'Please.'

'What are you doing?' yelled an accusing, worried voice from the dark: Elaya. 'Where are you?'

Hazel gripped his wrist, voice low. 'You can't let them see you like this.'

'I am sorry I did it,' he managed.

'It's fine, just go.'

He fired open the portal and stepped inside.

The light illuminated the others, scrambling through the woods towards their position. Elaya arrived first, blade held out levelly.

'What is going on out here?' Laglen came alongside Elaya. Everyone was there. Rowen and Maude's swords were drawn, ready for any danger.

Girvyn, back to normal, appeared through the door. 'It's fine. I am with Hazel.'

Elaya was scrutinising him with that slightly narrowed, eyes-slanting scowl. 'I've been searching for you!' she exclaimed. 'We've repeatedly told you to stick with us. To stay in the camp, and not to wander off. What if Crane had opened a portal and snatched you away?'

'How, Elaya?' Girvyn retorted, his expression unreadable. 'He would have to, one, know where we are, and two, have seen this exact same spot before to open his portal onto it!'

Elaya glared at him for a long moment. 'He sent the Drone Druid after you using scent, so let's not argue over details. Just do what I ask!'

'And no more use of the portal unattended or unnotified, okay?' Laglen added, disappointed.

'And why is Hazel crying?' asked Rowen.

Girvyn straightened. 'Because we worked out something Crane did that is very distressing for her. It was not a conversation that could happen in the dark, so I called the portal for light. I do not believe Crane can possibly know where to find us, but if he does then I can meet whatever comes through with creations from my own portal or, at worst, use it to flee. You do not need to keep coddling me like a baby.'

For some seconds no-one spoke. Then Elaya sheathed her sword noisily. 'Assuming you still need to eat as before, then Maude has caught a deer. Can we all agree on some feasting?'

∾

Later that night, Girvyn watched Hazel stare into the flames of the fire. Girvyn felt the heat in her eyes burning like a steaming cauldron.

'I watch your eyes follow my every move, Girvyn. Is there something I can help you with?'

Girvyn's gaze didn't waver. 'If my stare is too strong, I apologise. But turning away is the hardest test you ask of a man.'

'A man?' she teased, looking him up and down. 'I won't contest...'

'What is it that you see?'

'I see a burning distraction every time I look at you, Girvyn.'

'Then should we not go with this? Why resist what feels right? I didn't ask for it, nor can I stop it. Can you?'

Suddenly, she was in his arms. 'But Girvyn, we must stay focused on the mission.'

'But I can't ignore my heart, Hazel,' he whispered.

'Nor can I ignore mine.' She leaned in, and their lips met.

But just then, a voice interrupted. 'Girvyn, may we talk?'

Startled, Girvyn stumbled back. 'Freeze the structure,' he gasped, face flushing. 'Sunfire! Uncle always told me it's polite to knock before entering another's structure uninvited.'

'Girvyn, you forget I can see all structures.'

'You don't have to enter then! My shame is complete.' He dropped his head.

'Girvyn, I don't judge you for this. Many have done much worse. I am here to offer you a warning. Resist. It's tempting to use the Realm in this way. It offers one their deepest desires unchecked and indulged. For many, this is where the problems begin. If a Dream Traveller can't have something in the Waking, they fulfil it here; then the Dream side becomes their real! Often, not getting your own way in life, being turned down, and having to deal with disappointment and acceptance that one can't always get their own way makes a person. Hazel doesn't want you like this.' He flapped a flaming hand towards her frozen representation. 'It's not healthy to fulfil your desires in this way. Take the Baron, Kerrick. He has ruthlessly stepped on, double-crossed, used and killed to gain dominance over others. Look what happens to a man who is not checked. And he is on the Waking side!'

Girvyn frowned. 'It's not right that a person's deepest desires are viewed and judged by someone else! I can't even have a fantasy now? I am not hurting anyone.'

'I know you are not. I am not being critical.'

'I have all these feelings I don't understand, thrown into a mission I didn't request.' He sighed. 'This side, I can control the narrative. I am just trying to cope.'

Sunfire didn't reply immediately. Was he measuring him or reflecting? 'There is nothing wrong in having a crush on someone. Even someone older. For many, that is part of growing up. But here, where all your desires can be realised before any training or ethical considerations – you need to stay focused, not distracted.'

Girvyn's eyes narrowed. 'How do you know so much about Kerrick? Hold on, Hazel has only just rejected me. I thought you couldn't see the Waking side?'

'I can't, but I can see this side from all angles.'

'You are being evasive again; what are you not telling me? I am not stupid, you know. I don't trust you; you spy on me, and no one has ever heard of you before. Yet, you appear to me. Why?'

'I know this is hard to take in. But I am not your enemy. I am here to guide you, too. I have given you immense power, making yourself look older... that move was immature.'

'You always do that — change the subject. So, you *are* judging me!' Girvyn's frustration boiled over. 'Look, I know making myself look older was a mistake; I see that now. But we all make mistakes.' With a wave of his hand, he cleared away the image of Hazel, leaving them standing alone in the endless white expanse. 'I didn't ask for this, Sunfire, and I don't want this power. Why did you give it to me?' He let out an exasperated breath, his shoulders sagging. Even here, in a space he could control, his anxiety gnawed at him. 'I'm doing my best,' he said, his voice quieter as he dropped his head. Hesitating, he added, 'Everyone thinks I'm too young for this responsibility.' He made a face, glancing back up. 'I don't even experience things like other people. You were mad to give it to me.'

'That is precisely why you have it. Deep down within you is a care of others, is there not?'

Girvyn nodded mutely. 'How do you know that?'

'Would you not sacrifice yourself for the greater good of the many?'

'Wouldn't everyone?'

'Not everyone. You'll need that selflessness when the time comes.'

Girvyn's voice sharpened. 'What are you not telling me?'

But his question drifted unanswered into the emptiness.

Thirty-Two

He rolled sideways, felt his body shake. Voices from his dreams shouted at him. He shook once more, but this time the voice was clearer, targeting him alone. The chill of the ground pressed against his cheek, the scent of dampness filling his nostrils.

'Get up!' the voice commanded again.

He squeezed his eyes tighter. Why couldn't he open them? It felt as though he was trying to raise a portcullis with nothing but his bare hands.

Derrilyn sat up, felt his stomach jolt with queasiness. Was he going to be sick?

'Here, sniff this,' he heard the voice beside him say, felt a cloth press against his nose. 'Inhale deeply,' the voice said. It was Praleck.

'What is it?' Derrilyn managed.

'Delights from The East; it will help you wake up. You have been drugged.'

As soon as the odour shot into his brain, his eyes widened, and he became alert.

'What's going on?'

'Dremell and Nadine are gone,' Praleck replied grimly. 'It must have been co-ordinated across the camp.'

'Lady Adara, Jaden?' Derrilyn blurted. He searched around and found the druids sat against a tree, being attended to by one of Praleck's men.

'Are you ok?' Lady Adara said. She seemed groggy and slow.

Derrilyn nodded.

'Give us a few moments for our heads to clear,' Jaden said.

'Over here!' Donjul's interpreter called out, his voice carrying a note of urgency as Donjul pointed to the ground.

Derrilyn left the druids and joined Donjul, who spoke some more, and Alwad translated hurriedly. 'Their footsteps have left marks, just like the ones on the sand. They headed off in that direction,' he concluded, motioning.

Sward studied the tracks. 'He's right. With many horses, heading into the rough.'

'Are there any other members missing from our army?' Derrilyn said. Clearer thoughts began to cut through the haze.

'We're down by about twenty men, including the chef,' Praleck said. 'Keeping the purpose of our mission secret might have been a mistake,' he continued, his voice low. 'If we had shared the full truth with our men, that our aim was to eliminate a genuine evil, would this have happened?'

Derrilyn surveyed the camp. Soldiers scurried about, while the war committee convened around him, deliberating their next steps.

'After the library attack revealed the existence of the Travellers, we learned from Envoy Nark that he wanted all Travellers eliminated. The real oversight,' Derrilyn told them, 'was underestimating the threat posed by everyone knowing Nadine and Dremell's true nature.'

'And not knowing who to trust,' Praleck agreed. 'Saddle your horses, we're going after them.'

Lady Adara and Jaden arrived, studying the scene. They seemed like themselves again.

'Are you okay?' Lady Adara asked him softly.

Derrilyn gave a slow nod of his head. 'I'm sorry. My druid senses are not perfected yet. I didn't sense the danger.'

'The runner boys didn't know the soup was drugged. I scanned them at the time.'

'It was clever to send someone else to dispatch it,' Jaden added, looking away.

'Enough regret,' Sward told them, patting Derrilyn's shoulder. 'Don't worry, it's not your fault.'

'We need to get moving,' Lord Grisham said. 'Before it's too late. Donjul, lead us out.'

∼

Eight riders ventured into the forest, the rhythmic thump of the horses' hooves caressing the forest floor, filled the tense stillness that hung over them. Donjul and Maltip led them, sweeping the terrain. Each galloping path left a clear and unmistakable trail for all to perceive.

Lady Adara and Jaden followed behind. Lord Grisham, Sward, Praleck, and finally Derrilyn formed the rear guard. Just as Elaya's sudden revealing of the head had brought this group together in Rathnell, so the kidnap of the very two they had all sworn to protect now forged a common resolve among them.

As the seconds passed, turning into minutes, Derrilyn began to wonder whether they would see Nadine and Dremell again and, if they did, what they might find. Catastrophic visions inundated his consciousness.

Their journey continued in anxious silence for close to an hour, hampered by the dense woodland that hindered their pace. Donjul kept pointing to prints in the mud, uttering words that were unfamiliar to them, yet the meaning behind his actions was universally understood. Considering the arduousness of the terrain, Derrilyn surmised they had only covered some three leagues.

Yet, amidst their struggle, a nagging question arose: where were these tracks leading? If Derrilyn had planned the kidnapping, his instinct would have driven him to speed to a distant refuge. This track, however, led into the heart of the Lubin Forest.

Lady Adara halted, her countenance marked by a sombre intensity. The rest of the group stared at her questioningly.

'I know where they are going,' she declared, her voice laden with gravity. 'The Altar of Sacrifice.'

Praleck's reaction was immediate. 'Of course, the sacrificial altar at Pine Keep.'

'What is Pine Keep?' Maltip frowned.

Adara proceeded to enlighten them. 'Pine Keep is a man-made stone dais, surrounded by pine trees, which has stood for centuries.'

Lord Grisham chimed in, adding further context. 'Its origin and purpose remain shrouded in mystery, but fanatics have exploited it for sacrificial rituals.'

'We need to get there now!' Derrilyn urged and kicked the horse's flank. The horse reared up its front legs, then lurched into the trees.

∽

A few minutes before reaching the ceremonial site, Lady Adara signalled for the group to halt. Jaden dismounted and surveyed the surroundings, his gaze shifting back to Adara. 'I am sensing multiple auras,' he told her. 'Far more than the tracks indicated.'

Adara nodded. 'At least thirty,' she confirmed. 'We proceed silently.'

For Derrilyn, the atmosphere among them seemed to intertwine with fear and uncertainty.

Upon reaching the ridge, the scene spread out like a tableau of dread. A wooden platform encircled by majestic, towering pines. A multitude of figures scattered across the area. Some attendees wore masks fashioned after various animals: the sly fox, the lithe deer, and the savage wolf. These masked individuals stood with solemnity, each holding a staff planted in front of them. The sight painted a surreal display, evoking a sense of ancient rites and mysterious symbolism. Clay bowls brimming with squirrel skulls littered the area, the macabre remnants of past rituals.

The stillness of the adorned ceremonial leaders radiated a palpable tension. As Derrilyn's eyes darted from one to another, recognition dawned. Many of these men had been their companions during the journey, their true allegiances hidden behind the facade of solidarity. He gauged their auras. These weren't mere foot soldiers, but seasoned warriors.

At the centre of this harrowing spectacle were Nadine and Dremell, their voices silenced by gags, their hands bound behind their backs. They sat astride horses, their lives tethered by taut nooses looped around their necks, the ropes in turn affixed to an overhanging wooden structure.

The figure decorated in the guise of a wolf assumed the role of the executioner. Clutching a whip, he stood poised, ready to strike the horses' flanks. The brutal impact would propel the frightened animals into a desperate gallop, hurtling them into the surrounding trees. The ensuing jolt threatened to snap Nadine and Dremell's necks.

Derrilyn sensed Lady Adara's calculating scan, mapping out an attack plan. 'Jaden, aim for Nadine's rope, I'll take Dremell's' she said.

Donjul's voice reached his ears in a hushed whisper. His words carried quiet confidence. 'I can shoot a bird in full flight across the sands. Let me do this.'

Despite the heavy-sounding accent, the words were there. Jaden blinked in disbelief. 'All this time you speak our tongue?'

'I would rather dream in my own language. But we are in battle, so I speak yours now to you.'

Jaden measured the desert nomad, nodding. 'I trust in your exceptional marksmanship.' He holstered his bow, and drew a sword, joining the others. The group braced themselves, waiting for Lady Adara to instruct them.

Eyes focused down the line of the shaft, Lady Adara began instructing as new thoughts struck her. 'Jaden, lead the men down the hill. I need another arrow on the executioner, for when we free Nadine and Dremell, the executioner might go for them with his sword.'

Derrilyn felt his blood racing through his veins. 'I can be that arrow.'

With three arrows targeted, that left five in the rescue group.

'There are too many of them to take in hand-to-hand combat,' Adara said, sensing everyone's thoughts. 'Once we have removed the rope and the executioner, we can turn our arrows to the others. But they will return fire.'

'We need to protect the Dream Travellers from further attacks,' Derrilyn said.

'Let's go,' Lord Grisham agreed. 'We might even be able to talk them down.'

'You need to do it now,' Derrilyn said, his voice hissing. 'Look.'

The executioner had uncurled a scroll and began reading. 'Gather, brethren! Our sacred text commands us to rid ourselves of this unholy presence. These demons that have befallen our land, the Dreamers are responsible! We must act swiftly to protect our community from further harm! The Lord shall guide my hand. His divine providence has granted me the ability to discern the truth.' He addressed Nadine and Dremell. 'We stand today in the presence of evildoers, who have corrupted our land with their dark arts! As a devout servant of the Lord, it is my sacred duty to cleanse this community with death by hanging.'

'Stop!' came Jaden's loud cry.

Everyone stared at the top of the ridge as Jaden, Maltip, Lord Grisham, Sward, and Praleck, came down the slope.

'You know who we are!' Lord Grisham announced, his voice as sharp as the glinting steel in his outstretched hand. 'Put down your arms.'

'What? Hand over our weapons, and be split on a spit?' One of the men hollered, his mask quivered with his shaking rage. 'Like our brethren who you murdered, you cowards?!'

'No harm is done, stop this before anyone is hurt,' Sward shouted.

The executioner's voice boomed out. 'Stay back, Grisham, Sward, you dream lovers.'

'Heathens!' another masked man shouted.

Lord Grisham stared at the man in the mask. 'I know that voice. You betray your kingdom, Calum.'

'The Kingdom of Casper has betrayed us by joining this

devil alliance. Stand back! If you take a step further, we will make their horses bolt.'

'Think very carefully about this. We represent a sovereign alliance. Stand down, or you will face war with the Houses and kingdoms across the land!'

'Then your pitiful alliance will meet a religious crusade, Lord Grisham. One unlike any you have ever seen. We have soldiers in every kingdom, House, and armies across the land.'

'We are not your enemy. The Travellers with us are here to stop a greater evil.'

'Judgment has been made. God has spoken.'

The executioner held the whip aloft, poised to strike the horses' flanks, but a whizz sliced through the stillness. Then, in rapid succession, two further distinct twangs rang out; the swift release of arrows accompanied by the resounding thuds of their impact. The perfectly aimed shots severed the ropes, dropping the executioner, an arrow jutting out the eye of his mask.

Nadine and Dremell found themselves riding aimlessly with hands bound as chaos erupted around them.

Grisham charged, sword flying, and swept into a group of attackers. Sward and Maltip swung axes. Praleck, armed with a sword and shield and covered in Hoppenell armour, fought three men with the noble prowess of a seasoned knight. The din of clashing metal mixed with the cries of the dying. A fox-masked head rolled through the air. Other men fell where they stood. Jaden swayed, twisted, and ducked, while manoeuvring along the edge of the stage, taking on multiple adversaries at once.

Derrilyn drew an arrow to his cheek and released. Another man fell. More arrows followed from Donjul and Adara, thudding into the cult attackers, and now there were only eight left, ready to die for their cause. These, Derrilyn scanned, were the most skilled among the cultists.

Derrilyn set down his bow and unsheathed his sword. He wanted this. Until today he had never been in battle. A street fight yes, but nothing like this. He needed this. Was trained for this. Red auras deepened, issuing from the men's forms as their masks fell away, revealing determined, resolute faces; a solemn moment before the final stand. Eight against eight.

He left his position and came down the ridge.

'Be careful,' Lady Adara warned, coming to his side with Donjul, their blades drawn.

He reached the others and stood in a line, facing the men. There was no choosing or discussion on who took who. It just happened naturally.

The cultists tested their swords, their eyes narrowing into pinpricks, assessing what they might face.

A sword lunged towards Derrilyn, and he parried it away. An opening came, but he let it pass, preferring to follow Elaya's advice. He heard her words. *Let them lead. See what they can do. Assess their attack patterns.*

In battle, he had been taught, most men follow a favourable set of moves like a chess player with the same gambit each time.

What was his opponent capable of? Where did his patterns leave gaps?

He positioned himself as he had been taught. One foot slightly in front of another, allowing his attacker's force to determine his own movements. A lunge came. He blocked it, and they swapped positions, his attacker frowning at the shift in their location. Good, Derrilyn thought, he thinks I am toying with him.

A sideswipe came, and he deflected it, assessing his opponent's defence strength with a testing thrust. The zealot came again, and Derrilyn dealt with his combination, noting it, then another and another. Annoyance grew on the man's face, eyes narrowing, sparks now fiery shooting red.

The sounds of battle roared around him – shouting, grunts, and clashing steel – but he kept his focus on the man before him, sensing his twitching jaw, muscles, and tightening grip.

Derrilyn defended the grouping differently this time so as not to alert the other to the pattern they were creating.

The man growled. 'You fight like a tourney contestant.'

Derrilyn said nothing, kept his aspect unreadable, and his opponent came around. The combination repeated, a thrust, a reverse swing, and a chop.

Derrilyn sidestepped so the chop overextended, pivoting as he did so to punch him in the neck; a move Elaya relished. The man's eyes widened as he realised he was open, and vulnerable. A swing of his sword was all it took. Then his head rolled from his neck.

Derrilyn turned and saw his friends' astonished faces; their own opponents lay on the floor.

'Elaya has taught you well, young Derrilyn,' Lady Adara said admiringly.

Jaden nodded in appreciation. 'Many would have risked an attack to gain an end, but you waited.'

'I knew he couldn't take me, so if I stayed agile and defensive the opening would come to me.'

There was a cheer from his comrades and lots of slapping on his back; warm, elated faces filled his vision. Then there fell a hush. The group stood amidst the aftermath; the weight of their triumph settled upon them.

The prisoners were freed from their binds. Words seemed inadequate in the face of what they had endured. As Lady Adara beckoned them forward, there was an understanding that the bonds formed in the face of adversity would last a lifetime. The group led the newly liberated captives back to the ridge, where the horses patiently waited.

Derrilyn watched, filled with admiration for his steadfast friends; this group was a force to be reckoned with. Even if Crane was prepared for their arrival, they would prevail.

His reflection was interrupted by Nadine's outburst. 'What did I say about revealing our secret to the Orts. We've jeopardised all Travellers!'

Riding close, Derrilyn replied softly, 'You're right, and I apologise for not heeding your warning.'

Tears glistened in Nadine's eyes. 'It isn't your fault,' she sobbed, trying to control her emotions. 'You've been nothing but kind to me.'

Derrilyn cast one final look at the ceremonial grounds, then rode off, the remnants of the dark ritual dissipating into memory.

Thirty-Three

The next morning, Elaya began packing up the camp. Maude put out the fire and cleared away their tracks. Not that she needed to. In a short while, they would be horizon jumping to Wigginton.

Maude sent a sneaky glance at the pack horse, where a large pouch clinked against the saddle. Elaya had seen Maude look at the bag more than once since they'd started the journey: twenty gold pieces now for Lady Wigginton. Rattling away with every dropped hoof.

Maude came to Elaya's side. 'Can you assure me that, even though we have saved all this time horizon jumping, I will still get paid in full?'

Elaya went to the money bag, untied it, and waved it. 'Is this what you want?'

'Yes, you know why I am here.'

'You can't take your eyes off it. Money seems to be all you care about.'

'I am here to do a job and get paid. Not to talk to you and your company about anything else but the journey. It's ironic that if you'd known at the start Girvyn could horizon jump, you wouldn't have needed to hire me, would you?'

'But we did hire you. One hundred gold pieces for a month's work. Don't worry, you will still get paid the full amount.'

Maude sent her a sideward glance. 'I don't have to justify my fee to you! When you have money, you don't have to rely on people. I am not tied to a commander or an organisation! And even if it's just a pittance of a palace salary, you also get paid for the work you do.'

'No. I do not accept it.'

'What? What?' Maude exclaimed, her eyes flickering with a series of rapid blinks.

'There is nothing to buy with it. The Crown gives me my lodging. I eat in the barracks with my men.'

'You work for free?'

'I work out of loyalty, and receive housing and food. My family is the Crown.'

Maude shook her head. 'What do you do on your day off?'

'I practice my skills and see Laglen.'

Maude groaned. 'At least I have a life. And you are judging me!'

Elaya bared her teeth. 'I have a life. It's just not motivated by money, but by service, integrity and ethics.'

'Ethics! Don't talk to me about ethics. Every House and every ruling monarch is corrupt in some way. They are privileged, have not earned their position, are surrounded by private armies, and believe themselves above others. Some sovereignties even have the cheek to call for equality.' Maude's upper lip curled into a snarl. 'I never rely on others; family let you down.'

Elaya's voice softened. 'I was an orphan, and…'

'Everyone knows your story, Elaya. From a desert nomad to a street kid to Queen's Protector.'

'So what is your story?'

Maude paused and seemed to consider whether to tell her. 'A strict family from Casper brought me up. Not the most forgiving or accepting place for change or difference.'

'Are you different?'

Suddenly hesitant, Maude glanced away. 'I don't conform to the strict religious beliefs of Casper, that's all. Sorrel sent their first emissaries to Lale, when was it, sixty years ago? Then Lale brought that faith to Casper. As a little girl I heard in the grand basilica in Casper that God would see us rich in the afterlife, and we should follow what the kingdoms ask of us now, even if that made us poorer. In that moment, young as I was, I knew I would only believe in money and myself. Maybe that was a rejection of my father's oppressive doctrine. Maybe I was just built this way.' She shrugged.

'Is it not a child's place to follow her elders?'

Maude's eyes flashed with fury. 'I was legally my father's possession,' she growled 'until such time as he arranged a marriage, at which point I would become my husband's property. To symbolise this my name would be changed to the female form of his. Do you think *I* wanted that? If so, you don't see me at all. You may not like mercenaries much, but at least we are all equal before the same God, money, and we are a meritocracy. I don't judge you, so don't judge me.'

'But surely if you were dutiful to a loving father he would choose a good husband?' Elaya winced even as she said it, knowing it was a weak response to everything she had heard.

'You think it my duty to surrender my body to some man? To any man? And what if I desire something other than that, Elaya Faith?'

'Perhaps I have been hasty and ill-informed in my judgement of you,' Elaya said with genuine humility. 'I am sorry for this. Maybe you were also too quick to jump to conclusions about me?'

Maude's expression softened. Elaya felt her pulse quicken. She felt a rise in temperature from Maude, too; rising with the way her eyes seemed to search Elaya's features all at once. Using her druidic scan for personal curiosity to unravel the mystery of this enigmatic woman, felt ethically wrong. Yet, she couldn't resist the temptation.

Maude's mouth lifted to face hers. She came in close. Inches from lips to lips. Elaya saw a surge of purple aura, deepening with Maude's lustful gaze.

Surely she was not going to kiss her!

'Everything alright?' Laglen's gravelly voice brought them up sharp.

Elaya jumped back, that tingling sensation in her stomach subsiding. 'Maude and I were discussing the route.'

His gaze flicked between them. 'We are ready to horizon jump if you are.'

Maude cleared her throat, then lifted a finger and pointed. 'To the horizon then.'

∼

Wigginton Castle sat upon a hill surrounded by walls, a moat, and miles of flat land, which made attacking it hard unless an invading army was committed to a drawn-out siege war. But for the occupants inside the castle, the high ground and layers of defence made it a remote and secure keep. 'This is perfect,' Elaya said, viewing the estate from about a mile out. She had asked Girvyn to bring them well short of the hill. She didn't want to startle the estate guards by opening the portal close to the walls and preferred a traditional approach.

'Let's ride on from here, side by side so our number is plain to see.'

Maude scowled. Obviously, that went against her ranger instinct of being discreet. 'Is that wise? Why don't you stay with Girvyn and I ride on ahead and check they are expecting us?'

Elaya waved the idea away. 'After the kidnapping, the queen swapped locations of our hideout and sent a pigeon to Lady Wigginton. I have a second copy of the original request to Leverstock, so we can compare and verify each other. Let's just ride in together.' She moved in closer to Maude, her words hushed for only the tracker to hear. 'I've had concerns since Kerrick set his traps. He knew we were crossing that river. Kerrick has spies in Rathnell, officials secretly loyal to the Shadstone estate. And I don't know if the Privy is compromised. But if we don't go, where do we go instead? Eventually he may appear. One positive is that the Wigginton castle is high with flat plains that go to the horizon, so we'll be able to spot his approach. Our advantage is that Girvyn can jump us far away in an instant. You need to keep constant perimeter watch, though. If threat arrives, every second may be crucial to our escape and our survival. Okay?'

'Of course,' Maude said and clicked her steed ahead.

∽

About twenty minutes later, they arrived at the castle's base. A stone bridge led to the portcullis, but the drawbridge was up, and a twelve-foot moat separated them from the entrance. Two faces peered down at them from the castle parapet. A man and a woman with wary, zipping scans below grey windswept hair. Although she appeared spindly, the woman's voice was loud and strong.

'Identify yourself and your reason for being here!' she cried.

Elaya dismounted her horse, her steps light as she approached the bridge. Holding herself in a dignified manner, she announced, 'I am Elaya Faith, Queen's Protector to Queen Amelia and sworn guardian of Rathnell. I have a letter issued by Queen Amelia. I understand you have an identical copy?'

'We do,' Lord Wigginton said.

'This is addressed to Lord Leverstock, but I will read it as is...' She then unfurled the scroll in her hands. *'Dear Lord Leverstock, I approach you with urgent news. A shadowy menace grows, threatening our proud lands. Our hope, it seems, rests largely upon the young boy standing before you. He is inexperienced and requires intensive training to ready him for the challenges ahead. I beseech you to allow our party sanctuary within your esteemed walls for a duration of four weeks. Elaya will provide you with further information. For your troubles, I offer a sum of twenty gold pieces. Her Majesty Queen Amelia.'*

'Aye, I had to be sure,' the woman said, much softer. The gate chain began clicking, and the wooden drawbridge lowered.

When it settled into place, Lord and Lady Wigginton were waiting at the entrance to receive them. A few scruffy-looking castle staff remained close by, as did a few stockier, well-built men. Elaya scanned them and sensed workers and gatekeepers, all lacking in confidence.

Lady Wigginton waved them in, making an excited gesture. 'We received the pigeon a few days ago and were expecting you, but I needed to hear that letter to be sure it was you.'

'I understand, Your Grace. A wise precaution. But I need

to see your identical letter, too, before we enter your great keep.'

'Wise words, also,' Lady Wigginton said, and showed her the message.

Lord Wigginton spoke then, his voice thin and raspy. 'These days we run the estate with a minimum complement. But my men will take your horses to the stables. Come, you must be hungry.'

Elaya held out the bag of gold for Lady Wigginton to take.

Lady Wigginton waved it away. 'Nonsense, Elaya Faith. I will take no such thing from my cousin, Amelia. We have heard of the weighty reports that have befallen the land, though, as you can see, we are self-sufficient here and do not frequent even the closest towns and villages. But news has reached us of the missing babies, the summit, and the tale of demons in our land. We receive regular reports from Rathnell.'

'What you have heard is all true,' Laglen said.

'May I introduce Laglen? This is the boy's uncle.' Elaya then gestured to Girvyn.

Girvyn lifted a hand. 'Hello.'

'Master Girvyn, it is a pleasure. I look forward to this evening's feast to hear all about what makes you so special.'

Laglen interrupted. 'Direct such questions to me.'

Elaya introduced the others. Lady Wigginton hoisted an eyebrow. 'A ranger, a Forester, and a Highlander. What unusual company you keep, Elaya Faith.'

'These are indeed unusual times, which brings unusual company.'

Lord Wigginton chuckled long and colourfully. 'Since you are here, I am cheerful, to be sure.'

'And I am delighted indeed to meet the mighty Elaya Faith.' Lady Wigginton said. 'Your name sings far beyond the queendom of Rathnell. It has been over ten years since I have seen my cousin, Amelia, but we are honoured her protector resides with us.'

'Your own kindness has shown much bravery in our time of need. We all have a part to play in this fight. All I have done is raise my sword and brought us here, with the help of others.' Her voice descended into a flat, colourless monotone. 'The journey has cost us greatly.'

Lady Wigginton's expression dropped when Elaya finished. 'We have much to tell you too. Come in, freshen up, and we will talk at dinner.'

'A bath would be nice,' Laglen said.

'Then that you must have!' Lord Wigginton announced. All smiles and welcoming nods, they entered the keep.

∽

That night they feasted in the great hall. A bitter chill seeped through the stone walls, filling the air of the lofty chamber, relieved by potted fire torches scattered around the banquet table.

When Laglen had finished telling the story, he sat back and wiped the corner of his mouth using a napkin. 'There you have it.'

Lady Wigginton shook her head incredulously. 'That's quite a story.' She shifted straight to Girvyn. 'And, Master Girvyn, you are all new to this?'

Laglen interrupted. 'Until recently, he didn't even know about the Realm.'

Lord Wigginton scratched his chin, still looking at Girvyn. 'So remarkable.' He released a long soft whistle. 'What makes you and Crane so different to the other Dream Travellers, as you call them?'

Something tugged at Laglen. That was an unusual question to lead with. Most people's initial reaction had been scepticism. After what had happened on the bridge, anything was possible. Could Kerrick have killed the Wiggintons and replaced them with Realm forms? 'We are yet to learn why they are the only ones that possess the portal,' he replied carefully.

'I didn't want it, but Sunfire gave it to me,' Girvyn said.

'Who is Sunfire?'

'He is a Realm-based guardian,' Girvyn answered before Laglen could reply.

'He says he is,' Laglen corrected. 'But we really don't know.'

'Why give such power to a boy?' Lady Wigginton said.

'Indeed, Your Grace. Our thoughts entirely.'

They ate silently, then Lord Wigginton said, 'So how will you train him if his abilities are different to yours?'

Another unusual question, Laglen thought. He'd assumed if anything was untoward Elaya's druid senses would have picked it up instantly, but she had been fooled back on the bridge.

'Interesting point. When we train together, we will use the traditional method. I prefer to teach him the original rules of the Realm,' Laglen answered.

'It seems this portal blows away all of those traditions?' Lady Wigginton said, hoisting an eyebrow.

'Indeed, it does. It's beyond reckoning and incomprehension. And it's perilous! The Traveller sect I am part of has a saying, "What we create in the Realm stays in the Realm." The existence of an interdimensional doorway between the Realm and here is a massive world-ending scenario.'

'In the wrong hands it is,' Girvyn corrected.

'It *is* in the wrong hands,' Laglen told him, and shot up a facing palm. 'I am not referring to you.'

'I know you are not, Uncle.'

'And this portal allows you to jump across spaces you can see, or to places recalled from memory?' Lord Wigginton asked Laglen.

'Yes, that's what I said,' Girvyn answered.

'Fascinating,' Lord Wigginton said. 'And you brought your courageous company here doing these…?' he searched for the phrase. 'Horizon jumps?'

'Yes,' Girvyn said.

Lord Wigginton glanced down at his plate. 'It, therefore, does explain why so many people are interested in you, Master Girvyn. You could transport a whole army across continents in a flash.'

'We were told by messenger bird of the plot to kidnap Girvyn.' Lady Wigginton said to Laglen. 'When you recounted what happened, the kidnapping of Girvyn, I mean, that must have been terrifying for you all?'

'It was,' Girvyn told her.

'A second message has arrived since then and told us more,' she informed them. 'Were you aware Envoy Seskin orchestrated the plot? He has admitted it and will be extradited to Cundelly.'

'What?!' Elaya exclaimed. 'That slimy snake!'

'I knew he was up to something,' Hazel said and exchanged a nod with Girvyn. 'He was always complaining.'

'He was, wasn't he,' Girvyn agreed.

'Is Lale involved?' Laglen asked Lady Wigginton. 'Envoy Nark expressed stringent views on us. I have a hunch he would eradicate all Travellers if he could.'

'That is not confirmed. But you would be wise to suspect he might,' Lady Wigginton said.

'I didn't mention in my account that the other company going to the north to attack Crane suffered an assassination attempt on the two Dream Travellers in the group. Elaya's apprentice saved them,' Laglen said.

'It's like the burning of the druids all over again,' Elaya muttered.

Lord Wigginton growled. 'We will see hangings in the street for anyone that sleeps during the day.'

Lord and Lady Wigginton looked at each other. 'Interesting,' she mused.

Laglen tried to hide his frown, but he was sure it was rippling across his face. He wondered how the Lord and Lady kept up with these new and changing concepts. They didn't seem surprised by the Realm, seemed to accept, and understand it, and were very interested in Girvyn. Laglen had seen them give each other knowing stares more than once.

They continued their scrutiny of his nephew. 'It does seem you are of great value, Master Girvyn. But rest assured, you are safe here,' Lord Wigginton said.

'Thank you for your hospitality,' Girvyn said. 'Do you have many books here?'

'We have a small library. Why?'

Everyone started laughing, and Girvyn's cheeks went red. 'They tease me because I like reading.'

'No one is teasing,' Hazel said.

One of the waiters appeared holding out two plates of cooked food. 'What shall I do with these?'

'Take them outside to Maude and Rowen, you will find them patrolling the perimeter,' Elaya said.

'We had contemplated vacating the estate for a while.' Lady Wigginton said after they were alone again. 'Perhaps retreating to our coastal residence. We considered taking the minimal staff we employ with us.'

'We didn't expect you to leave,' Elaya said.

'We assumed you would want privacy.'

'This is your home, and we are your guests.'

'We have already given our staff the next eight weeks off, starting tomorrow,' Lord Wigginton told them.

'If you insist,' Elaya replied. 'We will leave the castle how we found it and hunt for our own game.'

'That's the thing,' Lady Wigginton said, casting a brief glance at Girvyn. 'We are considering whether to stay, just the two of us.'

Excited, Girvyn exclaimed, 'Oh, stay, please stay!'

Lady Wigginton's eyes glimmered. 'Maybe we will.'

However, Lord Wigginton's expression turned serious as he addressed Laglen. 'Can you tell us more about the dangers the world faces? What is this Crane like? And what do you think he is trying to do?'

Laglen responded gravely. 'He was always cruel. As a young man he used to torture people in hell constructs for fun. I have seen more than one of his punishment inventions. They are malevolent beyond imagining.'

'Just like hell is supposed to be,' Lady Wigginton conjectured.

'What he is up to is unclear. He has a portal and is bringing Realm demons through to the Waking. We know that. He is attacking settlements, kidnapping babies, and taking injured and the dead into his hell. We know that, too. And he seems to be converting them there; Girvyn saw him turn an innocent Forester into a Drone Druid.'

Hazel caught her breath, her distress evident. Laglen observed Girvyn offering her a reassuring smile, to which she responded with a faint one before averting her gaze.

'The death of Chieftain Glefforn and my Forester kindred must be avenged,' Hazel said, face hardening.

'We can't trust anyone,' Elaya added.

'I can portal us straight to his lair,' Girvyn offered matter-of-factly. 'All I have to do is think of a place I've been to, so maybe the portal can take us to the hell I visited when all of this began?'

'No!' Elaya and Laglen exclaimed simultaneously.

'That's a terrible idea, Girvyn,' Elaya growled.

'You are nowhere near ready for that,' Laglen said. 'Let the adults sort this out.' He regarded the Wiggintons again. 'But what is Crane doing? Why is he doing it? I cannot say.' Laglen finished. 'He needs to be stopped, not reasoned with.'

'Have you come to that conclusion then, Uncle?'

'I think we are beyond talk now.'

Lord Wigginton flapped a nonchalant hand. 'Whether it's global destruction, a takeover, revenge for something we do not know about, economic reasons, territorial gain. It's an act of war upon all of us, and that's enough reason to stand up and fight against him.'

'Those who wield the portal power will rule the world,' Lady Wigginton muttered.

'I don't want to rule the world. I am just learning the basics of the Realm, which is hard in itself,' Girvyn said.

'Thank the stars for you. You will save us,' Lord Wigginton told him.

Laglen objected. 'The plan isn't for Girvyn to save anyone. As we have already explained, an army is a day away from his stronghold. Perhaps though, when the time is right, Girvyn's portal can be used for the betterment of all humankind.'

Lady Wigginton shifted. 'Would you show us?'

Girvyn's eyes darted between them. 'Show you what?'

Lord Wigginton planted his elbows on the table, chin perched on knitted fingers. 'The portal, of course.'

'My uncle says I am not a court jester.'

Lady Wigginton laughed. 'Indeed you're not, Master Girvyn.' She smiled at Lord Wigginton. 'Darling, don't ask him such a thing. The boy needs to learn the creation traditions first and then relearn everything he has learned.'

Lord Wigginton sat forward. 'Have you brought anything through the portal yet? Tried it out?'

'Water and a rabid hybrid dog, the latter by accident,' Girvyn glanced at Hazel, then averted his gaze. 'It's dangerous, irresponsible, and elitist.'

'Well said, Girvyn,' Elaya commended. 'Using this power selfishly is a step closer to Crane, to yearning for world domination. You are wise to fear that.'

'The word we use is restraint.' Laglen fixed the Wiggintons with a penetrating stare. 'You seem to grasp the concepts we are telling you quickly. And accept them willingly. Is there something you are not telling us?'

'I admire your questioning instinct,' Lord Wigginton said, sitting back. 'Indeed, there is something.'

Lady Wigginton checked to ensure they were alone, then leaned forward. 'We are Dream Travellers!'

Laglen's mouth dropped open, and the rest of the table went silent, not a clank of cutlery on plates.

Lord Wigginton addressed Laglen. 'Remember when you talked about your Traveller sect? Lady Wigginton and I met in the Realm many decades ago and arranged to meet this side. I didn't know she was royal, nor did she know I had noble blood, with my family owning this estate. We fell in love in the Realm and discovered each other's lives in both dimensions. It was like falling in love twice. No one knows about our secret, not even our staff. We rarely leave the castle for royal visits.'

'Kindred spirits we are!' Lady Wigginton smiled. 'You can all close your mouths now!'

'And to you, Hazel, who do not Travel,' Lord Wigginton said. 'I trust you will keep our secret too? Just as you swore an oath of allegiance to protect Girvyn and Laglen?'

'Of course,' Hazel said.

'That does make sense,' Girvyn said. 'How can you have a loving marriage when one of you has a secret?' He looked at his uncle. 'I thought my uncle had a fatigue disease.'

They all laughed.

'We don't need anyone else,' Lady Wigginton said. 'We have each other, we have the Dream Plane, we keep ourselves to ourselves, and we do not enter other Travellers' worlds.'

'Don't you get bored?' Girvyn asked, sounding perplexed.

'Far from it. In fact the only thing boring is the time we must spend here. Our physical bodies are ageing, so we must look after them. They are essential to our survival, but all the fun is in the Realm. We have Realm created friends we visit. We take the most wonderful trips together, see technologically advanced societies. We learn more about ourselves and others on that side.'

'I assume you sleep a lot?'

'Yes, but not to the point of degradation of ourselves. We are healthy, as you can see. It's controlled.'

'Our life is full of colour,' Lord Wigginton said. 'Here is what you might call black and white.'

Lady Wigginton's eyes sparkled with enthusiasm. 'Consider this: you could journey to Cundelly or Stoer and spend a year there. They're both feasible destinations, but what might you truly discover about foreign cultures and, more importantly, yourself within that time? Certainly some new experiences, but likely nothing much more profound than that which you already know.' She paused for effect, letting her words sink in. 'Now imagine a different scenario. Suppose you crafted a majestic ship and dared to cross the ocean; a feat few have attempted. We've heard tales of settlers across the waters, with Amjad the enigmatic gateway to the eastern territories. The idea of forging new trade routes there tempts many, but the perilous voyage with its notorious risks dissuades most. Only Stoer has successfully made the journey, and they've guarded their newfound ties jealously. Many vessels have met their doom in the treacherous Gower Straits.'

She continued, 'Yet, if you dared to cross those waters and stayed in foreign lands for a year, imagine the wealth of experiences awaiting you! The journey would undoubtedly be fraught with challenges, but the what you would gain, in terms of personal growth and newfound wisdom, would be immense. Such a bold choice requires courage, yes, but the returns are exponentially rewarding.'

Lord Wigginton leaned forward. 'Master Girvyn,' he began, 'The sights and discoveries we've encountered in our voyages would boggle even the most imaginative minds. In one such venture, we crafted a world and allowed its progress to unfold unchecked and exponentially. The outcome presented a future where humans had inadvertently birthed their own overlords.' He let the weight of his words linger. 'Androids, born of our own innovation, evolved to possess intellects that dwarfed ours by magnitudes of millions. Yet, in a turn of events that was both humbling and astonishing, these superior entities did not view us as pests to be exterminated. Instead, they regarded us with a kind of benign affection.' He chuckled softly. 'Picture this: these intellectual titans, capable of so much more than we could ever comprehend, merely saw us as charming curiosities. They nurtured us, sustained us, and allowed our societies to flourish before their watchful eyes. Humans, under their care, were free to continue their lives, breeding and even socialising in public spaces, much like pets on a leisurely day out. It was as if we were delightful antiques from a bygone era, treasured by these machines for reasons we could scarcely fathom.'

'I don't really understand any of that. Uncle mentioned time differentials. Is that what you mean?'

'We call them time jumps.'

'But it doesn't prove anything,' Girvyn replied. 'It's just one possible future. The conditions you set are too variable to relate to our society. You make a world with your rules, then move it forward in time. What does it prove?'

'Nothing. You are quite correct. We are not trying to prove anything. We just want to expand our minds.'

'I see.' Girvyn shrugged. 'Also, I don't know what an android is.'

They all laughed.

'I would love to learn about the things you have seen,' Laglen said. 'Perhaps we can exchange experiences while we spend time together? Or join you in one of your constructs?'

'A splendid suggestion.'

'And your parents?' Laglen asked hesitantly. 'Were they...?'

'Sleepwalkers? Mine both were,' Lord Wigginton confirmed.

'Do you have any children?' Laglen asked them.

'No.'

'But you are a cousin to the queen?' Laglen said. 'Does that mean...?'

'No, the queen does not Travel.' Lady Wigginton shrugged. 'Amelia and I are related on my mother's side, but my father was the Traveller.'

'When the queen told us you were coming and what you were, we were obviously very excited to meet you and hear your experiences and see this amazing portal that Girvyn can summon,' Lady Wigginton said.

Laglen smiled, thinking. 'This does present an opportunity for Girvyn to hear different voices during his training. He has seen Travellers' windows in his Atrium. Having you here gives him a richer perspective. A deeper pool to immerse in, so to speak. Just don't ask Girvyn to do anything for you.'

'Like what?'

'Like bring through one of your favourite creations.'

Laglen could tell Lord and Lady Wigginton appreciated that his interactions were courteous, but he was also strong of mind and will, when needed. They stared at him until Lady Wigginton said, 'Of course, we respect your request and duly appreciate your caring instinct for your nephew. To ask such a thing of him would be dishonourable and deceitful, and it does not even come into our peripheral thinking.'

'It does beg the question, with Travellers being rare in the general population, how did we end up taking refuge with you? It seems too...' Laglen faltered.

'Lucky?' Lady Wigginton offered.

'Fortuitous.'

Lady Wigginton looked at her husband. 'Being Amelia's cousin, we received word via bird on the day of the demon attack in the library and were instructed to close our castle in case more monsters were loose. When we were told about this Traveller secret becoming public, it did read much like our own story, so we returned a message the same day to Amelia, offering to help.'

∽

A little while later, Laglen, Girvyn and the Wiggintons retired to the drawing room for after-dinner drinks before a lively fireplace to discuss all things Realm, and compare practices. It had been many years since Laglen had met Dream Travellers outside of his community. That time had been in dire and melancholy circumstances which he would rather forget; he had just lost his sister, Rosein, and was clouded by grief and regret. But in Lord and Lady Wigginton he saw two generous Travellers, eager to help. Before they started, it made sense, though, to develop a durable agreement on terms.

'I call us Dream Travellers. What do you call it?' Laglen asked.

'Sleepwalkers,' Lord Wigginton answered.

'Fair enough,' Laglen agreed with a nod.

'We use the terms structures and constructs to describe what we create.'

'Worlds, we call them worlds,' Lord Wigginton said.

'How many Sleepwalkers are in your sect?' Lady Wigginton asked; she sounded eager to get her next question in.

'There are five families in our community, including Crane's lineage. Tasmin has disappeared. So that leaves us,' he waved at Girvyn, 'Mora and Dremell, and Kalamayn and Nadine.'

'We hope to meet them.'

'I am sure you will.'

Girvyn was frowning. 'Why is there no covenant or guild like the druids have? Some collective council of representation?'

'We are a fragmented, disconnected people,' Lord Wigginton said. 'Until a few days ago, we thought it was just us, some rare and magical place we could visit that only we knew about. What about you, Laglen?'

Laglen shifted uneasily. 'Outside of my group, I did know

other Travellers once. Another community.' Words failed him. 'But I don't want to talk about it.'

'That's not like you, Uncle...?'

'It's immaterial now, and I have painful memories of those times,' was all he managed.

'Do none of you enter other Travellers dreams?' Girvyn asked them all.

'I think I have said this. One in a thousand might be a Traveller, Girvyn. That's a lot of weird and wonderful Ort dreams,' Laglen replied.

'Ort?' Lady Wigginton said.

'A name we use for non-Travellers. What do you call them?'

Lord Wigginton laughed. 'Just non-Sleepwalkers.'

'Ort is much easier to say,' Girvyn said.

Lady Wigginton dropped an amused snort. 'It's not like there is a global summit every year where we agree on enduring vocabularies.'

'What about this side? We call it the Waking,' Girvyn told them.

'Ah, we call it The Real.'

'Interesting,' Laglen commented, thinking. 'Does that mean you accept what you create is made up and not real? We debated this issue and decided not to call it the real, feeling that what we create is as real as anything here.'

'I get it; once it leaves your imagination and becomes a thing, it is alive.' Lady Wigginton lingered, considering. 'But it doesn't start off real; you must seed it.'

'That indulging, tingling sensation when you create. What do you call it?'

'We call it The Flow.'

'We call it The Pull. And the Atrium?' Laglen asked.

'The Atrium?'

'Sorry, I mean the white space where you look at all your windows.'

'We call it Home. What do you call the windows?'

It was Laglen's turn to laugh. 'We call them windows.'

'Windows! At last, an agreement!' Lord Wigginton declared.

'What about that deep place beyond The Flow,' Laglen used their term. 'Where The Flow meets the...'

'Ah, right. The Origin.'

'Makes sense. We call it The Source. Here is a big one; what do you think it is? Some of us think it's alive, do you?'

'Alive in the sense that it exists, yes, definitely,' she glanced at Lord Wigginton. 'It responds to our needs, whims, thoughts, wishes.'

'Even the white stars when we close our eyelids for sleep, they are alive too.' Lord Wigginton added, 'like a scouting party leading an army to base.'

'But alive in a sense that it's a sentient, thinking being, I am not sure,' she finished. 'It would have spoken to us by now.'

'Maybe it already is?' Girvyn said. They looked at him without replying, and he continued, 'Speaking to you, I mean. And I am not referring to Sunfire. Maybe you merely being present is what it wants. Thus, it gives you what you want, so you come back for more and more.'

'Very wise for one who has barely walked the substrata of imaginings,' Lady Wigginton said.

Girvyn stared into space for a moment, like he was returning from a dream. 'Thank you.'

Lady Wigginton regarded Laglen. 'What sort of worlds do you create?'

Girvyn scoffed. 'Flying metal boxes. Uncle likes to race around in speeding games.'

'I do other things too,' Laglen objected, red-faced. 'I did create a world and let it evolve.'

Girvyn smiled. 'He has an assistant that helps him. He is really nice.'

Laglen told them about his assistant, and they listened with raised eyebrows.

Lady Wigginton congratulated him. 'That's very clever and useful to keep your home organised.'

'I don't get it,' Girvyn said. 'This android you mentioned, it's just a made-up possible future. What do you learn from it?'

'We don't know what we will find. It's the experience of the new.'

Laglen was wrestling with something, and hadn't got to the bottom of it. 'What do you do when you accumulate all this knowledge?'

'What do you mean?' Lady Wigginton said, confused. 'Nothing. We just enjoy it.'

'It's entertaining, and enriches our lives,' Lord Wigginton added.

Laglen's nagging question had been answered. 'I get you,' he said, pondering. 'I get you.' He pointed at a cabinet of glass bottles containing orange liquids. 'Is that whisky?'

∼

Later that night, when they retired for bed, Girvyn sat in a chair in the shared quarters with his uncle. 'I like them.'

'I like them too.'

'Are we going to include them in what we are doing?'

'I think we already have. But they won't be joining us in the Realm to trap Crane. Mora has that covered.'

'They are so interesting! So into brain growth! I love it that they use the Realm to expand their minds.'

'There is no difference between them and me,' Laglen said tersely. 'Yes, they are into mind expansion. Good for them. That is their product; mine is racing around a track. But what is the difference? It's not like they are helping people with the things they learn. It's all self-indulgent, private consumption. Yes, they seemed dedicated to fitness; they walk around in the Waking and eat well, but then dive back in and indulge again. Just like me. I would look more negatively at them than you do. They could help people in the Waking, do so much more. They could go to every city and enlighten us with the things they have learned; make an impact as Kalamayn has. But they don't. They keep it all to themselves, pat themselves on the back and go to Realm dinner parties. What's the difference between them and me? At least I am honest with my vacuous, self-indulgent consumption.'

Girvyn tried to say something, but his mouth kept opening and closing.

'Come,' Laglen yawned and cupped his mouth. 'We have had a long day. It's time for sleep.'

'Realm?'

'No, just normal body resting, innocent dreams. Remember what I have said, when the lights begin to shine in your eyelids, just turn away from them in your mind and you will pass it up. Night, Girvyn.'

'Night, Uncle. Thanks for being by my side.'

'Always.'

Thirty-Four

Derrilyn listened to the committee members speak. They were all huddled close to the fire, voices low.

'Look, I'm fine, Derrilyn,' Dremell insisted. 'Nadine and I will sleep lighter from now on.'

'We will watch each other,' Nadine agreed. 'After what has happened, we would prefer to take control ourselves.'

Amusement passed across Lady Adara's face, before a resting stillness returned. 'Then having us watch over you too will be of no bother to you.'

Nadine's mouth opened, but no words escaped.

Derrilyn folded his arms. 'I won't leave your side until Crane is defeated. Just one more night, and it'll be over,' he said.

'We can take care of ourselves,' Dremell repeated, glancing at Nadine for support, but she awkwardly looked away.

'Look at it from our side,' Jaden added. 'It's shameful to admit it, but we have let you down. To let you get attacked for a third time would be amateurish.'

'I think we would all get sacked from the Druid Guild for

such negligence,' Lady Adara acknowledged, hiking an eyebrow.

'You're helping us. You will be saving us a great embarrassment,' Derrilyn insisted, unblinking. 'So, it's settled. Tonight, all three druids watch over you.'

Dremell let out a long sigh. 'Okay.'

Nadine rolled her eyes. 'But you're not following me to the toilet.'

'Well, I hadn't thought that far,' Derrilyn said, face unreadable. 'Maybe Lady Adara can handle that part.'

'I'll accompany you to the tree and look away; the rest is up to you,' Lady Adara joked.

Nadine groaned. 'This is all a bit much.'

Derrilyn shrugged. 'What about us? When we first met, you wouldn't even talk to me, and now I'm discussing your bathroom breaks.'

They all laughed, and the tension eased. Derrilyn exhaled a satisfied sigh. Amidst the gravity of their predicament and the camp's solemn mood, the joy of laughter provided a welcome respite.

Jaden grinned. 'It's amazing what a life-saving rescue can do for solidarity.'

'It was quite something, Jaden, watching you dance through those fanatics,' Dremell said. 'Leaving them dead at your feet.'

Nadine glanced at Lady Adara. 'And your archery skills were incredible. I can't believe you cut the rope with just one shot.'

'We don't take pleasure in killing,' Lady Adara asserted. For a moment, it seemed like a reprimand, but then she smiled. 'But it was an inevitable conclusion.'

'Everyone had a role to play in your rescue,' Derrilyn said. 'Lord Grisham, Maltip, Donjul. We made a great team.'

'Indeed, we did,' Lady Adara agreed. 'Indeed, we did.'

'And now we number five hundred and thirty,' Jaden said. 'The support from the Cundelly Druid Guild arrived today. I've been getting updates from them; did you know Seskin is dead?'

'What?' Derrilyn exclaimed.

'Seskin confessed to Girvyn's kidnapping.'

'Was it driven by religious motives?' Nadine asked.

'I don't think so. His motivations were political,' Jaden responded. 'He was apprehended and, signed a confession. Rathnell released him, and he was later killed in a bar fight.'

Derrilyn shook his head in disbelief.

'I overheard the fanatics talking.' Nadine said solemnly and began recounting her ordeal again. 'The initial attack wasn't intended to kill us in our sleep; it was a failed kidnapping attempt. They had planned a ceremonial execution all along.'

'It doesn't matter what their motivations are against the Dream Travellers,' Lady Adara interjected. 'Ignorance and hatred are never a rationale.'

∽

As the sun began to set later that day, the valiant group of eight rescuers recognised as the core members of the war council, gathered with Nadine and Dremell and a few other Highlanders and House members to strategise the upcoming assault.

Drawing them close, Dremell began explaining what was going to happen. 'This endeavour hinges upon a synchronised assault, spanning both the Dream Realm and the Waking,' he began, before pausing to ensure clarity among his comrades. 'By "the Waking," I refer to this very world we stand upon.

Our plan revolves around keeping our adversary engaged on one front while we strike him down at his most vulnerable moment on our side.'

Donjul spoke gruffly, 'We know this proposal, to preoccupy Crane, but how will it work in both worlds?'

Dremell looked at Donjul. 'My mother will lure Crane into her dream.'

'And how is she going to do that?' Lord Grisham asked Dremell.

Dremell explained, 'There exists an unwritten decree amongst Travellers, a code that discourages trespassing upon each other's worlds. Yet Crane has repeatedly shown contempt for such regulations. We shall capitalise on this audacity. My mother will create a window adorned with his own visage. It will materialise within his inner sanctum, beckoning him to enter.'

A chorus of bemused expressions glimmered in the flickering glow of the firelight. Lord Grisham, voicing the collective intrigue, inquired, 'But what if he refuses to take the bait?'

'We know Crane well enough to be sure he won't.' Nadine told him. 'Even though it might take some hours. Hold your position until I signal to proceed.'

'But how will we know when to attack?'

'The whole point of us being here is to tell you when Crane is pre-occupied in the Realm,' Dremell told Lord Grisham. 'Nadine will enter the Realm. When Crane enters my mother's trap, she will wake and inform us.'

'It is imperative that we withhold our assault until I return and give the signal,' Nadine repeated. 'We must know Crane is in the Realm preoccupied. If not he could bring his portal and his demon armies to bear.'

Dremell's gaze swept across the assembly, his conviction

unyielding. 'We enter his hut. If he is inside, we kill him while he sleeps,' he paused. 'If he isn't there, we search his stronghold and wait for him to come back.'

'It is going to be a long journey for nothing if he is not home,' Sward muttered.

'Realm food will not sustain him. He must return to this side to rest and eat,' Dremell said. 'If with one step, wherever you are, you could return to your home, would you not do so yourself?'

They all nodded, agreeing with the logic.

'I would have gone to my wife's bed, every night on this journey so far!' Praleck joked.

There were haughty laughs, while some of the others added stories of where they would go if the portal could take them anywhere.

Maltip interjected, bringing everyone back to the moment. 'Crane is never away from his fortress for long. A day, perhaps no more, shall be our waiting.'

'There we go!' Dremell said, pleased with himself. 'He will return!'

'We leave the horses at the base,' Maltip told them in a measured, low-sounding voice. 'There is a mountain track that serpents up the slope.'

'Serpents?' Lady Adara asked softly.

Cedar spoke to Maltip in the mother language they shared. 'Snakes?' he offered.

'Yes, this path snakes to the top, and will keep us busy from dawn to sun top. Right under his ledge is a lower level where we wait out of sight and sound. From there, twenty minutes carries us to his home.'

'What is this ledge like?' Praleck asked.

'It's wide and long,' Maltip replied.

'Sounds like a plateau,' Lady Adara ventured.

'When we get to this lower shelf, a few of us should climb to take a look,' Jaden suggested.

'We must attack in daylight, he will have the advantage at night,' Donjul said.

Dremell nodded in agreement. 'Are there any lingering queries or uncertainties?' His gaze encompassed the entire assembly.

Derrilyn, who had remained silent, letting the leaders' wisdom flow, glanced between Dremell and Nadine. 'I'm coming with you into this hut to keep you safe.'

Nadine smiled. 'So be it, young druid.'

'Anything else?' Dremell asked the assembly. When met with silence, he said, 'We are done then. It's sunset. Nadine and I must cross to the Realm to update our kindred.'

'Everyone get rest,' Nadine told them. 'You will need it.'

Thirty-Five

Girvyn hated change. He hated the worry it caused him even when he felt settled and peaceful. It just stirred in the background of his body, curdling his stomach. This time, though, he was not surprised to hear the horrifying personal account given by Dremell. Nor did he experience anything more than disbelief, which seemed an appropriate reaction at that moment. Perhaps, with so much change in his life, he was becoming more accustomed to managing his emotions.

Laglen let out a weary breath. 'Another attack?'

'Again, saved by the alliance. This time it took more than the druids to rescue us,' Dremell added.

'This is horrific,' Laglen muttered.

'We have quite a gathering,' Nadine told them. 'These seven days have heightened our purpose and solidarity. It's a formidable group.'

Dremell beamed. 'And Nadine has been making Ort friends.'

Nadine rolled her eyes. 'Baby steps.'

'There is more; fifty druids have bolstered our ranks,'

Dremell added, 'bringing the news of Seskin's involvement in Girvyn's kidnapping.'

'Yes, we heard, too. Word reached Wigginton by bird,' Laglen replied.

'He is dead,' Dremell told them.

Girvyn went to say good, but stopped himself. 'He had it coming.'

'Now fate must help us with Crane,' Laglen said.

Mora looked resolute. 'Well, we made it to the end line, if a little ruffled. Now we have to cross it and complete what we started.'

'Any news from your side, Father?' Nadine asked Kalamayn.

Kalamayn glanced at Mora. 'We have been practicing. Mora is ready for tomorrow.'

Mora pursed her lips. 'The Wiggintons, could they help us in the battle with Crane?'

Laglen folded his arms. 'They *are* helping us. I don't think we need them with us, Mora. We don't know what they can add. They might be a distraction. All you need to do is keep Crane busy.'

Mora nodded. 'We have more allies though. We need as many as we can gather.'

'They are very nice,' Girvyn told them.

'Girvyn, you are staying in the Waking, so just keep Laglen comfortable while he is in the Realm,' Mora said to him.

'Okay, Mora,' Girvyn answered.

'They have given us a nice ground floor chamber. It feels like a holiday,' Laglen said.

Girvyn let out a surprised snort. 'Uncle, when do we ever go on holiday?'

Dremell's voice broke up their light-hearted banter.

'Maltip is going to lead us to the slope where Crane's cabin is. When we reach it, Nadine will cross and wait with you.'

Laglen gave a serious nod. 'Okay, at that point then, Mora sends the invitation to Crane. Nadine, you wake when Crane appears and then tell the army.' He considered each of them in turn. 'Good luck everyone.'

Then, one by one, the Travellers began vanishing.

Thirty-Six

In the morning, Maude found Elaya in the stables, busy grooming the horses and tending to their feed.

'Why aren't you patrolling?' Elaya asked her.

'Rowen is in the tower.'

'I can do this, I don't need you here.'

Maude ignored her and picked up a broom. They worked in silence until Elaya addressed her.

'So, you must be enjoying earning such easy money?' Elaya remarked.

Maude shot her an incredulous look. She was surprised by Elaya's curtness. She thought they had reached some understanding, albeit laden with her yearning for her. She couldn't get Elaya out of her mind. Perhaps Elaya could sense this?

'This morning and last night,' Maude began, 'I've already scoured the perimeter, set up a series of traps to detect any watchers, and created a map of the surrounding terrain. I'm being paid for four weeks of hard work, and that's exactly what I'll provide.'

Maude observed that slow, sanctimonious nod, accompanied by a conceited tone that managed to be both self-righteous and patronising. 'You can still assess the site for further weaknesses, track the district for any riders or travellers, and hunt game. There's still plenty to do for your pay,' Elaya said.

She bit her lip, feeling a surge of frustration. Who did Elaya think she was? Maude was being compensated to perform a role, and she didn't need praise or criticism. She always did her job.

As she reflected on everything she had witnessed so far, a part of her was drawn to the idea of staying and fighting for the greater good, while another part wanted to run to the hills. The undeniable truth was that the world was changing, and it seemed to revolve around Girvyn. Maude had never believed in magic or sorcery despite encountering druids with extraordinary abilities. However, she had watched in astonishment as Girvyn summoned portals, whisking them away from perilous situations.

Amidst all the uncertainty, one thing remained constant: money. It had been her lifeline, providing shelter, food, and clothing. But it had also become an addiction, the pursuit of wealth and the satisfaction of completing tasks that earned it. Regardless of what happened with Crane or the strange events unfolding, currency would continue to hold sway over everything. It was reassuring to have one reliable beacon amid this topsy-turvy, impossible new reality.

She noticed Elaya glaring at her.

Maude grunted. 'You asked me to get you here. I have.'

'Once we get word that Crane is dead, we will see what happens,' Elaya said in that purring tone of hers; it was a sound modulated to the perfect level of condescension. Maude pushed back her ire and let Elaya continue, 'So, you keep scouting the perimeter for another two months.' Elaya raised her hand before Maude could speak. 'Don't worry, I will make sure you get your double pay.'

Maude cursed irritably, unable to contain herself any longer, 'Are we doing this again? What is your problem?'

'Apart from you being driven by profit, not honour, nothing.'

'Why do you even care? You hired me. I did what you asked me to. I did what I said I would.'

'I saw your face when Her Grace refused the gold. It's weighing down my bag, so you can have it. Take it as first payment.'

'Fine, I will.'

'Good, if it means that much to you.'

Maude stabbed the broom brush into the ground and pushed some dust away. 'I said, what's your problem?'

'Your guiltless, unwavering choices,' Elaya remarked.

'I think you envy that!' Maude stopped brushing, anger flaring. 'And you, noble Elaya Faith, wield your mighty sword for mere food, shelter, and a love for Queen Amelia. But she is old, and rumour has it she ails. What happens when she is gone? What happens when age means your sword is neither as fast nor as mighty? What happens when you are just another old woman with no patron? Will you have to beg Stasnier and his ilk for your meals and shelter? Will they throw you out into the street with the other destitutes? You will have no say in that. No power. Only faith. So, I'll tell you what: I will keep one of those gold pieces especially for you. Any time you want it, all you need to do is come to me and ask. That would kill you, wouldn't it? But are you truly confident you'll never have to? Do you truly have that much faith, Elaya?' Maude held the broom handle out levelly, brush facing Elaya. 'You chastise me for my values, but it seems to me you are the one who's lost.'

A loud crack echoed through the air, causing the broomstick to jerk sideways in Maude's grip. When she looked back at it, the brush had broken off the end.

Elaya thrust her own broom at Maude's face like an accusatory finger. 'Don't point your broom at me.'

Maude jabbed her stick at Elaya. 'Don't point that brush in my face.'

Elaya forcefully snapped off the brush from her broom, resulting in both of them brandishing wooden staffs. They began circling each other with quick, precise steps.

Maude couldn't contain her anger. 'Maybe you're growing slow already, Elaya? I've watched you in the tourneys each of these last eight years. You still won this year, but it was closer than before, wasn't it? You were winded and hurt and sweating beneath that calm facade, weren't you?'

'You seem more interested in my choices than your own!' Elaya retorted.

Maude let out a grunt as she lunged forward, wielding the stick with determination. It met Elaya's with a loud whack as she knocked it aside. They locked sticks. Maude threw a punch but found a block. They faced each other, noses almost touching.

'I think you are jealous of my bold life choices, stepping into unknown territories while you stay safe and sedentary,' Maude chided.

Elaya snorted. 'All you care about is yourself.'

'And all you care about is others. You have sacrificed yourself. When you can do so no longer, those you rely on will let you down and you will realise you wasted your talents for nothing.'

'You are the one wasting your existence. You have no meaningful connections. At least I touch people's lives,' Elaya spat.

Maude felt the warmth of Elaya's breath on her mouth.

Felt scattered drops of spittle land upon her nose and cheek. 'It doesn't matter when you are dead. When they are dead. No one will remember. At least I am living the now. You are too scared to live...' Should she say it? '...to love.'

Bodies pressed together. Chests heaving. Sweat touching sweat.

'Come!' Elaya pulled away. 'I'll show you who is scared! Who is slowing down!'

Maude could feel Elaya's rapid, shallow breath echo hers. She watched Elaya pull her tunic off over her head and throw it to the ground, revealing a single white tight vest, holding her firm stomach and breasts so flawlessly and moulded to her form.

Maude felt the heat too, but it was boiling in her brain. She stared at her wordlessly, her anger robbed of its target.

They clashed again. She felt Elaya's sun-kissed skin brush past hers. They parted, swapped positions, facing each other again.

'You're selfless, Elaya. I truly believe that about you. That it's not just an act as it is with most people.'

Elaya's eyes narrowed. 'I live to be noble in life and noble in death.'

'But if you let yourself be selfish for a moment, then what do you want?'

Elaya blinked and lowered the stick. 'What is it?'

Could she sense what she felt, Maude wondered. Maude's words trembled. 'Answer my question?'

For a moment, it felt as if the air between them crackled like the portal.

What seemed a constant distance between them, a forever undoable action, was no more. She was there in front of her. Hands on Elaya's neck, pulling her closer. She kissed Elaya's cheek, her neck, then looked her straight in the eyes, lips brushing, pulsing.

'No,' Elaya said. Her words were breathless, almost a kiss in itself. 'We mustn't.'

'Why?' Maude slipped her hand beneath her clothing, dipped a finger in the gentle curve of her back, following her soft, sweat covered skin until she reached the nape of her neck. She pulled her towards her. Felt her breasts press against hers.

'Because of Girvyn,' Elaya said, lips trembling.

Their eyes locked. 'Always thinking of others. Forget everyone else for a moment. What do you want?'

Maude felt Elaya's obliging lips, fast and passionate, multiple kisses, seeking out her mouth. Her warmth and softness sent shooting bolts of pleasure through her brain.

Elaya jerked back, wiping her lips with the back of her hand. A slow, lingering gesture that made Maude want more. To taste her again. To smell that hint of mint, jasmine, mixed with her body's scent.

Cheeks hot with pleasure, Maude took a moment to cool down, to measure her. Elaya's chest was heaving, her lashes lowered. 'I am not ready for this. My focus is on protecting Girvyn. Nothing else gets in the way.'

Maude sought so desperately to touch her again, to wipe a hair from her face, remain in her embrace and be a part of her presence, just for a moment longer. She took a step forward. Elaya didn't move.

'He won't need protecting forever; very soon he will be stronger than all of us,' Maude said.

Unexpectedly, daylight blasted in through the stable door.

They came apart, sudden embarrassed movements and murmuring emphasising the space between them. 'Ah, there you both are!' Girvyn declared. 'I have been looking for you.'

'Now you have found us,' Elaya replied swiftly, looking down.

Maude picked up the broomstick, saw it was missing the brush, and dropped it again.

'What happened to the brooms?' Girvyn asked, frowning. 'Have they broken?'

'Yes, we were sweeping too hard. What is it, Girvyn? How can we help?' Elaya said.

Girvyn straightened, scratching his head while he tried to remember. 'Uncle wants us all to gather for breakfast before he crosses to join the others.'

Elaya gestured cordially. 'Wonderful. Lead the way.'

Thirty-Seven

Nadine woke from the dream and rose to face the war committee. 'We are ready. Dremell is in position below the shelf. He says the area is empty, it's safe to climb.'

Derrilyn looked up. The Riddon Slope ascended into low clouds.

Maltip, at ease in his highland home, addressed them. His voice carried an authority. 'From this point onward, the terrain is rugged, so we proceed on foot,' he declared. 'Keep your weapons at the ready.'

Lord Grisham cast a glance back at the procession, pausing in thought. 'All the soldiers are prepped and informed now about the mission ahead.'

'Any objections?' Praleck asked.

'None. 'If there are any more zealot views, they have been focused into killing Crane,' Grisham said, then continued. 'The squires and support staff stay with the horses and protect the camp, anyone else that can fight, woman or man, will climb.'

Sward gave a slow nod. 'Before all this began, I had doubts about this alliance, this war committee, and even the stories we heard at the summit.' He looked at Lady Adara, blushing, 'And of the strength in others that were not noble or proven in battle. I was wrong to judge so quickly and am proud to fight beside you all.'

'You are not the only one that has been quick to judge, Lord Sward,' Nadine muttered, not meeting anyone's gaze.

Lord Grisham looked at Sward, then Nadine, then back at the assembled group. 'When we return from battle, let's talk about you marrying my daughter and joining our Houses, Lord Sward.'

There was a cheer, and Lord Grisham's voice lowered. 'Now we fight side by side. Give the call to climb.'

The drill Sargent called out. 'Company! Lead out!'

They began climbing, Sward came beside the Highlander as they ascended. 'How long will it take to get to this hut, Maltip?'

'About three hours. As we come close, the whole group must climb with caution.'

Derrilyn, Jaden and Lady Adara, followed. Lady Adara brought them close. 'When we get there, focus your druid scan on the spaces in front of you. Do not let our comrades' auras distract you. Check everything, even animals. For things may not be what they seem.'

∼

'It took ages to get everyone up the slope. It's jam-packed up here,' Nadine told them.

Laglen felt his nerves jangle. He looked at Mora, Kalamayn, and then back to Nadine. 'Where are you?'

'We've made it to just below the ridge without even being detected! It's where we would have been vulnerable, but we can get in there and at Crane no matter what comes at us.'

'What about the hut?' Mora asked.

'Our scouts have investigated; it is guarded by vigilant wolves, but not so many of them. The surrounding area is strewn with black rocks and charred vegetation.' She paused, while they stared at her. 'Yet an eerie calm hangs in the air.'

'My daughter.' Kalamayn's tone was serious and a little sad. 'Despite your mannerisms you have always been the kindest of hearts. You have never taken a life. Neither has Dremell. It is a reason I have been glad to have the two of you there, as backup for this moment, but also to support the other for what must be done. Are you certain you can do this?'

Nadine snorted and shook her head. 'I am far less soft than you think, Father. I will not hesitate, and nor do I believe will Dremell. This will be done, fear not.'

Laglen pursed his lips. Something didn't feel right about this. Something about the picture Nadine had painted seemed too convenient. Yet, since they had departed from the city, every moment had been fraught with tension and uncertainty. Perhaps he had spent too much time with Girvyn and his relentless questioning of everything. He tried to reassure himself that they had considered all the possibilities. That it would be fine, and that they'd covered all the angles.

Nadine seemed relaxed. 'So what now?'

Mora took a deep breath, smoothing down her dress, her touch filled with nervous anticipation. 'I will summon the window, adorned with Crane's image, to peer into his Atrium. A moment passed as she directed her thoughts towards The Pull. 'Now,' she stated, her expression darkening, 'we wait.'

∼

Dremell, ever watchful, readjusted Nadine's sleeping position, ensuring her comfort on the soft verge. He gazed over the ledge, tracing the contours of the majestic mountain shelf before him. The wooden cabin stood humbly, a single-story structure nestled amidst the rocky landscape. Its weathered facade exuded an air of mystery, featuring a low-pitched roof reminiscent of an ancient barn. Perched on a raised platform, a set of wooden steps led to a door embraced by a welcoming veranda. Two weathered chairs and a table faced a breathtaking panoramic view, as if nature itself were putting on a grand spectacle. The mountainside soared behind the cabin, a tapestry of stones, hardy alpine flora, and majestic spruce trees.

Dremell's gaze lingered, studying the scene with unwavering attention. The scars of past explosions marked the flat stone shelf, bearing witness to the dark history etched upon it. As a gentle breeze caressed his hair, he cautiously peered further up over the ledge, scanning every detail, seeking answers in every nook and cranny of the vista before him.

He waited there for some time. A surge of adrenaline coursed through his veins, making him on edge. Could it be that they had miscalculated and the cabin stood abandoned, its purpose transformed into a mere retreat? Was it possible that a new stronghold, more sinister and elusive, lurked elsewhere in the Waking, beyond their grasp?

The absence of creatures from the Dream Realm cast doubt in his mind. Just seven formidable wolves were scattered around the area. One wolf lounged on the lowest step, two more in proximity, and two pairs positioned on the far side of the ledge. They sat, an air of gravity surrounding them, their snouts pointed into the wind, their eyes following the dancing movements of birds.

Lady Adara approached Dremell's side. Her voice a whisper. 'What do you make of this, my friend?'

'Ask not I, what do your senses tell you? Do you perceive any hidden presence?'

Dremell watched Lady Adara's eyes moving from one wolf to another, her druidic abilities attuned to the subtle energies of the surroundings. With quiet unhurried focus, she extended her attention to the hut, delving into the depths of the cabin, searching for any traces of life.

'This was a foreseeable scenario,' she assured softly. 'I've done all I can. Our scans cannot sense a sleeping Traveller. I sense nothing inside. We wait to hear from Nadine that he is in the Realm. When the time comes, just go with caution.'

~

Amidst the sprawling whiteness, a dark shape caught their eye, flashing into existence. Crane's voice resonated through the structure. Mora tried to hide her startlement and glared at him while the others staggered back.

'I've been wondering how long you would take to notice my activities.' Crane seemed amused. 'Was that blatant signal for me just so we could chat, or do we have some feeble attempt at a trap for me to endure?' Crane stepped forward, head bowed, teasing them, a hint of a conceited grin concealed in the shadow of the cowl.

Arms folded, Mora challenged him. 'I see you still choose to wear those ridiculous robes. Reveal yourself.'

'I like to keep the hood drawn and the wind off my face.' His head turned to each of them. 'Was that little, or not so little, Nadine just exiting then? Was it something I said?' When his cowl reached Laglen, he paused, acknowledging him. 'Laglen.'

'Crane.' Laglen's voice stayed in a flat, detached tone. 'Well, I think she wanted to let us oldies talk this out.'

'Are we having a talk? Where is Tasmin, then? Couldn't she join us today?'

'You tell us? She's disappeared.'

'What a pity, I rather miss her sanctimony. She was always so ridiculously irreproachable.' He took another step. 'Well, I am sure wherever she is now she is keeping herself good company.'

Mora frowned. Was he laughing? It didn't matter, she thought, all they needed to do was to keep him busy while the team got inside the shack.

Kalamayn seemed to be mindful of the same idea, wanting to keep the conversation flowing. 'Have you come here to gloat?'

'Not to you. You are not worth my attention.'

Kalamayn clenched his fist, flailing it in front of his chin like a drunk.

'Oh, Kalamayn,' Crane laughed. 'All this posturing as some great scholar, and the minute someone hurls an insult at you your only recourse is fisticuffs. You prove my point perfectly.'

Kalamayn loosened his fist. 'You always were a coward.'

Mora stepped in front. 'What do you want, Crane?'

'You tell me? Inviting me through an image of myself on your window; are you trying to prod the lion?' He cocked his head. 'Or do you want to try and defeat me, Mora?'

Mora grew into a giant version of herself. 'We, the Traveller community, demand that you cease your foul activities in the Waking. Also, that you destroy your hideous demon creations and release all the children you have captive immediately.'

Crane chuckled. 'Is that all?'

The portal fired up behind him, revealing a black depth in the entrance of the door. Instead of entering it to escape, he remained ominous in his stillness. 'How sad, Lag and Kal, you let a woman face me. How very gallant of you, hiding behind your lack of connection to The Pull.' His silvery laugh sent a chill up their spines. 'Laglen, you know better than to confront me. Didn't you tell them what I can do?'

Mora threw Laglen a worried look. Any minute now, he would disappear from both dimensions, she thought. Just vanish out of existence as his Waking body released its last breath. They just needed to keep him preoccupied.

Twisting branches erupted beneath Crane's feet, grasping his legs and waist. Crane changed his form to water and just slid out of the clasp. A little further away, the water collected into a pool, then rose into a shape of a person, finally changing into the hooded figure again.

'So easy.'

'I have the power in my structure!' Mora roared in rage. 'Change your form to escape, if you will, but you can't hurt me!' A stream of fire burst from her fingers, and the others stood back from its unrelenting discharge.

Crane fell to his knees, and beneath the fire and smoke, let out a comical sound of suffering. 'Oh, it hurts, it hurts, it hurts... nothing. Shall I show you what pain really feels like, Mora?'

Slowly, through the dwindling smoke and flames, he stood up unharmed, and pointed his right arm towards her, flinging Mora across her Atrium.

∼

'Crane is in the Realm!' Nadine hissed.

Dremell almost leapt upwards, revealing his position to the wolves on the ledge above.

'We are safe to proceed!' Nadine insisted. 'But we may not have much time.'

Dremell's jaw twitched. 'This seems all too easy.'

Nadine's eyes gleamed with exhilaration. 'Shouldn't we put this down to great planning on our part? He is in the Realm, so right now he is asleep in the cabin, or it's empty. This is our chance to enter.'

Dremell considered Lady Adara. She looked at Maltip, Lord Grisham, Praleck, Derrilyn, Jaden, her gaze passing from one to the other in silent contemplation. 'We take out the wolves first. Seven archers shoot at once,' she said.

Matip lowered his bow and nocked an arrow, the others following suit. On a whispered count of three, they rose over the ledge and fired.

∼

Kalamayn's grip tightened on Laglen's arm as a deafening blast reverberated through the structure. 'How is it possible? How does Crane possess the full connection of The Pull within Mora's structure?!' Kalamayn cried.

Laglen struggled to find an answer. 'I... I don't know,' he replied. 'We must move away from the battle. If we become caught in its chaos we won't stand a chance of protecting ourselves.'

They vanished, reappearing moments later at a safe distance, far across the white void. Explosions erupted across the vastitude, sending shockwaves rippling through the air. Two figures zipped through the sky, locked in a fierce struggle.

Laglen's mind raced to find an explanation for how Crane

could create things in Mora's construct. 'It must be connected to his portal. Perhaps it is granting him power, enabling him to tap into the full potential of The Pull.'

'But how do we close it? How do we stop him?'

Explosions continued to rock the surroundings. Laglen eyed the battle for a long moment. 'We have nothing here, no Pull. All we can do is watch. We must trust in Mora's capabilities. It's her Atrium. She can match Crane's power.'

Kalamayn shook his head. 'They are two indestructible objects locked in a relentless struggle.'

'Mora's task is to keep him occupied, to divert his attention from the greater mission.'

Kalamayn's voice trembled with fear. 'I'm scared, Lag. This battle, it's overwhelming.'

'I am scared too, Kal. But we must stay out of harm's way and trust that the army will succeed. We have to believe in their strength and in Mora.'

∽

Dremell went to climb over the ledge, blade in hand, Nadine behind, when Derrilyn's whispering voice halted them in their tracks. 'Let me lead.'

'You don't know what's in here, Derrilyn,' Dremell replied. 'Who knows what volatile substances and toxins we might find.'

'Then we go together,' he replied resolutely. 'You don't know what you will find either.'

'Crane, I hope!' Nadine said.

'Let's just get this over with,' Dremell said.

Side by side, they walked towards the porch. The army followed, mounting the ledge, filling the sweeping plateau, waiting in collective silence. The wind whispered eerily.

Dremell and Nadine's determined strides took them towards the door of the cabin. They reached the first step and Dremell tested his weight on it. There was no give or noise, so he tried the next one.

At the front door, Derrilyn stood there, gripping the handle in his fist, and mouthed his words to them. 'Stay behind me.' He peered inside, his expression tense, a sword held in his other hand. However, he felt nothing. For a fleeting moment, he wondered if the Chattara had descended upon him, numbing his senses, as Elaya had warned it might, cruelly overwhelming him at the very moment when he needed them the most.

But he sensed them: Dremell and Nadine. A belligerent blend of green and orange. Calmness fighting fear.

Derrilyn twisted the handle, then pushed it, causing the door to creak open. They stood, waiting at the door, the limited daylight revealed a sparse, old-looking wooden interior. A musky smell rose to greet them. They saw a shelf with vials and beakers, cobwebs strewn across them, abandoned thread networks as old as the beakers themselves.

They came into the room. Nadine caught herself, her foot swept through a pile of ash, which kicked a cloud of it into the air. They stopped and waited for it to settle. When it did, they noticed other piles of ash around them; not thinly spread across the surfaces as they might expect, but heaps of it in different places.

Dremell gestured to the far corner, where a bed was pressed against the wall. There, lying still beneath a thick, heavy bedsheet, was Crane.

The cover was drawn right up over his body, covering every inch of him, including his head.

Eager, Dremell strode forward and whispered, 'This is it.'

Derrilyn knew that being in the Realm was not like

normal sleep. He had heard Elaya's stories about Laglen. There was no chance that their whispering would wake Crane up. Nevertheless, he brought a finger to his lips and scanned the sleeping figure. Again, he felt nothing, no colours, no reading, no aura.

He motioned for Dremell to continue.

Derrilyn moved to the base of the bed, keeping a close eye on the Traveller as he approached Crane's body.

Crane lay motionless, a frail outline beneath the covers.

With his right hand, Dremell raised a knife, while Derrilyn prepared to strike with his sword.

Then, with his other hand, Dremell seized the corner of the bedsheet and pulled it back.

∽

From the far side of Mora's structure, Laglen watched and winced as every shock wave reverberated through his being.

'We have no protection against this firepower.' Laglen held his breath. 'They could swat us like flies.'

Kalamayn cowered beside him. 'I've never seen anything like it,' he said. The dark pupils of his eyes reflected the billowing blasts of fire.

Another shudder resonated in the air. It was like seeing a war from the other side of a great lake.

'Mora is doing really well,' Kalamayn said.

'This is good!' Laglen announced. 'Because it delays Crane and gives the two young Travellers time.'

Kalamayn was jubilant. 'We distracted him as planned, any moment now...'

But the battle raged on, Mora slammed into Crane. She hit him as a shock wave came back at her, turning them both in a flight of somersaults. For a second, it seemed a moment of calm, a solace, or ceasefire, had befallen them, then they clashed again, and a sonic boom roared around the structure.

They grappled and gripped each other's wrist, twirling through the white expanse, faces turned into painful sneers, throwing energy from their eyes which locked between them before their faces. The energy intensified, compounding as two forces of equal strength built up between them. Mora sent a charge of energy from her midriff, throwing Crane backwards. Then he vanished from sight.

'Come on!' Mora bellowed, words reverberating through the Atrium like the voice of a god.

Crane reappeared, floating not far away. The material of his robe flapped gently as if caught in a breeze, adding drama to his appearance. 'Your powers do not affect me.'

'Nor yours me.'

Mora glided closer. No longer a giant, back to her Waking size, but a few inches added. 'Release the babies. Or you will die today.'

Never far from him, the portal waited obediently, following like a dutiful pet. 'Me? Die?' The words snapped, and the portal seemed to spark brighter as if it could manifest his agitation. 'Read the Book of Iraazka. All will be revealed. Then, now, and what is yet to come.'

A deafening clap of thunder echoed through the air as Mora sent Crane rolling backwards. When he eventually came to a stop, instead of launching a counterattack, he lowered himself to the ground and generated a thick, shimmering field around him in the shape of a dome.

Mora floated above him, summoning The Pull to form various weapons. Jets of fire shot out of thin air, only to glance off the dome. Armour-piercing projectiles smashed into the protective shielding, shaking the air. A billowing cloud of fire, smoke, and gases enveloped the field around Crane.

Mora glided around the eruption, her relentless assault continuing. She fired lasers, ice, cannonballs, sound waves, every weapon she could think of.

'What is he doing? Laglen gestured at the dome forcefield, where Crane was kneeling. 'Has he surrendered?'

'I don't know, but why is it taking so long? They have got to be in the cabin by now. What do we do?'

'We wait,' Laglen growled. 'We are not leaving her.'

Then, from Crane's waiting portal, dozens of demons issued into the white, each carrying a black circular object above its head. Every globe, sphere, ball, whatever it was, was ten feet in diameter, and the forward face showed an open door. It was hard to see inside it. It was dark. But there was a hollow within, a murky chamber.

Kalamayn's frown increased. 'What is he trying to do? Lock her within?'

The demons charged at Mora, extending the globes towards her to do exactly that; secure her within one of the spheres' gloomy inners.

Mora continued throwing shatterproof piercing weaponry, fire, smelted ore, boiling fat, and other earthly forces. The first line of demons came at her, and Laglen watched her swat them away with a thought. But more poured out.

This time, they were faster.

She sent a blast towards the portal opening to take them out at their source, and dozens burned before they could enter her structure, but the flaming door jumped and opened elsewhere, popping around her, letting out an inky blur of limbs and black twisted faces. Now, they came at her from every direction.

Mora unloaded all The Pull she could at them, twirling

while she did it, spreading her power in a 360 degree spin, but when one line fell, more came to replace it.

Then, suddenly, Crane was out of the forcefield, suspended in the air even as Mora was struck to the ground. She tried to rise, but an enormous pressure held her down like an ocean of water above her, threatening to crush her into nothing.

The black shapes mounted, closer than ever. Sneering, dribbling snouts in a frenzy of haste. Until one finally reached her side, sliding the sphere across the ground to scoop her up. That hollow, dark chamber took her; a cell, just big enough for one. She looked back and cast one final stricken gaze towards the distance, where Laglen and Kalamayn watched in silent horror. Then the door slammed shut.

All the weapons Mora had deployed – the lasers, fire, cannons, missiles, and the ensuing explosions and smoke it was causing – all came to a dead stop, and her structure hung in silence.

∼

From below the cover, fiery red eyes gleamed at Dremell, and a mouth contorted into a sinister grin-snarl. The creature emerged, unfurling from its compact form into a spiky monstrosity. It kept lifting, rising out from a hollowed pit beneath the bed, emitting a clicking sound. Multiple blade-like limbs extended outward, two batting away Dremell's knife and Derrilyn's sword even as the others poised in a deadly attack stance. In its full shape, it was three times the length of the bed, with the spiky apex of its structure reaching the ceiling.

In an instant, one of those razor limbs thrust through

Dremell's chest, sickeningly slurping out his back. He was lifted helplessly, writhing in agony.

Gulping for air, blood bubbling from his mouth, the Traveller tried to speak, but a soft hissing sound emitted from his throat. From a fang-filled central core, sprouted bristly limbs; two of these reached out and ensnarled Dremell. One looped around his neck and the other his torso. Then, with a swift, brutal twist, it cleaved him in half. A haze of crimson hung in the air while his lifeless body parts thudded to the floor.

Nadine crashed into a bedside table, toppling into one of the piles of ash. Derrilyn rushed to her, slashing at the creature. It retaliated, its legs snapping like whips. One swift thrust from Derrilyn, and the creature lost a leg, wobbling. Yet, it regained balance with its many limbs. Without hesitation, Derrilyn plunged his sword into its core. The beast jerked and released a ghastly hiss before collapsing like a defeated spider.

A rush of terror flooded Derrilyn's druid senses. The world outside had become a cacophony of screams, alarms, and battle cries. Across the mountainside, violence erupted.

∼

Crane hovered over the sphere, his robe flapping in an invisible breeze. 'Well, that was easy.' He cast his gaze momentarily towards the cowering Kalamayn, then to Laglen.

'Crane, please, let her go,' Laglen said.

'Here we go again, old friend; it always seems to be you and me at the end, with you begging for their safety.'

'Crane, don't do this.'

'Let me out! Let me out!' Mora screamed. 'I can't feel The Pull,' she whimpered.

'It's too late. It's already happened,' Crane said.

'No, please, Crane,' Laglen pleaded. 'You don't have to do this.'

Crane shrugged. 'Oh, but I do. None of this is my fault, by the way.'

Crane lifted his finger and pointed it at the sphere.

'Night's skies,' Laglen said in disbelief. 'What have we done?'

No light or blast or projectile released from his fingertips, but the sound of her screaming was unbearable to listen to.

Laglen leapt towards Crane to try and stop him. But the sphere exploded, sending a thousand pieces of shrapnel and flesh across the open structure.

A millisecond later, Laglen and Kalamayn appeared in their empty Atriums, where their hollow screams raged on.

Thirty-Eight

'ELAAAAYA!' The urgent call of Maude rang through the air before Elaya caught sight of her sprinting along the castle walls. Elaya sensed her distress aura.

Elaya sprang to meet her. 'What is it?' she cried, unsheathing her two swords from their back scabbards.

Maude's voice was breathless, her words tumbling out in a rush. 'There's something you must see.'

'Where?'

'Over the eastern wall.'

The Wiggintons emerged from the castle. 'What's going on?' Lord Wigginton asked. 'I heard shouting.'

'Maude has spotted something on the eastern horizon,' Elaya said.

'Come,' Maude insisted. 'You need to see this.'

As they hurried, Rowen and Hazel joined them, bows and expressions taut.

'We heard shouting, what is it?' Rowen said.

'Until I know what's going on, guard over Girvyn,' Elaya said to Hazel. 'He is in Laglen's quarters, watching over his sleeping body. Go to them.'

Hazel nodded and sped towards the castle.

They reached the watch tower. Maude pointed. 'It's moving fast. Five minutes ago, that was just a spec, now you can see its...'

They stood transfixed.

'Is that... a sandstorm?' Lady Wigginton said.

'There is no sand in these parts,' Maude said. 'The plain is flat moorland.'

'Wind does not arrive in such a manner,' Rowen said. 'In the mountains, I have witnessed its dance, and it never glides along the ground like that.'

'It's an army!' Elaya declared. 'An invasion.'

She swung away, fixating on the castle walls, sensing something amiss. 'Girvyn!' she exclaimed, nose flaring. 'I feel his distress aura. He is in danger!'

∽

In a large, comfortable chamber at the rear of Wigginton castle, Girvyn sat at the edge of Laglen's bed and watched over him. Girvyn stroked his brow. He had promised Laglen he wouldn't Travel, so there was little else he could do but make his uncle comfortable. It was not a situation entirely unfamiliar to him, caring for Laglen's sleeping form while his consciousness was in the Realm. But today felt different. His uncle was not indulging in harmless racing. Girvyn was overcome with worry, helpless and hapless while others fought for the common good.

Suddenly a gust of wind rushed into the room, toppling a potted plant from the windowsill. Girvyn made his way over to retrieve it, but as his hand extended into the sunlight an inexplicable darkness fell upon him. He glanced upwards, and to his astonishment, a silhouette obstructed his view.

In mere moments, the creature had entered, towering as high as a man, and broader. The dim light of the room brightened, revealing the entity's true form. Its torso was armoured with plates of grey metal, but it was the expansive wings that made it seem so massive. An acrid stench hung in the air as it spoke. 'Crane is expecting you,' it hissed, its mouth stretching into a malevolent grin.

Then the door was kicked open, revealing Hazel with a gleaming dagger. But before she could strike, a swift sweep of a wing sent her crashing to the ground, unconscious.

Girvyn sank to his knees, clutching his head in agony. His vision swirled, the edges darkening, even though the creature hadn't even laid a finger on him. The demon chuckled, 'Your headache is right on schedule.'

Its rough hide brushed Girvyn's arm, and he flinched at the prick on his skin. Girvyn fired up the portal, but before he could leap to safety, his eyesight faded to black. Nausea swept through him, and he collapsed.

∽

Elaya, Rowen, and Maude hurried towards Laglen's room, rounding the castle wall with urgency. As they did, they found a creature outside Laglen's open window. Elaya unleashed an arrow from her bow, striking the monstrous creature midway up its left wing. The creature stumbled against the wall, revealing Girvyn strapped to its back.

A forked tongue flickered between its jagged teeth. 'You're too late!' it hissed. 'Crane has won.'

Despite its size, it was agile, swinging its wing at Elaya and knocking her to the ground.

'Watch its stingers in its wings!' Rowen warned, pointing at the razor edging.

Maude's arrow struck its shoulder, and it bellowed more in frustration than pain. She tried to grab Girvyn's foot as the thing passed by her.

Elaya came back up and thrust her sword at its leathery side, but it bounced off. The impact reverberated through her arm.

The beast dropped to its knees, preparing to take flight.

'We can't let it escape!' Rowen warned, firing an arrow into its chest. This time it roared in pain, its eyes spiteful flames of red.

Maude had Girvyn's foot and was wrestling with it. 'I can't get him off it!'

'Its eyes!' Elaya yelled. 'Aim for its eyes!'

As the creature ascended, Elaya leaped, grabbing its leg, rising with it. She plunged her knife into its side, climbing higher.

Then, a twang echoed, followed by a heavy thud as the creature plummeted to the ground, collapsing onto its front. Elaya rolled out of the fall, while Girvyn, his still unconscious body stretched across its back, shuddered against the cushioned impact.

'Good shot, Rowen,' Elaya said, sending him a thankful nod.

Maude was trying to pick Girvyn off its back. 'Its spine is sticky.'

'Then unstick him and get him back inside. Check on Hazel, make sure she is okay.'

Rowen knelt beside Girvyn, tracing his finger across a black bruise. 'The razor has cut Girvyn's skin. He has been poisoned.'

~

Elaya stood at the south side of the castle, gazing out over the plains. The army was still some miles out but moving with dazzling speed.

Lady Wigginton's lips trembled, her pupils searching in their eye sockets. 'What do we do? Where do we go?!'

Seeing signs of shock, Elaya kept her voice steady. 'We stay calm. We can't outrun them, and we can't fight them.' Elaya paused, thinking. 'I don't know if Crane can make them military savvy. But this has Kerrick's hallmarks all over it. Send in an agile unit to take the prize, knock Girvyn out so he can't portal, then destroy the rest of us.'

'We are dead.' Lady Wigginton cried. 'We can't escape this. Dear Lord, help us.'

She understood why Lady Wigginton suffered stress. She was not a trained soldier and had lived in isolation for years. Moreover, perhaps she could imagine Realm-based monstrosities. But right now, she needed calm and focus. 'Where is Girvyn?' she asked Rowen.

'Girvyn is still unconscious in Laglen's room,' he answered. 'Maude is there with Hazel,' Rowen replied.

'Good,' she said, pausing. Elaya regarded the Wiggintons, hands gripping either shoulder. 'We can all escape if Girvyn wakes up, but we need time to examine what that creature did to him. Where's the strongest room in the castle that we can barricade ourselves in?'

'The armoury,' Lord Wigginton said.

Clearly disheartened, Lady Wigginton murmured, 'This is hopeless.'

'Focus!'

Lady Wigginton stared vacantly at Elaya.

'I need you to focus, Your Grace. Focus on your breathing, push away your fear.'

Lady Wigginton nodded mutely.

Elaya looked at Lord Wigginton. 'Tell me more.'

'We had it made during the kingdom wars. It's in the basement, surrounded by thick walls because experimental explosive powders were stored there. I don't know how long it will hold them off.'

Lady Wigginton yelped in surprise. 'I have an idea how I can wake Girvyn.'

Elaya smiled. 'Glad to have you back with us. Follow your idea, Your Grace. Rowen, get the others. Lord Wigginton, show me this armoury!'

Lady Wigginton picked up the front of her dress and sped towards the castle.

∽

Five minutes later, they assembled in the strongroom, an underground chamber measuring approximately ten feet wide and twenty feet deep.

Rowen shouldered Girvyn down the entrance stairs. With the help of Maude, he propped him against a wall, then went to retrieve Laglen. Hazel passed him in the corridor.

'Are you okay?' Rowen asked her.

'Yes, it was a minor injury.'

Maude inspected the door frame, carrying a pessimistic expression.

Elaya sensed what she was thinking. 'The weakest part is the door,' she said. 'It won't hold them back for long.' She glanced down at Girvyn, still unconscious. 'At least the corridor is narrow and will slow them down.'

The sound of Rowen's approaching footsteps reached their ears, Laglen hung over his right shoulder. Hazel helped Rowen place Laglen next to Girvyn, their comatose forms side-by-side, and then she inspected Girvyn's cheeks.

'Any luck?' Elaya asked Hazel, casting a quick glance back at her.

After a few moments, Hazel shook her head. 'Nothing,' she sighed, her voice heavy with worry. 'I tried water in his eyes, pinching him, but he remains unconscious.'

From the north side of the castle, a piercing shriek resonated through the air. They fell silent, listening, waiting for more sounds. When the next cry came, it was from above their heads.

'The advance party has arrived. Sounds like more wing demons. They're circling,' Elaya muttered.

High above, another shriek pierced the air.

Lord Wigginton grimaced. 'The moat and walls won't hold them back then.' He cursed, looking down the corridor. 'Where is Celia?'

Rowen drew an arrow and pointed it down the passage. 'Elaya,' he murmured. 'Something's not right...'

From the corridor's end, Lady Wigginton emerged, clutching a box. But Rowen's gaze was fixed on the shadow trailing her. Sensing a lurking danger, he fired an arrow over her head into the obscurity. A muffled thud followed by a menacing growl echoed back. Then, the shadow changed into a shape.

Lord Wigginton began shouting. 'Run, Celia!'

Hazel burst out of the door, dagger flying as she struck the hulking mass. She fell to the ground, stabbing her blade at a jumble of black whirling limbs.

Lady Wigginton reached the chamber, but before Hazel could get up and into it, a wicked black tail whipped out of the shadows and slammed the door shut, trapping her in the corridor with the beast.

They heard grappling sounds, shrieks, hissing, and Hazel's determined grunts on the others side of the door.

Maude barged into it, screaming in frustration, but the door was being held.

Elaya kicked at it, but it didn't budge an inch. There was a yelp and a scraping sound, then the door opened. Hazel stood there, blade in hand, hair ruffled above a staunch expression. 'You seem surprised?' she declared.

'Are you okay?' Maude said, impressed.

Hazel glanced back at the door. 'A blade to the eye is what stops them. Lock it,' she said, renewed strength in her voice.

Maude, with Rowen's assistance, positioned three wooden beams across the inside of the door, securing them through the cross-bar brackets embedded in the stone wall. This barricade stood as their final defence.

From high up in the castle came a thunderous boom. Even in the basement they felt the vibration, saw the dust sprinkle down from the ceiling. It came again, echoing like some ancient groan. They held their breath, captivated. Then a third rumble came. A hissing, slithering sound spread through the castle, growing rowdier and insistent. On the floors above them the ground quivered, resonating, bone-rattling tremors. The pounding of innumerable feet against the floor hammered in a frenzied rhythm. Gradually the whistling became something new, a deeper chord of guttural roars and howls, as if the very essence of darkness itself had been unleashed.

'They are inside,' Lord Wigginton said, his voice trembling amidst the cacophony of unholy vocalisations outside the door.

'Try again to wake him!' Elaya commanded, urgency lacing her words.

With trembling hands, Hazel shook Girvyn. His head jerked back and forth, but there was no response. 'I can't do it!' she screamed in frustration.

'Let me try!' Lady Wigginton took out phials from the box she had carried. She examined Girvyn and found three puncture wounds with black round the edges. 'The poison was put into his blood here, here and here.'

Lord Wigginton looked. 'It has the colour of a tincture of belladonna. This will be difficult, my dear.'

'They wanted him alive!' Elaya said through gritted teeth. 'So find a way to wake him!'

Using a soaked cloth, Lady Wigginton covered Girvyn's mouth, then began dabbing various bottles on his face, wrists, and ears. She placed the open bottle neck right under his nose as he breathed in, and he coughed suddenly, but remained unconscious.

'What's in the bottles?' Hazel asked them.

'Plant extracts,' Lord Wigginton said. 'We don't like mixing with others, so Celia is an amateur healer.' He encouraged his wife, 'Keep trying. It's working.'

A new voice penetrated the chaotic atmosphere, drawing their attention.

'Mora is dead.' Laglen rose to his feet; he cut a solemn figure.

'Are you sure?' Elaya asked.

'I saw it with my own eyes. We were thrown back into our own Atriums. She is gone.'

Elaya's expression stiffened. 'And we will meet the same fate unless you can wake your nephew!'

Laglen came to Girvyn's side and lifted an eyelid, his touch gentle. 'Girvyn!' he murmured. 'Can you hear me?' He addressed Lady Wigginton. 'How long has he been like this?'

'Too long,' she said, tapping a cream into the wounds.

A thunderous noise swept down the corridor towards them. When the demons arrived, it was like deafening thunder. Up close, they could discern distinct growls, could picture dripping snarls.

The door shook. The beams that held it shut rattled under the force exerted upon it. The frenzy of unworldly reverberations intensified; an eerie chorus that sent shivers down their spines. The door shook again, more forcefully this time, as if someone – or something – had violently collided with it.

And then, it stopped.

A mocking voice spoke, 'Come now, Elaya, old friend. How long do you think you are going to survive in there with no air? We can prolong your agony until you suffocate, which would be both boring and annoying, or we break in and kill you all, and put an end to your miserable existence. I gave you the chance and you turned it down. So now you are all going to die. Oh, how exquisitely painful it will be. So why don't you just be a good girl and open the door and we can do it quickly.'

Elaya hissed. 'Kerrick!'

She swung around. Was that a groan? Did Girvyn's eyelashes flicker?

Kerrick muttered something which they couldn't hear. Then, 'I am going to count to three, Elaya. If you don't open the door on three, I won't be able to hold them back any longer, I'm afraid. They are rather hungry, and angry. My way, you get a swift sword through the brain. Yours...' Elaya could picture his flamboyant gestures and his smug, pseudo-lamenting expression, 'it will be hideous.'

'One.'

Elaya looked back at the door, realisation hitting her. 'He thinks the poison is going to keep Girvyn unconscious!' she whispered. 'Otherwise he would just smash through!'

'Two.'

Laglen whispered. 'Elaya, now is the time for words, not

action. Taunt him. Use whatever's between you to delay him. Just get us time to bring Girvyn round.'

'Three.'

'How do I know you won't feed us to the monsters if I open this door?' Elaya directed her words to the door frame, gesturing manically at the others to keep trying to wake Girvyn. Hazel was fanning him using a discarded piece of wood. Lady Wigginton was dripping liquid into his eyes.

'You have my word,' Kerrick said.

'That doesn't mean much,' said Elaya.

'Open the door and I won't hand you over to Crane; I will give you all a fast death.'

'But how do I know your demons won't stop short a breath before death and torment us? That's what demons do, don't they?'

'Why are you stalling?' replied Kerrick. 'Girvyn won't wake up. You are just delaying the inevitable.'

Elaya checked Girvyn. His eyelids trembled. He let out a breath. Moved his head, flinched.

'He is waking,' Lady Wigginton said quietly.

Maude began instructing Elaya with whispering words: 'Your promises are as weak as your virility, Kerrick. Why should I trust them?"

Kerrick laughed. 'So my desert rose has a thorn! Well, well, Elaya. I need offer you nothing. It is simple generosity in respect of our long acquaintance. Open the door.'

'Ah but have you checked with your master if he will allow you to make such choices? He may whip you later for it, like a dog.'

Kerrick's voice was furious. 'I take commands from no one. I did not sell my talents into pathetic service to a weak queen as did you. You should have pledged your sword to me instead, but now you will die…' Kerrick fell silent. A demon said something in a raspy voice, words that were hard to hear. Heated whispers followed.

'What? Where?' A pause. 'Are you sure? A healer's kit?' Kerrick's voice boomed. 'Break it in!'

There was a great thud and the wood creaked in the doorframe. Dust dropped from the ceiling and the timbers groaned. Another crash. This time the whole wall shook. Outside rose a feverish clamour.

'We have run out of time!' Elaya shouted above the din. 'Move back!'

Sweeping everyone backwards, swords drawn, she readied for battle. Hazel and Rowen stretched their bow strings. Maude steadied her stance, levelling her blade.

Dust billowed again from the door, hiding the entire surface for a moment as the wood vibrated and moved in the frame. Splinters began tearing along the edge, the wooden runners rattling and jumping. One popped free and fell, which sent a wave of fervour outside, as the door gave some more.

It was as if the foundations themselves had joined the attack, trembling and quaking the entire castle from the stone groundworks upwards, dislodging mortar and sediment which had lain at rest for centuries. Powdery, silt-like dust and highland stone showered into the chamber as the door came away from the lintel. A roar burst through the widening gap.

When the door finally gave way, falling inwards, part of the wall came with it as the demons smashed through the stone. The door slammed onto the floor and the creatures surged over it like an angry tidal wave, filling the entire opening. Demons on top of demons, pushed like rats through cracks. Blazing eyes shot back at them. Hellish screams erupted from twisted faces.

Then they stopped. Covered in a dazzling blue cast. A canvas depicting hell's army. Caught in some frozen life-like mural, bits of broken wall suspended in mid-air.

'Shall we go?' Girvyn said, gesturing to the unknown in the rippling dark surface of the Realm door.

The demons fought against the invisible force. Bodies frozen in mid-movement. This wasn't a choke hold. It was some silent suspension. Their faces distorted in soundless strain.

One by one, the company vanished into the portal, until Elaya was the last one standing with Girvyn. She cast her gaze across the wall of unblinking paralysed demons until finding Kerrick's submerged mad and torn expression, sunken in seas of black twisted shapes.

'Look at you, Kerrick. It's a telling image. Suspended by hate.'

She patted Girvyn's cheek and stepped inside.

Thirty-Nine

Derrilyn kicked back the cabin door, his arm wrapped around Nadine's shoulder, guiding her forward. They were met with a deafening din of anguished screams as they gazed out onto the sprawling mountain plateau. What they witnessed was a nightmarish scene unfolding before them.

Huge, ape-like footmen and their monstrous allies charged down the mountainside with relentless determination, throwing soldiers aside with powerful swings of their forearms.

The earth shook beneath the horde's mass, and the air thickened with the foul odour of decay. A sudden spray of blood arced into the air, creating a gruesome red mist above the dying. Towering tormentors stomped through the ranks of soldiers, their muscular frames brimming with raw power, tossing soldiers into the air, crushing heads with relentless snapping claws.

More columns of ape-like demons descended from hidden positions above, smashing into the beleaguered line of soldiers attempting to hold their ground. The apes thrust their protruding tusks this way and that, hurling men into the air.

Amidst the chaos, clicking and jerking, beetle-like creatures scuttled about, using their spindly, serrated legs to cleave through soldiers with brutal efficiency. Above the mayhem, the air resounded with desperate pleas for mercy and the agonising cries of the dying.

Hovering over the battlefield were abominations with leathery wings, swooping down upon unsuspecting soldiers and tearing them apart with jagged claws and razor-sharp teeth.

But it wasn't just grotesque distortions of living flesh that instilled fear in the hearts of men. Alongside them were colossal demons of moving stone that lumbered forward, their massive limbs capable of crushing both armour and bone with ease.

Naked fear surged through Derrilyn as he caught sight of a Drone Druid. Its armoured upper body loomed over the crowd of men, swinging its great sword in a circle, cutting through soldiers as though they were mere weeds in a field.

For a slow, agonising moment, his eyes traversed the gruesome scene. He saw one man cleaved in two by a talon. Another, his chest split open with a single punch. He caught sight of faces. Final silent grimaces. Wild, vanishing snarls of people he knew. Donjul, of the Tologon tribe, was split by his own spear. Sward, of Andergine, torn limb from limb. Lord Grisham, of Trefgwyn, was flown into the air and disintegrated by a dive-bombing demon. Praleck, of Stoer, suffered the torment of two demons tossing him back and forth like a morsel of food.

His world was reduced to a tide of stabbing tusks, flashing claws, snarling fang-filled mouths, and screaming faces. For a fleeting moment Derrilyn caught a glimpse of a semblance of resistance, a flicker of hope. Maltip of The Highlands led his men valiantly, fighting back-to-back, and dispatching apes with metal tipped shafts…but then the chieftain was lifted into the air by a tusk-mounted assailant, vanishing in a surge of black, mottled skin.

Derrilyn watched in a state of shock and horror as the valiant Highlanders, once brave and mighty, resorted to hurling themselves off the precipice, choosing that desperate plunge rather than facing their leader's doom. Even a clean death was denied them; their desperate suicide attempts were met with sadistic glee by the winged demons, who snatched them from the air and callously tossed them back onto the plateau to become playthings for a final moment.

A blaring horn echoed off the mountain slopes. The call for retreat. It pealed again and he saw the coiled ram's tusk leave Lady Adara's lips. Standing beside her, Jaden swung his blade with desperate determination, employing two-handed, forceful strikes. Derrilyn's awe of them both was replaced by rising fear.

A sea of writhing shapes pulled Jaden away, leaving Lady Adara surrounded.

In that pivotal moment, Derrilyn's eyes met hers. Derrilyn had never seen such an expression on a face before, betraying incalculable distress. Shaking her head, she mouthed a single word to him: 'Hide!' Tears streamed down her cheeks.

The demons closed in. Every fibre of his being trembled as he witnessed Lady Adara being seized by the menacing talons of a winged demon and swept into the air. The bird carrying her circled high above, unleashing a chilling cry. And then, in a horrifying instant, Lady Adara was ripped apart, her remains descending rapidly into a swirling abyss of writhing shadows.

The sight etched itself into Derrilyn's mind, and he knew,

with profound sharpness, that her blood from this day would forever stain him.

At Derrilyn's side, Nadine stared blankly, whimpering, unable to talk or fight.

'We need to go!' Derrilyn cried, sweeping her along the cabin front wall towards the lower mountain shelf.

He suddenly became aware of a spider creature scuttling towards him, hissing and spraying a deadly venom. He picked up a veranda chair and threw it, which knocked it off the deck. Gripping Nadine's arm, he screamed, 'I can't carry you! We will die. You need to run!'

Shocked back to sensibility and wiping tears away, Nadine nodded with determination, lips quivering. They sprinted along the ledge, and two apes took chase, leaking primaeval snorts. They jumped to the lower ledge. Derrilyn landed, rolled, came up quickly, slicing one way then the other. The apes shrieked in anger, yellow blood oozing from the wounds. Noses flaring, they charged at him. Derrilyn rolled back, flicking one into the air, and thrusting upwards with his sword at the other, the blade jamming into the ape's neck. It landed on him, dead, but then he couldn't move.

Just as he felt the other weighty ape's feet approach his head, a swoosh cut through the air, followed by a squelching sound as a blade split its neck. The dead ape was dragged off him, and a hand appeared and helped him up.

'Thank you,' he said to Nadine. 'Let's go!'

They ran for minutes that felt like hours. The crushing roar of the dying echoed across the slopes around them, whistling off the mountain side like wailing wind. Winged demons circled above, emitting shrill sounds that chilled their souls. Rustling and rumbles of pursuers followed behind them. They jumped from track to rocky ridge, from paths to moss-covered ledges. Derrilyn risked a backward glance and veered right, towards a rocky formation in the mountain wall. 'There!' he hissed.

They leapt into a dark, shadowy opening, and at once felt the air grow colder, carrying a faint earthy scent mixed with the dampness of the cave. Derrilyn drew a finger to his lips as the sound of their pursuers grew louder. Then a flash of dark shapes passed by the cave entrance and disappeared.

'We can't stay in here long,' Nadine said in a whispered hiss. 'The winged demons must have seen us vanish!'

'We wait a moment then take a different route.'

'They have our scent,' Nadine insisted. She laid down on the cave floor. 'I'm sorry, I can't do this. I don't want to die like this. I am crossing to the Realm.'

'What?' Derrilyn said, flabbergasted.

'I don't want this to be my final moment. I'm sorry,' she said. 'In the Realm I can make the minutes we have left last years; I can slow down a structure and live inside it.'

'You are running away?'

'Thank you for everything,' she swallowed. 'Forgive me. Go, save yourself.'

Then she went still. Derrilyn blinked away the tears. When he heard noises outside the cavern entrance, he lifted his sword, planted his back foot in the cave sediment, and readied to face them.

∽

Nadine appeared in the white expanse of her Atrium, breath still rapid and shallow despite the calming ambience of her Realm home. Although it felt unjust and unfair to leave Derrilyn to face impending doom, she could not bear another moment in that harrowing reality. What use would she be anyway? Tormented by the spectre of death that surrounded her, haunted by the memories of Dremell's killing and the countless others who had been mercilessly massacred without a fair chance to fight back.

A blast sent her backwards onto the floor. She glanced up, shocked, expecting some pitiless finishing by Crane, and found Girvyn there instead.

'Nadine,' he spoke softly, his voice filled with concern. 'We were ambushed in Wigginton, but we managed to escape. Mora... Mora didn't make it.'

Nadine's tears streamed down her face as the weight of the loss hit her. The sheer totality of Crane's destructive rampage insurmountable.

She recounted the horrors of what she had seen, voice trembling.

Girvyn stood there, his jaw dropping as he absorbed her words. 'All of them... dead?' he uttered, struggling to comprehend the magnitude of the devastation that had unfolded.

'Leave me, Girvyn,' she said. 'I don't have much time. When I enter a structure, it will slow down and our time placement will be displaced. I have moments left to do it.'

'I am not leaving you. We're not leaving Derrilyn.'

'But how? You can't portal in. You can't imagine where we are. You haven't seen it.'

A hard smile played across Girvyn's lips. 'Show me!' He gestured. 'Paint it.'

'No, Girvyn. A painting would be blurry, vague. You could appear anywhere and die instantly. I won't take this risk with you."

'Make it look real then! I created a real-life replica of the Rathnell market. It Can be done. What have we got to lose? Even if it is your last, make this your greatest-ever structure. Find The Pull and draw the place your body lies in every beautiful detail.'

Nadine stood up, expression tight in concentration. As she drew The Pull into her being, the vast empty space of her structure began to fill with features. A sloping cavity wall, strewn rocks semi-protruding from a powdery cavern floor. The dark entrance, an oval shape stone opening as old as the mountain itself.

Girvyn regarded his portal, still flaring in the chamber behind him, and sent that image to the gate.

∼

In the confines of the cavern opening, Derrilyn defended his position. A brutish tusk came through the gap, its dark frame dimming the light on the walls around him. He saw more shapes arrive outside the cavern entrance. Tall, waiting demons folded powerful arms, and spindly insect-creatures scuttled up, clicking and humming in some angry melody.

He reminded himself to focus on one opponent at a time, disregarding that legions were lining up to confront him.

The first creature fell, and was replaced by another. Tears streamed down Derrilyn's cheeks as he fought for his life, discovering a reservoir of strength he hadn't known he possessed.

For years he had harboured a suppressed rage from his time as an outcast. Now, that pent-up anger surged, breaking free from the careful walls he had constructed around it during his time with Elaya. He no longer cared because he knew he was facing certain death, and he believed that Nadine, just like his parents, had abandoned him. Nevertheless, he resolved to keep fighting until the last vestiges of strength needed to lift his arm were drained from him.

'One at a time,' he told himself. 'Come on!' As he followed

this mantra, the next ape came through the entrance, and he fought it with a two-handed swing and a screaming shriek of rage. It fell and the next one came.

Then, a burst of dazzling blue illuminated the cave entrance behind him, surprising the demon caught in its light. The ape attempted to move forward, poised to attack, but an invisible force held it motionless.

He felt a hand on his shoulder and swung round, raising his sword.

'Derrilyn, no!' came Nadine's voice. 'It's me!'

'What? How?' Derrilyn lowered his sword.

She took his arm and led him to the portal. 'It's okay, come, I will take you to Elaya.'

In the blink of an eye, they found themselves standing in a serene forest clearing.

~

Many leagues away, Elaya perched on a fallen tree trunk, sighing in frustration. She scanned the forest. Apart from the quiet presence of animals, she sensed nothing. 'What are we doing here?' she muttered morosely. 'Where has Girvyn gone, Lag?'

Laglen's voice dripped with despair. 'I don't know. He said to wait.'

Maude looked around. 'I recognise where we are. We stopped here for a rest on the way to Wigginton.'

Lady Wigginton glanced at her husband. Hazel leaned against a tree, watching. Rowen stared into the fading light, bow drawn, arrow aimed at the dark.

'We can't stay here, Lag. We need a new plan,' Elaya muttered.

Laglen replied, in his own cloud of despondency, 'I know,

Elaya. But if he doesn't come back there's no point in us going anywhere. It's all over, and only hell awaits us.'

Maude muttered, 'If he comes back, do we just keep moving and hiding in the woods forever?'

Laglen admitted, 'I don't know.'

Elaya grumbled, 'We can only wait.'

Laglen kicked a stone. 'Crane was prepared for us in the Realm. He knew the entire plan.'

Then, the portal appeared beside them, revealing a rippling surface and the silhouette of a person within.

'We are going to Cundelly,' Nadine declared as she stepped into the clearing. Her face was covered in dirt, smudged by tears.

Elaya rose, sword drawn. 'Where is Girvyn?'

Another shape came through the portal. Elaya gasped. 'Derrilyn! Are you okay? What happened?'

Derrilyn, chest heaving, eyes burning with rage, could not meet Elaya's gaze.

The portal crackled and hummed, projecting a blinding light that revealed a new scene: a cluttered antique shop on the other side.

'Kal's shop?' Laglen exclaimed in astonishment. 'But how?'

Girvyn stood there, waving for them to enter and join him.

Nadine urgently addressed them, 'We need to go. We can't stay here. No one will know where we are at my father's shop. We need to hide out and regroup.'

Laglen, still baffled, stammered, 'Nadine, what happened on the slope?'

Nadine's voice broke, and she sobbed.

Forty

QUEEN AMELIA'S eyes narrowed further and further until her lids shut, and she sat back in her chair.

The four Privy Council members glanced at one another and remained silent.

Stasnier cleared his throat. 'Would you like me to repeat what was said, Ma'am?'

The queen didn't open her eyes. 'And how do we know this?'

'We received the message by a bird.'

'When did this happen?'

Cargya brandished the note. 'Two days ago, Your Majesty. The message came today.'

Amelia's eyes flicked open. 'How, if everyone is dead?'

Cargya fidgeted with her fingers. 'They left supply staff and squires with the horses at the base of the mountains, Ma'am. When no one came back, one of them climbed up to look.'

The room went silent.

'It was a bloodbath, Your Majesty,' Berenger said.

Stasnier shot Berenger a look. 'Perhaps Kerrick has spies

in the castle, or maybe the rot goes deeper than him and there is a mole of Crane's amongst us.'

Amelia fell silent. 'And Wigginton?' she asked.

'We lost contact three days ago.'

Ellis brandished a thin strip of paper. 'A note with no signature arrived today.' Ellis glanced down and read it: 'Wigginton compromised. Location moved. Training continuing.'

'Who sent this note?'

Stasnier continued speaking, 'It didn't say. It just said Wigginton compromised.'

A faint smile touched her lips. 'So, Elaya lives,' she whispered. 'Where did the bird originate from?'

'It wasn't a state bird, Ma'am,' Cargya said. 'No markings. It could have been any city on the continent. Countless mercenary homing stations are connected to Rathnell in even the smallest of settlements.

'It's significant that the bird could not be tracked back to its departure location,' Ellis said. 'If it's Elaya, she doesn't want to be found.'

'It is her,' the queen murmured. 'And she is right to trust no-one in this palace. I am angry with you all for your mismanagement. Crane was expecting our ambush in the mountains and attacked Wigginton too! Kerrick tells Crane of our plans, but who tells Kerrick? He was not in the summit, at the stables when we saw Girvyn's power, nor in the committee which formulated the attack plan. We need to find this mole,' the queen finished. Her gaze passed to each of them in turn. 'But the field of suspects is very wide, including castle staff... and you.'

Stasnier stood up. 'Your Majesty. Counsellors. As you know I am not a man who finds it easy to admit fault, but I must here. I have focused on earthly quarrels, human politics, but to the exclusion of this far greater threat that Crane poses.' Stasnier turned stiffly to the queen, and then bent awkwardly to one knee. 'I pledge that what strength I have left in life will go to this fight, the great and terrible fight of our times, and my first mission will be to find the traitor in our midst. I shall not rest until he, or she, is identified and brought to justice.'

The queen sat forward and went to speak, then lost all her breath in her chest and collapsed back in her chair.

∾

Hours later, Stasnier leaned out of his quarters' window, gazing across the night sky, relishing the cool breeze that refreshed his face. It had become his nightly ritual to survey the cityscape before retiring, to observe the glittering lights and the minuscule figures of people below and ponder over the day's events and his life in general.

A noise jolted Stasnier back to reality, and to his horror he found himself facing a monster as grotesque as the one that had attacked the library. Had Crane sent this creature to kill him? Fear coursed through him, causing him to stagger backwards. The creature advanced, its skin adorned with yellow and black bands of hardened texture that emitted eerie creaking sounds reminiscent of new saddle leather.

In a desperate bid for protection, Stasnier lunged towards the drawer of his writing desk, intending to retrieve a dagger. However the creature, anticipating his move, positioned itself between Stasnier and the desk, blocking his access.

'Don't even bother, Stasnier!' the creature jeered mockingly. 'You couldn't even pierce the skin.'

Stasnier took a step back, his eyes darting in all directions. 'Kerrick?! Where the hell are you?' he called out, searching for the source of the voice he'd recognised. The corrupt baron's company, though ominous, would be strangely comforting in this moment.

Kerrick's laughter echoed through the room. 'This is the funniest thing!'

'What?' Stasnier stammered, retreating until his back was pressed against the wall, clutching a chair with its legs out as a feeble defence. Although, the voice he heard seemed to originate from the creature before him.

'Kerrick?' Stasnier stiffened as he struggled to reconcile the voice and face. 'Is that you?'

'Yep.'

'But...? Have you changed into one of them?'

Kerrick laughed. 'Nope.' He laughed. 'Stasnier, put the chair down.'

'No.'

'Take a deep breath.' Kerrick sniggered,

'Is this really you? How do I know this isn't a trick?'

'Ask me a question that only you and I would know the answer to.'

Stasnier frowned, his brain still unable to associate the voice with the face. 'When we were children,' he said, shaking his head, disbelieving he was even asking the question, 'who was our maths teacher?'

The creature laughed. 'So easy. That would be Mescal.'

No! No! The words screamed in his mind. This wasn't a trick. This was Kerrick! After recent catastrophic events, somewhere, in some small, hopeful part of his mind, he had assumed the sides had been chosen, the game set, and he didn't have to do this anymore. Reluctantly, Stasnier lowered the chair, maintaining a cautious distance. 'You dare to show up here? The entire continent is after you.'

'This little gift is how we will talk; no more court corner whispering.'

Stasnier kept his distance. 'Be my guest and attend court; you will be in shackles before any hearing starts!' Stasnier faltered. 'You said gift?'

'It's a little gift from Crane,' the creature explained with the baron's voice. 'I am connected to its twin, allowing us to converse through them. Watching this creature mimic your cowering is hilarious.'

Stasnier looked around his chamber for open windows. 'How did it even get in my room? How did it get past the guards and infiltrate the castle?'

'It's a demon; it does demony things. It would make a marvellous assassin. I could kill people without even leaving my estate.'

'You do that anyway.'

'Yes, but I don't get to witness their final breath or deliver a cutting end line.'

'You are sick.'

'This is far more entertaining, and the communication is instantaneous.'

'What do you want?' Stasnier glared. 'What happened on the mountainside was not supposed to go down that way.'

'That was out of my control. I led the Wigginton attack, which, I might add, killed no one.'

'Which I am sure was not what you intended. What do you want?'

'Checking in for a report.'

'I sent you a pigeon when they left the city. There is nothing else to add. Don't expect these conversations to continue. We are done. We are on opposite sides now.'

The creature facing Stasnier seemed upset. 'One message, is that it? The rest of my team check in regularly.'

'Because they are scared of you.'

'And you are not?'

'I should have killed you when my father found you on the side of the road and brought you home.'

'Maybe you should have; and you had your chance. Now you are a weak, pathetic excuse of a man.'

'What you are doing is against humanity. You should have told me you were working with Crane.'

The creature towered over Stasnier, its fists raised. For a second, Stasnier thought it would strike him, but its hands unclenched. 'Don't forget our agreement. Or all the things you hold dear will diminish before your eyes.'

'They already have. How can you make this worse? The end of the world has begun, and you are clearing the path.'

'I am just ensuring I am on the winning side. So could you. Why not be a good little half-brother and suck it up and do what I ask?'

'We are not even related! You were adopted, then opted for the streets when you met Elaya,' Stasnier shot back.

'Great years, great years.'

'What, all eight of them?' Stasnier scoffed sarcastically. 'You don't get to hold an axe over my neck forever.'

'Oh, you're getting feisty. Just because I am not there to keep you in line, don't get cocky. You work for me.' Kerrick's voice turned cold. 'And if you choose to deviate from that, I will kill everyone you care about, including your children. You know that…Answer me?'

'I do know that,' Stasnier muttered. 'Better than anyone.'

'Good, because once I ruin the Glencast family name, I will kill everyone you love. My loans of gold earned by my ingenuity and hard work saved your father from embarrassment. While you whored and gambled away the family fortune to leave your wife and children destitute. Your mansion is paid for with my credit. Your wife's dresses, your children's schooling. All that you earn and every cut and bribe you take from your duties pays only the interest on my loans, as you know. With one boring little word to call in those debts, I can destroy you and your family name forever. Is that what you want? Are you really feeling that brave?'

Stasnier moved away, keeping his back to the creature, and gazed afar. 'You don't need to threaten me. I have supported your twisted pursuits at great personal risk.'

'I don't care about your personal risk. You always use that excuse to delay doing everything I ask.' Kerrick's voice dripped with disdain. The demon pointed a thick hand at Stasnier. 'The potions, are you still administering them to Amelia?'

Stasnier opened his mouth to respond but thought better of it, choosing to remain silent. It was a skill he had honed from a young age, particularly when dealing with Kerrick. If not for him, would Stasnier have become the quick-thinking strategist he was today? Throughout his life, forced upon him by Kerrick, he had learned to navigate the conflicting forces of self-interest and self-preservation. He needed to rely on those skills more than ever to navigate this precarious path.

'You know I disagree with this. You *were* one heartbeat away from ascending anyway. By publicly supporting Crane, you have ruined it. And anyway, consider the countless meetings and obligations you would have to fulfil. Do you really want all that tedium? Amelia is barely able to walk across a room half the time, and she signs whatever I put in front of her. Why mess up something that works so well? You rule, but you keep your freedom,'

'Do you think I will be that sort of king, pandering to the fops of the court and pathetic traditions? No Stasnier, I will

RULE. I will take the throne by force, once Crane's work is done.'

The Kerrick demon stared at Stasnier intently for a long moment before throwing its head back in uproarious laughter. 'Just keep administering the doses. I have eyes everywhere, and I'll know if you fail. Don't think I'm unaware of what's happening down there. Understood?'

Stasnier's face ran through a gamut of emotions. Finally, he let out one begrudging word. 'Yes.'

'Yes what?' The demon flexed its hand, wanting violence.

'Yes. I understand.'

Forty-One

Crane took a moment to reflect on what Boud had said. He picked up an extravagant gilt embroidered jewellery box, turned it around in his fingers to inspect the reverse, and then put it back on the mahogany writing table. He had seen it a thousand times. Everything in the room had remained the same since he had made it some twenty years ago. There was a slight musty smell to the air, as if the wood and books had endured for centuries.

Boud watched silently, leaning back in the leather chair, weaved fingers poised in his lap. 'We can't turn back now. You have come this far.'

'I know.' Crane sighed. 'I am not hesitating. It's just…'

'Just what?'

'So many deaths, and so much more to come.'

'You know what you must do to regain what is rightfully yours.'

'It's all I have ever thought about since this all began.'

Boud shrugged and stood up. 'You follow the map, and you get what you want.' He came to stand before Crane. 'It's months, that's it.'

'Thank you for keeping me focused all these years.'

'It's what you created me for.'

'I didn't; I created you as a child so we could grow up together.'

'We both know I'm not that same person anymore. Girvyn saw to that.'

Crane clenched a fist, then exhaled and released the tension. 'So much suffering. It's all Girvyn's fault.'

'Yours is the greatest and longest suffering.'

'I know.'

'And it is his fault. Not yours.'

Crane nodded, deliberating. 'He has settled into his powers very easily.'

'And we know why. All is as it should be,' Boud said.

'So much will change,' Crane said gently. 'I just want the noise to stop.'

'It will. I promise you.' Boud's voice grew harder. 'He started this. Don't forget that.' Boud took his hand. Crane didn't blink. Instead, he held him close. They stood like that for many minutes. When Crane returned to the Waking, he realised they had held each other for hours.

Forty-Two

Elaya checked on Derrilyn, ensuring he was still asleep. She closed the door and ascended the basement steps to the cluttered antique shop floor. Scattered throughout the shop, the others awaited her, seated in display chairs amidst the packed items. Kalamayn tensed whenever someone stood up to examine something. The maze of treasures was unfamiliar to many, and Kalamayn hurriedly corrected anything that got moved on a shelf. Elaya had advised him not to worry about the stock, and felt his anxiety was misdirected. A week into their new hideout, the "closed" sign hanging on the door, everyone was feeling anxious.

'How is Derrilyn?' Laglen asked Elaya.

'He is the same.'

'How long will he stay like this?' Nadine said, concern in her voice.

'The Chattara works differently for each of us. The massacre has precipitated its start, which is not an ideal way to begin the process. Like a trauma might quicken childbirth.'

'Is there anything I can do?' she asked. 'I want to help. It's the least I can do to repay his kindness.' She glanced away, tears filling her eyes.

Elaya shook her head. They fell silent, lost in unsettled thoughts.

'We have been so naïve and made many mistakes,' Laglen muttered.

'So much has been lost,' Rowen said. 'Not just hundreds of lives but hope. We just sit here and mourn the dead. What's the plan?'

Hazel's head jerked, interest piqued.

'To stay safe,' Laglen replied. 'And consolidate.'

Nadine murmured. 'We don't have a plan, and – no offense – the best of us are dead.'

Hazel sighed, head returning to its customary droop.

'I want to send a message to my people,' Rowen moaned.

Elaya interjected. 'I told you, we can't do that.'

'But you sent a bird to the queen. I have lost my father!'

Laglen glanced at Rowen, then down at his hands. 'Hazel has lost her father.' He mumbled. 'Rathnell, Stoer, Cundelly, Trefgwyn. The Druid Guild...' His words trailed off. 'Every community has suffered.'

'And the Travellers,' Kalamayn muttered.

Elaya sighed sadly and sent Rowen a sympathetic look. 'We cannot risk being found.'

'Crane has outmatched us at every turn,' Kalamayn said. 'We should have worked out the worst possible scenario and planned for it. Whether Crane had spies, or whether his portal allows him to cross without sleeping or grants power in another author's structure,' Kalamayn couldn't look at Nadine. 'We took too much for granted. Risked everything, and lost.'

The room lapsed into silence, the only faint noises coming from the city outside the window.

'Yes, we have lost.' Girvyn's voice brought everyone's heads up. He stood. 'Yes, we have lost so much. Mora and Dremell, the army drawn from across the world. Do not think that I diminish their sacrifice, but we always knew this plan might fail, didn't we? All it means is that now the way forward is clear. It is me. However untrained and untested. Maybe we should have chosen this way from the beginning, but perhaps the time that our fallen comrades have bought us will prove crucial. I am coming into my power, but I cannot do this alone. I need all of you.'

Laglen shook his head. 'We're no use. Kal and I were mere spectators to Crane's might.'

'Perhaps, Uncle, but I can lend force to your wisdom. I can be your hands and you my eyes.'

'What do you mean?' Laglen was frowning, unsure.

'I mean, just tell me what you want me to do.'

Figures of Note

Dream Travellers

Crane: A Dream Traveller whose dark ambitions threaten the balance of worlds.

Dremell: Son of Mora and best friend to Nadine, determined to stop Crane.

Girvyn: A 14-year-old book lover from Rathnell, and nephew of Laglen. On a quest to discover his true self.

Kalamayn: A Dream Traveller from Cundelly and Nadine's father, known for his passion for intricate constructs and celebrated for inventing library cataloguing systems.

Laglen: A Rathnell Library scribe and Girvyn's uncle, with a penchant for thrilling, high-octane escapist dreams.

Mora: A strong-willed Dream Traveller from Cundelly, and mother of Dremell. Known for her sharp critical mind.

Nadine: Daughter of Kalamayn, and Dremell's best friend. Prefers solitude and distrusts Orts.

Sunfire: A mysterious guardian from the Dream Realm.

The Queendom of Rathnell

Alwad: Interpreter for Donjul and a researcher of desert culture at the Rathnell Library.

Amelia: The aging Queen of Rathnell, troubled by her growing fragility.

Berenger: Vice-Chair of the Privy Council, known for his obsequiousness and sharp quill.

Brennen: A reclusive academic who lives in the secret tunnels of Rathnell Castle. Friends with Elaya and Laglen.

Cargya: The only woman on the Privy Council and a former Chair, respected for her pragmatic leadership.

Derrilyn: Apprentice to Elaya and a druid in training. Brimming with potential.

Elaya Faith: The Queen's Protector and a skilled druid. Once a refugee from the southern deserts, she's now a sworn guardian of Rathnell and a mentor to many.

Ellis: The longest-serving member of the Rathnell Privy Council, steeped in tradition.

Finlack Shadstone: The son of Baron Kerrick Shadstone.

Kerrick Shadstone: A shrewd and unscrupulous baron with ambitions for greater influence.

Maude: A skilled ranger from Rathnell's East District, known for her tracking prowess.

Stasnier Glencast: Chair of the Privy Council and the Queen's chief advisor, often viewed as a schemer.

Tarith: A royal guard under Elaya's command, tasked with protecting Girvyn.

Notable Figures from Other Houses, Kingdoms, and Factions

Lady Adara: A powerful druid and the respected leader of the Druid Guild.

Cedar: A moderate Forester from the Elm Tribe, open to peace talks.

Donjul: Leader of the Tologon Desert Nomads.

Glefforn: Chief of the Elm Tribe Foresters, escorting Hazel to the summit. Deeply distrustful of Highlanders.

Grisham: Envoy from House Trefgwyn, regarded as an honourable and trustworthy Lord.

Hazel: A courageous survivor of the Sycamore Foresters, arriving at the summit to recount Crane's attack.

Jaden: A druid and ally of Lady Adara.

Jakub: Envoy from Casper and friend to Nark.

Maltip: Highlander leader and father to Rowen. His distrust of Foresters stems from a long-standing war.

Nark: A zealous envoy from Lale, with a reputation as an uncompromising arbiter.

Praleck: Envoy and general from Stoer, a kingdom allied with Hoppenell through armour trade.

Rowen: Highlander son of Maltip, intrigued by Hazel's call for peace despite his distrust of Foresters.

Seskin: Envoy from Cundelly, striving to bolster ties with Rathnell to counter the Casper-Stoer alliance.

Sevada: A brilliant young envoy from Hoppenell, representing its unmatched armour trade.

Sward: The younger son of Andergine House, pursuing a marital alliance with Trefgwyn. Known for his terse demeanour and misogynistic views.

The Wigginton Estate

Lady Celia Wigginton: The Queen's cousin, living in isolation in the Wigginton estate.

Lord Humphrey Wigginton: Husband to Lady Wigginton.

Coming Soon

Continue the story of The Dream Traveller Series in

The Dream Traveller: Rising Storm
2025

The Dream Traveller: Storm Born
2025

Author's Note

Thank you for reaching the end of my book. I hope you enjoyed it and are left wanting more.

For me, the allure of fantasy and science fiction is deeply rooted in their subtle power to illuminate present-day issues. I've always perceived the Dream Realm not merely as a spiritual or astral plane, but as a more ominous space where indulgence finds room.

Imagine if every daydream could materialise into reality? I think for my characters, the Travellers at least, they face the ongoing battle of self-restraint. Bring in a portal and a sociopath and along comes the carnage.

These days, a coffee, and a muffin cost more than an audible download, but it's the investment, your time, that I am truly grateful for. Having got to the end, I'm keen to hear what you think, so if you have a moment, I would be grateful if you could leave a review on Goodreads or Amazon. If you find my photography website, it shows you the way to my writing pages.

Until next time,
John

Acknowledgments

This story has been a long time in the making, and with projects that span such durations, there are invariably many contributors. From English teachers to editors, friends to family, and passionate supporters, this has truly been a collaborative journey. Although the list of individuals to thank is extensive, I deeply appreciate each person's impact on this project.

First, my gratitude goes to Helen, who reviewed my initial draft three decades ago and shared insights not taught in classrooms. To my sister, Chantelle, my first reader: Chantelle, at times it felt as if I was writing for you alone, so profound was your enthusiasm. Dan May deserves special mention for the joy we found in plotting and experimenting together.

I extend my thanks to early test readers Auntie Jean, Conrad Cheney, Sarah Constantinou, and Cristina Christou Michael, whose engagement sustained me through the early stages. Friends-turned-editors Peter Darrell, Sarah Stephens, and Nadia Danaos-Ueberall provided indispensable advice that elevated the work.

Becky Stradwick illuminated the path with her manuscript assessment, and Iain Maloney at BPA offered crucial mentorship. Ivan Mulcahy provided invaluable publication advice, and Freddy Sawyer contributed critical insights into character development.

Andy Snow-Ellis crafted the typography and offered a lifetime of creative support. Michael R Miller paved the way to publication, a milestone in my writing career.

To recent test readers – Katie Heath, Peter McCartney, Segun Olusanya, Mike Staples, Andy Hodgson, Clare Brown, Sarah Skinner, Laura Payne-Stanley, Stella Enright, Effie Pitts, Phil Green, Mandy Stanfield, Emma Murray-Jones, and Charlotte Le Blond – thank you for affirming the strengths of my work and identifying areas for improvement.

To David White, Camilla Collins, Hazel McClennon, Chris Bunce, and Caroline Knapman: your enduring encouragement has meant the world. To Sarah Church, for her exceptional marketing support.

Mum, your unwavering support from start to finish has been more than any son could ask for. Liz and Theo, your understanding and encouragement have been the bedrock of this process. My debt to your patience is immeasurable.

Chris Knapman contributed cover art and maps, which are just the tip of the iceberg. Your dedication over the last five years – including plotting, reading, proofreading, and supporting – has been extraordinary.

Finally, to my editor, David Imrie, who went beyond the traditional role of an editor by not only fixing but also teaching and refining every aspect of this work: this book would not have been possible without your thorough dedication and expertise.

Any faults found within this work are solely my responsibility. However, the credit for any qualities readers may discover belongs to the remarkable group of individuals who have supported and contributed to this journey.

Printed in Great Britain
by Amazon